THE
EMPTY
DIARY

a Modern Gothic Romance

by Ajeeb Prince

THE EMPTY DIARY

This is a fictional story set in an imaginary modern reality.
Names, characters, places, and incidents are created from the
imagination of the author. Any resemblance to actual events,
organizations, practices, or persons, living or dead,
is entirely coincidental.

Print in the United States of America
U.S. Virgin Islands

ISBN #: 979-8-9914597-0-9
ISBN #: 979-8-9914597-1-6

Edited By: Hawaii Hill-Allen

First Edition: August 2024

ABOUT THE AUTHOR

Ajeeb "Yojee" Prince is an author born in Philadelphia, PA, and raised on the island of St. Croix in the U.S Virgin Islands from the age of four. Along with his pursuits as a writer and novelist, he is an active member of the Virgin Islands community as a group facilitator, teaching life skills and advocating for substance prevention. Prince has always been fascinated by the art of storytelling and worldbuilding for longer than he can remember.

Although he was considered dyslexic and a terrible speller at a young age, his love for reading and writing were undeniable. In fact, he realized how much he enjoyed history because of the plethora of stories from the past and how it brought humanity to the present time.

Ajeeb Prince hopes his writing will inspire generations of readers, storytellers and creators, whether literary or any other field or endeavor. However, actively assisting others to bring their own stories and worlds to life is the most gratifying.

STORIES BY AUTHOR

<u>Published</u>
Scenic Drive
10 Steps to Killing a King

<u>Unpublished</u>
The Finest Vintage of Tomorrows
The Curious Mr. Wrinkle
Jubilee
(Dead/Death) With Me
Ten Thousand Moons
Mermaids Beneath the Moon

STORY DISCLAIMERS

This story is broken into three perspectives,
Walter, Yvette, and *Dr. Linda Pierce*.
Walter and Yvette's chapters are written in normal print
as they are the story's main narrators.
Unlike most of my stories, the point of view might change
throughout the chapters and will be separated by a:

*   *   *

*Dr. Linda Pierce is the character being told this story
throughout her therapy sessions with Walter.
Her point of view is written in Italics.*

TABLE OF CONTENT

Prologue

THE MORNING THE DOCTOR MET THE D'ARTAGNANS
was a memorable one, but for all the wrong reasons. Sometimes
with the plethora of clients and paperwork, days and nights
could be a blur or even clustered altogether. However, this case
permeated her mind more than most and made her question the
impossible. Even if she wanted to, one case she could never
forget was the case of Walter D'Artagnan.

With adult patients, psychiatrists find themselves put in
many heavy situations with their patients — raged by injustices,
grieving beyond belief, disconnection from a lover, even being
misunderstood or misinterpreted. Somehow, at the age of
sixteen, Walter D'Artagnan seemed to be plagued by all four...
and more.

It was the last week of April when Dr. Linda Pierce met the
D'Artagnan's. When she arrived, the doctor spoke a kind word

to her receptionist, Lana, and complimented the sunflower in her hair.

"Thank you, Doctor," she said warmly. Lana wore her welcoming smile as always. However, when she turned towards the doctor's door, that smile was replaced with gloom. "They are already here, doctor. They were early, so I let them sit in your office to wait."

"Thank you, Lana."

Dr. Pierce relieved her shoulders of her dark trench coat and smoothed down her black skirt. Her receptionist handed her another file for the mountain of others, but she was more interested in the coffee she was handed second — business before pleasure, of course. She felt a bit irked since she couldn't enjoy it alone. She usually didn't, but it was still a bother. With a sip of her morning relief, the doctor enjoyed the warmth and solace of the moment she had to spare.

"Why do I do this to myself," Dr. Pierce muttered aloud, feeling the words slip out her mouth.

"They need your help," Lana said sincerely; desperately even.

The doctor shook her head solemnly. "That's not what I mean. I need to get here earlier so I have time with my coffee." It was only half a lie, but it would ease Lana's mind. "How were the parents' demeanor? Did they seem sad? Angry? Worried?"

Lana thought for a moment. "Vacant, I'd say, like neither of them really knew how to feel." She paused, then said, "You always told me that these situations should be handled with care... and caution."

"Any case should be handled with care and caution, but I did say that because they should be. When you don't know what's going on with your own child, it's not vacancy you feel. It's fear.

8

Sometimes it can cause a family to break down completely. We aren't here to elicit anything harmful. This family has already gone through a lot, so caution and tact are paramount in these delicate situations."

Lana looked worried now and her innocent eyes were beginning to bear the weight. "Could they really be frightened of their own child?"

Dr. Pierce lowered her voice and said, "Maybe not 'frightened of' but 'frightened for.' When you fear something you can't understand and it is harbored within your child... well, that can be a nightmare... especially when you feel that your child might be a danger."

"But to who?" Lana whispered. "Isn't he just a teenager?"

"A danger to them... to himself." Dr. Pierce felt herself smiling sadly. She knew how empathic Lana was and hoped to simmer some of her worries. "Don't worry, they came to the right place."

It was only after Linda Pierce met Walter D'Artagnan that she would rethink that assertion.

Dr. Pierce felt the uneasiness in the room when she entered her office. Mr. and Mrs. D'Artagnan were sitting in front of her desk — uncomfortably, she wagered. The fatigue in their eyes caught the doctor's attention; angry eyes, somber eyes.

"Good morning," Dr. Pierce welcomed with a warm smile. Both parents seemed just as Lana said: quite vacant. "I'm sorry I was late. Traffic this morning was impossible, frankly."

The father spoke first. "Thank you for seeing us, doctor. I believe you've already met Harriet. I'm Walter's father, Lawrence."

Mrs. D'Artagnan was a short, buxom woman with a flat nose and wide hips. She wore bright purple scrubs and her square glasses sat in front of her slightly swollen brown eyes. She only grinned nervously when the doctor's eyes met hers. Mr. D'Artagnan was lean and fit and, even when he sat, she could tell he was quite tall. His chin was square, his eyebrows were thick, and his hair was a short afro of curls. Dry oil stained his hands and darkened his fingers, while his overalls were faded and looked more bright gray than blue. Both D'Artagnans didn't seem pleased to be there; the father especially.

Dr. Pierce shook the mother's hand and habit directed her to the father, but both forgot the oil.

"Sorry about that." Mr. D'Artagnan's hand receded. "We had an early client this morning."

"I can relate." Dr. Pierce grinned as she sat behind her desk. "Thank you for coming, both of you. I know seeking... this kind of help is never easy and even harder when it's for your child. Tell me what's been happening and please... take your time."

The D'Artagnan's shared dreadful looks with one another. The mother spoke up and her voice was cloaked with sorrow.

"I can't even remember when it all began," she said, wiping a falling tear from behind her glasses and sniffling. "Our son, Walter, he... he seems to be going through... quite some interesting changes, you can say." She paused for a moment. "I'm not really sure how to describe it."

The doctor nodded. "Take your time. I know at his age, children are still finding themselves and going through different phases. It can be hard for parents to keep up."

Mr. D'Artagnan snorted. "When it involves seeing ghosts or hallucinating, I'm sure this is no phase."

"Ghosts?" Dr. Pierce squinted her eyes suspiciously but fixed her lips so she wouldn't smile or smirk. The paranormal always seemed quite ridiculous to her, but the doctor didn't want

10

to appear insulting towards the parents. "Mr. and Mrs. D'Artagnan, I personally wouldn't recommend a medium, but my receptionist, Lana, could provide you with any—"

"Dr. Pierce," Mr. D'Artagnan cut her off abruptly. "Please don't mistake me, I'm not even open to the possibility that there are ghosts at play here, but... Walter turned sixteen last year. He's too old for imaginary friends, I'd say. Sometimes he's in his room talking to himself as if someone else is there and I can tell if he was on the phone or not. I'm not that old."

Dr. Pierce nodded and kept silent. She understood what he meant but didn't comment on it and allowed them to continue.

"And all this has only started recently," Mrs. D'Artagnan added then turned to the father. "It might have been after the funeral."

"There was a funeral recently?" Dr. Pierce flitted her attention back and forth between the parents.

"His cousin, Samuel. But... But it's not just that. Yes, Walter might be seeing things, it is possible, but... I've seen him mumbling in his sleep. Sometimes he blacks-out for a time and I don't know where he goes. And then there is..." She sighed in frustration. "All this started out of nowhere. I... I don't know what's going to happen next and I don't know what's happening to our son now. It's like he's haunted or..."

Mrs. D'Artagnan broke off her sentence and Mr. D'Artagnan began rubbing her back to calm her.

Dr. Pierce gave the parents a moment to themselves before asking, "How close were Walter and his cousin?"

"They were more like brothers than cousins," Mr. D'Artagnan admitted.

"That must have been a sad time for him. Tell me about these changes you mentioned. Any shifts in behavior, perhaps? Would *you say he reacted out of character when he heard the news of his cousin?"*

Mrs. D'Artagnan sniffed. "Not necessarily. I don't know. He was silent, I know — when he heard the news, when he saw the body at the funeral, when he helped lift Samuel's casket in and out of the church. I don't fault him for that. Eventually, he cried about it, so nothing seemed out of the ordinary. He just needed time. But grief is not what brought us here, Dr. Pierce. He seems more than just troubled."

The doctor nodded solemnly. "Frankly, I wouldn't be surprised if he were not troubled at all. Children go through many changes during their teenage years. Sophomores will have SATs on their mind soon, graduation and getting into college. But with Walter — the loss of a brother, keeping up with friends and schoolwork, as well as trying to main a relationship with both of you — it could be a bit much for a young man to bear all at once, and with the pandemic, there were some many lives lost in so little time. It's quite hard not to affect all of us in some way. Walter might be seeking some attention that he doesn't feel he is receiving; consciously or subconsciously." Dr. Pierce shifted in her seat, hoping to get a bit more comfortable. "Tell me, has your son displayed excessive irritation or aggression? A spike in anger, perhaps?"

"No!" Mrs. D'Artagnan seemed appalled by the question. "Walter is a good boy. A sweet boy. He gets rowdy at times, but what teenage boy doesn't?"

"All teens can be quite rowdy. However, a good person can become aggravated, aggressive or angry, Mrs. D'Artagnan. Those are emotions we all feel. It's where we direct those emotions and how we express them that makes us good people. I have no reason to believe that Walter is a bad child based on what you've told me. He has interests most boys his age share

12

*and he has a few friends to spend time with. You've even
provided me with report cards and academic achievements to
make your case. He seems like an average student, academically
— above average, at times — but... such records and attributes
don't help me understand his mental state."*

*"Aggravated, maybe," Mr. D'Artagnan chimed in
impatiently. "Disturbed and delusional, certainly, but Harriet is
right. Walter is usually rational for his age — even with his
smart mouth — but this... this is not normal... not for him."*

*Dr. Pierce nodded. She had already jotted some thoughts in
her notes, but she still needed a clearer picture. "Is there
anything else you find different? Not just different but
noticeable?"*

*Mrs. D'Artagnan made a small grin, a happy one. "Well,
there is a girl I think he's been seeing. I'm not really sure
though. He's very vague about it."*

"Is that a problem for him?"

"A distraction, maybe," Mr. D'Artagnan interjected.

*"Girls can be more than just a distraction to some teenage
boys," Dr. Pierce added. "It might even cause them to act out
hoping to gain certain attentions."*

*"Oh no, Yvette is a nice young lady; very polite, very bright.
Walter seems to have been interested in her for some time. She
seems good for him too. She did lose her mother awhile back
and they might both be going through the same feelings. I can't
really say."*

"And you don't believe that all this is about grief?"

*"It's more than just that," Mr. D'Artagnan added. "I'm sure
of it."*

*Fortunately, Dr. Pierce's mug was to her lips and hid the
awkward smile that ran across them.* The paranormal, *she*

thought again. Even so, the entire story seemed so vague and filled with holes. When her lips softened, she rested her mug down and said, "Forgive me, but this all seems quite odd to me. I'm inclined to believe everything you're telling me, nothing you've said has made me feel otherwise. However, I'm also inclined to believe that there is something you aren't telling me."

Mr. D'Artagnan nodded in agreement. "Yes, doctor. There is something our son isn't telling us. Now you understand how we feel and why we are here."

- Session One-

Wednesday, May 5th

**THE DAY FINALLY CAME WHEN DR. PIERCE MET
WALTER D'ARTAGNAN**

    *The town of Centralia had recently experienced a drought for
some time and the temperature was hotter than it needed to be
during spring. Thankfully, there were many sheets of rain that
afternoon. Although it was quite sudden, the rattles on the glass
were a welcoming change.*

    *She had just finished a late lunch and was enjoying an
afternoon cup of chai alone when she began reviewing the file
sitting on the desk beside her. Even though new sessions began
after meeting him, Walter D'Artagnan's file remained close by.
After the comments Mrs. D'Artagnan' made during their last
meeting, a second file found its way beside Walter's. The abrupt
end of sessions with this second client was already a cause for
concern, but now Dr. Pierce wondered if Walter was connected
to it. She might have been getting ahead of herself, but it was
something to keep in mind when she met the young man.*

Hallucinations, *she thought. Dr. Pierce had heard the story of Walter's hallway incident that occurred several weeks prior. It made her shiver when she heard that. It wasn't paranormal, but it frightened her. Still, she surmised that something was disturbing his mental well-being. A tactful approach was usually the preferred, but Walter's story was far from usual.*

Outside her office door, the doctor was met by Mr. D'Artagnan with his sixteen-year-old son at his side. The man wore a pleasant grin, but his son wore a scowl.

"Good afternoon, Dr. Pierce," Mr. D'Artagnan greeted her. His palm was less strained than their last meeting, but the doctor was still a bit hesitant to shake it. To not appear rude, she did, but briefly.

"It's good to see you, Mr. D'Artagnan." Dr. Pierce then shifted her attention to the young man. "And you must be Walter. I'm Dr. Linda Pierce."

The teenage boy gave the doctor a fake smile. His father nudged him roughly and he spoke up. "Good afternoon," said Walter reluctantly.

She shook his hand also and his palms were noticeably less rough than his father's. However, Walter D'Artagnan did have his father's lanky frame, just not as tall along with his mother's comeliness. A bit of peach fuzz hung from his chin, and he had several pimples on his cheeks like most his age. An unsmiling teen was common, and Walter's was no less unsettling. His eyes, however, were deep and two-toned; a dark brown inside and a lighter shade surrounding it. They were quite handsome as well; the kind young girls are usually fond of. Still, there was a coldness to them, and although she sensed no resentment in him, Dr. Pierce had been wrong before.

"Well, it's four o'clock now," the doctor announced. *"Shall we get started?"*

Mr. D'Artagnan nodded, then turned to his son. "Don't give the woman a hard time, Walter. She's here to help you."

Once his father was gone, Dr. Pierce ushered the young man into her office and gestured toward the couches. "Sit wherever you like. However, leave your coat on the rack by the door, please."

While the young man hung up his coat, the doctor gathered her pen and pad. Walter found a spot at the end of the sofa; noticeably, the closest seat to the door. Taking note of that, the doctor sat in her armchair, folded her legs, and rested her notepad and pen on her lap.

"I don't want to be here," were the first words Walter spoke *when they were alone in her office. Still unsmiling, the young man shifted in his seat several times until he was comfortable.*

"There is nothing to worry or be afraid—"

"I'm not afraid," he interrupted sternly, his tone icy.

The doctor nodded solemnly. Your parents are though. Doesn't that frighten you? *When those words ran in her mind, she remembered how it felt being Walter's age and being asked that about her own parents. It made her feel terrible. Instead, Dr. Pierce swallowed that impulse.*

"Well, what are you not afraid of?" she asked. *"Is there something specific that you're referring to?"*

Walter turned away from her saying nothing, but his irritation was plain to see.

"I heard you're quite the artist," she said, *hoping to cut the tension in the air and find something she could work with. "Have you drawn anything new lately?"*

"No," the boy replied quickly, avoiding eye contact.

18

"Why is that? Has it been hard lately?" He shrugged his shoulders, so she went on. *"Sometimes that could be hard when we are grieving. Can you tell me about your cousin... Samuel?"* She had nearly forgotten the name.

"I don't want to talk about it."

Dr. Pierce felt herself frowning and noticed he said *"it"* and not *"him."* Keeping that bit to herself, she asked. *"Have you ever talked to anyone about him since he has passed?"*

He shook his head. *"No. Not really."*

"Not really? Have you tried?"

"No," Walter clarified. *"Just... no."*

Dr. Pierce stayed quiet, letting the silence linger for a moment. *"I hope you understand why you are here, Walter."*

"I do," he admitted. *"But—"* Suddenly he stopped and grew silent again.

Curious, she thought. *"You are allowed to speak your mind here, Walter."*

"Nothing." Walter's voice was still flat and uninterested.

"Nothing you say here will ever be repeated to anyone, I assure you. I pride myself in confidentiality."

"Confidentiality?"

"Absolutely. I am not allowed to tell your parents, or anyone about anything you say in these sessions... unless, of course, I believe you are a harm to yourself or anyone else."

"I know what confidentiality means." His words were sharp, but Walter drew back, regretting his outburst. Still, she can see his teeth clenched as he said, *"I'm sorry, but... I'm not a danger to anyone. I don't know how to prove that to you."*

"I don't think so either," Dr. Pierce assured him. *"However, the only way I can be certain is if you talk to me and tell me how*

you are feeling. That's how you can prove it to everyone, Walter. I'm here to help you."

The young man sighed and scowled. *"I don't know what you want me to say."*

"We can talk about anything, really." Even with that certainty, Walter held his silence. Dr. Pierce waited a moment then went on. *"Did you and your cousin have a lot of fun together?"*

Without looking at her, Walter nodded. He was quiet for a moment, but he was slowly opening up. *"Samuel was older than me, but we were close... Well... not so much before he died, but..."* He fell silent for a moment then continued. *"He liked having me around. I never really knew why but I never thought about it either. I was just... I don't know... just happy to spend time with my older cousin. He introduced me to most anime I watch, he would always beat me and my best friend at basketball and video games..."* He paused for a moment. *"Yeah. We had a lot of fun times together. Brotherly stuff, I guess."*

Dr. Pierce grinned. She could hear how nervous Walter was but could feel how warmly he spoke. *"He seemed like a big brother to you."*

Walter nodded. *"You can say that. I never had a brother so... you know. He wasn't the best influence, I know, but... it wasn't like Samuel had me around everywhere he went. I was still a few years younger than him, so I never saw any of that..."* He trailed off, reclaiming his silence once again.

"I see. Well, I'm happy to hear that he cared for you and saw the good in you."

Walter smirked a little. *"He liked that I was into comics and video games and wasn't the kind of kid who was always making trouble. If I was doing anything stupid or acting out and my dad wasn't around, he would try and twist my neck himself." He paused again with his lips ajar; possibly reliving an old memory. "But he always had my back and made sure I learned my lessons. I think he expected a lot of good things from me. That's why he was always frustrated when I messed up, when I argued with my mom, or when I was doing badly in school. Stuff like that. He often tried to do my father's job when my father wasn't around."*

"It must have been hard when he died."

Walter nodded. "It was... but I had Yvette."

The doctor felt a grin on her lips. "A special friend of yours?"

Walter smirked a little. "Something like that."

"From what I understand, Yvette knew Samuel also. Am I correct?"

He fell silent again. His eyes became fixated on the door, his attention far from the doctor now.

"Walter?" she called, but he made no move or reaction. "Walter?"

He wasn't there... not really.

Saturday, February 28th

FOR MOST OF LAST YEAR, THERE WAS A GLOBAL
gloom in the air that changed the lives of many, but in that time,
nothing changed Walter's life more than the day he learned of
his cousin's death. That gloom in the air lingered longer than
everyone had hoped, but it wasn't a sickness that took Samuel.
Walter didn't know what was worse but knew both were
frightening ways to die.

The funeral was held on a gray afternoon, but the dark clouds
never shed a tear. The smoggy air had a sour taste on Walter's
tongue as well and the aftertaste lingered.

The halls of Cousin Lily's home were filled with cries and
wails, but Walter heard just as many cynical, even cruel mutters.
Attendees were courteous enough to keep their mutters from
Cousin Lily — behind shut doors, in the corners, the yard,
beyond earshot — but he had heard enough to know the
prevalence of that disdain. It was no secret that Samuel was
involved with what many would call "wrong crowds" and was

even punished by the law before eighteen. Being detained and behind iron bars could change a person: but bad deeds are never truly replaced by the good that might follow — at least, not really. Such muttering mourners might agree to that. Still, Samuel was family and that mattered to him more than some bad decisions. Still, Walter didn't really understand and wouldn't pretend like he did.

Even so, he was trying to find a way to retreat from all the mourners and family members. His mother's arms were wrapped around her first cousin, Lily, and rocking side to side hoping to simmer her sorrows. Hearing her balling for her deceased son brought an uncomfortable rumble to Walter's stomach. Now her only child was gone, and Lillian Russell was a mother more in name. She was still a grandmother though and would do anything for her grandson, Michael. There was some solace in that. However, the feeling of incompleteness would never fade away. Walter knew that feeling, but his parents could come together to become complete again if they wanted. Samuel was gone and that wouldn't change; deeming his son to live without a solid memory of his own father.

A few mourners even came to Walter with their condolences — a few of Samuel's friends, one of his old co-workers, and an ex-girlfriend. Walter didn't recognize their faces but somehow, they knew his, or he just couldn't remember. Samuel might have been five years older, but his cousin liked carrying Walter on adventures, even at a young age... *Although, that didn't last long,* he thought. Be that as it may, he smiled and gave them hugs and even allowed a few to wet his shoulders with their tears.

Walter's mother had recruited a few other women to try and calm Cousin Lily; keeping her from getting up from the couch, he surmised. Understandably, they couldn't stop her from crying, however.

He remembered how tightly Cousin Lily hugged him when he gave her his condolences. The way she held him so tightly and cried into him, he felt like he might cry also. Still, he felt he had lingered too long in the sorrow, and was trying to edge his way out before he became too pensive.

Walter made his way to the dining room. The family photos on the wall were a distraction for a time, but they were still memories; all that remained. Although Samuel was her only child, no one would guess that from all the photos on the wall of him and other cousins around his age. Walter found the only one with him and Samuel together. He could remember when it was captured, but Walter might have been seven or eight and Samuel was thirteen. The two were sitting on the porch, making silly poses while standing back-to-back. It must have been a hot summer day since they were both shirtless. *He was probably taking me to the basketball court or something,* Walter deduced. Although there were only memories left, Walter struggled to remember it all.

"Walter?"

When he turned around, he saw his cousin Ciara, walking around the dining table. She seemed a bit surprised to see him. Even her approaching steps seemed a bit careful, like she wasn't sure if it were him or not.

"I almost didn't recognize you. You've gotten taller and everything."

Walter smirked. His father was a bit taller than him, and his mother was quite short so Walter was sadly stuck in the middle.

"That's funny," he said dryly, his face barely softening. "I barely feel like I've grown."

She ignored his tone and hugged her cousin anyway. "How would you know, stupid?"

Walter's face broke into a smile. "Oh, yeah. Right."

Ciara was always taller than him with her long legs, arms, and neck. Her tone was a shade darker, her golden-brown hair laid straight above her shoulders, and her black dress had a short V in the middle. When she approached him, her sleeves and hemline swayed with her steps.

Ciara was on her way to the backyard and welcomed him to join her. Surprisingly, she was chuckling when she did.

"You look even worse than me being stuck in here," she said, beckoning him to follow.

"You said it, not me," Walter said smirking yet agreed all the same. Exiting the house with her might make him feel better about himself. It wasn't as if he were the only one who felt a bit claustrophobic. He went on to lead the way to the back door himself, with Ciara following behind as quietly as she could. It would be ill of her to be seen tittering at their cousin's funeral.

The subtle cool breeze Walter felt as he stepped through the door was freeing. Still, he couldn't ignore the unsmiling sourness still permeating the air. There was some solace being there with Ciara. She was better at dealing with loss than him. Losing her father at six might have played a part in that, unfortunately.

Nonetheless, the smile she wore while she slipped off her heels and knelt beside Cousin Lily's flower garden was pleasant. Roses, lilies, tulips, and others — Walter couldn't name them all — they might have been the only colorful things he had seen all day. His favorite color had always been black, but not when everyone was wearing it. That wasn't pleasant.

Samuel and Ciara's mothers were sisters. The women were close in blood but that might have been it. Walter's mother wasn't too fond of Cousin Lily either, but family was family. On the other hand, Walter and Samuel were closer than cousins, while Ciara was an older sister to them both. All three of them were only children so they had their own sibling relationships with one another. Ciara would always warn Samuel about his terrible choices and Walter about spending too much time with him. Even with how close the three of them were, it was seemingly all she could do. After she graduated, she went away to study medicine and that was that. Now, she had returned home from school once again for another funeral; a funeral neither her nor Walter expected to happen.

The red apple tree in the middle of the yard didn't add to the color. It had no foliage, and it was several months before it bloomed. The backyard wasn't as vibrant as Walter was used to. The last time he bit into one of Cousin Lily's red apples, the taste was sweet, and juice ran down the corner of his lips. She had always been an avid gardener who often put Walter and Samuel to work. Although Walter wasn't too fond of reaping, sowing or tilling, it would make the boys' moms happy. Walter's mother was always a bit jealous of her older cousin's green thumb. However, she didn't hide it as well as she thought.

Even when she slipped out of her high heels to walk across the grass, Ciara was still taller than Walter. She seemed peaceful to see how much the garden had grown while her toes brushed the freshly mown grass. However, that peace was soon interrupted as her purse began to vibrate.

"You gotta be kidding me." Annoyed, she pulled out her phone and ignored a call.

"What's wrong with you?"

She sulked. "It's this guy I'm seeing. He's nice but the clingy type, you know? Being away for a few days proved that already. He has to go, Walter."

He smirked. *Honest as always*, he thought. Ciara hadn't changed in the last three years. There was always some curtness when she spoke. It was her charm and Walter grew accustomed to it years ago.

"But you look dead," she added without preamble.

"Yeah, I guess," Walter agreed without really thinking. "I don't know. Funerals are kind of... weird, you know?"

Ciara snorted. "No. Funerals are stupid."

"How would you do it then?" He was curious. "You know, the mourning part?"

"I don't know. Something less dreary. We should be celebrating him, you know?"

Walter shrugged. "Yeah, I get it. I'm used to you playing pranks on him or something, not trying to be all nice."

Ciara shot him a side grin. "He is our family, Walter. He was hard-headed, overly passionate and a terrible decision-maker, but I loved him." She paused for a moment and her voice turned eerily low. "But he was haunted, Walter. We both know that. We just don't know what that was."

Silently, Walter made a sunken nod.

Ciara frowned. "I feel terrible for his son; another boy raised without his father. It's... tragic." She sighed. "Auntie Lily told me how Michael screamed when Samuel didn't come home the next morning. I can't even imagine what Samuel's wife is feeling right now. I barely know her, but I can tell how distraught she is."

Walter nodded solemnly. "I wanted to go and talk to her, but... I don't know what to say, you know? I felt like it has been

27

years — I mean — Samuel barely even talked to me before his wedding… or after. Even at the wedding, he was still so cold. We shouldn't have left… I… I shouldn't have left things the way they were. Now he's gone."

"That was a few years ago, Walter," Ciara reminded him strongly. "You are young, and he was a father. He should have known better and not put that pressure on you. Still, you have to stop blaming yourself and let it go. They were happy… They got married… You didn't do anything to change that, nor did you pull that trigger."

Walter wasn't convinced, but he nodded nonetheless, staying nothing.

"You just have to forgive yourself, Walter. That's it—"

"Oh, shut up, Ciara." Walter was growing irritated. "Forgive myself? What does that even mean?"

His cousin scowled. "Hey! Don't forget who you're talking to and start raising your voice at me. I'm not your child."

Walter took a deep breath and scratched an itch at the back of his neck. "Sorry, I didn't mean—"

"Forget about it." Ciara waved it off and got over it.

From her bag, she withdrew a flask from her pouch. She took a swig then smirked as she tilted it in his direction. Walter grinned then took a swig himself. The taste of the rum and the metal brim was disgusting but… *Might come in handy*, he thought.

"Keep that down before someone sees you. I can still get in trouble, you know."

Walter looked around first then took another sip and handed it back. The harsh taste barely simmered in his mouth before Ciara nudged his shoulder to get his attention.

"What?"

"Hey, that's Charlotte's sister, right? Yvette?"

When Walter faced the back door, he felt his lips part a bit. The girl was escorting an elderly woman through the pathway and up the stairs to the back door. She wore a delicate smile as she was assisting the woman inside. The gloom in the air seemed to disperse when Walter spied her smile through her thick curls.

"Yeah," Walter finally responded to his cousin. "I saw her at the church earlier."

"Well, duh. Oh, wait… you two go to Centralia High together now, right?"

Walter nodded, keeping his eyes away from Yvette. "Yup."

She turned away from her and grinned at her cousin. "She's really cute. You ever try to—"

"Ciara, we're at a wake," Walter said stiffly.

"Oh, hush, Walter. Relax." Ciara dipped down to grab her heels then waved to get Yvette's attention. His cousin began approaching her, so Walter slowly followed, hoping to ignore the nervousness in his knees. Even so, his steps never buckled.

Yvette Anders was the girl he always had eyes for. She was a bit shorter than him and petite. Her eyes were big and brown, her nose was a bit flat while she had wide lips with a heavy lower lip. She wore a maroon dress with a violet belt tight around her waist. When the wind blew, her skirts flowed like Ciara's sleeves. Her short heels matched the color of her dress and a crystal pendant hung from her short, silver necklace that complemented the crystals dangling from her ears. Walter didn't know how he should feel at that moment, but he couldn't deny his attraction to her.

"I can't remember the last time I saw you," Yvette was saying to Ciara when Walter made his approach. "You look so pretty."

"Why, thank you," said Ciara while whipping her hips from side to side so her dress could sway a little.

Yvette chuckled. "How's college?"

Ciara sighed. "Annoying and I have to leave tomorrow morning to get back before class on Monday. And med school is only going to get worse, so… Exciting!" She chuckled exhaustedly. "Anyways, what about you? Still writing, right?"

Yvette nodded. "Yeah. I wrote for the school newspaper last year."

"Not this year too?"

"Yeah, I am. Just from home. I actually haven't gone back to school yet." Yvette looked quite uncomfortable saying that. "I've just been keeping up at home for the first semester, but I have to go back for the second. My dad thinks it would be good for me."

Ciara nodded as she smiled sadly. "I understand."

"I'm sorry about what happened to Samuel," Yvette said solemnly.

"I'm sorry too. And about your mom. I'm sorry that I never—"

"It's okay. I wasn't really in the mood for talking, honestly. Thank you though."

"Sure."

Walter was slowly drawing closer when Yvette turned to him. When her soft eyes looked up at his, he felt his lips curl into a tiny grin on their own.

"Hey, Walter," she said sweetly yet her voice shifted to a melancholy tone as she began giving her condolences. "I'm so sorry about Samuel. I know you two were really close."

Walter nodded sedately. "Thanks, Yvette." He paused for a moment, nervously, then thought of something to say. "How is your sister holding up?"

She sighed. "I don't really know. She barely talks these days but... it's understandable. I can't imagine what she's feeling right now. I try to speak with her and see if she's okay, but she barely responds. I guess..." She paused for a moment then said, "I guess that's how I was when my mom died."

Walter?

Suddenly, Walter heard a feminine voice in his ears, but he wasn't certain where it was coming from. He turned, thinking someone was close by and was calling for him, but Ciara was already gone and only Yvette remained. Strangely, he couldn't remember seeing his cousin leave, nor could he remember this recognized yet unfamiliar voice.

Yvette must not have heard anyone as she continued. "I know it must be hard for you to lose your cousin. If it wasn't for him, we may not have met. Well, officially, at least. Remember?"

Walter made a grin that matched the one she was now wearing. "I remember. You swore I was someone else, didn't you?"

"You spooked me," Yvette replied honestly while she nodded, "and I was already spooked that day. I didn't need it to happen again. But I don't think I ever apologized for that. I'm sorry."

Walter remembered that day well. It was during seventh grade and the two of them were in the cafeteria line waiting for their turn to grab lunch. If it wasn't for his best friend, Art, he wouldn't have bumped into Yvette, nor would she think he tried to grab her inappropriately.

"Don't worry about it," Walter assured her then took the blame for himself. "It was my fault."

"I shouldn't have acted like that though. It was a terrible day, but still... Sorry."

"Oh, I could tell. Everyone could tell." He laughed a little. "Who cares about it anymore? No worries."

Yvette tittered lightly and Walter smiled. However, the laughs didn't last long. Eventually Walter realized he never gave her his condolences.

"Hey, about your mom," he began, "I never got to say how sorry I was. I hadn't seen you since she died. I know it was already difficult when she got the virus, but..."

Flustered with dismay, Yvette nervously grabbed an ear while slightly turning away from him. "You don't have to say anything, Walter, but... thank you." She paused for a moment then said, "I honestly thought she was getting better but... I guess she wasn't. It makes me more... more angry than sad."

Walter nodded but he didn't know what to say. Even so, Yvette spoke up before he could think of a way to respond as she turned towards him with a soft grin.

"I know you and Samuel were close but he's in a better place. It might sound a bit stupid and cliché, but he is. If it wasn't for his son, he might not have been doing his best to right his wrongs and be a better person. I don't know, but — I guess after a while... it all just catches up to you—" She paused with a light gasp. Aghast, Yvette faced him fully. "I'm sorry. I don't know why... I shouldn't have said that."

"No," Walter replied, "it's fine. You're... not wrong." Honestly, he didn't know what to say or how to feel. He and his cousin had their own history that he was sure she knew nothing about.

His cousin Samuel had made some decisions in his life that their family weren't proud of. He had already spent time behind bars as a juvenile. Although he was young, that didn't make it any more condonable by the family. Samuel had tried to earn his money legitimately, and, with a wife and son at nineteen, he was desperate to provide. Still, Samuel was dealt terrible cards, and instead of him spending time behind bars again, or righting his wrongs on the outside, he was killed, leaving no chances for redemption. It might have been worse if Samuel was a target... or maybe he was... Still, bullets — whether stray or deliberate — know no name. He might have been just in the wrong place at the wrong time, but not everyone chose to believe that. As for Walter, he didn't know what to believe, all he knew was what he heard.

There was an awkward silence, but Walter nervously said, "I thought I was going to fail your mom's class, you know?"

"Don't," said Yvette abruptly, yet her face read regret. "I mean... sorry, Walter, but... I still can't talk about her. It feels... weird talking about my mom. I guess... I'm just not ready yet."

"I understand. You're ready when you're ready." Yvette didn't seem to react, so Walter went on. "She's always with you, you know? Your mom? She's always there for you and always will be. My mom always says stuff like that."

Yvette smiled softly. "She's right though. Thank you. I hope you've been taking her advice too."

"I do." He had to admit. "It's kind of hard not to."

Walter?

There it was again, the same voice from before, but clearer now. Even so, Yvette continued, oblivious to its call.

"So," she said, "when was the last time you saw your cousin? I remember you used to be around each other all the time. What happened?"

"I… I honestly don't remember." That was a lie. Walter knew well enough what happened between him and Samuel. "We didn't really end on good terms the last time we talked but don't remember what happened. He kind of… hated me, honestly."

Yvette seemed surprised by that. Her lips parted for a moment before they locked together in an awkward and thin smile "I doubt that. Whatever it was, I'm sure he wouldn't hold a grudge forever. You two were close. You were family. You still are family."

"I don't know. I guess." Walter was still unconvinced and even a bit bothered. Yvette could have been right, but he didn't want to elaborate on that or even think of it at all. It wasn't the time, and it definitely wasn't the place. Be that as it may, it didn't seem necessary to bother her with cousin conflicts. *It wouldn't change anything,* he thought bitterly.

Yvette smirked uncomfortably then turned back to the house. "I need to go check on my sister, make sure she's okay. Maybe we can talk later?"

He nodded. "Sure. I don't want to hold you hostage."

Yvette smiled. She looked like she was about to say something to him. Walter could see a bit of hesitation on her face, but Yvette stayed silent as she returned inside taking her smile with her. He didn't want to pry so he let her go.

"Walter?"

Dr. Pierce was practically hollering. Walter turned back to the doctor quickly with a look of confusion on his face. The doctor was concerned and even taken aback.

34

"Are you okay?" she asked. "You blacked out for a few minutes. I was calling your name."

"I'm... fine," he said, rubbing his temples. "I was... thinking of... something. I'm sorry."

The doctor stayed silent for a moment before asking, "Is there anything you want to share with me?"

Despite the question, Dr. Pierce could tell that she was beginning to annoy him already, but leaving was out of the question for him and staying silent was out of the question for them both.

The doctor thought she knew what was on his mind, and she might even get him to tell her, but she gave him a moment.

Walter huffed and most likely felt her eyes on him. "I'm not trying to evade anything."

"And I don't think you are," she lied. "I'm here to help you communicate on how you feel."

"Why? What else did my parents tell you? Did they also tell you that I used to play with fire as a little kid too? That I used to play with matches and steal my dad's old lighters? Does that make me a pyromancer?"

The doctor sighed patiently before deciding to correct him. "No, Walter, your parents didn't tell me about that, and I don't think that makes you a pyromaniac. Still, it sounds to me that you've always had a creative mind... probably even enjoyed fantasy stories."

Walter shrugged, looking a bit embarrassed. "Yeah, I guess."

Dr. Pierce studied his face a bit and saw the uneasiness. "I don't want to make you uncomfortable, Walter, and forgive me if I do, but whatever it is that worries you — whether it's Samuel or something or someone else — you have the floor to tell me. Like I said before, anything you say in here is strictly between

35

the two of us. Confidentiality is very important to me, I assure you."

Walter smiled slyly. *"Confidentiality,"* he repeated under his breath. *"Okay, Doc. I want to say this, there are things that I wish were different between me and my cousin, yeah, and of course, I miss him. But…"* There was a bit of hesitation, possibly a knot in his throat, but he continued. *"But this isn't about Samuel."*

Then Dr. Pierce had a thought. *"Is this about the girl? Your mom told me about her. What is her name?"*

Suddenly, Walter grew silent again, as if the mention of Yvette had shocked him. *"Yvette,"* he finally muttered.

"Yvette?" the doctor said, as if she wasn't already aware of the young lady in question.

"Yvette Anders."

The doctor nodded. *"And what is she to you?"*

"She's… Well…" Walter was hesitant again. *"Honestly, I don't know what she is to me anymore."*

"Oh…" Dr. Pierce paused, a bit surprised by his answer. *"I see. What does your incident at school have to do with her?"*

"It's a lot to explain." Walter shook his head. *"But… I don't think you're going to believe me."*

"Try me."

Walter took a deep breath and asked, *"If I gave you a book and told you that anything you write inside of it will come to life, would you believe me?"*

With a slight tilt of her head, Dr. Pierce put on a confusing look. However, she gave it some thought then gave her response. *"Anything is possible,"* she said politely. *"Sometimes, writing everything down can help bring out that bad energy we feel is getting in the way, or holding us back. Seeing everything written down could help bring perspective and clarity in our lives. Have you ever heard of the Law of—"*

"That's not what I'm talking about," Walter interrupted. "I'm not talking about something... metaphorical or the Law of Attraction. I know what that is. That's not what this is."

Dr. Linda Pierce shifted in her seat, folded her legs and studied Walter's look. His face had grown even more sour than when she first met him. His unblinking eyes looked directly into hers, making it hard to dismiss his statement as some kind of fantasy. Those eyes, they looked angry and hurt. They looked honest.

Eventually, the doctor said, "I don't know how to answer that question, honestly, but I'm willing to listen if you are willing to explain it all to me."

Monday, March 16th

WALTER ARRIVED AT HIS THIRD-PERIOD BIOLOGY class a bit early that morning and was already a bit frustrated. He had forgotten to finish his homework the night before, and incomplete assignments were what had him on punishment now. Honestly, he began worrying about his grade in Biology, seeing how often his homework would slip his mind. The sciences were his weakest subjects by far, but he still enjoyed learning about them; usually on his own without a teacher in front of him or perched over his shoulder.

Most of the class was already there when Walter entered. Besides greeting two classmates close to the door, he didn't take a moment to socialize. Quickly, he began reading though the chapter he was supposed to read over the weekend. Mr. Vega pompously enjoyed reminding the class of how many days of the weekend there were whenever a student forgot their homework on Mondays.

Speaking of, the meager and balding Mr. Vega walked into the classroom as the bell rang over the intercom. Walter already had his textbook out, skimming through the chapter he was supposed to read last night, and Mr. Vega had already spotted him. Pretending not to notice, Walter quickly dropped his eyes back to the book, just hoping he seemed oblivious to the teacher's arrival.

"Good morning," Mr. Vega addressed the class as he scratched his thick mustache. "Quiet down. Quiet down now."

The students settled into their seats and fell silent before giving the teacher their attention — not as quickly as Mr. Vega would have hoped, however. Some of them tittered at the shine on Mr. Vega's bald spot. A joke at school was that Mr. Vega sheened his bald head every morning. The man was always well dressed with his suits pressed perfectly, so it seemed fitting. His shoes were never scuffed and even when he took his jacket off, he laid it down softly on the back of his chair like it was newly laundered. *It wouldn't look right without a bit of shine on his head to top it off,* Walter often thought. By now, Vega's shiny head was so famous that students would say "bling" whenever he walked past just for a laugh.

"I trust everyone read last night's chapter?" Mr. Vega asked, getting right into his lesson for the day.

Most of the class sulked at this, while Walter just kept his mouth shut and pretended not to hear him. Instead, he continued skimming through the chapter sneakily. He had barely read halfway through the chapter and was far behind. He simply turned the pages, flitting his eyes from paragraph to paragraph, hoping to find a few context clues. It was better than knowing nothing at all.

Mr. Vega threw the students a curveball. "So, I'm assuming you all would be prepared for a pop quiz then?"

The class instantly sulked all at once, and Walter couldn't help but join in, even groaning through his teeth. Teachers reviewing reading assignments with the entire class was annoying enough.

"Come on, Mr. Vega. Wouldn't you rather I have more brainpower to bring this school a championship? We haven't won one in years."

However, Mr. Vega wasn't convinced nor impressed. "Yes, Mr. Sims, we are all very proud of what the basketball team has accomplished this year. However, as I'm sure you know, that is not enough to exempt you or any other players from participating in my class. Now, enough whining, all of you. All you had to do was read a chapter this weekend. If you did, then you shouldn't have a problem, should you?" He didn't wait to hear any replies; maybe knowing more whining was coming. "Clear your desks. You will only need a sheet of loose-leaf."

"We have to write down the questions too?" one of the girls winced. In fact, nearly everyone was bothered by then.

"Well, Ms. Langdon, and with your penmanship, you need all the practice you can get." A few students tittered when he said that. "Quiet! Now, let's buckle down. We have much to go over today."

None of the students seemed to have the energy to quarrel or even respond anymore. Walter wouldn't care if someone did. It just meant more class time would be wasted, although he wasn't brave enough to raise a revolt himself. Certainly, he wasn't the only one who hadn't read the chapter, but it didn't matter now.

Mr. Vega began writing random questions on the board — but honestly, they weren't random at all. There were a few words and terms that were familiar to Walter, but the answers eluded him. It wasn't as if he had much time to absorb all the information, but he knew that was his fault.

As Walter was writing down the questions and already stumbling over the answers, a teenage girl entered the classroom. Her brown curls hung over her shoulders and her big brown eyes looked nervously at the teacher. Silently, she peeked over at her classmates in their chairs with her textbook pressed against her chest. She was wearing a dark midnight blue — denim jacket and jeans — and Walter thought it was a good color on her, so much so that he didn't realize how much he was staring.

"Good morning," she greeted. Her eyes flitted towards the students and back towards him. Those heavy eyes and stern lips gave her a sad scowl.

Mr. Vega turned to see the young woman standing a few steps from the doorway. "Well, good morning, Ms. Anders," he announced. "It's good to have you here today."

Yvette Anders slowly approached the teacher and handed him a sheet of paper. He barely read it before he nodded and muttered something to her. Walter couldn't hear anything amongst the other mutters between the students, not knowing why he was so curious.

"Everyone, I want you all to welcome Yvette Anders. She has been away from us due to a… family matter. Some of you might know why. No matter, we will respect her space. Now, Yvette, there is a free desk in the third row. Right there. Behind Ms. Livingston."

Yvette nodded then shuffled over to her seat. Walter's eyes were on her, and they only returned to the board when she sat behind the vacant desk. There was a row of students between Walter's seat and hers but he kept his attention on the board.

"Yvette, we are about to have a pop quiz," Mr. Vega announced to her. "Were you able to read the chapter during the weekend?"

Yvette nodded.

"Good. All you need is a loose-leaf."

Eventually, the boy who sat in-between then shifted his head down to write on his paper, giving Walter the chance to steal a glance at Yvette. She must have noticed because she peaked over at him. Walter felt a slight rumble in his chest as their eyes met. She shot him a little smirk and he responded with his own. The rumble only simmered when she returned her attention to the board.

As Walter paused in-between his story, Dr. Pierce took the time to ask. "How did it feel to see Yvette in school after so long?"

He shrugged. "Seeing her at school... I was happy she was there. I figured that meant that she was better... Well, not better, but... You know? I don't know."

"I understand and that's fine. It can be hard to explain ourselves at times."

Still, Walter seemed to be deep in thought. "I was worried about her, you know... when I heard about her mom. Everyone was asking her about it and giving their condolences. I didn't want to bother her, you know? I honestly didn't know what to say to her."

She nodded. "I understand. That was nice of you, Walter. Giving her some time to adjust back into school."

"I guess." A tiny grin reached his lips.

Dr. Pierce nodded solemnly. "Do you remember the first time you two spoke?"

42

"Well..."

If he were being honest, Walter couldn't remember whether it was later that week, or the week after that when he first spoke to her. It was the final minutes of the lunch period though and Walter had his face in his locker. His best friend, Art, was beside him and excited about their last win. The basketball team was on their way to the first championship appearance in years.

"Thirty-three years, Walter," Art reminded him. "We haven't won a championship since my mom was in school, and you know, my mom is old."

Walter snickered. "I'm going to tell her you said that."

Art snorted. "I'm not worried about that. You know I have to tell her that as many times as I can. She's always trying to play me one-on-one, or race me in the parking lot like she can keep up. She can't."

"Your mom is cool, bro. It is kind of weird when parents try to prove they are still young or whatever." If he were being honest, Art's mother was always fun to be around and had a young, jovial way about her. Even his stoic dad made deadpan jokes from time to time. Walter always felt like their second son when around the Wright family.

Arthur Wright had been Walter's best friend for... well, he wasn't quite sure how long. The boys went on a double date once in ninth grade, and one of their dates — he couldn't remember which one — asked them how they met. Neither could answer the question. They hadn't been friends since kindergarten or anything like that, but they always shared the same grade. They just remembered getting along quite quickly and became fast friends. They both agreed it was either during second or third grade, but since they were both on different class teams, they never shared classes together in elementary school. Nevertheless, from elementary to junior high and high school, the two were close like brothers.

Although they were both the same age, Art was always shorter yet stockier than Walter. The first week of their freshmen year, some joked that he skipped junior high entirely. Of course, Walter wasn't necessarily tall either, 5'9 to be exact and thankfully still growing. Art was somewhere around 5'5 possibly, but still his legs and arms were a bit larger than usual for his age.

Ironically, Art wasn't into art... not really, at least. He was an athlete at heart. The height had never been his hindrance. Even with his short stature, there wasn't a sport that he wasn't good at — exemplary even. He was strong, swift, and skilled.

Art went on to say, "My mom has been so excited about the championship that she's been giving me new challenges every day when I come home from school. She said she's trying to keep me sharp."

"Yeah, bro. She's proud of you. I'm proud of you... or whatever."

"Shut up," Art snorted then chuckled as he nudged his arm.

As Walter closed his locker to walk to class, he bumped right into a girl passing by in the hall. The textbook and paper that once pressed against her chest fell from her hands. The textbook hit the tile with a thump while the papers spread and glided across the floor. In shock, they both stared at one another for a moment then knelt to collect her belongings.

"Sorry," said Walter.

Yvette smirked slyly. "You like bumping into me, don't you?"

They both stood and Walter handed her what he collected. There was a shine in her eyes that glistened like amber glass. The way her lips curled softly when she smiled made him grin uncontrollably.

"Maybe the third time I should do it on purpose," Walter replied slickly, his eyes looking square into hers.

"Then we're going to have to fight."

He couldn't tell how she did it, but her threat sounded sweet and charming.

It wasn't until Yvette's friend Hazel called her and reminded her that they were going to be late for class that the two were brought out of their daze.

"I'm coming," Yvette said then turned back to him. "See you later, Walter."

"Later."

Walter saw Yvette peak back at him once more as she continued down the hall before vanishing around the corner.

Dr. Pierce was listening to his story in the hallway, thinking he might recall the incident, but the story was taking a lighter tone. "Sounds hopeful. Seems like she was interested in you, Walter."

"Maybe," he replied scornfully while shifting his seat. "I wish it would have happened that way. It would have been less embarrassing."

"Oh." Dr. Pierce was surprised. "It's not? Then... what happened?"

When Walter bumped into Yvette that day, it wasn't just papers and a textbook that fell. Her friend Hazel wasn't walking beside her either but her teacher, Mr. Mullen. When the textbook

45

and papers escaped her hands, her elbow suddenly lifted and knocked the cup of coffee from her teacher's hands, and it splashed onto his chestnut suit. Walter gasped at the mess, and he felt worse when coffee fell onto Yvette's papers. They were all watching him now — the teacher, the students in the hall, Art and, of course, Yvette. She was shocked and her eyes flitted between her stained papers, Mr. Mullen and the culprit.

"Oh, snap! I'm sorry," Walter suddenly apologized. He quickly knelt before Yvette did and began collecting her belongings briskly, starting with the textbook and scattered coffee-free papers. Yvette handled most of the papers herself, grabbing the stained ones last and more carefully. They were already beginning to stick to the floor.

Then Walter spotted a slender leather book that seemed to slide underneath him. Strangely, when he grabbed it, the old stiff bindings seemed to have a certain kind of weight to it. The book wasn't heavy by any means, but it had an unmistakable presence. In fact, he felt a subtle and peculiar pulse in between his fingers when he held it. However, before he could comprehend what he was holding, Yvette snatched it away roughly, swiftly disappearing amongst her other belongings.

"I'm sorry about that... both of you," Walter said earnestly. "Art distracted me."

Mr. Mullen was a plump man with a gray beard and completely bald. He began brushing the dripping coffee off his white shirt, bright blue tie, and his creamy brown suit. *The coffee blends in with the suit, at least,* Walter thought, hoping he couldn't show what he was thinking.

"That's quite alright, son," Mr. Mullen said unconcerned. "It could have been worse."

Yvette, however, was not so kind. "You like bumping into me, don't you?" she said, lips twisted in anger, but her eyes seemed close to tears. "Maybe the third time it should be on purpose, huh?"

"Don't be so brash, Yvette," Mr. Mullen said courteously. "Mistakes happen and that was already the worst of it. I will speak with Mrs. Mars myself regarding your assignment. I will make certain she gives you enough time to set it straight. No harm done."

No harm done? When Walter heard that it was Mrs. Mars's assignment he ruined, he felt his heart thump as though it were his own homework. Mrs. Mars was a speech teacher. Calling her rough was an understatement, and saying she was precise was only half the story. Mistakes on her assignments were just as bad as not following one of her unwritten directions. Every student that ever had her class knew of, and warned others of her ridiculous assignments. Walter went through the torment himself last semester and passed, fortunately.

"It's good to see you again, Walter." Yvette gave him a thin smile, but her voice was sour. Then she walked ahead of her teacher with her stained homework and scowl. Walter felt foolish and Yvette's reaction didn't make it any better.

On the other hand, Art was seconds from bursting into laughter. His cheeks were already puffed up and his lips were pressed behind his fist. "Good thing the coffee didn't get on Yvette too," he said, a burst of laughter flying out of him. Art was holding his stomach and wiping his eyes at his best friend's expense.

"Why didn't you say anything?" Walter demanded, less amused.

"Because it was more fun to watch." Art snickers a bit more than says, "Come on, lover boy. Let's get to class."

"What?" Walter was taken aback. "Lover boy? What are you… talking about?"

Art snickered on and shook his head, possibly taking note of Walter's hesitation. "Nothing, man," he said, tittering. "I just see that you still have a thing for Yvette."

"I don't—"

"You don't have to lie to me either, bro. I already know."

Walter sulked. "Whatever, man. Let's just get to class. I really don't feel like having this conversation right now."

Wednesday, March 31st

YVETTE WAS WEARING ORANGE TODAY; A LONG
sweater and a fuzzy, sunny beanie topped with a large white
cotton ball. Her dark curls had an extra bounce to them today,
and even danced and swung with every step, counting her
tempo. Even the cotton ball on top made a silly wobble when
she walked. Orange was kind to her. Her big brown eyes seemed
to have more of a shine to them than usual. Walter didn't know
why he hadn't realized that before; maybe he had never seen her
wearing that color, or maybe he wasn't paying attention as much
as he thought.

The two didn't have any classes together that day, but he did
see her during lunchtime in the library. He figured drawing in
the library would be a good way to pass the time that afternoon,
since Art was practicing with the basketball team that day.
Sometimes he and Art would play chess with a few students
during boring lunch periods, and Walter was surprised to see
Yvette there playing against the leader of the chess club himself,

Lenny Hale. Around them were a few other chess club members, spectating the half a dozen pieces on the board, more Yvette's than Lenny's.

Now, if the chess club were a band of tough guys, they might roam the hallways like the football players, with Lenny Hale in the center causing the most trouble. In fact, Lenny was the reason Walter and Art often came back to the library. Those boring lunch breaks weren't so boring around the chessboard when Lenny started running his mouth. The best was when Art played against him. So much smack and insults flew across the board in whispers and hisses. It was quite funny actually.

Although Lenny had the symptoms of a nerd and could correctly answer most questions posed to him, he was more jock in appearance. He had the build of a linebacker or tight end with his large arms and chest with broad shoulders, but had a mind made for a scientist and a pair of thick glasses for good measure. Even with his frame, Lenard Hale was no bully but protected his less combative companions. Although he was a sort of rival to them, Walter and Art respected that about him.

For a while, Walter joined the other spectators and watched Lenny and his opponent trading off moves over the board. Eventually Yvette spotted him amongst the group. A confident smile was on her lips and the twinkle was in her eye. She made her next move and saw Lenny's frustrated response.

"Three more moves and I win," Yvette announced gleefully. Walter observed the board and noticed she had trapped his king.

Seeing Lenny smack his hands together in frustration quickly caught everyone's attention and nearly caused Walter to laugh aloud.

You don't look so smart with that look on your face, Lenny, he thought playfully while shaking his head. If Yvette wasn't there, he might have said it boldly but decided to hold his tongue. His competitive side could often be as pungent as his best friend's.

"You've realized that you have nowhere to go, don't you?" said Yvette. Her smile grew wider and a little chuckle slipped between her lips.

For some reason, Yvette reminded Walter of a cartoon character. She seemed so alive and colorful. She probably wanted to say aloud how much of a fool she was making out of Lenny like Walter and Art often did.

Soon, Lenny stood, seeing his loss was coming. He cursed and was nearly kicked out of the library when a passing librarian heard him.

"Now, who's next? Walter?" A confident look smeared across Yvette's lips as she claimed her next victim.

"Oh please, Walter is trash," said Lenny.

"Whatever, bro." Walter turned to the clock on the wall, just realizing how much time had already passed. "I don't think we have enough time. Lunch is almost over already."

When he said that, Lenny and his minions peeked at the clock all at once like meerkats. Realizing the bell was minutes from ringing, they began packing up the chessboard and gathering their own things.

However, Lenny had a response. "That's enough time for you to lose."

"Whatever, just get the board back where it belongs before you get yourself in problems with Mr. Hale."

Yvette was collecting her belongings as well, noticeably slower than the others. "Lenny just knows that would have been three wins in a row for me, and we would have tied."

Walter nearly laughed out loud. "Well, I'd rather not disappoint you, Yvette."

51

She snorted. "Trust me, Lenny knows I'm going to be the first to get four straight wins during lunch and break his record."

"Stupid record," Walter blurted. "Art wants to break Lenny's record too. He just liked seeing Lenny lose.

"How about you put your money in your mouth, Walter," said Lenny.

There was a silence in the room and Walter's eyes squinted and lips curled as he tried not to laugh. Yvette shook her head with disappointment, yet her snickers were playful ones.

"The saying is: 'Put your money where your mouth is,' Lenny," she corrected.

"Oh, right," Lenny said, stumped. "What does Art always say? Oh, yeah. How about, 'See me on the board?'"

Walter chuckled. "That sounds weird coming out your mouth, you know that right?"

"Then how about my favorite line?"

"Oh no…"

"You remember it, right?"

"Bro—"

"You want to dance, D'Artagnan?"

"Oh my God, no." Walter shook his head, less amused. He even saw Yvette chuckling at that. "I hate when you say that. I'm not a musketeer, bro. And that still sounds so suspect. I hate it so much."

"You know I got to mess with you," Lenny chuckled as he put his backpack on. "Come by the library tomorrow. You can help me win four in a row."

"Whatever, bro."

Walter and Lenny bumped their fists before the chess club captain led his club-mates out the library.

"Well," Yvette said, getting his attention again, "You two are friendly."

Walter snickered at her sarcastic tone. "I don't know about Lenny, but I'm always friendly. We just like cracking on each other. It's just the charm, I guess."

"Your charm, huh? Well, I'd hate to see Mean Walter." The way she chuckled in response made him less bothered by the "Mean Walter" comment. Even so, he couldn't help but laugh as well.

"I'm just glad you beat Lenny," he added. "Just to shut him up. You realize he wasn't talking all that crap when you were beating him."

Yvette smirked. "Thanks. He's just cocky and the cockier someone gets, the less they think. Once I found a weak spot to exploit, it was basically over after that." She giggled. "It's a shame, really. He's a good player, but Lenny's confidence is his downfall. Now Carmen, she's good. Better than Lenny and he knows it. She's too quiet to be the leader though... plus I never actually beat her."

"Yeah, I heard she was really good but I've actually never played Carmen before. Art probably has. You know, I actually think she has a thing for him."

"Maybe. Art is pretty expressive, and she is quite timid. He might frighten her instead."

Walter shrugged with less concern but Yvette giggled a little and shook her head, seemingly realizing how ignorant he could be.

"I can't remember the last time I saw you in the library," said Yvette curiously. "What were you up to?"

"Nothing really. I was going to draw something... or something, but you... you guys distracted me." Catching his own words before they slipped out, Walter hoped he didn't sound like Yvette herself was the distraction.

"Oh, I didn't know you draw," she said. Yvette surveyed the table to make sure she had everything.

"Hey, about last week, you know, in the hallway with the coffee and—"

"Oh. It was just an accident. You don't need to apologize, but I should. It was my first week back at school and I was just… a little on edge. I couldn't finish all my work when I was home and fell a bit behind too. The coffee falling on my speech assignment…" She sighed. "It all just happened at the worst time. I'm so glad Mr. Mullen was there to talk to Mrs. Mars for me. Oh, and I have a test for her class next week. I can't forget that." With that, Yvette sulked, remembering something else to add to her plate.

Walter nodded but then had a thought. "Speaking of tests, you know we have one on Friday for Mr. Vega too, and I was… you know… we have to study, right?"

Yvette smirked a bit then nodded in agreement. "We *do* have to study."

"And, you know, I might need your help passing this test."

"Do you know that you say, 'you know' all the time?"

When she said that, it made Walter snicker. Yvette was sharp, there was no doubt about that. "Yeah, my mom tells me that all the time."

"Eww…" Yvette made a funny yet disgusted face. "Are you comparing me to your mom?"

"What? No. I'm just—"

She started laughing, so much so that one of the librarians had to quiet her. Her laugh simmered down, and light giggles took its place. "You should have seen your face. Seriously."

"Okay, okay," Walter said with a chuckle. He opened the library door to the semi-crowded hallway and held it open for Yvette to step out first. "You got me. So, what's up, you want to study together tomorrow?"

"Study together? It kind of sounded like you were going to ask me to tutor you, Walter."

"Did it sound like that?" She nodded with a smirk. "Well, I think I'm fine but maybe I can tutor you instead, or help you study for your Speech test. I know things too, you know. I was able to pass Mrs. Mars's class." *Should I have said that?* Walter was enjoying his time talking to Yvette, but he wasn't sure if he said too much in his attempts to be charming. Committing didn't bother him, it was the impulse of offering.

However, Yvette chuckled and hid her lips with a hand. "You're silly. Thanks, but I'm going to study with my friend Gina."

"Oh, that's cool."

"No, I mean... I'm studying for my Speech test with her. We already agreed. I'm sorry, I should have said that the first time."

"No worries."

Suddenly, the school bell began ringing throughout the halls. Teachers and students were already making their way towards their classes, and the two of them needed to do the same. However, Yvette hadn't made her way to leave nor answered his question.

"So, tomorrow after school before the late buses come?" he suggested.

Yvette wore a soft smile and slouched to the side with her sharp stare. The way her eyes looked up at him, there was nothing else Walter would rather see. However, she turned away from him for a moment and held onto an ear nervously.

"Sure," Yvette answered when facing him again, her smile now stretching across her face. Her brown eyes were a bit shiny now and her dimples dug deep.

Walter held back the eagerness to smile as well. It was no date, but being alone and studying with Yvette could lead to various conversations and outcomes.

"Okay. Sounds good." Once again, Walter didn't know what to really say but figured that was enough.

"But Walter," Yvette added, "make sure you're not trying to bump into me again. I'll be watching you."

Without another word, Yvette turned away and walked down the hall, taking her big brown eyes and smile with her. He watched the extra bounce in her hair and the way it danced with every step. It swung to her rhythm, and the cotton ball on top made a silly wobble when she walked.

*   *   *

It had been her second year as a reporter for the high school newspaper, the Hallway Herald, but things had changed since Yvette's freshman year. There were fewer student reporters now and the budget was spent elsewhere. With the peak of social media, the paper had become less relevant in the hallways throughout the years. Even so, Yvette was proud of her words and, fortunately, there were enough readers in and out of school to keep the paper afloat. The Editor-in-Chief, Mr. Mullen, would eventually commission a website to keep up with the "social" trend. There were even a few students working on an app as well, but that seemed far off and might not be ready until next

year. Frankly, Yvette really wasn't into the whole social media
frenzy like most of her peers, but even she knew that digital was
widely preferable.

With her time away from school, Yvette had to give up her
pursuit to be the managing editor of the *Hallway Herald*. The
uncertainty of being the initial student-in-charge and leading the
others wasn't enough to hinder her. Failure was easier to
swallow. However, it wasn't fear or failure that changed
everything. After their last managing editor graduated, a coveted
seat became a vacant one. Mr. Mullen might have thought she
would make a good choice, but she wasn't able to prove it nor
earn the position. It was her mother who inspired Yvette to
pursue the position, but it was her mother's passing that changed
all that. Soon after she stopped attending school and the position
was no longer in her reach.

Now, the tall and fit Georgia-Lee held the lead position,
while Yvette was at the same post as before. It might have
bothered her some, but not enough to wish ill on her new leader.
Georgia-Lee Singer was always curt, but becoming the
managing editor made her strict and quite mean at times. The
newspaper meant a lot to her, Yvette couldn't deny that. Still,
there was a part of her that couldn't abate the thought that she
could do the job better.

Whenever she submitted a new story to the paper, there was a
bit of jealousy there and today was no different. Even for a
school newspaper, Yvette took her job just as seriously as her
grades. She was the most investigative of their teenage reporters
and they all knew it. This was where most of her pride lingered.
She wanted to be rewarded for that, for all of it... but she
wasn't.

Be that as it may, Georgia-Lee was a junior so Yvette knew
she might get her chance once she graduated, but the thought of

it made her sulk. Being in-charge for her senior year alone didn't sit well with her. Yvette didn't know if she should feel hopeful or terrible for thinking that way. Even so, it was undeniably there. Her pride weighed down on her and her pride weighed a ton. Still, Georgia-Lee had always been a good and honest friend to her, and even reminded Yvette of her older sister.

"I like it," said Georgia-Lee with a little chuckle.

Her newest article was a dive into these strange, old dolls Mrs. Strickland's eleventh grade Chemistry class found on one of her many outdoor experiments. She and her students were by the river a few acres behind the school's football field, and were searching for a certain kind of moss that apparently grew an obscure color. However, a few students stumbled upon the dolls while searching the grounds, and the focus shifted. The dolls had tiny black buttons for eyes, but, without even a hump for a nose or a carved mouth, their faces looked incomplete. Those creepy half-faces became more intriguing than some funny colored moss.

Mrs. Redding herself surmised that the dolls might have been made by students over two centuries ago, around the time the school first opened. The dolls were undoubtedly old, but Yvette wondered what the purpose of them might be, seeing as though they barely had faces. However, when she finally saw them for herself, she was taken aback by the look of them. There was an eeriness in those eyes as she stared back at her, and she didn't like how familiar the half-faces were. It didn't deter her fascination or from writing the article, but those faces... they resurfaced old memories she would rather forget.

On the other hand, Georgia-Lee found it all to be quite funny and tittered from time to time as she read. "All this weird fear over some stupid clay dolls?"

"Ceramic, actually," Yvette corrected.

Georgia-Lee laughed, leaning back in her chair shaking her head. "I heard that Rose girl was freaking out over them too, like they were coming to life or something." She rolled her eyes. "People believe all kinds of crazy things, don't they?"

Yvette shrugged, unsure of how to respond. "Yeah, I guess so."

One of Mrs. Redding's students, Molly Rose, insisted that the dolls might have been made by some woods witches many years ago, and were possibly possessed. She swore she saw the dolls heads turn and move when they thought no one was looking. Supposedly, she wasn't the only one who had seen it — one or two others, possibly — but Molly was the only one who spoke up about it. Of course, not many believed her, but she swore and swore, and the gossip grew and grew. By the time Yvette jumped on the story, Molly Rose had nothing more to say on the matter.

She's afraid people might think she's crazy, Yvette knew and shared that fear.

Still, she was curious about Molly's statement and wondered about these witches she mentioned. Eventually, she found an article nearly a century old about several students who disappeared without a trace. Soon after, a local theory surfaced about a group of witches who kidnapped them, sacrificed them to their queer and terrible gods; locking the children's souls into certain objects to do their "divine" bidding. Of course, this wasn't something Yvette wanted to omit from her story. Nevertheless, without Molly's statement as a segway, it would all be baseless. It might not have been the best story to delve into when Yvette was returning back to school, but the curiosity was hard to ignore.

It all felt too close to home.

59

Nonetheless, it all was newsworthy — a high school and town exclusive in a sort of macabre way. Fortunately, Yvette masked the ghastly with some charm and color.

"I didn't know you were into that kind of stuff," Georgia-Lee went on.

"History and good stories are what I'm into, really." Yvette shrugged but was secretly indulging in the praise. "When I heard about the experiment, I told Mrs. Redding about Dr. Harris."

"Oh yeah, the archeologist. Where did you find him?"

"My mom knew him for a long time. She introduced me when I was in fifth grade, I think. So, Mrs. Redding got in touch with him and the two of them started an experiment together with the class. Afterwards, they reported their findings to me."

"So not only did you get the information you needed for the report, but you got Mrs. Redding and *this* Dr. Harris to do most of the investigating for you." Georgia-Lee gave her a devilish smirk. "Sneaky, Yvette. Very sneaky."

Yvette felt her lips curled a smile, not knowing how it even got there. "Not really. It just worked out that way. I'm a journalist, not a scientist. I made sure to credit them, of course."

Georgia-Lee shrugged. "Well, either way, well done. Dr. Harris definitely pulled everything together, but I like how you left a bit of mystery at the end. It's well written also. Just needs a little editing. Some of the sentence structure could be tweaked. We can go over it together. I'll show you what I mean."

"Sure," Yvette agreed, although she was a bit annoyed that it wasn't perfect. It was what she strived for.

Georgia-Lee turned her rotating chair to face her completely. "How do you feel about your first article since you've been back?"

Yvette shrugged and smirked. "It feels good... to be back and everything, I mean. And hey, thanks for being so cool with letting me write a few articles from home."

Georgia-Lee cleared her throat. "If I'm being honest, I never told Mr. Mullen but I was a bit against it."

Yvette's eyes narrowed suspiciously. "Why?"

"After everything that happened with your mom, I figured it was better if you didn't know all the crap going on around here. I thought it would be too much for you right now after your mom, and then Samuel. I mean, this is basically an elective, so who really cares? But, Mr. Mullen was... 'excited to have her words back in the paper' I think was what he said. Anyways, I'm happy you're back either way. I missed you — you know that — but I didn't want to overwhelm you if you're already doing school work from home."

Yvette grinned uncomfortably but understood what Georgia-Lee meant. Even though she didn't agree with her editor, she tried to let it go but failed to do so.

"I understand but... I don't know... The distraction was good for me. I could still feel like I was in school even when I wasn't. I could — somehow — feel normal again. Does that make any sense?"

Georgia-Lee nodded solemnly then said, "You're right. I'm sorry. I didn't want to impose, I was... I was just a little worried about you."

When she grinned this time, Yvette felt a bit warmer inside. "Thanks, Georgia-Lee."

"I know you've probably been hearing this question all day every day, but..." Georgia-Lee paused. "I'm not going to ask. I just hope you're okay."

Yvette sighed. "I'm fine... considering, but I couldn't stay home forever."

"I know. I miss her too, Yvette." A soft smile ran across her face. "Did I ever tell you that your mom's class was the first class I ever failed?"

"Oh... Really?" Yvette was shocked. Georgia-Lee Singer was always one of the top students in her class, so failing didn't seem to suit her. "I never knew that."

"Your mom was a bit frightening when she wanted to be... and funny... and sweet... I never understood how she could pull that off. I admired that about her. Even though I failed her class once, I took her class again during summer school in seventh grade." She smiled. "I'm glad she pushed me the way she did. She saw something in me and... Honestly, if it weren't for your mom, I probably wouldn't be here. It was her that got me into reading more but I didn't think I would have ever fallen in love with writing. Seeing your writing reminds me of hers. It's like you both have the same voice."

It was real; the smile on Yvette's face as well as the knot in her throat. She wanted to be mad at Georgia-Lee. Knowing that she couldn't remember her mother's voice on her own, yet her friend did, made Yvette a bit resentful. She knew what she meant — a writer's voice, a common description — but the word still triggered her nonetheless. A part of her wanted to be mad at her mother for unknowingly pushing Georgia-Lee into the position Yvette coveted most. Still, it should have been a bittersweet moment, she knew, but there was nothing sweet about it... not really.

Be that as it may, she was learning how to hide such things, so she masked her frustration with a pleasant look. "Thank... Thank you," she muttered. Suddenly, it became strenuous to speak.

The two girls were then distracted as a bright flash went off between them. Disturbed, the Hallway Herald's managing editor turned to her left angrily.

"Donnie!" Georgia-Lee nearly screamed, "How many times do I have to ask you to put that camera down? You're driving me crazy already."

Chuckling with a Canon in his meaty hands, Donnie — a chubby sophomore with red curls above his snout of a nose — was always jolly behind a camera. He was funny... at times, Yvette could admit that. However, Georgia-Lee saw him more as a chip in her spine.

"Come on, Gee-Lee," said Donnie with his cheeks a bit pink. "The best pictures—"

As he spoke, Georgia-Lee growled and balled up a blank sheet of paper angrily. "I told you to stop calling me that." With a quick huff, she threw the paper at Donnie, and he laughed as it bounced off his stomach then flopped to the floor. Georgia-Lee rolled her eyes. She might have missed the mark she was aiming for, but Yvette couldn't tell.

"—are when they are out of nowhere," said Donnie, finishing his sentence.

"Then take a picture of... of..." (She scanned the room.) "... of Samara then."

When she heard her name, Samara, with her long brunette hair and curious gray eyes, tilted her head from behind her laptop as she heard her name being called. "What was that?" she asked, her concentration broken.

"Nothing," said Donnie as he lifted his camera. "Say cheese."

"Oh, my—" Samara quickly ducked behind her screen to hide from the flash. "Donnie, not now. I'm editing."

The photographer looked down at his camera, and his titters simmered to utter disappointment. "I can only see your hair and your laptop." He shrugged. "It's fine. You're editing. I can make that work — Oh, yeah—" Donnie turned back to Georgia-Lee. "Jacob was feeling sick, and he was sent home, so… he won't be able to have that article ready this afternoon."

With a large stressful breath, Georgia-Lee sulked. "Why didn't he call me?"

"Because it was right before lunch," Donnie said candidly. "He looks pretty bad. I saw him. He probably got the virus for something."

Samara looked up at the cameraman. "Don't joke about that, Donnie," she scolded. Her frightened eyes flitted towards Yvette then quickly shifted back to the screen in front of her.. By then, everyone had heard the story of how her mother died… or at least the story that was told. Just the thought of the lie made her ears burn uncomfortably.

"And why are you telling me this now?" Georgia-Lee snapped.

Donnie shrugged. "I've been here for — what — ten minutes? I just remembered."

She grunted. "And you are already annoying me." Georgia-Lee was through, and her irritated grunt spoke volumes. Turning back to Yvette, she took several deep breaths to calm down.

"Do you need some help?" Yvette asked sincerely, leaning in closer to her, yet already regretting the question.

"Yes… Yes, I do." She quickly turned to her laptop. "I need you to call Jacob and have him email you his article right now so you can finish it before the period is over."

"What?" Yvette didn't really like that idea but had a feeling that something like this was coming. "Me?"

"Donnie and Lyle have already finished the layouts and most of the edits are nearly done. We are still behind, and I need Jacob's article today. Please, Yvette. If Mr. Mullen was here, he would suggest that you finish it too."

Needless to say, Yvette wasn't too thrilled about having to finish another's article. She liked Jacob's work and didn't feel comfortable mixing her words with his. It might have been a bit selfish, but it was the way she was. However, Georgia-Lee needed her, so she swallowed her pride and complied.

The front door to 7013 Wilk St. always made a slight creek when it was opened. Even if she wanted, it was kind of impossible for her to sneak in and out of the house. Nonetheless, Yvette pushed the front door open with a shoulder knowing how difficult it could be at times. A good thud nearly knocked the wind out of her, and she gripped her history book tightly before it fell to the wooden floor. As soon as she walked through the door, her neighbor's dog, Po, ran towards her. His eyes and mouth were wide open joyfully, while his black and white fur swayed with his rhythmic gait. His arms opened wide as he rose and hugged her, pushing her textbook against her chest.

"Okay, Po, okay," said Yvette exhaustedly. Still, she took a moment to rub his furry side. "I missed you too."

Although Po wasn't their dog, they took care of him whenever his elderly owner was incapacitated for a time. Po had become part of the family and a reoccurring visitor at the Anders house.

"Yvette?"

Suddenly she heard her father's voice coming from the basement. Excitedly, Po dropped from his hug and ran down the hall towards the basement stairs. Within seconds she could hear his four paws running down the steps — four paws that sounded more like a dozen.

"It's me," she called. She dropped her textbook on the couch then rested her bag on the floor. "That's better," she muttered, relieved by the loss of weight on her back. She took a quick look around the living room, and didn't see any duckling blanket laying on the leather couch or by the stairs. Even the glass table didn't have any toys or food stains on it so she knew her nephew wasn't home yet. A moment alone once her father was gone is all she really wanted right now.

The basement was a little less cluttered than it was that morning. Old boxes labeled in permanent marker were piled in the corner, and scattered tools that once laid across the floor unorganized were now hung up in their rightful places. Her father didn't get far besides that. Aside from the old paperwork on the table, there was a box sitting beside him. Laid out in front of him was a bouquet of pictures. When she saw him, he was wiping his pinkish eyes.

"Hey, sweetheart," Mr. Anders greeted her with a soft smile.

Yvette smiled, hugged him tightly and giggled after kissing his hairy cheek. "Hey, Dad." A single tear was starting to fall so she wiped it away from him.

"I haven't been crying long," he promised, his handsome smile only growing. Yvette's father was a stocky man, fit as well with large arms and a broad chest. He had big brown eyes like his daughter's and his chin held a thicker beard than she was accustomed to. It had become a bit more unkempt and overgrown. It often tickled her when she hugged him and made her feel like a little kid again.

Turning to the table, she saw that her father was looking at pictures of her parents' wedding. One picture got her attention more than the others. It showed her parents in all-white, smiling after they were named husband and wife. Between them stood her sister, Charlotte, who wore the largest smile fit for a five-year old. Wrapped in white lace and snuggled into her mother was one-year old Yvette who looked at the camera with wide unblinking eyes. Seeing it made her happy and sad all at once.

"I got distracted," her father admitted. Yvette Anders was only sixteen but still knew how immersive the past could be; maybe more than most. She herself was still living in it every day.

"Come on," Yvette said sweetly with a smile. "Let's put these pictures away and... I'll finish sweeping up for you."

Yvette's parents met five or so years before she was born. Her father, Maurice Anders, was a single father who lost his first wife due to childbirth, leaving him heartbroken, widowed and with a newborn daughter to raise. Going through therapy was a challenge for him. From what her sister had told her, he was living with guilt and fear, thinking he could have done something to prevent his wife's death. Yvette might have felt a bit neglected since he hadn't confided in her like he did Charlotte, but it was only until the death of his second wife that those feelings resurfaced. Margaret Reyes was the woman who loved him when he thought it would never happen again, and now she was gone. Yvette could only imagine how awful her father would feel to talk about it with Yvette. However, soon he met Ms. Reyes, a fellow teacher working at the same junior high school — the school where Yvette first met Walter on that unforgettable day in the cafeteria.

Maurice Anders met Margaret Reyes during a staff meeting after school one day. The two were organizing a field trip together with both their English classes sometime after. A few years later, they were organizing a wedding after the birth of their daughter. Although he was heartbroken, their father tried to stay strong for his daughters; however hard it was. Now, Maurice Anders had lost another wife... another piece of his heart.

Charlotte, however, had lost a second mother. She never knew her own, so Yvette could tell that her sister didn't really know how to feel even if she would never admit that. Charlotte was very supportive to Yvette knowing how hurt she was. On the other hand, when Charlotte lost her young husband and became a widow herself, their father was there for her the most. They both knew what it felt like to lose a spouse and be left with an infant on their own. Yvette felt guilty of that. She might be able to help them in their grief, but she wasn't sure if she should. Such thoughts made her secret feel even heavier than it already was.

The Anders House knew about loss like many others, but this family experienced enough to last a lifetime... and more. They were devastated, all three. Still, the truth of Margaret Anders's death was kept a secret from the rest of the world, only residing in their humble home. Her old doctor might have known as well but wasn't quite sure if that counted or not.

Still, it was the three Anders who remembered the blood... Yvette most of all.

Once the pictures were stacked back in the box and the floor was swept, Yvette's father asked her the time. He wasn't running late yet, however, they began to return upstairs, and Po followed.

"I made your favorite," her father told her as they entered the kitchen. "Shrimp Alfredo. It's still warm. I made it maybe an hour ago. A minute or so in the microwave should be good enough.."

Yvette grinned. "Thanks, Dad." It wasn't really her favorite anymore, but she rather not bother him with that.

"The best way to thank me is to eat it." His voice was less cordial now. "I'm tired of making you food after school and you barely eat it. You keep doing that and I will stop making you food all together. Do you understand?"

Yvette nodded slowly. "I'm sorry. I've had so much on my mind... and school—"

"I understand, sweetheart, but I've heard it all before. Now, did you hear what I said?"

Defeated, Yvette nodded once again, this time a bit more sorrowful. "Yes, Dad. I hear you. Sorry."

Graciously, her father kissed his daughter on the forehead and thanked her before asking her to start the coffee maker while he made his way upstairs, leaving Po to rub his fur against her.

Sometime after, she was sitting on the countertop next to a half-eaten bowl of food, and was tying her father's tie for him. Regardless of how many times he did it, the tie would often dangle unevenly from his neck. Her father was stretching his head towards the ceiling, but Yvette still had to work around his long chin and beard.

"So," he asked, "How has school been so far?"

"It's fine," Yvette replied, halfway done with his tie. "The paper isn't doing too well though."

"No?" Her father was surprised. "The *Hallway Herald* was always popular in my day."

69

"In your day—" Yvette evened out his tie, "— you didn't have Snapchat and Instagram and all that."

Her father nodded as he grabbed his coffee. "True, but there is nothing a good storyteller can't do to reel a reader in. You have talent, Yvette. Where's the talent in Instagram?"

Yvette chuckled a little. "You'd be surprised."

"I rather not find out. What about the report you did on the dolls? It was written well, just needed some editing. What did Mr. Mullen think?"

"He wasn't there today. He's sick, I guess. Georgia-Lee liked it. I think he will like it too."

Her father smiled. "I know he will. Now, tell me, how do I look?"

Funny enough, her father's question reminded Yvette of her mother. He would ask his wife that same question every morning. To Margaret Anders, her husband was always handsome, whether he was rugged or barbered or even clean shaven. Yvette felt sad by that but smirked nonetheless as she looked at him in his black security uniform with gold trimming, silver badge, and utility belt with his pistol attached. Yvette stared at his weapon for a moment. *I'm still not used to this,* she thought. Her father would often leave home in suits with classwork, now he was wearing a gun and badge. Although her father didn't seem happy about working security again — something he hadn't done since his days in college — Yvette didn't have the heart to convince him that he would be happier returning to school. Still, she had mixed emotions about that.

Maybe he was waiting for some time before returning to teaching, she often thought hopefully. *Maybe he will return next year, even to a different school. I don't care.* She just wanted her father to be happy.

Suddenly, Yvette swore she saw blood drip onto the kitchen floor. She could see it forming beneath his sleeve, and a messy stain conjured on his wrists turning his black cuffs to a deep crimson.

Drip, drip, drip, blood fell to the floor.

She blinked and her mother stood in her father's place with bloody wrists with her sharp eyes crying tears of red. Yvette quickly shut her eyes, heart thumping, skin shivering.

"Sweetheart?"

Yvette looked up to see her father, haunted. Her mother was gone... for now and her father was there once again.

It's not real, she told herself.

"Are you okay?" he asked, putting his hands on her shoulders.

Yvette flitted her eyes to the floor then to his wrists. There was no blood to be found. She had been hallucinating again.

"Sorry, Dad. I was just—" She stopped herself and turned to her father with a forced smile. "You look great. Very handsome."

Mr. Anders approached her and rested his hands on her shoulders. "Your mother?"

Yvette quickly shook her head. "No," she lied.

Her fathers didn't seem convinced, but he let it go for now. "If you want to talk about it later, we can, okay?"

Grimly, Yvette leaned into him and wrapped her arms around him. "Okay."

Mr. Anders embraced his daughter tightly then placed a warm kiss on her forehead. "I love you, sweetheart."

"I love you too, Dad."

71

Before he walked out the kitchen and out the door, her father then pointed at her bowl of food. "Make sure you eat all of that, Yvette."

She grinned nervously. "I will."

With a nod and a grin, her father left saying his farewells. She waited until she heard her father pulling off before getting up from the counter. She went to the sink and scraped the rest of her food out the bowl. She ran the water, and soon, the garbage disposal was dicing her dinner down the drain.

It didn't take long for Yvette to settle in her bedroom. She fished in her book bag to pull out a little leather book. Ominously, Yvette stared at the old bindings for a moment before sitting at her desk. She opened to the middle where there were a few less stains then grabbed a pen. She took a deep breath then wrote a name down on the page.

Margaret Anders.

Once she leaned back in her chair, Yvette felt a warm, tender hand rest upon her cheek. Her lips parted and curled at the touch. There standing beside her was an older comely woman with crimson-colored lips, short nappy curls, and cheeks with dimples dug deep.

"Well, hello, sweetheart," the woman said sweetly with a soft smile.

Yvette smiled as well, showing her matching dimples as she took the woman's warm hand. "Hi, Mom."

*   *   *

"Do you mind if I ask you something?" Dr. Pierce spoke up.

Lowly, Walter nodded and looked up to give her his attention. "What did Yvette tell you about her mother?"

Walter seemed a bit baffled by the question. "What do you mean?"

"Well, I know at the beginning she didn't really talk to you about it. Did she ever talk to you about her?"

"Why do you ask?"

"If she talked about her then it tells me two things: she really trusts you, but, also, seeing that you both lost someone close to you and you both mourn Samuel, it might add to what you have been experiencing."

"We did talk about her... sometimes, but... but not really, you know? There was an article about her, so almost everyone knew what happened and how she died."

Dr. Pierce nodded. She had read the article herself when Mrs. Anders passed away. It was a pleasant farewell. "I understand. I'm happy to know you've been there for her, Walter, and that she has been there for you."

He sighed, nodding. "I think we needed each other... you know?"

"I do." The doctor checked the time. "We still have some time today. This book you asked me about, the one that if you write something down in it, it will come true."

"Well—"

"Not word for word, but... has it helped?" Walter was a bit baffled by the question. Instead, she rephrased a little. "Do the two of you write different intentions into the book and try to visualize or manifest it? Has it helped to make the—"

"No..." Walter said bleakly. "No, that's not what it is?"

Dr. Pierce leaned in her chair with her notepad to her side and eyes a bit squinted. "Then what kind of book do you mean?"

Thursday, April 1ˢᵗ

THE DAY SEEMED TO SLUG ON. CLASSES WERE MORE
boring than usual. Walter was issued enough homework to stay
busy for the night. With his mother's punishment, she would
make sure his assignments were done. Even so, he was looking
forward to studying with Yvette after school. However, it didn't
help the day move any quicker.

When the bell for lunch came along, Walter was relieved,
hoping this period would slug on like the other. *That never
happens though,* he thought bitterly. Still, the school day will
come to an end and that gave him more solace than he was used
to.

Wrapped in his brown paper back was his old reliable
sandwich he was also looking forward to, his peanut butter and
jelly; a classic yet simple comfort. Across from Walter sat Art
who wasn't really hungry, but was eating Walter's pear for him.
They were talking about the basketball game Walter missed,
when Art was distracted by the buxom Nurse Jane who had just

entered the lunchroom in her lilac scrubs. His best friend once admitted to Walter that he sometimes wished he was always sick or injured; just to be sent to the nurse's office often. Walter thought it was quite silly, but he couldn't deny that Nurse Jane was attractive with her wide hips and thighs, but he liked her long brunette hair most of all. Most of the boys in school would stand in a line outside her office with their cuts and bruises, coughs, and sniffles, staring and gawking at the alluring nurse.

A year prior, when both boys were freshmen, they were talking to a few other students and debating who was the prettiest teacher in school — teenage boy stuff.

"Ms. Bellamy," was Walter's answer. She was his Algebra teacher last year. She was a shapely woman with long legs, beautiful long jet-black hair, a honey sweet voice and — unlike most women in their school — unmarried. "She could give me homework everyday if she wanted and I'll never forget." Even then, the lazy teenager always handed in his homework to Ms. Bellamy on time every time. Walter's strongest subject was indeed math, but that was beside the point.

"Mrs. Redding," said Hopper, an energetic sophomore who they used to hang out with before he moved to Pittsburgh. "And I'm taking Chemistry II next year, so I hope I get her class." He didn't. His parents had divorced before the year was even over, and he was living with his grandmother by the second semester.

"Nurse Jane," said Art, sitting on the opposite side of Walter. Of course, he was reminded of the rules, but didn't care. "I know she's not a teacher but... Honestly, just look at her. I should convince her to teach Health class instead."

"Yeah, I wouldn't mind that," Walter added. Anyone would be a better Health teacher than Mr. Wattley... or Dr. Wattley as he liked to be called; which was strange to Walter. It seemed silly to be a doctor teaching a stupid Health class in a stupid old high school.

"We can hold classes at my house," Art went on. "One on one classes, if you know what I mean."

Hopper laughed. "I don't think *you* even know what you mean, Art."

Like it was yesterday, Walter remembered snickering as he shook his head. Art wasn't laughing though. He was serious, which made it even more hilarious.

Unfortunately for the two, Walter and Art didn't have any classes together since their freshman year. The school might have known that when the two of them are in the same class they are often talkative; not only amongst themselves but with everyone else. Regardless of how disturbing they could be, Walter and Art would usually get good grades — if Walter finishes all his homework, of course. Unfortunately, not every teacher could be Ms. Bellamy. Walter couldn't remember how they got on that subject in the first place. Puberty was all the rage back then. Although the conversation didn't last long, Walter still remembered Art's answer, making it more memorable.

Now, as the two sophomore boys sat in the lunchroom, Art was still infatuated by Nurse Jane. Just like a year before, Walter just watched and shook his head as his friend stared.

"Don't stare too long, Art," Walter implored as the doors closed and the nurse was out of sight. "You're already drooling."

Without thinking, Art wiped his dry lip. When he realized there was no drool there, his friend began to laugh. "Don't be a loser," he said, taking a bite out of the pear.

Walter might stop for now, but it had become a yearlong running joke that he wouldn't let his best friend forget. "It's just funny, bro."

Art sulked. "It's not," he said dully, unmistakably less interested in his friend's comments.

"What are we talking about?"

The boys turned to see they were joined by Art's teammate, Kevin Kittle. Kevin was a handsome boy, olive tone, gray-green eyes and his hair was faded on the bottom with a cluster of thick curls on top. He was tall and fit — being a seventeen-year-old senior — and had noticeably more than just some peach fuzz on his chin. Underneath his arm was a basketball and he placed it on the table as he sat.

"What's up, Walter?" Kevin asked. He didn't wait for an answer and turned to Art. "One more week, bro."

Suddenly, Art became unexpectedly hype. He dropped the half-eaten pear and took the ball in his hands. The championship game was soon approaching, and it was all Kevin and Art would talk about.

"One more week," Art repeated jubilantly as he smacked his palm against the ball.

"This is our last chance before I graduate, and I plan to make it count."

"I know you're not worried, are you?"

"Worried?"

"I don't know, bro. You sound a little scared."

"Scared? Bro, I'm tryna make sure you're not scared. Plus, we all got to be on it. I'm not tryna get all the way to the championship and lose."

"Lose?" The look on Art's face would make someone think he was offended. "Who said anything about losing?"

78

Kevin chuckled. "Yeah, you're right." The teammates did some secret handshake Walter didn't know so he took a bite of his sandwich and observed. "Don't forget we're having that players' meeting right after school — 3:20 on the dot. Don't be late, Art."

Art spread his hands. "When am I ever late?"

"Hey, you know what Coach always says. 'Tardiness on this team is not like tardiness in the classroom. Less time in practice—'"

"'—less time in-game.' I know the saying. It's just as annoying when you say it. Maybe more, actually."

Kevin snorted before turning to Walter. "Walt, make sure your boy doesn't forget."

Walter frowned slightly. "Please don't call me Walt."

"Oh, right. I forgot you don't like that. Why not? I never asked."

"You did," Walter reminded him flatly. "Walter Taylor from third grade."

Art laughed. "I remember him. He mooned the entire school during an assembly once. That kid was crazy."

"Right, and they called him Walt. So, I'm Walter."

Kevin chuckled. "I get it."

"Can we get back on topic here," Art said, still hype. "You're asking Walter to remind me about practice? You can't depend on Walter to remember anything. He's like... an old man. You didn't know that?"

Walter snorted as well. "I've got nothing to say, because... he's not lying." He had to shake his head and smirk while admitting that.

"I feel you," Kevin chuckled. "I have problems remembering homework sometimes. I'm failing Mr. Witherspoon's class right now because of that."

"That's probably because Witherspoon is an asshole," Walter said coldly.

Art nodded. "Yeah, let's not get into Witherspoon."

Kevin nodded as he stood. "You know how teachers are. Anyways, Art, make sure you're there after school. No excuses."

Art waved him off. "I won't forget."

"You better not. I'll see you guys later." Kevin walked off with the ball twirling on a finger, passed several students and sat at a crowded table on the opposite end of the cafeteria.

Soon after, Walter saw Art staring again and thought that Nurse Jane had walked back in the lunchroom or something. It wasn't the nurse who had his attention. Walter turned around to see a girl side eyeing Art. She had skin like dark chocolate, long legs with sharp dark eyes and a flat nose. She sat at the end of a table amongst a few other girls, hoping to hide in plain sight. The smile she wore was soft and directed towards his best friend. Walter didn't know her, but she did have a nice smile. When she saw the two of them looking at her, she quickly averted her eyes. Art was grinning too, but his lips tightened in embarrassment when he saw Walter's sly grin.

"What are you looking at?" he asked, trying to appear clueless.

"I was going to ask you the same thing." Walter subtly tilted his head toward the girl. "She's cute. Who's she?"

Art sneaked another peak, seeming pleased that she was distracted by her friends and didn't see him. "That's Trisha."

"Trisha, huh?"

"Shut up."

Walter chuckled a bit. "She's your classmate?"

Art nodded. "Yeah, in my World History class. I like her and... I think she likes me too, but..." He paused. "I tried talking to her once. I just get really nervous, you know?"

Walter nodded solemnly. "I know exactly what you mean."

Art took the pear in hand and took another bite. "Oh yeah." He chewed and said, "Like you and Yvette."

The name rocked Walter and he was puzzled. *Why would you bring her up?*

"Yvette Anders?" Art said, clarifying unnecessarily. "You know who I'm talking about. She went to junior high with—"

"I know who Yvette Anders is."

"Then why are you acting all surprised when I said her name?"

"The better question is: why are you even bringing her up?"

"Nope." Art shot down the question right away. "I asked my mine first, Walter. Go on."

Annoyed a bit now, Walter sighed showing it. "I'm not surprised, you just... caught me off guard. That's it."

"Caught you off guard?" he said slowly and purposely, pretending he hadn't heard him.

Walter shook his head, grinning and knowing he was defeated. "I don't have to explain anything to you."

Art gave him a slick smile and shook his head as well. "Honestly, I'm surprised you hadn't tried to talk to her already. Who cares about the whole coffee thing anymore? Who cares about the lunchroom thing in seventh grade? Who cares? She probably already forgot about that... or maybe not."

Walter snorted. "You know as well as I do that she was dating — whatever his name was — in eighth and ninth grade. I

81

wanted to ask her out after they broke up but... then... you know."

Art sighed slightly. "No, you're right. I get it."

"What about you and... World History?" He had already forgotten the name.

"I met Trisha this semester. It's not the same. I get what you are saying about Yvette being in a relationship once and everything that happened, but what about now?" He paused and Walter didn't respond. "You see, no answer. I'm right, it's not the same. I might be nervous to talk to Trisha for a month or so, you have been nervous to talk to Yvette for three years. And I mean 'talk' talk, not like a friend—"

"I can't really say she's my friend, bro."

"Doesn't matter. She's not your 'friend' friend either. Don't pretend like we never had this conversation before."

If Walter was being honest with himself, he knew Art was right. Admitting it aloud to himself would be difficult, however. So instead, he said, "Well, I'm meeting her after school today. We're going to study together for Mr. Vega's Biology test tomorrow. Well, she's more tutoring me than anything, but—"

"Really?" Art interrupted, impressed and surprised all at once. "Smooth. It's actually perfect. You can stroke her ego and still find time to—"

"Wait... Stroke her ego?"

Now, Art seemed baffled and even unconvinced. "Don't pretend like you don't know how these smart girls are."

Walter shook his head. "No, I don't," he said a bit coldly.

"Right. Of course you don't. You like the dumb ones. At least they like you back though." Walter punched Art's arm hard enough that it caused more than just a sting. Art laughed it off.

"Trust me, I don't care how sweet she is… or smart… or funny… or pretty—"

"Art—" Walter interrupted with a voice that grew less friendly.

"I'm joking. You see, already defending her. Let me just remind you, Yvette Anders is not your girlfriend. The knight-in-shining-armor thing doesn't work — doesn't look good on you either."

Walter smirked, still shaking his head. "Don't pretend like I don't already know that, bro."

"I'm happy for you," Art said genuinely. "Good luck during your studying — I mean — tutoring session. Next thing I know you'll be telling me that 'Ms. Anders' is your new favorite teacher."

Surprisingly to him, Yvette arrived at the library a few minutes after him. He had already found a table in the corner before she arrived. The yellow she wore was as bright as her welcoming smile. It colored her shirt and socks, a wrist of bracelets, small hoops dangling from her ears and even the hair tie that held her curls in one. Her denim jacket matched her jeans as well; monochromes of sky and baby blue. She was indeed bright, but orange was still his favorite color on her.

"I thought you would get here before me," Walter admitted as he greeted her.

Yvette chuckled as she took off her bag and sat at the head of the table. "And here I thought the same thing… or maybe that you would forget." She gave him a side smile and she rested her Biology book beside his own where they hogged the corner.

Walter nodded. "No, I remembered."

She got comfortable in her seat. "Remembering stuff, huh? That's a first." She chuckled. "Honestly, I was thinking of not coming at all, but that would have been a terrible April Fool's joke."

With her unexpected quip, Walter couldn't help but laugh. He had forgotten what day it was and it caught him off guard. "That wouldn't be a good joke."

"I thought so too. Honestly, I wished we weren't having this test tomorrow. I swear, Mr. Vega loves giving them out. It's like his hobby or something."

"I just think he has a thing for giving out failing grades." His words were blatant and quite bold — harsh, even — but he meant it... some of it at least. Mr. Vega was far from his favorite teacher. However, to lighten the mood, Walter drew in closer and muttered, "I think he gets off on it."

Lips agape, Yvette shook her head then chuckled. "I was joking, Walter. You are terrible."

"I was joking too," said Walter, laughing at his half-lie. "Why worry about this stupid test anyways? I have an excuse. I forget things. You? I'm used to you being the top of the class."

She snorted. "I wish I was top of the class. I'm not even 'top of the newspaper.'"

"So? I've read your work and it's always good to me. Some are pretty dull, but yours are always interesting, even if it is a boring topic."

Seemingly a bit stunned, Yvette stared at him for a moment. "You've read my articles before?"

"Sure. I've read a few last year. I read the one about the dolls the other day too. I liked it. Seemed a bit spooky to me — not too spooky, though — like a subtle spooky, if that makes sense."

Yvette pointed at him as her lips separated in excitement. "That's what I was going for!" She even smacked his shoulder with glee. "Walter!? That's so awesome!"

"Oh." Surprised, he chuckled and said, "Well, I think you did… do that well." Frankly, he didn't expect such an excited response, so he didn't have the words ready for it.

"I never would have guessed that you read my work or even read the paper, for that matter."

"Sometimes." He shrugged. "I'm a curious person."

Yvette was blushing now. "Thanks, Walter. That's sweet of you. And thanks for what you said about stupid tests… and for calling them stupid."

A light smile came to his lips, both for what she said and what he just remembered. "To be honest, I thought you might have interviewed that Molly girl. Wasn't she the one who was saying the dolls were moving or something… like they were possessed?"

Yvette groaned a little. "Yeah. I tried talking to her about it, but with everyone calling her crazy, she was too scared to talk to me. I don't blame her. High schoolers are like hounds…"

"Or vultures."

When Yvette tittered and smiled, it was soft and subtle. Without warning, Walter felt his chest ring like the school bell; his heart quaking nervously underneath. Yvette grazed an ear with her fingers as she turned to get her notebook, but the smile was still there — still subtle, still soft, still bright like sunbursts.

"You have the notes from class yesterday, right?" she asked.

Walter quickly turned to his copy book, and began flipping through the pages to the date in question. "Yeah, I got it."

"Good. Maybe we should start with the notes first, reviewing what we know will—" She paused while taking a closer look at Walter's notebook and his small spiky penmanship.

"What?" He began surveying the page, looking for something strange. "My handwriting isn't the best, but—"

"No, stupid." She giggled and leaned up for a better view. Beside his notes was a drawing of a rooster sitting on a fence with the moon above him, while eagerly looking at his watch around his wing. "This is cute," she said, then chuckled. "Kind of silly too."

"Yeah. Just some pictures I draw when I'm bored in class."

"You have more in here?"

"A few."

Curiously, Yvette began reaching her hand out to turn the page, then caught herself. "May I?"

His sketches inside had honestly slipped his mind. No one really looked at his notebooks — only teachers and parents were that nosey. He wasn't sure if he wanted Yvette to see or not. Not many had. Still, he eventually nodded. After all... *She likes one of them, she might like the others.*

Resting her chin on the back of her palm, Yvette began flipping through the pages, exploring the sketched and shaded drawings inside. They were usually silly stuff — bears dressed as construction workers sitting stories high on a steel beam, while eating honeyed ice cream, a sun and dark cloud facing one another wearing boxing gloves and scowls, a male mouse handing a female one a bouquet of cheese, even a black and white bat hanging upside down and playing chess with all gray pieces — senseless silly stuff.

"It's just a habit," he told her. "I started doing that in my math book back when I was in elementary school."

86

Yvette chuckled. "I see you draw a lot of animals."

Walter snorted playfully. "Yeah, I liked animals growing up, but my parents never let me get a pet, so… you know. It just became my thing, I guess. I don't only draw animals though, as you saw."

Yvette leaned in closer for a better look at one specific drawing. It was their teacher looking up at a falling anvil that was seconds from crushing him. Walter even drew a large, bright shine coming off his bald head.

Walter laughed a little when he saw it. "Oh yeah, I drew this one not too long ago. Maybe two weeks ago."

"Oh, my god!" She covered her mouth, hoping not to laugh aloud, but he could see the shock on her face. "Is that Mr. Vega?" Yvette looked up to see a smirk run across his lips. "You really are terrible."

"I really don't like Mr. Vega."

She giggled. "I can tell. Honestly, Walter, they're really good. I mean, this looks just like him."

Walter was a little surprised. His father had only seen a few, his best friend might have seen a bit more, but Walter felt strangely satisfied letting Yvette see all the drawings she pleased. Page by page, she went through the book; smiling, chuckling, pointing and asking questions. It gave him a certain delight that — until Yvette saw them — he didn't know he coveted.

"You're really good, Walter," Yvette told him. She then grew silent as she lingered on a black bird — maybe raven, maybe crow, Walter couldn't remember which — with a pipe between his beak, a black top hat and a monocle perched on his visible eye. One of its wings tried to hide the menacing smile between his beak with his dark feathers, while the other was wrapped

87

around an ebony cane with a rat's skull pommel. The only part of the drawing with any other color was the skull. It was filled in with an eerie yellow. *Gilded bones,* he reflected. *The bird is a crow. I remember now.*

"This one is very… ominous," Yvette went on. Her tone was a curious one. "I really like it though. And the skull too. It's pretty."

"Pretty?" He shot her a side eye and an eyebrow rose in sly, silly suspicion.

"Well, you colored it yellow, and I like yellow." she giggled. "But… is the skull supposed to be gold?"

"Well, not solid gold, but—"

"Gilded?"

Walter smirked. "Yeah… gilded."

Yvette was smiling again. "You really have talent. I know I keep saying it, but it's true. I can't even draw stickmen straight."

That made Walter laugh. "That's because you're a writer."

"What's that supposed to mean?"

"Well, aren't all words just a bunch of stick-people? Or like… piles of stickmen body parts? You've had a lot of practice with that."

Yvette eventually began laughing and shaking her head. "Shut up, Walter. You are ridiculous… but very creative." The pair tried not to bother anyone else in the library, but it was a dumb joke that couldn't be ignored.

A moment later, a girl Yvette knew from class came over to the table, and in her hands was a bundle of borrowed books. Walter couldn't remember her name — it wasn't like he knew her in the first place — but the girl gave Yvette her condolences. She was saying how sorry she was, how she would miss Mrs. Anders and how much she meant to her as a teacher. Yvette was kind and thanked her, but did look a bit bothered when the girl was out of sight.

"Are you okay?" Walter asked, a bit confused.

"It's nothing... Just..." Yvette was hesitant until the venting came. "If I'm being honest, I don't like to get condolences anymore. I mean... I can't be mad at her. She was just being nice but... I don't know. I'm not really mad at anyone. It just feels overwhelming having to be reminded that my mom is gone. Like... I really didn't like when Mr. Vega put me on the spot, and started announcing what I'm going through to the entire class like everyone doesn't already know. Why couldn't he just leave it alone, like..." Her voice sunk back down. "...like it never happened?"

He wasn't used to this. Yvette was being honest with him; open, vulnerable. He wanted to say something to assure her. Something smart, or witty — not too imposing — but assuring in some way. Nothing stupid, of course, but something. So, he spoke his mind, hoping the words wouldn't fail him nor come out tripping over his lips.

"You shouldn't blame him. It seemed like he was trying to protect you... in his own way. You know how nosey people are. Plus... your mom meant a lot to many students here, even teachers. It might have been a bit uncomfortable, but I think it was important that people know not to bother you about it. You should talk about it when you feel comfortable, and no one should pressure you. And... I don't know... that's just... you know, my opinion. At least that way no one can say they weren't warned about it. A..." He paused for a moment, searching for the word he was looking for. "Not really a warning... Well, kind of. Umm... A deterrence, I guess."

The words came out but he wasn't sure if they were exactly the words she needed. Nonetheless, waiting for Yvette's response was the troubling part. He wasn't telling her that he loved her or anything of that sort, yet all those words couldn't stop the butterflies and their razor wings. The swarm inside him simply flapped on violently.

However, the silence lingered for a moment. Wondering what she might be thinking, wondering what her reaction could be, he tried to stay patient. Her eyes shifted downward for a moment before she shook her head.

"No, no, you're right, Walter," she agreed although she spoke quite sedately. "I guess... I guess I never saw it like that."

There was another pause, long enough for a smirk and a stare. It was a sight to see but came without preamble.

"What is it?" Walter asked with his own to match.

"Nothing. I just… I never knew you could be so sweet. That's all."

Walter snickered. "Sometimes."

"When you want to be, right?" She tittered. "Now, come on. Let's get to work."

The two didn't have much time to talk and talk, so they started to study. Although they were studying, Walter couldn't help but make a few jokes just to hear Yvette laugh. Even the librarian had to quiet them twice. It was fun. Walter truly believed that Yvette enjoyed it as much as he did, but, most importantly, she was a great tutor and would make a great teacher if she wanted to be. *Must be in the family.*

Eventually, Yvette began fishing through the crevasses of her backpack, but then remembered she had forgotten her eraser home that day. This bothered her. "I only do my notes in pencil," she went on to tell him. "I hate scribbling over words when I make mistakes. It just makes everything look so… sloppy. Even worse, sometimes it can be hard to read my mistakes, especially when my mistakes aren't really mistakes. So... I guess the mistake... was that... I thought it was a mistake... when it wasn't?" Her head cocked to the side before she looked over at Walter. "Does that make sense?"

"Well... I think so. I don't know. You said 'mistake' a lot."

Yvette chuckled a bit while taking another gander amongst her things. Eventually, she gave up. "You don't have an extra eraser, do you?"

"Yeah. Somewhere in my bag. Are you okay?" *Stupid question.*

Yvette shook her head at first. Her ringlets swayed from shoulder to shoulder only to rise and fall when she nodded. "Yeah... Yeah. That just bothers me — took me through a..." She paused for a moment; eyes flitting toward her bag then her textbook, deep in thought. "Sorry, Walter. I just hate when I forget things. It can make me... a bit rattled honestly."

"Hey, don't worry about it. Trust me, I know exactly what you mean." He was forgetful so often that it surprised him when he remembered. "I think I have one in the front pocket of my book bag." He couldn't remember if it was or not, but Yvette zipped open the pocket and fished inside. She seemed to be having trouble finding one, however, she suddenly froze and locked eyes with him.

"What's—" Suddenly, Walter remembered and felt a bit stupid.

Yvette pulled out his pocket knife with a hard plastic hilt painted in deep olive green. Curious, she lifted the blade up to see the ebony metal with its sharp silver edge. It was two fingers thick while the hilt was slightly wider.

"Why do you have this in here?" she asked, baffled yet intrigued.

91

"Well…" He was hesitant at first, but then joked and said, "It's not an eraser, I know that."

The knife fell back into the bag as it left her fingers. "But… why?" She seemed more curious than concerned.

"I got it from Samuel, actually. Honestly, it's been in there so long that I never took it out. But… you never know when you might need it."

Yvette shrugged with a sad look. "I guess." She zipped the bag shut. "Well… no eraser in there."

Walter went into the depth of the side pocket in his jeans. One by one, he laid a sharpener on the table, kept the zippo lighter in his hand, then placed an old, crumpled receipt beside the sharpener. His eraser was underneath everything. He was ready to hand her the eraser, but Yvette was more curious about the glittering silver lighter in his hand. She pointed. "And what's that there?"

Walter handed it to her. Seeing what it was, she hid it behind her fingers from any would be prying eyes. Yvette took a gander above both her shoulders before her fingers spread open. Ironically, the way her fingers spread; they resembled the eagle wings engraved in the metal. Wings, eyes, body, and beak — all cloaked in polished silver. Yvette's fingers massaged the metal, feeling its smooth yet rigid surface. She even gave out a little titter as the touch of its texture gave her fingers a bit of a tickle. Silver on silver rang as the lighter tapped one of the three rings on her right hand. Walter then realized that no matter what jewelry she might wear, those rings always bedecked the same fingers. He couldn't remember a time when she wasn't wearing them.

"And why do you have a lighter in your pocket?" she muttered. "Did you forget that was in there too?"

Walter snickered from the sudden slyness in her eyes. "Okay, the lighter was my dad's once. I never want to lose it, so I always keep it close. Just like my eraser, apparently."

She made a silly little snort. "But why a lighter?" she asked curiously.

He shrugged. "I always liked it as a kid. It felt cool. Plus, the sound it makes when it opens—" Before he could finish his sentence, Yvette opened the top of the lighter, beheading the eagle with a satisfying click. "You see. I don't know if he gave it to me or if I just stole it, honestly, but he never took it back. There is no gas in it so it's not dangerous or anything. Just a keepsake, really." He hadn't realized he was scratching the back of his neck as he spoke until after. He did love fire growing up and watching things burn, but didn't think that was something he should share.

"Mm," she hummed. When she closed the top, it clicked back together like a clasp, and she returned the eagle's eyes and beak where they belonged. "It's pretty," she said, seemingly abandoning the eraser still in Walter's hand.

"Pretty?" That word again.

"It is," she said, eyes rolling yet her lips gave out a few chuckles. "A pocketknife in your bag and a lighter in your pocket. You're such a boy."

The two met four years ago when both began their seventh-grade year in junior high school. They didn't share any classes together that year, but Walter remembers seeing her at their orientation for the first time, and here and there during school.

It was Samuel who introduced the two. However, that wasn't entirely true. Art would say that Walter and Yvette first met in the lunchroom in the seventh grade. The boys were talking about something Walter couldn't recall, but he ended up bumping into the girl in front of him. His hand might have grazed her butt, he couldn't be sure, but the girl was certain he did. The girl was twelve-year old Yvette.

"What's your problem?" she snarled, lips tight and nostrils flared.

"My bad," Walter apologized with his hands raised. "I didn't mean to bump into you."

She eyed him suspiciously for a moment. "What's your name?"

"Walter."

"You like touching girls' butts, Walter? You like being sneaky?"

That took twelve-year old Walter aback. "No... I..."

Yvette's arms were folded now. "Try thinking of a lie faster next time, Walter. I might believe you." Her sarcasm was cold, and her eyes rolled; sharply, heavily... but they were pretty, even then

"Well, what's your name?" he figured he'd ask.

When she looked back at him, her eyes weren't as sharp but they stared at him a while. It wasn't for too long, however. Walter could remember her hair whipping as she turned away, grabbed a burger and said nothing.

It wasn't until after that lunchroom misunderstanding — a week after, perhaps — that his cousin picked him up from school and Yvette was already in the backseat. Samuel did warn him that Charlotte and her sister were riding with them, but he didn't expect it to be her. In fact, it wasn't until a few times after that car ride that he chose to even remember her name. *Yvette Anders, huh?* He didn't know it then, but Walter would never forget the name.

As the two were going over the notes from class, Yvette opened her history book searching for the answer to a question neither of them knew. When she did, the book opened and, in between the pages, a little brown leather book was resting inside. It was much smaller than a normal notebook, but not small enough to fit in someone's back pocket. With a little grin, she took the slender book from between the pages then stuck it back inside a few chapters ahead.

"Sorry about that," said Yvette.

Her apologies made Walter wonder why she said that to begin with. He didn't give it much thought but that didn't make it any less strange. "What is that?" he asked, just as curious as Yvette was with the eagle lighter.

"Um… Just a sketchbook."

In response, Walter pushed his lips to the side in an unconvincing way. "Oh really? A sketchbook? What do you draw in it? Crooked stickmen?"

Yvette hit Walter's shoulder playfully. He chuckled, but there was a bit of a sting to it. "Oh, shut up, Walter."

"Just saying," he replied with a little chuckle. Although he was still a bit curious, he decided to let it go and continue studying. They had already wasted enough time.

After an hour or so, a screech blared over the intercom as an announcement was being made. "Attention students attending after school programs, to anyone who is taking the late buses, they are parked outside the school and will be departing soon. Thank you and enjoy the rest of your day."

When she heard that, Yvette quickly rose from her seat and began to gather her belongings. "I have to go," she blurted. "My dad works tonight so I need to get home before he leaves the house. I have to watch my nephew tonight until my sister gets home."

"Oh." Walter stood to gather his things as well. "Well, let me walk you to your bus."

Yvette looked up at him suddenly, pausing for a moment. "Oh... No, I probably won't get there in time if you do. I'm sorry. I'll just see you tomorrow, okay? Maybe we can study some more in the morning before class?"

"Sure." Walter understood and nodded, hiding his disappointment well enough. "I'll see you tomorrow then."

With a biology book in hand, Yvette gave him a little grin, a good-bye, and she scurried out the library door. The library wasn't fun after that. It was dull.

Walter wasn't in a rush to return home as Yvette was, so he sort of lagged his way out of school. Fortunately, his mother allowed him to stay after school to study. It was a leeway he was thankful for. She had him on punishment since last week and she was already annoying without it. Why he was on punishment is not important, however, the lack of entertainment at home made his time spent with Yvette even more enjoyable. *Let's just say, I'll think twice before being forgetful and a childish liar.* The lying part was his mother's most burning pet peeve. It wasn't as if he didn't know that already. Forgetting to finish a few homework assignments was scarcely an issue. Lying about doing homework when he hadn't, made his mother livid.

On his way walking home, Walter felt a strange lump within the bindings of his textbook, then he realized it wasn't his book at all. The bindings were smoother, and he could feel the wording more easily beneath his fingers. There was no mistake that the textbook wasn't his, even without the square lump between the pages. Upon opening the textbook Walter was greeted by the slender brown book that sat snuggly inside.

When he held it close to examine it, he remembered the abnormal feeling it gave him. Inspecting more closely, there didn't seem to be anything particularly special about it. It even looked too small to be anything more than a little sketch book or a lineless notepad. There were no words on the front or back covers, just faded brown bindings that were a bit cracked and scuffed. He respected her privacy, but his curiosity was hungry, so his eyes feasted inside.

Peculiar enough, he found nothing inside. Mottled brown stains spread and bled from page to page and were especially thick in the corners. These blots were particularly rougher while the untouched areas were quite smooth for some old book. Although it was strange, it seemed more fitting to be trash than a secret.

A crack of thunder nearby caught his attention, and gray clouds were gathering and drifting. He closed Yvette's textbook with the book inside and continued home, hoping to beat the rain. Remembering his forgetful nature, Walter had to make sure he reminded himself not to leave her textbook at home.

Harriet D'Artagnan made her favorite food that night, something she usually does to punish him further. Instead of threatening not to feed him like his father had done before, his mother would serve her son the worst. When she laid a plate of mashed potatoes, grilled chicken and mixed vegetables, everything was covered in a thick sea of mushroom sauce. These mushrooms weren't diced to hide the taste or texture but there were many large slices swimming in its shallow sauce. Walter was already preparing to vomit.

"You better make sure you eat everything on that plate," his mother said sternly. "Everything on that plate is good for you."

"Mushrooms?" Walter winced. "Really?"

She wasn't pleased. "All of it, Walter. When you are done, I want you to get the kitchen cleaned up — and the next time I walk in your room, and your school clothes are still on that unmade bed or yours, we're going to have a problem. Now get to it. You don't have all night. And don't forget to pack a container for your father. He might come by for some food later."

Walter shook his head. "We don't have any more containers. He took them all, remember? I couldn't find any this morning for my lunch."

His mother sighed with disgust. "That man... I keep telling him to bring back my Tupperware containers and he never remembers."

With that, his mother shook her head while walking out the dining area, leaving her son to suffer through the mushrooms on his plate.

Walter's mother's maiden name was Barker, and she was named after her late grandmother. Harriet Barker had been a nurse since before her only son was born, but it made her a bit bitter throughout the years; less sympathetic, ironically. Although she eventually became the head nurse of the hospital, she was, as she would say... "Overworked, underpaid, and exhausted."

When young Harriet Barker was interning during her junior year in high school, she met Lawrence D'Artagnan, a fellow junior from a rival school. Their schools' conflict history was so terrible that Harriet almost felt unremorseful to see the boy's badly broken leg. She had no way of knowing that his boy

98

would be her future lover and husband. Walter remembered
laughing so hard when his father told him the story.

"My mother can truly be cold, can't she?" Walter asked his
father, comically and, of course, confidentially. Walter knew
those words would never reach his lips if his mother and her
scowl were around.

Even so, Lawrence D'Artagnan laughed. "She can be warm
too."

"Yeah, maybe to everyone else."

Walter's parents might have had the strangest high school
sweetheart story ever, but Mr. and Mrs. D'Artagnan were
together for years after that. They loved one another deeply,
however, when Walter was eight, the divorce came like an
avalanche; cold and unescapable.

His father was a mechanic who owned his own business and
three separate shops around the city. He was a great father to
Walter, he was a great businessman to his patrons, but both his
ex-wives would probably say he wasn't fit to be a husband.
Walter was eleven when his father remarried, only to sign
another set of divorce papers two years later. Walter never cared
for his stepmother, but he did feel a bit guilty yet happier when
his father was single again.

Even so, Walter knew his mother still loved his father. He
guessed the distance between them nurtured their co-parent
relationship. Later, it seemed like their fractured friendship had
been mended, but he didn't really know. He would occasionally
see his father flirting with his mother, and sometimes she smiles
up at him, silently allowing it. Walter only hoped the smiles
would last at some point and their broken family wouldn't be so
broken anymore. It had been another two years since his father's

second divorce, but Walter wasn't sure what was possible between his parents.

That night was a quiet one. Walter's mother was exhausted after dinner, and was already dozing off in her bed. He finished cleaning the kitchen and wrapping his father's plate in Saran wrap. However, his father never came and eventually called and said he had to work late. There were some equipment issues at his shop that needed his attention, so neither Walter nor his mother argued. Walter was used to it while his mother was as well, but she might have been too exhausted to indulge. Ever since his second divorce, she'd made extra food just in case he was coming by. It had been several years since the three of them sat down at a table, and had dinner together as a family. Walter never saw the big deal about it, but he could see how much it mattered to his mother. He just wanted them to be a real family again. Be that as it may, wishful thinking is nothing but that, wishful. *Time will tell,* he figured.

Since he couldn't watch any television for another two weeks, Walter finished his homework in no time then spent an hour going over what he and Yvette studied for the biology test tomorrow. While he was studying, his mind ran across the empty little book again. That curiosity captured his attention, overtook his mind, and it couldn't be ignored.

Nonetheless, Walter thought nothing of it for now and finished up his studying for the night. It was still early so he decided he would draw a picture for Yvette in the little sketchbook. Whatever it was, the book seemed too old and derelict for Yvette to care if it returned to her with a harmless drawing inside. *She might even like it.*

By the time he began making a new Captain Long Ears drawing, he could hear his mother snoring from her bedroom. Walter often wondered how his father and her would sleep in the same room when they both snore so loudly. Even so, his mother's snores were muffled when he got up to close his door, and he returned to work on the captain's nose. Walter gave the crime fighting bunny a smile and raised one of his arms in a wave. Above his open lips, Walter drew a comic bubble that said, "Hi, Yvette." He shaded him a bit — giving him an afternoon shadow — and made a few subtle strokes around his fur to appear a bit more scuffed from battle.

When he was through, Walter was satisfied with his picture. It was different from most of his sketches. Captain Long Ears usually wore a stern scowl as he fought criminals and supervillains. Walter never drew the bunny smiling, but a smile was worth it for Yvette.

"Hi, Yvette."

Suddenly Walter turned around in his chair as he heard a high-pitched voice conjured behind him. As if his drawing jumped off the page and found color, Captain Long Ears was waving at Walter with his scruffy fur wisped back and forth upon him. However, when the captain had a good look at him, his lips curled downward to a recognizable scowl.

"You're not Yvette," said Captain Long Ears disappointedly. Even his fist balled up and his eyes squinted towards Walter. "Wait, you're Walter." His voice was gleeful now and spiced with pep. "I thought you were your father, Dr. D'Artagnan." He even flitted his furry head from side to side, making sure the coast was clear of his kidnapper. Only Walter was there, lurking; surprised and suspicious.

"What the—" His voice was slow, and Walter just realized that both his eyes and mouth were wide open in disbelief. *What is this?* Walter was frightened and wouldn't dare turn away or even move. The bunny was nearly naked like the original stuffed animal the captain was based off. Just like the stuffed animal,

101

baby rattles played in his tummy when he moved. The only clothing he wore was a fitted white shirt with three words sewn in bright and bold baby blue letters: *It's a Boy.*

It was ironic though. His mother would tell him how a lot of people thought he was a girl. He even remembered his mother telling him about a time when he was four years old, and he threatened to prove it to a woman he wasn't a girl. Determined, his hands were already at his belt buckle. Fortunately, his mother was there to stop him. Till that day, Walter had no idea what his father would do if he were there, or if he even knew about it. Seeing those bold blue letters and hearing those baby rattles was strange and even insane.

Captain Long Ears's grin suddenly returned as he spotted Walter's basketball sitting in the corner. Like a living cartoon, the bunny bounced from Walter's bed and grabbed the ball with his paws. "You have a basketball!" he nearly shouted.

"Wait—"

Walter tried to stop him, but he lifted his furry body in the air and began to glide while bouncing the ball. Walter was able to grab him by the ears and threw him back on the bed. The way the bunny's fur tingled his palms... frankly, it freaked him out completely. To add insult to injury, his ball bounced several times, so it was too late. The snoring in his mother's room had already stopped.

"Walter?!" she bellowed. "I know you're not bouncing that ball in my house!"

"No," Walter called back nervously. "My ball fell on the floor. Sorry."

"Don't mess around with it and that won't happen. Now, get ready for bed before your punishment is extended."

Walter sighed lightly so she wouldn't hear him. "Okay, Mom."

With his own stern scowl, Walter turned to Captain Long Ears who curled up on his pillow looking a bit frightened. It wasn't until that moment that Walter heard the rattling coming from the bunny's stomach. "I…" Walter lowered his voice to a mutter. "I told you not to bounce the basketball. I'm already on punishment."

"Oh, right," said Captain Long Ears nervously. "I'm sorry. I forgot."

"You forgot? I… I never told you about my— It doesn't even matter. How did you even get here?"

He didn't wait for an answer. Walter turned to the diary ominously and was a bit frightened. The drawing was still on the stained page, and he began to stare. The disbelief was unwavering.

"Well… technically," the captain shrugged, "You never said not to bounce the basketball. You said, 'Wait!' So, if we're splitting furs… Why are you staring at me?"

Walter didn't know how to answer that but realized he was staring and turned back to the old book. All he could do was stare at the drawing instead, wondering if it were all real. "I'm dreaming, right? This is… I must have dozed off or—"

Suddenly, his door opened, and Walter nearly jumped in fear. His mother was at his door, peeking her head inside. Seeing her frightened him since she might see Captain Long Ears on his bed. However, she didn't acknowledge him or seem to hear the rattling he made when he shook. Instead, her sleepy look was on Walter only.

"It's getting late. Did your father pass by?"

Walter shook her head as his eyes flitted towards the captain then back to his mother. "No, Dad never came by."

Walter's mother sulked then said, "Get that butt in the shower then into bed, and make sure you leave your homework out so I can check it. Anything undone and you'll meet a literal rude awakening."

He already knew that, but he nodded all the same. "Okay."

With that, Harriet D'Artagnan vanished behind the door and left it slightly open.

"Was that the evil witch Wexly?" the captain asked nervously, his stomach rattling as he shook.

Walter could have just answered, but instead he started to ask, "How are you—"

"Check the book." The bunny jumped up to his feet then walked to the edge of the bed. "You drew me in it, didn't you? It's still there."

"I…" No matter how hesitant he might have found himself, the truth was plain to see. The drawing was there and Captain Long Ears was here. "I'm going to take a shower."

Walter rushed into the bathroom, nearly forgetting his towel and snapped the door shut. He rested his body against it, shocked and confused. It was as if he were hallucinating, but he saw the drawing and he even felt the fur on his palms. *That was no dream, yet… it couldn't be real either.*

Before long, Walter stood bare beneath the shower. As the water washed over him, so did a plethora of questions. He was starting to understand why Yvette seemed a bit spooked when she saw the book appear inside her textbook pages. That book was no normal secret… it was… something else entirely.

After he was washed, dressed and left his homework out in the living room for his mother, Walter returned, ready to see the captain still bouncing and rattling on his bed. However, Walter was alone when he walked through his bedroom door. He even called after him.

"Captain," he whispered, but there was no response.

Walter looked down at the open book on his desk. However, as if it was never there at all, the drawing he made for Yvette had vanished. No cloudy marks were left, no vestiges of the drawing remained on the page. Walter even flipped through them back and forth, as if the bunny might have hopped to another. There was nothing.

The little brown book laid there... unmarked and empty.

"You don't believe me."

Dr. Pierce must have had an unconvincing look on her face without even knowing. If she was being honest, she was quite engaged in his story and wasn't paying attention to how she appeared anymore.

"I didn't say I don't believe you, Walter," she replied sincerely but the look on her face might have something else entirely. "I didn't say anything."

"Exactly," was his response. "You aren't saying anything. You aren't even writing anything down anymore."

"Should I be writing something down?" The doctor tried her best not to sound too spiteful towards a child, teenager or not.

That question made Walter sulk and shifted positions on the couch. "I don't know... I... You're the doctor, right? You tell me."

She sighed heavily and might have even shrugged a bit, if she dared, but she remained courteous amongst the rude tone. "I don't know what you want me to say, Walter. It sounds like—"

"Like I made it up? Is that what you were going to say? Is that what you think? That I'm crazy? I'm not crazy. I swear, everyone thinks that or thinks I'm paranoid and that I'm seeing things but—"

"Walter, I don't think that at all."

"No. Don't try to... You know what, I'm sitting here in front of you like it really makes a difference. You probably don't need to write anything anymore anyways because obviously I'm crazy, right? Right?!"

"Walter! Walter. You need to calm down." Shouting was never a method the doctor would use in the office. Shouting was no method at all, in her eyes. Still, she shouted, and Walter sighed, staying silent. Even so, he was panting now. Dr. Pierce remained calm and went on. "I don't think you're crazy. I don't. But if you are being honest with me—"

"I am—"

"Listen to me, Walter. If you're being honest with me then I will be honest with you. I can understand why your family would be concerned about all of this, but I'm here to listen and help you. I'm not here to judge."

Walter nodded. "I'm sorry."

Dr. Pierce wasn't that bothered, so his apology wasn't necessary, but it simmered him down and Walter took his seat back on the couch. She looked at the clock and saw that they still had some time left to continue. "Tell me what happened the next day when you gave Yvette her book back."

Friday, April 2nd

MR. VEGA'S BIOLOGY CLASS WAS THE PERIOD
before lunchtime. It was probably why Walter hated it so much
— well, beside the fact that he hated biology. His mother always
told him that he shouldn't hate, but even his father agreed that
most science subjects were a reasonable exception. Fortunately,
Yvette made the class a bit more bearable.

When he walked into class, she was already there, resting her
head on her desk. She wore a purple jacket with white strings
and faded blue jeans with silver stitching. As Walter approached
her, she raised her head to face him. She wore an exhausted and
unpleasant look. Even her eyes held bags as if she hadn't slept at
all.

"Hey... Hey, Walter," she said before a small series of
coughs.

"Hey," he said, smiling nervously. "Are you okay?"

Yvette coughed. "Yeah, just an itchy throat." She cleared it, covering a few light hocks with her fist then took a few sips of her bottled water. She began apologizing, her voice a bit clearer. "Sorry that I left so suddenly yesterday."

"Oh, don't be," Walter replied. "I get it. You do look tired today, though."

Yvette made a sigh that slowly turned to a yawn. "Michael can be... a lot at times, plus my sister got home late last night so... there's that. I had to watch him a little longer than I wanted. I love him but... well, you know how little kids can be."

Walter nodded. "Yeah, annoying." They both chuckled a bit and Walter thought of her nephew. "How is Michael anyway?"

Yvette smiled. "He's doing okay, but he's teething so..." When she giggled, it formed into another soft yawn.

Walter remembered seeing little Michael a few times already. He was tiny but had a lot of energy and strength, and he was barely one year old. Michael was no doubt like his father.

Walter grinned. "Does Michael have a big head like his daddy?"

She grinned. "Kind of. Don't tell my sister that, okay? But... he's just a bigger handful the older he gets. I don't blame him for being restless. I haven't really slept well the last few nights either; especially last night." Walter was about to ask her why, curiously concerned. Yvette must have sensed it. "Just a lot on my mind, really. So... you have my textbook with you... right?"

"Yeah, I have it here." Walter grabbed it from his backpack and the two exchanged books. He suddenly missed her pristine copy. The overused one had wrinkled corners and countless pen marks inside and out. Frankly, it was quite unwelcoming.

"It wasn't until I got home that I realized I took your book by mistake," Yvette told him. "Sorry about that."

Walter waved it off. "Don't be. Your textbook is way better than mine. I even put in some extra study time last night, you know, taking advantage."

Yvette chuckled and shook her head, but she looked so tired. He was inclined to ask her if everything was okay, until he remembered he already had. Still, he only hoped she was being truthful with him. Even if he wanted to ask, it was too late. Mr. Vega had just walked into the classroom, so Walter had no choice but to let it go.

"Alright, everyone. Settle down and take your seats." Mr. Vega rested his briefcase on his desk, and his coat on the back of his chair as always. "You have five minutes before I hand out the test. I suggest you use that time wisely."

When the announcement was over, Yvette gave Walter a soft smile. "Good luck," she said, sweetly yet wearily.

"Thanks," he replied courteously. "You too."

Walter sat at his own desk and started reviewing the notes he and Yvette went over. It was several minutes before he peeked over to her. Worryingly, she seemed conflicted; staring down at the pages, entranced by the words before her. Something was on her mind, something strange or wrong, and he could only guess what it was. But when she turned over at him, she seemed a bit irked. The grimace she had for him made him uneasy. *Is she mad at me or something? Was it something I said... or didn't say?*

"Alright, your time to study is over," Mr. Vega announced not long after, his voice booming against the walls. Some of the students were sulking and he was ready for it. "Enough! Clean your desks. All of you were given a sufficient amount of time.

Spend more time studying at home and you'll be more prepared."

Walter honestly felt confident about the test. He remembered most of the notes from the previous day, but began replaying the memory of their time studying together. That all made Walter wonder increasingly more if he had done something to upset her.

Class seemed a bit longer than usual. Walter was being attentive, but his mind often drifted to Yvette and the angry look she had. It was queer to see her unengaging and even uninterested in class. She didn't raise her hand to answer a question, nor comment on the lecture throughout. Some others might have noticed like Walter did, but Mr. Vega didn't seem bothered by it or didn't show it.

Once class was over, Yvette was the first one out the door and this didn't go unnoticed. However, when Walter exited the classroom, Yvette was standing right outside. He already knew she was waiting for him.

"Are you ok?" Walter asked. "You seemed a bit—"

"Give it back," Yvette abruptly cut him off.

"Yvette, I don't—"

"Don't lie to me, Walter," she said painfully. "You know what I am talking about. I know you do."

Then he bit his lip, just remembering that he hadn't grabbed the book from his desk and put it back where it belonged. *Oh, crap,* he said to himself. "I do," he admitted, and his words took her aback a bit. "I left it at home this morning. I was running a bit late today and forgot it on my desk."

"Why would—" Yvette suddenly fell silent. She stared up at him for a moment, lips agape and her eyes flitting between his own. "You used it." It wasn't a question, but she seemed more worried than angry.

110

Walter nodded, hoping he looked as genuine as he felt.
"Look, I'm really sorry. You can come with me and get it from
my house later if you like. You know I don't live that far. Maybe
we can talk about it then—"

"I don't want to talk about it," she said suddenly,
unpleasantly, roughly. However, soon she softened. "I'm sorry,
Walter. I... I can meet you after school."

Walter didn't respond right away. He quietly nodded but
should see how uncomfortable she was. "Okay. Meet out front
after the last bell."

Yvette, however, barely responded at all. She peaked up at
him and nodded but couldn't face him for long. Averting her
attention from him, Yvette turned away and walked down the
hall without another word.

Throughout the rest of the day, all he could think of was
Yvette and her little brown book. It would be foolish to think
that something like that wouldn't be precious to her; maybe
even something she couldn't live without. Seeing a stupid sketch
coming to life with some old notepad was indeed astonishing.
He began to wonder what Yvette used it for. She admitted being
a terrible artist. It made him wonder if simply writing in the
book might bring words to life as well. Walter's curiosity
peaked and he wondered most of all how it came to be in her
possession initially.

"Walter."

He was sitting in the lunchroom when his best friend called
him to grab his attention. Art was trying to tell him about the
basketball game; another Walter missed due to his punishment.
Art was too excited to talk about anything else besides
basketball, and Walter couldn't blame him but couldn't share his

excitement either. Seeing how exhausted and drained Yvette seemed without it for a night was unsettling, and permeated his thoughts. Cracked bindings and stained parchment-like pages flipped and turned relentlessly in his mind. The thought pulsed so violently that everything else seemed to be nonexistent.

"Walter!?" Art called again. "You good, bro?"

"Sorry," said Walter as he looked up at his friend. "What were you saying?"

"Are you alright, man?" Art asked with an eyebrow slightly raised. "You looked like you blacked out for a minute. Are you even here right now?"

Confused, Walter didn't know what he meant. "What are you talking about, Art? I'm sitting right here. What kind of question is that?"

"It's a legitimate question. You've been looking real... distracted lately. A little distant like you're not really here. Are you sure everything is okay with you?"

Walter nodded. "Yeah." Although he had his sandwich wrapped up and sitting in front of him, Walter was far from hungry.

"Oh yeah, I never asked about how it went yesterday."

A little baffled, Walter asked, "Yesterday? Oh yeah, I told you about that." *Maybe I should have just kept that a secret.*

"She's been on your mind, huh?" Art guessed. Before Walter could deny anything, he continued. "Don't feel any way about it. I think about Trisha a lot. You and Yvette do have some history, so I get it if she's on your mind."

"Yesterday was fine, and to answer your question... No. Yvette is not on my mind. Just... other things." A half-truth seemed to be the best option.

However... "You're lying." Art knew him well.

Walter sulked. "Just a little bit."

"What happened?"

"It's a little complicated. She was a little annoyed with me this morning."

"Sounds familiar," Art chuckled, then tried to look serious. "Let me stop joking. Look, you said it's complicated, so I know you're not going to tell me everything, but don't worry about all that. You're worried that you probably turned her off, I get it, but you shouldn't worry too much. And I know you've been going through a lot after Samuel died, but don't let that sadness cloud your judgment, you know. It would be her loss if she held something against you just because you annoyed her a little. Still, if you let it bother you... Well, the last thing you want is to lose the girl you really like when you're the cause of it."

"Yeah, you're right," Walter agreed.

"Honestly, I kind of want you and Yvette to happen. You seem pretty good together... or whatever." He chuckled a little then asked, "So, you're going to spend some time with her again soon, right? Take her out or something?"

"Yeah... I guess. She's coming by my house later today. I forgot to bring her something today so–"

"Oh... slick." Art snickered then his voice went up an octave. "'Oh, Yvette, just follow me home, I have something to show you.' Nice." Whether he was attempting some stupidly chivalrous tone or... whatever that was, Walter ignored him and shook his head. Even so, a small grin appeared on his lips, even as his friend played his situation for a laugh.

"I don't even sound like that," he said with a little chuckle. "I'm serious. She's just following me to grab something she forgot at the library. That's all." Another half-truth.

113

Art shrugged. In a more serious tone, he said, "Sounds like she trusts you though. That's a good sign."

The scenario might have made Walter nervous, but he did think of that. He doubted Yvette would follow him home if she didn't trust him somewhat. Even so, it was the mysterious book she wanted. Walter had to remember that.

"I don't want to be a hypocrite or anything because I might be nervous around Trisha at times, but I just met her. You know Yvette and she might feel the same way you do. You just have to figure that out."

Walter shook his head. "The most annoying part."

Art followed with, "Trust me, I know, but the ball is in your court now, bro."

If he was being honest with himself, Art was right about all of it. In fact, he usually was. The boys didn't usually see things differently, but he was better at putting things into perspective. Walter always appreciated him for that.

Fortunately for Walter, his mother wasn't home when he and Yvette arrived that afternoon. Knowing her, she would have reminded him of his punishment in front of his guest, embarrassing him in the process. Then when she was gone, his mother would have pestered him about Yvette, asking a million and one questions. He wasn't sure if he should use the word "pester" when speaking about his mother, but… she could definitely be an annoyance.

What was also fortunate was that his bedroom was clean when Yvette stepped inside. Walter had to remind himself that he did clean it the night before last — his mother orders, of course. It was on his mind before they arrived. He even had her wait in the living room to check and make sure before allowing her upstairs. When she entered, he could see her surveying the area, making eye contact with the dresser, bookshelf, the semi-cluttered desk, and his surprisingly made-up bed.

"I heard you can tell a lot about a person by whether or not they make their bed in the morning," she said, shooting him a side glance.

Walter smirked as he observed her, wonderingly and intently. "What does mine say about me?"

She tried to not to show it, but Walter saw her soft smile she wore for a moment. Even so, her voice became considerably less cordial when she spoke again. "So... where is my diary?"

"Diary?" Walter asked. Somehow, calling it that seemed a bit strange to him. He closed his sketchbook on his desk, and there it was, laying underneath. "Is that what you call it?"

Yvette quickly picked it up and gripped it in her hands. There was an instant smile that appeared on her face as her fingers locked together, embracing its old bindings. However, her blissful moment was disturbed.

"What did you say?" she asked, her eyes still entranced on the old book in her hands.

"Um..." He hesitated for a moment. "I didn't know you called it a diary. There is nothing inside so... It's just a bit strange, you know."

When Yvette finally looked at him, her bliss seemed to escape her completely. "I have to go, Walter." She turned to leave but Walter stopped her.

"Wait, Yvette."

"Tell me the truth," she said sternly, her curls whipping around as she swung back to face him. "Did you really forget my diary home or were you trying to steal it from me?"

"Steal it? What?" Walter honestly couldn't fathom why she would think that. "Of course not. Leaving the book home was an accident. I'm forgetful, I admit it, but I'm not a thief. If I were a thief, would I even tell you I had it? You should know me well enough to know that I wouldn't steal from anyone." He paused for a moment. "I know this... diary must be a secret, right? I know what it can do, but I wouldn't steal it from you or tell anyone. I'm not that kind of person."

"I don't know that." Her voice was angry yet sad, giving her quite a confused expression.

Even so, Walter felt himself grimace. "Are you serious?"

With a thick sigh, Yvette sat at the foot of his bed, looking overwhelmed and frankly exhausted. Walter calmed down, deciding to wait and see what she would say.

"That's not true," she admitted calmly, while nervously itching the back of her ear. "I don't trust many people anymore, Walter. Not really. It's hard for me, especially since my mom died. I do trust you, it's just..." She bit her bottom lip and turned her face away from him. "It's just important to me. I hope you understand that."

Dubiously, Walter sat beside her, leaving enough space between them. "How did you even find this... diary?"

"It's a long story," said Yvette.

A long time was something he couldn't afford with his mother coming home soon. However, his curiosity was unwavering and unavoidable. "If you're willing to tell me then I'll listen."

Yvette made a relieving sigh. "I found it amongst my mom's stuff."

"Your mom?" Walter's tilted and as his eyes squinted. "So, this was hers?"

Yvette shrugged. "I guess so. I didn't know what it was at first since it was just empty and looked very old, but it was my mom's so... I don't know... I felt a strange connection like a weird yet... familiar feeling. Does that make sense?"

"Yeah... I think so." Walter's thoughts lingered on how it felt when he first held the book. It indeed felt strange but didn't feel familiar to anything he had before.

"I don't know..." Yvette sighed heavily. "It made me curious and wonder what it was... before I used it and realized what it really was."

"How did you find out?"

"It was a day after I went to see this doctor. I was feeling really broken up about my mom, so the doctor told me I should write to my mom and say what I wanted to tell her; like a pen pal or something. But... instead of using the notebook she gave me—"

"You used this book."

Yvette nodded as she swallowed nervously. "I call it a diary because it's what made sense to me at the time. Is that weird?"

Walter shook his head. "No, that makes sense to me. What happened after that?"

"Well, I wrote the first time before I returned to school. When the doctor suggested, I didn't try it right away. I didn't really trust her, but... that doesn't matter. Maybe I was just doubtful about writing a letter to my mom that she wouldn't actually read. I was just tired of crying all the time, so I just thought I would try it.

"So, I decided to write a letter to my mom about my day; I wasn't sure what else to write. It was a hard day for me, and she was the only one I wanted to talk to. I was in my room

117

writing…" She paused for a moment, seemingly deep in thought. "But then… I wasn't in my room anymore."

"What do you mean?" Walter asked curiously, eyes squinted slightly with disbelief.

"Eventually, everything around me changed. I wasn't in my room anymore. When I wrote in the diary about what happened in the library, it was like the diary was showing it to me. Like…" She paused for a moment then went on. "I was in the public library where I spent most of that day. And, as clearly as I see you now, I saw myself sitting at the table studying. I nearly screamed and hugged myself, hoping I was still me. That's when I realized I was reliving my memory of earlier that day."

Lips agape, Walter stared into Yvette's honest eyes a bit shocked. *So… the book does work the same way when you write in it,* Walter thought, confirming his theory. It all seemed so obvious now, but the level of influence the diary had on the world around them was quite astonishing if not frightening.

"So, everything you wrote in the diary was appearing around you… like a dream even."

Yvette tilted her head. "Maybe… Well, no. It isn't a dream, but… it did feel like I was. Dreaming, I mean. But it was a clear memory. I even saw when this guy bumping into the table and spilled my juice over all my papers. I was so angry. That's probably why I remembered his face. But…" She paused again. "What spooked me was that most of the people in the library had no face."

Once again, Walter's eyes squinted in confusion. "No face?"

Yvette nodded. "Some of the faces have some facial features — like one had a beard, another only had a nose with glasses resting on it, but… that's it."

"No eyes… mouth—"

"Nothing. It was… creepy. The only faces I could see were those I recognized or ones I already knew. Some had hair on their heads, and most of them wore gray and… distorted clothing? I really didn't know what it was."

Walter thought it over for a moment. "Diary," he said aloud as he pondered. "So, the diary doesn't just recreate what you write or draw inside of it, but… it creates based on your memories too."

Yvette nodded in agreement. "That's what I thought. When I was in the memory, I saw the man who spilled my drink all over my papers. I was already so angry that day… That's probably why I can remember his face so clearly in the memory, even clearer than the few people I knew who were there."

"Anyways, the man apologized and scurried off, leaving me to clean up the mess. So, while my past self was angry and trying to clean the table, I followed him. His face began fading away the further he got and he headed towards the door." She paused again, head cocked, and her mind was seemingly trying to recall everything. "When the man walked outside, there weren't any cars or trees or people walking past. It was just… an all-white nothingness. He walked through it and… the white just seemed to swallow him."

Walter was speechless as he listened — eyes wide, lips agape. To relive a memory already astounded him, but he couldn't deny how frightening it all would be. "I wouldn't know how to feel, honestly. I would probably think it was all a dream."

Yvette nodded as she looked down at her fidgeting fingers. "I thought it was a dream too, but it wasn't." She sighed then sniffled. "That's what my mother told me."

119

For a moment, Walter wasn't quite sure he heard her correctly. "Your mother?"

Yvette wiped away a tear then nodded once more. "When I was in the memory, I heard her speak to me. When I turned around, she was there, standing right behind me. I still remember what she said. 'This is not a dream, sweetheart. Just another memory.'"

"Oh, wow," Walter muttered, stupefied by her story.

In seemingly an instant, his astonishment was trumped by his fear. Reliving a memory might bring joy or even sadness, and to see a dead loved-one was already frightening enough in dreams, but to see a theoretical ghost haunting memories was daunting. Even when she wrote a memory in the diary, it conjured more than what was written on the page. Her feelings and intentions were what truly mattered. This was discouraging to Walter, uncertain of what dark, suppressed feelings the diary might surface. He only hoped that the memories of her mother weren't tarnished or used against her.

"Honestly, reliving old memories is terrifying," Yvette went on, "but I still call it my diary. I don't know why, but... I just do. I guess... a reminder, ironically. I haven't relived memories in a while, but... at the beginning it was hard not to, though I knew I had to stop." Her lips parted again, but the words failed to come. Instead, her eyes sank and so did her shoulders.

Exhausted, Yvette rested the diary between them, but Walter couldn't help but stare at the brown book. "If this was your mom's," he said looking back up at her, "does your dad know about it too?"

"No," she replied, then she didn't seem too certain. "Actually, I don't know. I don't think so. I doubt I would find it myself if he did."

It made sense to Walter, so he nodded, but then asked, "Where do you think she got it from?"

Yvette shrugged. "I sometimes asked myself that." She suddenly fell silent and began fidgeting with her fingers again. Walter then recognized the three silver rings on her right hand, and how she calmed down after she massaged the metal. Walter realized that she wore them religiously, no matter her outfit or color.

"Were those rings hers too?" he asked, redirecting the subject for a moment.

Yvette nodded with a grin and stretched out her hand to give him a better look. Walter took her hand gently, feeling her soft palm and made his own tingle. It was strange but he liked it.

Looking down at her hand in his, Yvette smirked and said, "She had tiny hands too."

A smile appeared on his lips and when she saw it, Yvette sniffled, and her lips stretched to a smile as well. However, it was short lived. "After she died..." Unable to speak any further, her voice trailed off... and so did her smile.

Walter nodded patiently. "It's okay. I get it." He knew what she meant but left it at that.

The three rings were simple, sleek, and all-silver. Instead of a crowned jewel or gem, they were engraved by a rose, a smiling mask, and an ankh respectively. Each centerpiece had a word encrusted on its side — the ankh for Life, the smiling mask for Laugh and the rose for Love.

"I like them," Walter said, smirking.

"Thank you." Just for a moment, Yvette's tiny smile returned. "She had good taste."

Both Walter and Yvette held a part of their parents with them; locked within silver rings and silver wings. Speaking of held,

Walter eventually let her hand go before she pulled away on her own. *Too long and I'm a creep,* he told himself. Although she didn't seem bothered with her hand in his, Walter let his fingers slide away.

He asked, "Is this why you didn't sleep well last night?"

"It…" She was hesitant again, taking the same hand and gently grasping an ear. "It helps me with my schoolwork. It makes it easy when I can see everything — especially history and… I don't know… Does that make sense?"

"No, I get it. Well… I mean yes, I get it… You know what I mean, right?"

Yvette chuckled as she watched him fumble on his words. "Yeah, Walter. I know what you mean."

Walter wanted to reach out to her and console her if he could. Ultimately, he kept his hands to himself. He could tell her everything would be fine, and no one would find out about the diary, but it didn't seem like that was enough. Instead, he sat there and thought of something to lighten the mood.

"You know, I always wanted to draw my own comic one day," he began. "You know, something different… something relatable—"

"Something silly?" Yvette added with a sly smirk.

She knows me well. He grinned. "Yeah. Something silly too. Your diary would really come in handy for that. Like you said, you get to see everything."

Nervously, Yvette turned to him and apologized. "I'm sorry, Walter. I shouldn't have accused you of anything. I should have known you wouldn't steal from me or lie to me." She paused for a moment. "Honestly, it feels kind of good — I don't know — just having someone who understands… someone to share that kind of stuff with. It makes me feel… a bit better."

Walter smiled at that, but it wasn't as sweet as the one Yvette was wearing. "Your secret is safe with me. I promise you. Do you want to know how I discovered how the diary works?"

As he hoped, Yvette seemed interested.

"Some back story first. When I was a little kid, I used to have this stuffed white rabbit. It was my favorite toy as a baby. It even had a rattle inside its belly, so every time I shook it, it would make those silly sounds babies like. I had it for a long time, but one day... I couldn't find it. I have no clue what happened to him. He was just gone. My dad might have taken it... maybe. I don't know."

"That's terrible," Yvette replied sadly. "Why would he do that?"

Walter shrugged. "He thought I got too old for it, and I didn't want to get rid of it, but... I don't know. I started making these drawings of him going on these crazy adventures — fighting lions and tigers, saving princesses, you know... whatever super-bunnies do."

She chuckled. "Super-bunnies?"

"Yeah. I even drew him on the moon once, shooting zombie aliens with lasers and plasma cannons. I don't know what happened to most of those drawings, but I do remember what I drew though."

Yvette began to giggle, hiding her lips behind her palm. Her bracelets even jingled as they fell down her arm. "Zombie aliens, Walter?"

"What?" He laughed. "I can't even remember how old I was. Sometime in elementary. Maybe third grade. I don't even know if I met Art before or after I lost my bunny. That was half my life ago."

"Let me guess, you used to draw them in your notebooks too?"

"You know me well."

Yvette's giggles continued. "I think I saw a drawing in your book of a bunny fighting... something. It was probably zombie aliens."

Walter shrugged with his laugh. "Probably."

"What was the bunny's name?"

"Oh, right. I called him Captain Long Ears."

Yvette was laughing hysterically now. "Captain Long Ears? Seriously?"

"Like I said—" The way she was laughing distracted him for a moment and made his lips curl upward. "Hey, I was a little kid when I came up with all this stuff."

With her lips still curled upward, Yvette playfully patted his shoulder. "I'm sorry if I sound mean but... It's a silly name, you have to admit that much."

Walter sarcastically squinted his eyes to appear angered. "Don't make fun of eight-year-old Walter. He can't defend himself."

"Oh, so you *do* remember how old you were?"

"Well... I don't really know how old I was when I lost him, but I was eight in third grade so... you know..." He shrugged. "Look, I'm estimating, here, okay."

"Okay. Estimating." Yvette playfully rolled her eyes. "You're funny, Walter."

As the laughs simmered down, Walter proceeded to tell her about his imaginary bunny hopping and bouncing around his room; even down to the fact that he almost got in trouble for it. Yvette laughed and laughed when she heard the story, but then felt horrible for laughing at his misadventure.

Suddenly, Yvette opened the diary, her laughs simmering. "I want to give you something." Without warning, she ripped out several pages and handed them to Walter with a gentle grin.

Walter was a bit stunned. "Really?"

Yvette nodded. "I hope this can count as a sorry."

He examined the pages. "Less stains."

"Yeah," she said sweetly. "Maybe you can recreate some of your animal drawings and see them come to life."

Walter smiled at that, then had a sudden thought. "Wouldn't the animals see me and maybe attack me because I like lions and tigers and bears, you know."

Yvette chuckled. "Well... maybe that's not the best idea because I don't know. I don't even know if they can hurt you or not... or what else it can do. I'm curious to find out more about the diary, but it might be dangerous. Just be careful, Walter. It's easy to get attached to it."

Dangerous, Walter said to himself. The weight of the word was heavy. There was a sense of anticipation there.

"Can I ask you something?" she said.

"Sure. What's up?"

"I honestly need to know." Yvette took a breath. "If you knew you could use this diary to see anything... relive old memories or... or see someone you haven't seen in years just by writing their name, would you do it?"

Walter wasn't sure how to respond to that. "I don't... know honestly." *I would have never thought to ask myself that.* Walter pondered for a moment, then a thought ran through his head. *Does she—*

"Never mind. It's nothing important." Yvette shook her head and grabbed the diary once again.

"Why?" Walter wasn't certain whether he should pry or not, but when the question slipped out of him, he let it and followed up. "Do you?"

"No, I... I don't. I... I honestly have to go. Sorry. Maybe we can talk about it again another time." The diary was shoved into her bag, and she was on her way out the room.

Before Walter could try to provide her some kind of clarity, they both heard the front door open downstairs. Fortunately, his bedroom door was open or neither of them might have heard it.

Yvette turned to him, troubled. "Your mom?" she whispered, and Walter nodded. "Is she going to get mad if she sees me up here?"

They were already in Walter's room, and he was already on punishment, but he knew a white lie that might help.

"Walter?" His mother called.

He stood suddenly and called back, "I'm upstairs."

"Well, come downstairs. I have groceries in the car."

"I'll alright, I'm coming down now."

"And tell your guest to come down here with you."

How did she... Walter suddenly felt stupid. He had forgotten about Yvette's shoes sitting beside his. *It's not like I could sneak her out anyways. I'm not going to treat her like that kind of girl.*

"Don't worry," he murmured to her. "I'll just say you came to get your notebook you forgot in class or something."

"Are you sure?" she asked uncomfortably.

"Yeah, just follow my lead."

The uncomfortable feeling was plainly still there but Yvette nodded. She stayed closely behind him as Walter led her down to the living room where his mother stood with an unpleasant face, sharp eyes, and her hands on her hips. However, when she saw Yvette behind him, a bit of surprise suddenly mixed in with her unpleasantness.

"Hey, mom," Walter greeted her, not knowing what else to say. "This is Yvette. You remember her, right?"

"Hi, Mrs. D'Artagnan," Yvette waved, greeting the woman nervously.

"She just came by to get her notebook," he added, seeing as though his mother had yet to respond.

"Yvette?" his mother finally spoke, but with an inquisitive tone. "Charlotte's sister, right?"

Still nervous, Yvette forced a grin. "Yeah, we met at Samuel's funeral."

"Oh yes, I remember." She was wearing a smile now as her hands left her hips and her arms opened. "Come give me a hug. You don't have to be afraid."

Yvette's eyes flitted back to Walter before she accepted his mother's embrace. She made an uncomfortable smile and Walter had his own to match. Even so, his mother's hugs were warm and soon Yvette's smile turned pleasant.

"How has your sister been?" his mother asked when she let the girl go. "And her little boy?"

"They're both doing good, but I'm sorry, I have to get home before my father leaves for work."

Walter told his mother he would walk Yvette to the bus and be right back. Fortunately, she didn't protest. When the two got down the block and out of earshot, they both began laughing with one another.

"I'm sorry about my mom," Walter apologized. He was already prepared to hear her million and one questions when he got back.

127

"I was a little frightened," Yvette admitted. "I'm just glad she remembered me, and I wasn't some stranger to her."

"True," he agreed.

Yvette turned to him and folded her arms. "Plus, I don't know how many girls you bring to your house to 'get something you forgot.'"

Walter snorted. "Well, there is a first for everything, right?"

A shy smirk crept across her face as she turned around and continued down the block. "Come on, the buses should be passing soon." It wasn't until they arrived at the bus stop that Yvette turned back to him to say, "Thank you."

"For what?"

She shrugged. "For understanding... For being in my corner... I don't know, just... thank you."

Walter grinned. "Sure."

"Give me your phone." Yvette took it, added her number to his contacts then handed it back. "Text me so I have your number too, okay?"

Walter nodded, half-expecting her just to text her phone herself but he was proven wrong. "Sure."

From their peripherals, the two could see the bus coming towards them and heard the roar of the engine steadily rising as it approached.

"So, I'll see you on Monday?" Yvette asked with optimism in her voice. The bus pulled up beside her and slid its door open.

Walter nodded. "You will."

*   *   *

Yvette lied to Walter and felt terrible about that — her father had the night off and she hadn't forgotten. Her lie stemmed from her frustration with him, but once it was dead and gone, she wasn't really mad at him at all. She liked talking to Walter, and strangely, a part of her didn't want to leave. Yvette wasn't a people person, and usually didn't find interest in talking with others who weren't like her or shared similar interests; especially boys. Her ex-boyfriend was another writer, but anti-social and barely expressive. In fact, most of her friends were quite cynical — Hazel, the least — but it wasn't until her mother died, that Yvette realized she wasn't that different from the cynical or pretentious.

However, Walter was fun to be around and made her smile often. He wasn't a boasting wise guy nor was he afraid to speak his mind. Yvette admired that about him. He seemed comfortable with himself and confident as well. These attributes were indeed attractive. Still, a part of her was cautious of him… even afraid.

When she entered the house, her father was sitting on the couch with his lips open and his eyes shut. The television was showing some detective show, and the music and excitement muffled the squeaky door behind her. Yvette was happy to see him sleeping. He needed the rest desperately. Before and after the pandemic, she had never seen him so exhausted.

Po came to greet her though and she rubbed his fur pleasantly. "I missed you too, Po," she always told him. She sometimes forgot he wasn't truly their dog.

The rest of the house was quiet. Charlotte must've already dropped off Michael and set off to work. Yvette knew she wouldn't be able to really talk to her sister about Walter that night, but she had so many thoughts. Charlotte would listen and reason with Yvette in her own sisterly way. Since her sister had already left for work, Yvette felt a little anxious. Even so, it was Friday so there was some solace in that.

Fridays were the only days that Yvette refused to do homework or articles. She didn't even go in her room when she got home. Exhausted, she sat next to her father and rested her head on his shoulder. He jerked a bit when he awoke and found his daughter resting on him.

"Hey…" He coughed. "Hey, sweetheart."

She looked up at him. "Hey, Dad," she greeted. "You were drooling again."

Wiping his lips, her father snorted when he felt how dry they already were. "No, I wasn't." Then he made a silly smile knowing his daughter was messing with him. "How was school?"

She nodded, thinking of her diary — back in her bag, back in her possession, and back where it belonged. "It was good." Staring towards the television as her lips curled to a satisfied grin; her dimples dug deep and dark.

It might have been an hour or so, but Yvette fell asleep and woke up alone on the couch. She rose from a pillow set beneath her cheek; ironically, her cheek was moist with drool. After she went to use the bathroom and returned downstairs, she found her father in the kitchen with Charlotte's son in his arms. He was heating his grandson's baby bottle by the sink while Michael was making adorable baby noises. When he smiled, a couple of bottom teeth peaked from behind his lips.

"Hey you," Yvette said sweetly, with her voice an octave higher. When did you get here?"

Michael's two-teeth smile peered her way as he stretched out his tiny, chubby arms towards her. So, Auntie Yvette took her nephew in her arms, relieving her father of the baby weight.

"Charlotte dropped him back off when you were sleeping," he said, letting Micheal go then turning the baby bottle under the pouring hot water from the sink.

"Oh. I thought he was staying with his grandmother tonight?"

"Charlotte thought so too but something happened, so he'll go over there in the morning. I'm glad I was home. You've been stuck with him all week."

Yvette smiled at her nephew while rubbing his delicate head and speaking in the same higher octave. "I wouldn't mind."

Her father turned off the sink. "You wouldn't get to take a nap though, and it looked like you really needed it." He held out the warm bottle. "And speaking of mind, would you mind feeding him while I order some food? Unless you feel like cooking because I don't."

Willingly, she nodded and took the bottle.

By the next hour, Michael dozed off and Yvette and her father were on the living room floor sharing a box of pizza, and playing a game of Scrabble while her father played music by Foo Fighters on his phone. Even Po sat with them with his nose resting in her father's lap.

It had been a while since Yvette and her father spent time together. Charlotte was more of a daddy's girl than her sister, but Yvette missed their father-daughter time. Even after their game, they enjoyed a movie. Michael slept between them, but as soon as he got fussy and tossed and turned, his grandfather held and rocked him gently back to sleep. Yvette couldn't remember ever seeing a baby in her father's arms. The way he coddled her nephew, she smiled thinking how he once held her that way and soothed her to sleep as well. Yvette even felt herself giggling when she imagined the little boy in his arms calling her father

"Granddad" when he gets older. Charlotte was already calling him "Granddaddy" or "Old Man" quite often. That always made Yvette laugh.

Her father turned to her. "What?" The movie was paused, so he was a little lost.

Yvette shook her head. "It's nothing. I was just… thinking about something."

Michael finally simmered, so her father rested him back in his bassinet then sat back on the couch and resumed the movie. "Something funny happened today in school?"

"No, not really, just… something someone said to me today." Her titters simmered but a smile remained as she turned back to the screen. She didn't want to tell her father she was laughing at him, but the smile she wore wasn't for him. Unexpectedly, the thought of Walter crept into her mind and dwelled there for a moment.

"A boy," he said. It was no question and her father sounded so certain when he said it. Even Po looked up at her with his wet nose and curious eyes.

"What?" she asked as her eyes flitted in between her father and the dog.

Her father shrugged. "Just guessing really. You're at that age. Can't shelter you *too* much like I tried to do with Charlotte." He paused for a moment then tensed up and faced his daughter. "You're not having sex, are you?"

"Dad! No!"

"Are you sure—"

"Dad, yes! I'm pretty sure I'm not having sex."

"I trust you will make the right decisions. I don't expect you to be sneaking any boys in my house."

"Dad!" Yvette nearly yelled. "I'm not having sex, okay?"

132

Her father nodded. "Well, I know how… pushy boys can be and how curious young girls are—"

"I'm not that curious, Dad."

There was a certain smirk her father would wear when he believed his daughters — or wanted to — but still needed to be convinced. Even when she told the truth, Yvette was still a little frightened of that look, as if she were lying and didn't know it yet. This moment was no different.

"Sweetheart," he went on. "I can't always be there to protect you, so it's important to me that you are protecting yourself. How can I protect you if I don't know what's going on in your life? I'm not going to kill the boy, whoever he is. I didn't do anything to the last one, did I? You remember how long you kept him a secret from your mother and I?"

Fourteen months, she reflected. *Parents hate secrets, don't they?* Still, it was a good feat. Only Charlotte knew of her first boyfriend — Terrance Blount, curly hair, short nose, and dark eyes. He was gentle and smart but wasn't that courageous. It wasn't necessary for her — not really — but it wasn't in him either, and that did matter to her. He might have been too terrified to meet her father eventually anyway. It didn't matter now. By ninth grade, they were attending different high schools, and by that Christmas break, it was over.

"I remember," she admitted. However, it was followed by a lie. "But no. I'm not interested in anyone."

Once the movie was over, her father stayed with Micheal and put on sports highlights while Yvette freshened up, and settled in her room for the night. She kept her door open, knowing Michael might start crying for… something and would help her father if necessary. When she was finally alone, however, she went into her bag to retrieve her diary. She sighed a bit, wrote a name down, and waited.

Soon after, Yvette felt a woman's hand rest gently upon her shoulder. "I missed you too, sweetheart." Yvette smiled as she already knew what was on her mind. She indeed missed hearing her mother's voice and faced her with delight.

Margaret Anders was wearing the same outfit as always; her slim black overcoat, olive green knee high dress, silver heels and a necklace of pearls. Her nappy curls hung above her shoulders and her lips were painted a dark red. The woman smiled softly when she saw her daughter, as if she hadn't seen her in weeks. They embraced lovingly, wearing matching smiles on their lips and matching rings on their fingers.

"I'm sorry," said Yvette lowly. "I didn't have the diary last night. I had it in my textbook, but Walter took mine by mistake, so he had it last night and—" Her mother didn't particularly react to anything her daughter was saying and Yvette felt a bit worried by this. "I'm sorry... I'm sorry..." One didn't seem like enough and she apologized twice for good measure.

Her mother quieted her. "Hush, sweetheart. It's okay. I understand. I'm just glad you were okay without me. You know how much your mother worries." They both sat at the foot of the bed, Yvette being held the entire way down in her warm hands.

"So, tell me about this boy."

Yvette squinted a bit. "Don't you remember Walter? Walter D'Artagnan? He's Samuel's cousin. You taught him English in eighth grade."

Her mother smiled. "I do remember him. Mr. D'Artagnan. A creative boy. Easily distracted, but creative. I always caught him drawing in my class."

Yvette smirked. *That sounds like him.*

"What do you think of him?"

Honestly, she didn't know how to answer that. Walter seemed like someone she can trust. Still, she hoped she wouldn't regret ripping pages out of the diary for him. Even so, Walter seemed just as nice as he always was, but he was older now, and Yvette couldn't stop herself from smiling at that. He was just as joking and ridiculous as ever — but he was more mature now, someone she felt comfortable telling her secrets to, even if she wasn't sure if she should. It was all so sudden. She only knew what he told her, and everything he said could have been lies. Still, she couldn't truly hate him for that when she was doing the same; keeping secrets, telling lies. Yvette couldn't deny that she was projecting a bit.

"I don't know," Yvette ultimately told her mother.

"Do you like him?"

"Um…" That was another question that Yvette didn't have an answer for. She felt like she did. Walter was always funny, quite charming, and had a handsome smile to match. If she was being honest with herself, she liked the look of him more now than when she first met him in seventh grade. But his eyes — those bi-chrome pools of brown and gold — she could drown in them. Even when she first met him in the cafeteria, it was hard not to stare into them, even with her scowl. Just seeing him in her mind made her cheeks swell and her dimples dig. "Walter is… nice." That was all she was willing to say.

"Well, that doesn't answer my question."

"Well, I don't know," Yvette said, slightly annoyed. Prying usually rubbed her the wrong way and her mother wasn't exempt from that. "Can we not talk about it?"

Her mother smiled. "It's fine, sweetheart. You've already said enough."

Yvette already knew what that meant but she stayed quiet. Soon after, Michael was crying in her sister's room. She heard her father coming up the stairs with tired steps. "I'll get him," she told him. "You and Charlotte had him all day."

Her father nodded with a light smile, but he continued past and dragged his feet across the carpet to his bedroom. "Thanks, sweetheart. I think I'm going to lay down. Just call me if you need me."

Yvette was met with slow, spinning lights that shone around the room in bright blue stars. The music box was playing its lullaby above the crib, but Michael's cries were higher than that. Yvette gently reached down and raised his head to her shoulder. Sweat was beading over his eyes, so she let his blanket fall back to the crib. She hushed him and he slowly simmered down.

"That's how you were when you were a baby," her mother whispered behind her. "You would fuss and fuss and always keep your father and I up at night."

"I know, Mom, I know. You told me so many times. Every time you see a whining baby, you bring it up."

Margaret Anders smiled at her daughter. "A proud parent always brags about their children."

Yvette grinned and shook her head. "Don't remind me."

Nights when Michael was restless and his mother was not home, Yvette would take him in her room so he wouldn't be alone. She sat on the bed with Michael on her lap. He gripped onto her pen, and she held his hand tightly then began writing a phrase beneath her mother's name. "A puppet orchestra with an audience of sheep." It wasn't in her best penmanship, but it was readable.

A few dozen tiny stuffed sheep gathered all around Michael, and the baby boy giggled as their soft fur tickled his sides. At the end of the bed, a miniature big band of stuffed animals with their petite instruments were conjured as well. They started playing a few songs for Michael and the animals even danced as they strummed, banged, and tooted. There were monkeys on the drums, three giraffes on the trumpets and three elephants holding the tuba, trombone, and French horn respectively. There were rabbits on saxophones and clarinets, puppies and kittens holding violins and guitars, while a rainbow of birds held their flutes at their beaks with bright, bold wings. Standing before the band was a well-dressed puppet conductor, who waved his smooth-point baton without strings or fingers.

Yvette snuggled next to Michael and her mother spectated and sat behind them. After a few songs to make Michael laugh, the orchestra played a few lullabies that beckoned his head to the pillow and drifted him off to sleep.

As for Yvette, she couldn't remember when she drifted off to sleep again herself. Vaguely, she could recall her sister coming into the room for Michael, but she wasn't sure if the orchestra was still playing. What she did hear was a sudden crack or pop like she was sleeping in a fireplace. When she rose from her bed, it was sudden and she couldn't tell if she was waking from a dream, or if she was in one. Nonetheless, whatever the sporadic sound was split the silence in half. The room was dark, Yvette was alone, and she couldn't tell where it came from.

What was that? she asked herself.

Steadily, Yvette moved towards the door and peaked through the empty hallway. She went to Charlotte's door first and peaked in. Her sister was in her bed hidden beneath her blankets while her son slept beside her in his crib; the blue star lights still danced on the ceiling above. As for her father, he was asleep as well with the covers barely over his legs. Even Po was sleeping

137

undisturbed on the carpet. *Did no one else hear that or am I hearing things?*

Curiously and cautiously, Yvette began descending the stairs. It was a bit dark in the living room, but nothing she could see seemed out of place. It might have been a bit too quiet outside for a Friday night, but she didn't put much thought into that detail.

My mind is playing tricks on me, she surmised. Even so, she couldn't be shocked.

"No. I heard it too."

The sudden voice spooked her, and she turned around to see a teenage boy sitting on the couch with his silver lighter in his hand, and dressed in black from head to toe. He looked like a shadow sitting there. The way he constantly opened and closed the lighter in his hand, it sounded like the seconds of a clock. She slowly walked around the couch to get a better look at him.

"Walter?" she gasped, surprised and confused. "How did you—"

"It might have just been our imagination," he said ominously, darkly. The boy turned to face her and wore Walter's unruffled face. "What do you think?"

Her body soon felt numb. Even her lips struggled with her words. "This... This is... a dream... right?"

"I don't know. I guess we won't know... until we wake up..."

"We?" She didn't understand.

He stood from the couch and approached her; the lighter was still opening and closing, counting the seconds. "Maybe you never fell asleep at all."

Yvette shook her head and took a step back. "No... No, then you won't be here."

He grinned. "Here. Catch." He threw the lighter and Yvette
caught it in her hands. She could feel the silver — wings and
beak — and she could feel the heat. When she opened it, a
bright spark ignited, and an orange flame appeared on its own.
The metal was instantly hot, and the tips of her fingers began to
burn. However, the top of the lighter now weighed a ton and
Yvette couldn't close it. Sweat beaded on her forehead as she
struggled and struggled — her breath growing heavy and
pushing in-between her gritted teeth — until the boy held her
hands and shut the lighter himself. The grasp was tight and
Yvette couldn't help but look up at him.

"It's not that hard to close, is it?" he said with a little smirk.
"I guess you just needed a little help."

"What's going on, Walter?" Yvette asked, searching his sharp
eyes as if they were maps to an answer. "Is this... Is this the
diary?"

The boy shrugged nonchalantly, giving no answer at all.
However, he peaked over her shoulder and looked down. "Did
you see that?"

Her bottom lips hung ajar, her eyes still searching his own
for... something. "See what?"

She slowly turned around, Yvette's hands still in his. She still
didn't understand until she looked down and her heart sunk in
her chest. Her hands left Walter's grasp and cupped over her
mouth before she screamed. It didn't matter. She screamed but
her voice wasn't there.

"I know. It's frightening, but we can't wake the rest of the
family, can we?"

Yvette was shaking and struggling to breath. She didn't want
to look, but her eyes struggled to turn away. The body on the
floor, the blood; it brought back a burning memory. Those dead

eyes staring back at her made her feel like she might throw up...
but she couldn't turn away. Something wouldn't let her.

"Why are you showing me this?" she wept, wondering
wholeheartedly why the diary was showing her worst fear.
"You've never done this before."

"Are you going to tell him?"

Yvette slowly shook her head, her eyes still unwillingly
undeterred. She didn't need to ask who "him" was.

"Good, because he is not special. We can't have him finding
out about this. There is only so much he can know."

Yvette fell to her knees as she felt her body nearly give out.
Her eyes finally began to water, and goosebumps ran across her
arms as she hugged herself tightly. The boy and the body were
gone, and Yvette never felt so alone. Her tears fell and poured
down her cheeks, but no one could hear her cry.

Saturday, April 3rd

DEEP IN THE HEART OF FOREST COVE, WAS A LARGE
pond where Walter's father often took him to go fishing. It was a
place where locals visit to enjoy the water and scenery. In
certain areas, the water was so clear that fish could be seen
swimming. Walter might have liked watching them when he was
younger, and even tried catching them with his hands, but
fishing overall was quite boring. Nonetheless, Walter always
enjoyed spending time with his father.

Mr. D'Artagnan and his son arrived at the lake early that
Saturday morning. Beside another man with his younger son and
daughter, no one else was there that early, not yet. Walter's
father had a special area they occupied every time. He didn't
own a boat yet, but his special area was on a short and shaded
cliff overlooking a section of the lake where it was accessible to
many fish. As for Walter, even with all the fish around, it was
never a sport he was good at, nor did he find it to be any sport to
begin with. He was too impatient and suffered from spontaneous

boredom, so fishing was one chronic boredom attack. Since he never really saw it as a sport to begin with, he didn't believe he needed to be athletic to do it. That was until he tried to reel in a large one that got the best of him, nearly pulling him into the lake with it. If his father hadn't caught him and cut the line, he might have been pulled in. His father would only laugh at Walter even more than he already was. It was embarrassing, but he found the humor of it all. His father was sillier than he might have seemed and always knew how to make anything fun when they spent time together.

The two were at the lake for about an hour and his father was reeling in his second fish for the day. He added it to their first cooler than grabbed two cold pilsners from the second. He opened them both and handed one to Walter. Their glasses rang as his father tapped his bottle with his son's. Walter hesitated for a moment.

"One beer won't hurt you," he said before taking his first sip. "Just don't tell your mom and she won't find out."

Walter nodded and chucked a bit. "I don't need more problems."

The boy and his father shared a laugh and enjoyed the beers together. His father knew he was on punishment, but he was more lenient than his mother. Still, there wasn't much Walter could really get away with when it came to either of his parents.

"How is your mom doing?" he asked. That morning when he picked Walter up, his mother had already left for work. His father did tend to arrive late at times so he and his ex-wife would often miss one another — sometimes just by minutes. He sometimes wondered if that was intentional.

"You should ask her yourself," Walter told him boldly. He could remember how tense his body was after he said that, but he steered into the skid. "You used to be around more often. You should come by and spend some time… I mean — you know — when you can." His father nodded, staying silent, seemingly thinking of something deeply. "Moms said that you need to bring back her Tupperware containers."

"Yeah, you're right, Walter. I used to be around more often, and I keep forgetting about her Tupperware. Make sure you remind me to give them to you when I drop you back home."

Walter nodded. "I'll try and remember, but that's going to be a challenge."

His father snorted and shook his head. "I will do the same." They both smiled with their beers, and, the funny thing was, they both sipped and sighed in unison. Then his father turned to his son and said, "Hey, I wanted to ask you something. What do you think… well… More like, how do you feel about your mom and I getting back together?"

"What?" Walter was surprised. "Really? How? You hardly ever see her."

His father snorted once more. "Just because you are not around when I do see her doesn't mean we don't see each other. I always find time for you and your mom. You know that, Walter."

"I mean…" He honestly didn't know what to say or how to feel. It wasn't like a small part of him didn't want his parents to get back together, but it felt so sudden. According to his father, it wasn't sudden at all, but Walter sat slightly conflicted. "Did you talk to Moms about it?"

"We aren't talking about her, we are talking about you." His father's tone was very stern and candid but genuine. Walter knew how serious he was.

"I think that once you and Moms are happy then I'm happy.

"No, seriously, Walter—"

"No… seriously, Dad. I mean it. You're my parents and I love you both. Why would I be against it? I guess… all I can say is… good luck?"

His father chuckled. "Why good luck?"

"You know why," Walter said with a little laugh. "Or… maybe I should say be careful instead."

"You know better than me."

The two of them laughed for a while. It might have been at his mother's expense, but she would probably laugh at that too. It might have been hard to believe, but Walter's mother wasn't just a mean middle-aged woman, scorned and sour — although Walter often wondered how his jokey and care-free father could win his mother's heart all those years ago. Love, he guessed, not truly knowing what it really meant. Even so, his mother was loving and loved to smile so it wasn't unlikely. No matter if they were married or not Lawrence and Harriet D'Artagnan always loved one another and couldn't trail too far away from each other.

"Did your mother ever tell you that she wanted a dozen children?"

Surprised, Walter was taken aback. "A dozen?"

His father laughed. "Could you imagine twelve of you running around your mother's house?"

"No. She has her hands full already, as she likes to say."

"My thoughts, exactly. But it's true." He sighed. "She just wanted many children to love… but it didn't work out that way."

Walter nodded silently, not really knowing what to say. The pain that ran across his father's face caught his eye. Then he grinned. "I hope the two of you get back together." His words seemed to fly out of him and made him question if he truly meant it. Walter never knew why his parents divorced so he only hoped it wouldn't occur again.

Then his mind trailed to Yvette. *We're different*, he admitted. *Me and Yvette. But did it really matter? There is no "me and Yvette." But, my parents were able to find each other... but does that even matter?* He couldn't say.

"Hey Dad," Walter got his father's attention. "Can I ask you something?"

"Of course. What's on your mind, Son?"

A knot tied his words and breath together and gave his throat a bit of a squeeze. "It's nothing. Never mind."

His father snorted. "There is nothing you need to worry about, Walter. If there is something on your mind, don't be afraid to say it."

Walter sighed. "Well, there is this girl at school..." He decided to keep it vague and Yvette anonymous. "I like her, I really do, but... I guess I'm just a little afraid to be honest with her about it."

His father nodded. "Don't know how to tell her how you feel?"

Reluctantly, he shook his head. "No, I don't."

"Really?" His father was a bit shocked. This caught Walter off guard. "I don't get it. It's not like you never had a girlfriend before. I've seen you talking to a few girls in school... in the neighborhood... I guess this girl is a special one."

Walter turned away, peeking at the other family where the father was helping his son keep his fishing rod steady. "I guess."

"So, what's the real problem?" his father asked.

"I don't know," he claimed, then made a little shrug as he turned away from the other family. That was a lie. He knew well what his hindrance was, but it seemed so stupid to him that he wouldn't dare say it aloud.

"This all reminds me of when I was your age," his father said. "You know, I had the same problem for a while. There were girls that I liked and some even liked me back. I wasn't afraid to talk to them and flirt with them a little — throw on the charm, you know — but there was always that one girl that I liked more than anyone else. I was afraid to talk to her... a long time, actually. Her life seemed so put together and... well, mine really wasn't." He wrapped an arm around his son and grasped his shoulder firm. "But, trust me, Walter, that's all a phase. Even so — and I can't speak for every man when I say this — but it seems like there is always that one girl that grabs your attention more than the rest, and just the thought of being rejected by her is frightening. You never know, she might feel the same way, but you won't know if you don't muster the courage to find out. If she doesn't feel the same then that's okay. You are going to meet a lot of girls in your life, Walter, many suitors. But, you have to be honest with yourself, and with them."

Walter thought about what his father said, and felt a bit better knowing he wasn't the only young man who had gone through the same. Be that as it may, everything his father said did make Walter a bit curious.

"You said almost every guy goes through this and so did you, right?"

His father nodded. "Right."

"So, who was yours?"

His father grinned. "Your mom."

Walter's eyes widened. "Really?"

"That's right, and, if I didn't have the guts to tell her how I felt, you and I wouldn't be having this conversation right now."

His father paused for a moment and turned entire body towards his son. "Look, Walter, I am truly sorry. I haven't been around like I should for the past few years. You know I didn't really know my father so there were times that I didn't know what to do and… well, I don't want you to feel the same. I'm happy you came to me with this because I want you to know that I'm always here for you. I want you to be confident in who you are, and once you have that confidence in yourself, there is nothing you can't do. It's okay to be afraid sometimes, but you can never let that fear hold you back or change what makes you… you. Do you understand me?"

His father was right, and the solace in his words made Walter stronger. He wasn't about to run to Yvette's house like some madman, to fall to his knees to confess some love for her. That would be ludicrous, he knew, but he felt self-assured and willing. He only wondered if he was ready, then he thought of Yvette. Her loss, her mother, her family — these things plagued her which concerned him. It made him ask himself, *Is Yvette ready for all that?*

The two spent a few hours by the lake, and Walter never even got a nibble on his line. However, his father caught enough to be satisfied. That afternoon they fried a few fish for dinner, while the rest were stuffed into the freezer and his father set some aside for his mother. "I hope I don't forget to take those to her too," he said.

Walter chuckled. "And her Tupperware."

"Right," his father said, pointing and winking at him.

The fish was delicious. Not only did he catch them all, but his father seasoned them to perfection. Eating was certainly Walter's favorite part of fishing. Plucking out bones, however, was less fun. Even eating fish could sometimes be a stupid sport but worth it.

The two watched a few old movies with dinner; "real movies" Walter's father called them. However, in the middle of the third, it was after sunset, and his father had already drifted to sleep and was snoring heavily. Walter barely finished the movie on his own — since he could barely hear it — instead, Yvette Anders was on his mind and the world around him seemed muffled. He wanted to see her but wasn't sure what he would even say to her. So, instead of sitting there listening to his father basically gargling, Walter went upstairs into his second bedroom.

This room was smaller than the one at his mother's. Having two bedrooms was a bit annoying at times. Walter was constantly split between two places which meant there were two rooms he had to keep tidy. Ultimately, that also gave him double the chores. *Maybe it might be good if my parents got back together after all,* he thought slyly. However, before he digressed, Walter came up to his room for a reason, and the reason was in his book bag.

Locked within two random pages of his geometry textbook were the pages from the diary. Walter sat on his bed for a moment with his pencil to the page. A few moments passed and he hadn't written anything inside. The empty pages stared back at him. He was nervous to write anything. Be that as it may, Walter swallowed his next breath then wrote a name down on the paper.

Yvette Anders.

It wasn't long after he wrote her name down, Walter heard her voice beside him, and, although he knew it was coming, a part of him still couldn't believe it.

"Walter?"

He turned to his left, and... there she was, sitting on his bed with her big brown eyes seeming vacant. However, when their eyes first met, her lips curled into a gentle smile. She was beautiful as ever and Walter stared in amazement. She wore the same dark color she wore on Friday, clean and freshly pressed — like she was wearing a memory of yesterday. Walter stood with shock and astonishment, and her subtle eyes followed him while she stayed seated and silent.

"Y... Yvette?" Walter stuttered a little.

She giggled. "Surprised to see me?"

"No, I just..." Walter took a back step towards her and knelt down. Her eyes continued to follow him the entire way and locked when they were on the same level. Walter raised a hand and gently rested it upon her cheek. He couldn't imagine how, but she was real. Walter could feel her skin beneath his palm, and her curls that lightly grazed the back of his hand.

Gently, she placed her hand upon his and smiled. "It's warm."

So are yours, is what he wanted to say.

With his heart pumping. He rose back up and glanced down at the name written in his spiky handwriting. Its magic wasn't new to him. He had used the pages several times since then, but to see an exact replica of Yvette was a little overwhelming.

There was a squeak, so he turned back and faced his bed to see... her... as she stood. "What's wrong?" She stepped towards him with a subtle pace as her legs nearly crossed with every step. "Aren't you happy to see me?"

"Of course, I..." Walter's tongue was caught again; by what, he didn't know. Somehow, he felt more rattled in front of this Yvette than the real one. The way she looked at him gave him a frightening comfort. What is this? The room was growing heavier in tension.

"Walter?" Her head cocked to the side. "Do I make you nervous?"

His response came out in a nervous yet warm gasp. "Yes."

Her smile showed itself again. "You don't have to be nervous with me, you know that... don't you?"

"I, umm..." He was hesitant again. "I... actually wanted to ask you something."

"Did you?" she asked sweetly. "You can ask me anything, but you already know that."

"Umm... Well, I wanted to ask..." Walter was hesitant. "Wait... Wait, hold on." He paced for a moment trying to find his confidence.

A giggle slipped between her lips. Walter wanted to smile, but he kept his lips at bay. "Okay. You said you wanted to ask me something, right?"

Walter had to remember it wasn't really her. "Yvette, I want to ask if... if you..." Walter became hesitant again and grunted heavily. "Why is it so hard to talk to you?"

Her smile was now gone. Her arms folded and she stared at him a bit vacantly. "It seems to me like you are the one making it harder on yourself. Don't you think I like you back?"

She's right. This isn't even Yvette. Why am I making this so hard on myself? And does she? Does she like me too? The girl before him was nothing more than a dream or like looking in a mirror — the reflection of a girl who wasn't even present — or whatever.

But this... this is so much more than that.

Walter faced her again, took a deep breath and said, "I wanted to ask you... if you wanted to go out sometime?"

The smile she made was what Walter liked so much to see, laying beautifully beneath big brown eyes flitting back and forth between his own. "Sure. I would love to."

The Yvette before him made the same subtle smile. It was surprising to hear how open she was to him. It wasn't Yvette at all, but he couldn't help but feel the same comfort, yet a deep disquiet.

"You would?" Walter asked, a bit surprised. Then he asked himself, *Would Yvette actually say that? Would she really feel that way?*

Suddenly, Yvette moved closer to Walter. Her footsteps knocked against the floor so slowly, and her eyes were sunken a bit as her voice lowered and softened. "This is what you want, right? Isn't is... what you want... Walter?"

After a moment of silent astonishment, Walter felt his lips draw closer, slowly open and say, "Yes."

The memory must have faded as Walter opened his eyes. They were sunken and sad. As he was telling Dr. Pierce his story, he often paused and blankly stared for a time. He might have been reliving vivid memories, but Linda Pierce couldn't truly believe his story. Some old leather book that brings written or drawn content to life seemed to come out of a fantasy tale, or a comic book filled with magic and mystery.

"What happened after that?" the doctor asked stoically. "With Yvette, I mean. It seems to me that you were trying to practice a certain... intimacy with this... projection of her. What did you—"

"I wasn't being... inappropriate with this... copy... if that's what you mean," Walter interrupted uncomfortably. "It's like... practicing in the mirror, but seeing the other person instead of

yourself... In a way, you kind of still see yourself for... " His
voice trailed off.

"Go on," the doctor implored.

Walter sighed. "I mustered all my courage to — funny
enough — not lean in and kiss her." Admitting that seemed to
fatigue him. "Even so, she disappeared right in front of me, and
when I looked back down at the diary, her name was gone."

"And how did that feel?"

"I don't know, Doc," he said, shaking his head. Then he
paused for a moment and said, "It reminded me that none of it
was real; not really. But it felt so real and... I almost lost
myself."

With a quick snort, the doctor began scanning through her
few pages of notes. "Your father gave me his own observation.
Do you remember what happened after you used the diary that
night?"

Walter was baffled. "What observation?"

Dr. Pierce pushed her glasses back above the bridge of her
nose. "He told me he found you in the living room flipping
through channels hours past midnight. You weren't blinking and
you were staring into the screen continuingly changing the
channel. He tried calling you several times, but you never
answered nor responded. You just sat there — staring blankly at
the screen... like a dead man. Eventually you walked back into
your room and into your bed but—" She stopped herself, seeing
the blank expression on his face. "Do you have any memory of
that, Walter?" She already knew his response, but she needed to
hear him say it.

With his lips slightly parted, Walter stared in disbelief,
seemingly lost in thought. "I was... Are you serious?" Walter
asked, frightened.

"I got a recollection from your mother as well. If I'm not mistaken..." Once again, she consulted her notes.

"What did she say?"

"The night after that, do you remember walking out onto the lawn and waking up when it started to rain?"

Walter's eyes averted from the doctor to the floor, to the couch, then back to the doctor. "I remember that."

"You do?" She was relieved to hear that.

He nodded. "It's very vague, but... but I remember walking back into my room and... I was a little wet. I... I thought that was just a stupid dream, you know?" His confused eyes bore into hers. "Doc... are you saying... I've been sleepwalking?"

Ding.

Before she could answer, the timer went off and took Walter's attention. Dr. Pierce faced him disappointedly. "I wished we had more time to delve further into this, but sadly our time is over for today, but..."

The doctor's voice trailed off for a moment and that brought a worried look to Walter's face. "What is it?" he asked.

"I want you to understand how serious this all is. Sleepwalking is a frightening thing for both yourself, and the people closest to you. I hope you are starting to understand why your parents are so worried?"

Walter nodded, but that was all she could get out of him.

The doctor stood and smoothed down her skirt. "I would like to return to this story next week, Walter. I believe reliving these events could give us a broader understanding of what we are dealing with here. Would you agree?"

"What do you mean?" he blurted angrily. She was used to such aggression, but Walter's caught her off guard. "I told you what it is. It's the diary."

153

"So, are we blaming the diary for your sleepwalking as well?"

Walter grimaced and grunted. "I don't know," he admitted tensely as he averted his eyes away again.

"Well, you haven't finished your story yet. You will need to tell me more about what happened with all of this — the diary, Yvette, Samuel, all of it — for me to fully understand and help you. However, the solace I can provide you is that you are not alone. I want to believe you, Walter. Keep convincing me."

When he nodded, an exhausted sigh escaped his lips. "Thanks for at least not lying to me."

Dr. Pierce grinned. "Your welcome, Walter. You will be here next week, won't you?"

He nodded again. "I will be here."

Dr. Pierce wanted to believe him but couldn't. She sighed and said, "I've heard those words before. I need you to be sure that you won't fight this and come to our sessions willingly." Dr. Pierce couldn't afford to lose another patient so early in the year. Still, she kept that to herself.

"No, I won't." Walter shook his head. "I will be here. I promise."

Dr. Pierce put her glasses to the side and then nodded. "I hope so. Do you feel comfortable returning to school?"

He nodded. "I think so. I have to see Yvette. I..." His voice fell to silence. She was curious of what he had to say but decided not to pry. Their next session would be the time for that.

"Before you go..." Instead, she went into her desk, received a black notebook and held it out to him. "Whenever you have thoughts, anything you want to remember, anything at all... I want you to write it down in this book. It can be your own diary... or journal if you'd rather..." The look on Walter's face

154

made her worried that she might have used the wrong word. She made sure to keep the young man's trigger in mind, respectfully. Even so, she asked, "Something wrong? You don't have to worry about anyone reading what you write. It's for your eyes only... if you like."

"It's not that," he said. "Can I... Can I get a different color?"

"Oh," The doctor was a bit surprised. "Boys usually ask for the black ones... or blues... or reds... Any color you prefer? I have them all."

Walter's eyes averted for a moment, but when he turned back to her, a soft smile was stroked across Walter's lips. "Orange."

- Session Two

Wednesday, May 12th

IT HAD BEEN TWO WEEKS SINCE WALTER'S INCIDENT;
the incident that initially brought him to the doctor. Honestly,
Dr. Pierce was a bit taken back when she heard the story from
Mrs. D'Artagnan's lips. Ghosts were her first thought. Centralia
High wasn't free of its own macabre history and controversy,
and the hallways weren't entirely clean. She kept that bit to
herself though, figuring there was no need to bring this up to the
parents. Even so, the doctor only hoped that the story didn't turn
too ghastly.

Neither his father nor mother knew what Walter had seen
that day in the hallway at his school. Dr. Pierce didn't want to
come to the thought that Walter might be lying to everyone,
trying to escape from something that no one might understand.
Bullies could have threatened the young man's life for all
anyone knew. Possibly, the boy would rather devise a colorful
tale of a magical diary being the culprit for his behavior and
some conduit for hallucinations than own up to the truth. None

of the teachers or staff reportedly knew about the incident until after nor did they know what caused it. Even so, Linda Pierce hoped to hear the truth of it from Walter D'Artagnan himself; sooner rather than later.

When the young man arrived, he was a bit more pleasant than the week prior. He wore a thin grin when he entered and greeted the doctor with a less sunken and detached approach. She even observed him sitting in the same spot on the couch, which was common to most his age; like desks at school. Still, he seemed quite comfortable there while his demeanor was more calming than before. Dr. Pierce was quite pleased to see this.

"You seem... calmer today," Dr. Pierce commented while gingerly sitting across from him in her own comfortable armchair.

Walter nodded with his tiny grin in the corner of his lips. "I'm trying to be."

"That's good. I'm glad you're here. I know it's not easy being the patient in the room, but if it makes you feel any better, most of us have therapists of our own. Life's not easy for us or anyone. Just because I have 'doctor' in front of my name, does not mean I have all the answers. No one does. We all need someone to speak about things sometimes and give us some perspective. Don't you agree?"

Wide-eyed, Walter nodded although he seemed to have many questions in his head. "Yeah... Yeah, that makes sense."

"That's why we work together — doctor and patient — to get through everything. You don't have a broken leg and need me to fix it. No. You may not be able to do this without me, but I can't do anything for you without you."

A small grin appeared on Walter's lips as he nodded. It was quite hard for him to keep eye contact, but that invisible shield

*he held during their first meeting was lowered now. It was still
there; an unseen silver lining silhouette.*

"*So,*" *Dr. Pierce began,* "*how have you been, Walter?*"

He shrugged. "*I've been fine, I guess.*"

"*Fine is good. I like to think even guesses can be optimistic in
some ways. Yes, it can lead to progression — our goal, of
course. She paused for a moment as her patient nodded.* "*Has
anything new happened since last week? Anything you would
like to speak about? Anything you think I should know?*"

"*Like what?*"

"*Anything at all. Remember, it's just you and me, Walter. You
can always speak your mind here.*"

*The young man was silent for a moment but eventually just
shrugged.* "*I don't know. I'm not really sure what to say. What
are you looking for?*"

Dr. Pierce felt herself grin. "*Good question. Overall,
everything you say will give me some insight to determine what
is at play here and how I can help you with all of this. The core
of that is most important, won't you agree?*"

Walter began sulking and the doctor knew why. This diary,
she thought.

"*I already told you,*" *he muttered, less bothered than their
first meeting.* "*It's hard to believe but I'm telling you the truth.*"

The doctor sighed, patient yet hesitant. "*Listen to me
carefully. I need you to understand how… puzzling this all is. I
think even you can imagine that it would be hard for someone to
believe your story. It's, as they say, 'A hard pill to swallow.'*"

*Walter didn't respond. She waited, hoping he would, but he
didn't. Instead, he sat there, slowly returning to his sunken state,
reminding her of her first impression of him. It had become too
familiar at this point, and she wouldn't allow any process to be
in vain. Still, his shield didn't raise, but it was still at his side.*

Even though Walter seemed just as saddened as last Wednesday, he was a bit more sympathetic. "I'm sorry, Doc."

Dr. Pierce was sad for him, but she felt herself grin when he called her "Doc."

"This is all overwhelming, I know," she said warmly, "but I'm still here and I still want you to convince me. Let's continue your story from last week. Reliving these events and acknowledging what occurred can really help me understand and clarify some things. This diary is a way you and Yvette deal with grief, I'm not here to judge that. I'm simply here to understand. Remember, it's your parents who are worried about you and, frankly, so am I. Can you help me and maybe we can help your parents as well... and even Yvette? Help her too?"

Walter nodded. Although he was a bit sunken, he seemed to understand. "Yeah, you're right."

"The only thing I care about is understanding what is affecting you, and I'm sorry if I don't understand. But that's what I'm here to do, to understand more about this diary."

Walter fell silent again, seemingly far off in a distant memory as his face seemed to vacate before her. She was hoping he had something to say or would even debate or plead his case, but he only sat there, seemingly in an old memory.

"What's on your mind?" the doctor asked, her head cocked to one side curiously.

"I wanted to ask you something," he said. "Something personal, if you don't mind."

"Depends on the question."

"True." He sighed. "Have you ever lost someone? Someone close? Someone that can never be replaced?"

The question caught her heart. Linda Pierce felt herself drift into a memory; a sweet memory of a close someone, an irreplaceable someone. However, although this person was

160

someone she loved dearly, she could feel the hole they left behind and the love that once filled it. When they were gone, no matter how much she wanted them back, the love of her life would never return. It was all very sobering, and even numbing. Dwelling in such an empty place brought her no peace.

However, the doctor smiled sadly. "We all have someone who—"

"I know but..." Walter was hesitant. "It's just... nothing. It's nothing."

She sighed, still holding her sad smile. "When you love someone, Walter," she said lowly, "they can never be replaced."

He was silent for a moment before asking. "What does that feel like?"

"Walter, we are here to talk about you—"

"Please... What does that feel like?"

His voice grew adamant; no anger nor desperation, but adamant all the same. She took notice.

Dr. Pierce centered herself while gathering her thoughts. "It can feel like life as you know it is over. There is an emptiness left inside you that... that never really goes away." She felt sunken for a moment, until she remembered where she was and cleared her throat. "But that's based on my opinion. Therefore, it's best to develop coping regiments to help when you feel that emptiness."

With his lips parted in astonishment, Walter muttered, "That's what Yvette must be feeling like. Every day."

"It's unfortunately prevalent. To lose a parent at that young of an age, and in the way that—" Before the doctor could say too much, she stopped herself and bit her tongue. "It's... indescribable. Why don't we continue with the story, Walter? We still haven't gotten to the incident in the hallway at school. You know what I'm talking about, don't you?"

161

Walter nodded contently. "I remember."

Once her notepad was in her hand, Dr. Pierce shifted in her seat to get comfortable and rested it down on her folded legs. "Whenever you are ready."

Tuesday, April 20th

SOMETIMES AFTER SCHOOL, WALTER'S FATHER
would take his son to his mechanic shop with him to teach him
the trade. Walter didn't really care for it, but he liked the money
he made. Neither his father nor his mother were fond of
allowances, so it was the only cash Walter would make
throughout the week. He never complained — at least not too
much. He would rather not hear his father's response to that.

On the days he didn't work with his father, Walter would lie
to his mother saying he was staying to study after school. In
actuality, Walter was more interested in spending time with
Yvette rather than anything else. It was challenging to see Yvette
the following weeks, however. He had only gotten the diary
pages recently, but it felt like months ago. Besides their biology
class and several times in the hallway, Walter barely saw her. It
was undeniable that she was most likely still gaining her bearing
while at school. Of course, her obligations at the newspaper kept
her busy just as Art was with the team more and more as the

championship crept closer. She didn't seem upset with him or anything, but she didn't seem to have time for him either. Art's absence didn't bother him, yet Yvette's did. Walter didn't like feeling that way, but he couldn't control it.

Once while in class, Walter drew Captain Long Ears sitting on Mr. Vega's head during one of his lessons and had the bunny gyrate on the man's bald head. When he turned to Yvette, she was trying her hardest not to laugh. It was funny, yet Yvette wanted to strangle him for almost getting them in trouble.

It was over a week before the two spent any real time together. Not too far from their school, there was a park nearby where they spent nearly the entire afternoon. All they needed was the diary and one another to stay entertained. Walter drew out crudely grown characters while Yvette wrote little short stories to go with it. With constant laughs and titters, they watched as the diary would play out the story for them better than any screen. Regardless of where they went, anytime a passerby saw them they would stare, wondering what Walter and Yvette were watching that only they could see. Neither of them cared, in fact, when some people walked by, baffled and even concerned, it only made them laugh even harder once they were alone again.

"What are you drawing?" Yvette asked him once. He was keeping the diary away from her and soon she felt something tiny crawling beside her ear. She nearly jumped until a ladybug the size of a fingernail flew in front of her nose and landed on her hand where her thumb and index joined. She smiled when she saw it and even petted the shiny shell. "It's so pretty. I've never pet a ladybug before... or seen one this big. And the shell... orange instead of red. That's cool." Her smile stretched. "Did you know?"

Walter was confused. "Did I know... what?"

164

"That orange is my favorite color, silly."

He smiled. "Well, I like it on you."

She giggled a bit. "Thanks," she said; sweetly, graciously. "And you? What's your favorite?"

"Black, of course."

"Of course." Yvette leaned into the diary a bit. "How did you do that, anyway?"

"Do what?"

She parted her lips to explain, but instead, she snatched the diary then gleefully took a look. Sketched inside was a tiny ladybug with a dotted swirling line trailing behind it and its wings and shell spread out from its back. Written below the drawing were instructions telling the orange insect to fly from behind her ear and onto the back of her hand.

"I never tried that before," she said, seeing how they usually let the diary play out the story how it wanted. "You drew a picture but told it what to do. That's amazing."

Walter shrugged. "I just thought of it. I figured I'd give it a try, you know?"

That's how their diary stories started.

Later that Wednesday, they were in the library and they drew his favorite character, Captain Long Ears. He appeared on the table before them, the furry white rabbit with his large beady eyes, long fluffy ears with gold fabric at the tips, and stitchings in baby blue above his rattling belly. Captain Long Ears jumped onto another table and began dancing on the head of a sleeping student. Yvette tried not to laugh at first, but she couldn't help it after a while and a laugh burst through her lips. This was the first time a librarian tried to keep them quiet. Honestly it was hard to do so as the captain started making funny faces, and even licked his finger and gave the student a wet willy. There were so many barks of laughter between them that they were soon asked to leave.

It was fine. Yvette needed to get home and Walter's punishment had yet to be over and it was only a matter of time before his mother expected him home. When she went home that night, Yvette was left alone. Her father was working and so was her sister, so Yvette was babysitting her nephew while she took time to study and talk with her mother. Yvette found a book her and her mother would read together and read it to her. Fortunately, the story was sweet enough for Michael to fall asleep and snooze a few hours before his mother and grandfather came home. Not long after, Yvette fell asleep beside the book and diary.

As for Walter, he had a certain project he was working on in his spare time. During the night before he went to sleep, he would write Yvette's name on the stained and mystical parchment ripped from the diary. The Yvette the diary conjured would sit on his bed with her legs crossed and try to hold her smile while Walter sketched her. Walter was already through with most of her face, but he spent the most time perfecting her eyes. *They had to be just right.*

But on this night, *this* Yvette was very fidgety.

"You're moving around again," Walter told her.

"I'm sorry but it's hard sitting like this for too long," she said. "You've been drawing for over two hours tonight."

"Honestly, I didn't think you could get tired," Walter replied boldly. When he looked up at the Yvette on his bed, her arms were folded now and the smile on her face had turned sour. "Sorry, I didn't mean it like that." It wasn't really Yvette, but Walter still felt bad. He sat beside her to show how far he had gotten with the drawing. "What do you think?"

The same gentle smile that Yvette always made ran across her lips. She took the sketch book in her hand and her grin grew wider by the moment. Walter watched as she took a few fingers and gently ran them across the drawn dimpled cheeks.

"It looks just like me," she said, only to correct herself pensively. "I mean... it looks just like her."

Walter felt a little bad about that too. It might not have been the real Yvette but it seemed like she was... in some strange way. Every time Walter wrote her name, the Yvette that appears always seemed to become increasingly more lifelike. When he first started his drawing, she didn't mind sitting still for long periods of time. She stayed so still she could have mistaken her for a life-size doll. Now she was becoming moody, distracted, head-strong and unsatisfied.

Hoping to ease her mind, Walter drew a rose on the page, and like magic, the rose appeared in his hand for her, but it was orange, not red. When Yvette saw it, she blushed and took it in her hands. "For me?" Walter nodded as she tried to hide her gleeful face behind sunset pedals. When she playfully turned back to him with her sharp eyes gazing deep into his, he smiled. "You are sweet, Walter. Do you know that? I wish I really were Yvette. You would certainly make me happy... like you always do."

Although she was using Yvette's voice and her demeanor, a part of him didn't want to believe anything she said, remembering that she wasn't who she appeared to be... not really. She might have just been saying all the things Walter wanted to hear. Nonetheless, that satisfaction was reserved for the real Yvette, not a manifestation . All he could ask himself was, *Is that really what Yvette would say?*

"I may not be her," she went on, "but I can be." As she said that, Yvette slowly leaned in to kiss him. She was inches away but he could almost feel her lips against his… her embrace. Once again, he kept his distance. However, unlike before, she grinned lightly and didn't tease him by disappearing. No. She was there.

Four fingers slid up to his neck and her thumb caressed his cheek, hoping to bring him back to her. Although it was the comfort he wanted to explore with Yvette — the comfort he had thought of many times — Walter quickly stood and stepped away from her. *I can't,* he thought then wondered, *What are you?*

Her eyes turned wide as she looked up at him. "What do you mean?" The way she asked that, so aghast and hurt, it was like she read his mind.

"I want you gone," Walter told her. It wasn't easy, however. He had to be curt with her… and himself.

The way she looked at him, eyes wide and lips parted, she couldn't believe what she was hearing. "What?" she asked desperately. "But… But why?"

The sweet innocence in her voice disturbed and even angered him. "I can't write your name anymore. I'm sorry."

Baffled, she tried to grasp his arm. "Walter…"

He pulled back, not wanting to be sucked back into her. For a moment he stared as those big brown eyes bore into his. His heart was racing, thumping and skipping; a strange tune to a strange feeling. *Dread,* he guessed; but that's all it was, a guess. All he knew was that there was an eerie power about her presence and he had to get away from it. So, he left the room leaving the fake Yvette on the bed and her name in the diary. He tried using the orange notebook he got from the doctor to write his thoughts or draw instead, but there was nothing like the diary.

Walter felt overwhelmed and went downstairs to find his mother in the kitchen. She asked him to make some popcorn because there was a movie she wanted to watch with him. She reminded him he was still on punishment, but she wanted to spend some time with her son. "Plus, you've been cooped up in that room," she added. Then she gave him a motherly smile and said, "I've gotten good reviews from your teachers too, so I guess more time for studying is helping, huh?"

Honestly, Walter couldn't be sure if his mother was being a bit sarcastic or not, but he nodded and enjoyed the praise. Plus, a good movie might be the distraction he needed.

For most of the night, he and his mother watched an interesting drama with most of the main characters gifted with magical abilities. It was the kind of story that Walter would often draw; the kind of story his mother knew he enjoyed. However, throughout the movie, he would peek up the stairs periodically hoping Yvette wouldn't show. Seeing her standing at the top of the stairs might have frightened him out of his mind. She didn't, but, somehow, Walter felt like he was being watched.

Midway through the movie, his mother turned to him and told him how she heard of the conversation he had with his father about his parents possibly rekindling their relationship. It was quite strange and sudden, and made Walter think that having this conversation was the point of their whole movie night. Harriet D'Artagnan wasn't known for leniency. Still, that didn't matter though. It even made Walter chuckle a little. He liked seeing them spend time together and "rekindling" as his mother put it. He's not sure if he ever heard that word used before that.

"So, you *have* been seeing Dad without telling me?" A large smirk ran across her son's face. Hearing his mother say it for herself did make it all the more enjoyable.

"Your father felt it was better if he told you himself, and I agreed wholeheartedly."

Walter snorted lowly, unable to fight the urge. "I'm just a little surprised you didn't tell me… seeing how it's Dad and all."

"I don't have to tell you everything, Walter." Just the tone alone, Walter knew his mother was setting him straight. "That's why you have two parents."

Without a good response to give to that, Walter let it go. An angry mother is the last thing he wanted, no matter what her movie night was meant for.

"So, tell me about Yvette," his mother said and this caught Walter off guard. "You like this girl?"

"Can we not talk about her?"

"Well, you seem to be very interested in her," his mother pointed out. "You've been spending some time with her. I remember she was a smart one — her sister too — so that's good if you're going to be spending your time with someone. Maybe I should thank her for your grades improving."

"Maybe," Walter said flatly, unsure of a different answer to give.

"So, is she your girlfriend?"

"No, we're… just friends."

His mother rolled his eyes and grunted. "I've heard that before."

Walter smirked, surprised. "What do you mean by that?"

"You don't think I remember how those little girls used to call my house when you were in — what — *fifth* grade? You're not as slick as you think you are, Walter."

An uncontrollable little laugh escaped him as he shook his head. "It's just the charm, Mom."

She snorted, not hiding it at all. "That charm better not get any of these little girls pregnant, you hear me?"

"Woah…" Walter rose his hands in defeat. "I'm not doing anything, okay?"

She rolled her eyes as she turned back to the movie. "'It's the charm.' Boy?!" She made a laugh, light and modest. "Just like your father, I swear."

"Dad told me about when he first asked you out and how he was a bit… frightened I guess — I don't know what word he would use to describe it — but I guess he was—"

"Nervous?" His mother's smile was showing more teeth now. Walter nodded. "Yeah."

"That's because your father is afraid to talk about how he feels. He's loving and caring and great at showing it, but you can't ask him how he feels. Either he won't know what to say or he won't have any answer at all. That lack of communication can be frustrating at times. Sometimes, I just want to hear him say—"

His mother paused suddenly as she seemed to step into a world that only she could see. She went from a grand smile to sour frown, then a forced grin to a pleasant smile.

"Are you okay?" Walter asked.

She sighed. "I'm fine. Your father had me laughing the other day about that first time we met in the hospital. You know the story, how much I wanted to hate him since he came from a rival school — you can't imagine how bad that rivalry was back in our day — but I couldn't deny how I felt. He couldn't tell me the same, but I was young, so I accepted him being a bit… reserved with his feelings. In a way I still do, it is just who he is."

171

It was a bit strange seeing his mother all flustered like that. An influx of emotions seemed to be escaping her.

The curious feeling grew inside him and got the best of him. "Why did you and Dad get a divorce? You always said I had to wait until I was older to know. I was young when it happened, but—"

"And you are still young, Walter."

"But I'm not a little kid anymore, Mom. Can't you tell me what happened? You two might be trying to get back together, but I don't even know why you two broke up in the first place. You tell me to go ask Dad about... whatever, I get it, but this? I mean, it seemed like you were madder when it happened. I figured you didn't love Dad anymore or hated him or—"

"Never!" The tone sounded as if she was slightly offended. "I have always and will always love your father. We share so much. We share you, the most important thing to both of us. You know that, right?"

"Yes," he nodded. "And you asked me the same thing when you two got divorced. I don't always remember stuff, but I do remember that."

His mother sighed. "Like I said before, you father and I share you, and for a few years before the divorce, we were trying to have another child — something more to share — hopefully to bring us... closer. I... I don't know, sweetheart."

Without warning, Walter's lips curled into a thin smile, just by the possibility of having a younger sibling — a brother, a sister, he didn't care which. However, seeing his mother frowning in nostalgic sorrow, his thin grin melted away.

She continued. "Unfortunately, we found out that — I don't want to get into any details — but... well, I wasn't strong enough to give birth to any more children and... It made me feel so weak and worth—" Then she stopped. She might have nearly said something personal she didn't want to divulge to him. Walter was already curious, but he decided not to pry seeing how open his mother was being and how hurt it seemed to make her. He was about to embrace her, when she sniffed and went on.

"Your father was there for me, always by my side during that time, but he never told me how he felt. I didn't know if he was sad, disappointed with me... hated me—" Another pause. "That caused the worst argument we ever had. I blame myself just as much as he blames himself, but... for years we blamed each other even more. We tried to stay together for you — we truly did, Walter — but it was hard. He never disrespected me or treated me wrong, but sometimes I felt like I barely knew him. When that happened, along with other stupid things we were already arguing about, we couldn't go on."

Speechless, Walter stayed quiet and soaked in everything his mother was revealing to him. He never expected the reason to be such a sensitive one. Even if she had told him years ago, he would have never understood. It would have just made everything worse. On the other hand, Walter was saddened for his mother. She wanted twelve and she got him. *I can't imagine how you feel, Mom.* Walter even saw as her eyes began to water. Unhindered, he wrapped his arm around his mother and she chuckled lightly as she gently rested her cheek on her son's shoulder, snuggling into him.

"I'm so happy that I have you, Walter," his mother said sweetly. "I wouldn't know what I would do without you. I hope you know how much you mean to me. You are the most important thing to me, and I felt like I disappointed you when I couldn't have more children. I know at least one other sibling is all you ever wanted growing up and I'm sorry we couldn't do that for you."

To assure his mother, Walter rested a kiss above her brow and said, "I'm happy I have you too, Mom. You could never disappoint me. Maybe — I don't know — that's just how it was… how it was supposed to be? Do I sound horrible?"

Even with the tears, his mother smiled and Walter could feel it against him. He liked to see his mother's smile. It was nice. It was like Yvette's.

"No, sweetheart," she assured him. "I just wanted to be a mother. I always thought a dozen children would be a solid number. I would have so many children to love… take care of… and have take care of me and their father. I imagined a dining room table with fourteen seats; a seat for everyone."

"Dinner times would be absolutely—"

"Insane!" His mother laughed.

Walter joined in, but when the laughs faded away, he frowned. "Would having more children have brought you two back together… like you wanted?"

His mother gave a sad smile as she shook her head. "No, because that's not what would have kept us together. Your father and I had to acknowledge that. I don't care that I didn't have more children, because I was blessed with you, Walter. You have enough love for a dozen children, because those dozen children are you."

Walter was smiling now. "Thanks, Mom." She was his mother, of course, but still… *She has never said anything so sweet.* He hugged her even tighter and held her for a while, but couldn't tell how long.

Walter didn't remember going to bed that night. He did drift off on the couch but when he woke up, he was in his bed, shutting off his old alarm clock on his end table and taking a fuzzy look at the time. Even getting out of bed, getting clean and ready for school, eating breakfast and all that, it all seemed to come by in vague pictures and blurs. He felt a bit woozy at times and his legs could have been mistaken for noodles. His breakfast cereal and buttered toast helped but little. It wasn't until he arrived at school that he felt a bit better. He slipped into the nurse's office for an aspirin then was off to class. *Good thing I didn't have Art with me. I might not get to class on time.*

It wasn't until lunchtime that day that Walter was approached by Yvette. The bell had just rung and Walter had just opened his locker when she called his name. She was wearing purple today — her sweater with a short V of buttons and hair tie that held her thick dark curls that laid gently on one shoulder.

"Hey, Walter," said Yvette, her brown eyes were bright and becoming yet somehow sad and worrisome. The pink in her eyes clashed with her purple. Just seeing them made him abandon his locker completely.

"Hey." His tone was wary. "Are you okay?"

So was hers. "Can I talk to you for a moment? In private?"

"Yeah, sure," he replied, shutting his locker.

Walter followed her outside the main building towards the courtyard where several walkways stretched towards a few small buildings, the gymnasium and the football field. Tall trees with wide branches and thick leaves dotted the walkways, and served as perfect shades for the benches beneath them. Most of the shaded benches were occupied, so Yvette led Walter to an archway leading to the science labs.

"What's going on, Yvette?" he asked. "Is everything okay?"

"Yeah, sure, but... I'm sorry, Walter. I thought about what you said and it made me feel terrible."

Walter was confused but he tried not to show it too much. "What do you mean?"

She gently grasped one of her ears. "I... lied to you."

175

Unfortunately, Walter was even more confused, and felt the strain in his face as he tried to hide it. Eventually his face relaxed, allowing his eyes to squint and his head to slightly cock to the side. "Lied to me? When?" Yvette seemed too honest to lie, but he had been wrong before.

"Remember when I asked you if you would ever write a name in my diary just to see someone who died?"

Walter nodded, lips agape but saying nothing.

She sighed heavily. "I wanted to know if I was the only one who might feel that way because... that's why I use it. With the diary, I... I get to see my mom again."

Slowly, Walter's eyes widened, burning with surprise. "Wait... You're serious." It wasn't a question. The honesty and vulnerability was apparent.

Yvette nodded. "Losing her was very hard and... the diary... it helps me with..." She paused for a moment, her finger massaging her right ear gently. "If I could see her and talk to her then... I thought maybe it wouldn't hurt as much. Before the diary, I couldn't even remember what my mother's voice sounded like."

Walter didn't know what to say. He never lost a parent, so he couldn't even fathom what she was going through. Divorce wasn't the same as death. *Death was permanent,* he thought, only to second guess that.

She went on. "Ever since I found it and I learned what it can do, I've been talking with my mother and... it comforts me. Just hearing her voice comforts me."

"But..." Still a bit speechless, Walter mustered out the words "But it's not—"

"—not really her, I know. I have no idea what it is but... when I see her, it's like... it's like she never left." Yvette turned to Walter with his eyes widened. "If my last doctor knew she

176

would call me obsessed. How could I blame her? I can't eat without the diary. I can't sleep without the diary." She sighed. "I wanted to hate you so bad when you had it. It was only one night yet I was practically numb. I couldn't stand it…'" Then she paused as her lips fell agape. "Wait, Walter, am I broken? Tell me the truth. Is this what broken feels like? I'm not broken, right?"

"Hey, calm down." Without thinking, Walter reached out to her and held her shoulders gently, hoping to comfort her. When she looked up at him, her eyes were filled with unfallen tears. "You're not broken, Yvette. Only your heart is. You lost your mom. No one can expect you not to feel hurt or… even alone. It's okay."

Yvette turned away from him and began wiping the tears in her eyes. "I don't like crying. It's so ugly." Walter couldn't help but snicker at that and she matches him with her own. "Thanks, Walter. I didn't think anyone would understand that."

"You'd be surprised," Walter replied. "It's hard losing someone and I don't think that ever really goes away. It might be harder to let go… you know?"

Yvette shook her head, her eyes sunken. "I don't want to let go."

Walter couldn't judge her but he didn't know what to say either. The diary had become so important to her life. She might have been obsessed with it, but it was her mother she coveted and it would be difficult to take that away from her. He could only wonder what he would do if he were in her shoes. It made him think of the fake Yvette again, posing for his sketch only to wish he hadn't.

"You're right though, Walter," she said, fortunately regaining his attention. "I guess it's just easier said than done. But… I won't just give up on her so quickly. It would be like... like losing her again."

"You won't lose her, Yvette," Walter assured her, hoping to ease her mind a bit. "No one is asking you to give her up. You can't. That's impossible... Because she lives within you... You know... in your heart."

Hearing Walter say that brought a bit of warmth to her smile. "I heard that saying before and you are right. That's a very sweet thing to say."

Walter made a nervous grin. "I'm only worried that all this might make you a bit... unhinged."

Suddenly, his next words took that warm and sweet feeling away. "Unhinged? You think I'm unhinged?" Her tone had changed completely, leaving a bitter and cold unpleasantness.

"No, I don't mean it like—"

Yvette shook her head, disturbed. "Then what do you mean?"

"You were the one asking me if you were broken and I said no—"

"Well of course not because you think I'm unhinged now."

"It's like... the same thing, Yvette—"

"It's not."

Walter sighed heavily. "Fine, you're right, it's not the same. I don't think you are unhinged, Yvette. I don't think you're broken or... damaged or anything. I know you are going through a lot, but... but look at what this book is doing to you. I saw how you looked on Friday. How exhausted you were without it for only one night. You just admitted that. You looked like you were working in a graveyard. It's not healthy, Yvette. You're the smartest person I know, but I don't get how you don't see it that way."

Yvette wiped her eyes and sniffed as she turned and stepped away from him. She folded her arms at first before finding one of her ears to hold onto. She was even shivering now but Walter kept his distance.

"You're right," she finally stated. "I thought I was fine. The doctor said I was fine, but… I just miss her so much. But... It's true. I am obsessed."

"Maybe you are, Yvette, but it doesn't make you broken or unhinged or whatever. You lost your mom. Just going through that is hard. You have your family that loves you, but this, you're going through this alone. I'm good at keeping secrets, so you don't have to worry about that. But Yvette, your mom, your real mom, she wouldn't want you living in the past forever." As Walter spoke, he realized that a part of him was talking to himself.

Still shivering, Yvette faced him with watery eyes. "Can I get a hug?"

Walter grinned and embraced her. Her cheek rested on his chest and he rubbed her back gently. "You're going to be okay," Walter said warmly. More thoughts came to mind of what he wanted to tell her — how much he cared about her, that he would be there for her and that she wouldn't be alone once he was there — but he didn't. It didn't seem like the optimal time. Not yet.

Yvette looked up at him. "Thank you, Walter. I'm... I'm sorry for lashing out like that. Do you forgive me?"

"Of course, I do," Walter assured her, but he couldn't hide his curiosity. "But, why did you tell me all this?"

Her cheeks snuggled into his chest a bit more as if she was hiding from him. "I don't know," she said. "Like you said, I shouldn't go through this alone. Sometimes I feel like I'm drowning. But when you found out, I was afraid, but… it's nice… having someone to share this with, I mean."

Walter was surprised to hear her say that. His lips even curled to make a smile. When she let go of him, his lips straightened as his teeth locked together behind his shut lips. Yvette's eyes were still a bit watery, but she still wore her soft smile. Just the way she was looking at him, he still wanted to tell her how he felt right then and there — take her by the waist, pull her into him and feel her lips against his. But he had to stop himself. *That won't make her feel better*, he surmised. *Only me.*

The two made their way back into the main building with a slow stroll. Neither really spoke. Walter himself was tongue-tied and he could only imagine what was on Yvette's mind. Most likely filled with mixed feelings; sadness and confusion most likely.

They arrived at Yvette's locker not long after. She had to make her way to the newsroom for the rest of lunch and needed to grab a few things. "I really appreciate you being so cool with me sharing all this with you."

"Don't worry about it," he assured her. "I understand. However, if you do want to thank me, you can allow me to escort you to the newsroom."

With the sly smile she responded with, Walter knew her well enough now to know when she was being playful. "Oh, really?" The tone of her voice even reminded him of when he was being silly.

"Yeah, I mean… this school is crazy."

Yvette giggled. "Sure."

The soft smile she wore still made Walter nervous all over again. He really wanted to tell her how he felt, even if he second guessed it a moment ago. Now he was in the hallway with students and faculty walking past him and he began to overthink it all. Be that as it may, the longer he waited, the less chance Yvette might reciprocate.

Yvette opened her locker with a sulk. "I swear I open this locker ten times a day. So many books. I should just have two lockers."

Walter abandoned his confession for now. Instead, he replied to her. "Like a fat kid who needs two seats?"

"See, you're terrible," she said. Even so, she was giggling. "But yes, Walter. My school schedule is a fat kid. And now you're making me sound terrible too."

"If it makes you feel any better, I go to my locker ten times a day too, but it's mainly because I'm always forgetting something."

Yvette shook her head. "No, no, it doesn't help," she jested. Chuckling, she received a textbook and a small binder. Walter felt so warm inside that he felt his lips open to speak.

However, before Walter could muster that confidence his father told him about, he was interrupted as the human basketball himself, Kevin Kittle, moseyed on over to Yvette's locker with such swagger in his steps.

"Hey, what's up, Yvette?" he said, his basketball married to his armpit.

Yvette turned to him, not seeing his approach. "Kevin. Hey. What's up?"

"I wanted to thank you for helping me prepare for my test the other day. I ended up passing so..." he nodded, "...you were a big help."

"I knew you would. You didn't even really need me, Kevin. You know the work, but like I told you, you're just not preparing for tests properly."

"Right. Thanks for that. I really needed to pass that test. I might not be playing if I didn't."

"Well, I'm glad I could help 'cause the team needs you."

"You already know. So, you're going to be at the game, right?"

Yvette nodded. "Yeah, I'll be there. Hazel and Stefan will be working on the article for the team and Donnie is taking pictures, but I think we are all going. Not sure yet though."

He nodded. "Cool."

Walter stood there, his eyes flitting back and forth between them.

Kevin went on. "Well, make sure you tell your boy Donnie to bring his best camera because I plan on flying." Sarcastically, he slammed over Yvette with the ball in his hand, and it made her snicker but gesture back a bit. Whether the snicker was genuine or not, Walter couldn't be sure. Even so, she seemed a bit crowded.

"So, my brother is having a little party after the game," Kevin announced, suave and as swaggering as he closed the distance.

Seemingly surprised, she said. "Oh, really? You guys are *that* confident, huh?"

"Of course, we are. It doesn't matter if we win the game. It just gives my brother a reason to have a party, honestly. But I'd rather hold up the trophy at the party than not."

Yvette seemed convinced. "I can understand that."

Kevin then took a step closer. "So... the party... you want to come with me?"

Surprised and even shunned, Yvette's lips grew slightly agape while Walter who was taken aback entirely. He had his chance, and here comes the basketball star stepping on his toes.

"Really?" Yvette eventually replied nervously, but still surprised. "You mean, like... like a date?"

"Yeah... like a date."

"Umm…" Yvette was silent for a moment. She even glanced at Walter with a nervous look as her lips parted. He didn't know what to say or if it was wiser to stay quiet. Even so, when she turned back to Kevin, she said, "Sure. Sounds like… like fun."

"Great." *Well, aren't you pleased with yourself,* Walter thought wickedly. Kevin went on to say, "I'll text you the information for the party." He then turned to Walter, acknowledging his presence for the first time. "You're coming to the party too, right?"

Walter might have been a bit annoyed, but he nodded in agreement anyway. "Yeah, you know I will be there," he replied in a flatter tone than he wanted. "I got to celebrate with my boy, Art, right?"

"Good, because you know he would be mad if you didn't come." Boy talk was over as quickly as it started. Kevin returned his attention to his future date. "So, I'll see you there?"

Yvette nodded slowly, her hand holding on to the back of an ear. "Okay."

Kevin nodded. "I'll see you later then."

Yvette gave him a little wave. When he was gone, she then turned back to Walter who was stunned and raddled but hoping he wasn't projecting.

"Sorry about that," she apologized to him. "I didn't… except that."

Walter couldn't stay around Yvette anymore. He felt defeated and being around her wouldn't make it any better or less awkward for him. With everyone that passed in the hallway so close to his shame, it only felt worse by the second. *Why didn't you just ask her, you twit?* thought Walter; bereft and bothered, baffled and beaten.

"Hey, I just remembered," Walter lied, "I have to meet with Art before class to give him something. I guess it's back to my locker for the eleventh time." He chuckled lightly hoping he would feel less terrible. It didn't help. "I know... I'm hopeless."

"No, I wasn't—" Yvette was hesitant but let it go. "I... I guess I will see you later then."

Walter nodded. "Sure. I'll... see you..." With that, he awkwardly walked away towards his locker. Annoyance was boiling within him. He hated that he didn't take that chance when he had. Walter planned to attend the championship game and even the party to celebrate with his best friend, but now Walter was feeling a bit deterred and unsure if he should even go at all.

Friday, April 23rd

THE LAST DAY OF THE WEEK FELT MORE LIKE A
monday than a Friday. Not only did the day snail by, but Walter
felt a bit alone. Art was with the team and getting ready for the
championship game, while Yvette spent most of her day in the
newsroom preparing for next week's issue. Even when he saw
her in the hallway or during Biology class, she was very
occupied and distracted. Walter didn't want to bother her since it
was a busy day for her, but ever since Kevin took Walter's shot
and asked Yvette out before him, he strangely felt rather better
now with the space between them. She was still sweet when she
saw him — herself, really — but her presence made him
uncomfortable now and he couldn't be around her for too long;
at least not now.

Out of all the guys in this school, why Kevin Kittle? Walter
wondered. Even Art had nothing but nice things to say about his
fellow teammate. Kevin might have been loud at times, but he
wasn't unlikeable. His high-spirited nature was well-liked on

and off the court, besides entertaining. Walter couldn't even hate him properly. Instead, he hated himself for letting opportunities to ask Yvette himself pass.

When he got home that day, he tried calling his father, but he was too busy to talk. "I will call you back around six when I should be free," he told him before rushing off the phone and back to work. That would be nearly three hours Walter would be waiting to talk to him, however, his impatience was unbearable. Ciara came to mind as well, but he was deterred, thinking she might be in class at the time. Fidgeting, he even started playing with his father's lighter for a time, listening to its clicks as he repeatedly opened and closed it. It was awkwardly soothing to him, usually, but it wasn't helping him now.

Walter thought of his cousin, Samuel. He was always comfortable around the girls and never really seemed to be afraid of anything. There were times when he was younger that Walter wished he was more like his cousin and wanted his bravery at least.

He wasn't sure if he should, but Walter's impatience permeated his mind increasingly more once he was home and alone. He could spend time on his phone or sneak on his PS4 before his mother got home, but he was too distracted. So, disregarding his hesitation, Walter grabbed a page of the diary and wrote down a name.

Samuel Winston.

A moment passed and Samuel appeared before him with his arms folded, his thin goatee freshly barbered, and wearing a pair of fitted jeans and baby blue polo shirt. It was the same clothes he wore the night he died. In fact, Walter swore he saw blood stains on his cousin's clothes and a gaping bullet wound above his left eye. It was sudden, but he knew what he saw. Just for a moment, Samuel had the look of a walking cadaver.

Now, the blood was gone, the bullet wound was gone, but even as his cousin stood there, Walter couldn't escape the memory.

"Well, well, well," said Samuel. He would always say that whenever he saw Walter like some cliché villain. "I can't remember the last time I saw you, cousin. How you been?"

"I can't believe it," Walter said aloud, even snorting a bit at the absurdity of it all. It was baffling to say the least but there Samuel sat, dark brown eyes staring back at him.

"Can't believe what?" Samuel asked, eyes squinting. He sat at Walter's desk and stared at his cousin. "Something you have to say?"

"It just... I haven't seen you in so long. It's kind of weird, you know?"

Samuel shrugged. "It is kind of weird. Being here. Anyways, what's on your mind, cousin?"

"What are you—"

"Man, I'm hungry." Samuel stretched his arms out and even yawned like was waking from a long nap.

"Hungry?"

"I haven't had a bite in... well, I don't actually remember that either." Samuel shook his head. "Can you even imagine what that is like? Wait, don't answer that. Do you have any — like — food or something? Death can make you hungry..." He made another heavy yawn. "...and tiring, I swear."

Tiring... Really? Walter had heard that death and sleep were close cousins. "What kind of question is that?"

Samuel chuckled with amusement. "I'm just joking, cousin. So sensitive, I swear. Anyways, what happened yesterday? Choked with Yvette, huh?"

"No, I just... Wait, how do you know that?"

187

"Well, I know what you know, so that's how this all works — well… it's kind of hard to explain. Anyways — and more importantly — I personally don't know why you are so bent on this girl. I mean, she literally decided to go out with some other guy… right in front of you. I could spell it out more clearly for you, but I'm sure you get it. You should leave her alone, cousin. You're acting like there aren't other girls who would like you. You're… handsome, or whatever. You might not be the most trustworthy, but… well, we all have our flaws, right?"

Walter gritted his teeth knowing his cousin said that just for spite. "Don't bring that up—"

"I wasn't," Samuel said dryly. Then he asked, "What is so special about Yvette anyway?"

"You were the one who introduced me to her," Walter reminded him.

"So?" Samuel spread his hands. "Don't blame me for your strange infatuation. How was I supposed to know how you would feel?"

"I don't… I'm not—" Walter was hesitant. "I'm not obsessed with her or anything if that's what you mean."

Samuel looked confused. "Obsessed? Who said anything about you being obsessed?"

Ignoring that, Walter went on. "I'm happy with whoever she decides to go to the party with. I don't care."

Samuel snorted. "Yes, you do. Wait, let me guess. You care about her happiness more than you care about your own or something boring like that?"

"It's not as glamorous as you make it sound, but — more or less — yes. She's not like everyone else, cousin. Plus, she makes me… think about things… I guess."

Samuel snorted again. "Yeah, you are right, Walter. She is basically a nerd. The girl might as well have the braces and

188

glasses on to prove it. And, for the record, every girl you like is funny or smart or interesting or shares your interest or whatever is 'not like everyone else.' You are smart enough to know that by now. Like I told you before, it's just a trick the brain does on you. Makes you think someone is so special when they are — more or less — probably not." Samuel made himself smile. "You see what I did there?"

Walter didn't respond to that. Samuel always had little sayings or proverbs for such occasions, like: "If you can't back up what you say, don't expect anything one else to back them up for you," or "You can't help someone else if you can barely help yourself."

Walter thought about that and decided to back up what he did as well. "Yesterday... She was being really honest with me. I could tell she was vulnerable. I didn't think it would be a good time to bombard her like that. I mean... I'm right, right? It was bad timing?"

His cousin snickered and leaned back in the chair. "It wasn't bad timing for the other guy, I'll tell you that."

"Seriously..."

Samuel shrugged. "Why even ask me?"

"I thought you could help me. I didn't... ask you to be here just to talk about—"

"No? So why did you ask me here, Walter? I'll tell you why. You asked me here so I can save you from yourself. Am I right?"

Walter snorted, defeated and, too drained to fight back. He conceded. "Fine. Yes, you are right. I don't know. Yvette makes me think a lot and I don't want to do or say anything stupid. Does that make any sense?"

"Not really. You say stupid stuff all the time. She got you thinking but not doing enough."

"What?" Walter was confused. "What does that mean?"

"You know exactly what I'm talking about. Yvette knows how you feel and she spends a lot of time with you. Why don't you think about that and tell me what does that mean?"

"Does it really matter now?" Walter sat on his bed, not thinking about it at all. "Yvette is going out with Kevin. You remember Kevin, right? Kevin Kittle?"

Samuel pushed up his lip. "Do you remember Kevin? Did you forget how this works already?"

"But I think that—"

"Stop it, Walter," Samuel urged. "Stop with all the overthinking. Yvette isn't here."

"No, seriously. Listen to me. You saw how upset she was. It didn't seem right to ask her out. She was upset, and she was… also vulnerable. It just… didn't seem right." Walter just found himself reiterating, then he felt annoyed, then stupid. All his whinging would get him nowhere.

Samuel nodded solemnly. "You know, I was always proud of you for one thing, Cousin, knowing right from wrong. Other times you can be destructive… or delusional."

"Knowing the right from wrong hasn't helped me much so far."

"That's because other times you can be destructive or delusional."

Walter gritted his teeth. "Do you want to talk about—"

"Do you?"

Suddenly, Walter felt a pain in his chest — a knot, most like — twisting, tightening and tugging within him. Hot air pushed through his nostrils in frustration. Samuel always had a way of stirring him up. He was a good enabler and his younger cousin was no match.

"Fine." Walter rubbed the peach hairs on his chin. "I do want to talk about it."

Samuel scuffed. "Okay. You start."

Walter stood and began pacing for a bit. "I hated myself for telling Ch—"

"Keep her name... out of your mouth."

Walter had heard those words before. "I didn't say anything that would cause her to think that you were cheating—"

"How do you know that?"

"You said that I was smart, right? I know that girl Jaime was just a friend but she was into you. What was I supposed to say when your girl asked me who she was. I told her the truth and omitted that Jaime was into you. Would you rather I not say anything and stand there like a damn idiot?" He didn't wait for an answer. "I know you wouldn't cheat on her, but it isn't my fault if she didn't know that too." Walter sat back down on the bed and sighed. "It wasn't my place and I'm... I'm sorry."

Samuel nodded solemnly, his eyes never leaving his cousin's. "I don't forgive you."

Hearing those words, they stuck into Walter deeply and they were razor sharp. "You don't?"

Samuel stood to tower over him. "Your big mouth nearly caused my engagement to crumble. Did you even stop and think about that? Did you ever even realize that?" He snorted. "'It isn't your fault if she didn't know that too.' Please, Walter. Where did you get that crap from?"

Walter would have shrugged if he wasn't utterly upset. "I have no idea... but it makes sense to me."

His cousin snorted. "Did Yvette teach you that?"

"I already said I don't know but it makes sense to me. Look, I'm sorry. I didn't mean for any of that to happen. I tried talking to you about it—"

"On my wedding day!" Samuel yelled and reminded him bitterly. "You tried to talk to me about it… on my wedding day. Do you hear how ridiculous that sounds?" The grimace he wore was as stern as steel.

"I barely saw you before that."

"I was a father, Walter. I didn't have time to make you feel better about yourself. That wasn't my job. That's your job. It's not my job, it's not your parents job, it's not Yvette's job — it's yours." His words struck Walter hard. The truth was as cold as death itself.

Walter fell silent and took a deep breath. "You're right," he admitted. "It wasn't your job, and it wasn't my job or even my business to meddle in your relationship. But I want you to know how sorry I am. I know I almost—"

"Don't." Samuel cut him off abruptly. "If you say sorry one more time…" He paused. "You don't know what you did and you don't understand what you caused. I was going to be a man and tell her about Jamie myself and ease her mind, but you had to open your big stupid mouth and talk about things you don't understand."

Utterly beaten, Walter felt worse than before the conversation started. However, even if this Samuel hadn't given him the forgiveness and closure he coveted, the only solace he had was knowing that he wouldn't find what he wanted here. *I will never find it,* he thought. *Samuel is gone. I can't change that.*

Walter sighed, even heavier than the last. "I just know that if I didn't apologize I would have felt worse about myself knowing I won't have that chance."

"No, it's fine," Samuel snapped at him. "I don't need all those extra words. They don't mean anything anyway. You need to stop pretending that you really care though. You might know right from wrong, Walter, but the only one you care about is yourself. I know that which means you know that." When he was through, he shrugged and sat back. "What else is there to say?"

Before he could even dare to respond, Walter heard his phone ring on his desk. Art was calling. He must have been on his way to pick him up. Walter answered after two rings.

"On your way?" he answered the call.

"Yeah," Art said with his voice booming on speakerphone along with gusts of wind in the background. "I'll be there in five."

He told his best friend he would be ready, then hung up. Walter took a moment to center himself then turned to see Samuel still sitting there patiently. His eyes bore into his cousin's, and Walter felt that razor sharp point at his throat. Annoyed and feeling fatigued, he only wished his cousin had already disappeared and the diary was empty again.

"I have to go," Walter told him.

Samuel smiled; a sinister smile. "That thought that you have in your head... I can hear it. I can see it. So, since you are my cousin, I'll give you this one piece of advice."

Walter looked at him in disbelief, but his stern scowl was used to mask it. "Yeah. What is that?"

Samuel leaned in a bit. "Don't overthink it."

*   *   *

The gymnasium was so loud with the stands full of students and fans jumping in excitement. Unbelievably, Yvette was amongst all the rage. She might not have been particularly comfortable within the crowd, but it was exciting for her to cheer on the basketball team with everyone else. She was always filled with school spirit and being a school reporter made her express it more than ever. It would be good for the *Hallway Herald* to report on a championship game again. She felt a little jealous knowing she won't get to report it herself.

Donnie seemed less thrilled with the crowd than even Yvette usually was; but he wasn't like her. He enjoyed the parties and the crowds, but when he was holding a camera, his demeanor would change to a young mother holding a newborn baby. Throughout the game, he had to basically hug it closely to keep it safe.

Although this was the case, Yvette felt great seeing the gym bedecked in their school colors and the stands full of screaming fans raising their hands every time their team scored a basket. It may have only been the second quarter, but they were up by eight by then and their momentum was building. That momentum, however, was juxtaposed with Donnie's annoyance.

"I swear," he nearly cursed. "If one of these people knock over my camera—" He didn't even finish his sentence before grunted heavily as he tried to take a photo of the court once again. Yvette couldn't remember seeing him so agitated. Another grunt came from his throat, a deeper and thicker one. "Someone is going to owe me a new camera, I swear."

"Calm down, Donnie," Yvette said nicely, trying to be heard above the crowd as the opposing team closed the gap by five. "Why don't you take pictures around the court like you were doing earlier?"

"My legs were killing me."

Sitting with Yvette and Donnie were the twin sport reporters, Stefan and Hazel Penn. Stefan was less cordial than Yvette, even with how silly he looked with a mess of powdered cheese caking his fingers and thin mustache.

194

"What did you expect?" he said, licking his lanky fingers. His dark eyes still pressed to the game before him. Stefan was taller than most boys at the school. Standing next to him especially was a bit overwhelming to Yvette as sometimes she would get swallowed by his shadow. However, with him and Donnie sitting below her and Hazel, it was comfortable for her.

"These people are going crazy," Donnie continued complaining. No one could really blame him. His father gifted him an expensive camera that he was glued to. "My dad will literally kill me if something happens to this camera. Do you know how much this thing cost?"

"Just be careful," Stefan replied. "We may not get another championship run anytime soon. Only good vibes today, Donnie. Damn... I wish I was playing, man."

Yvette remembered when Stefan was a part of the basketball team in ninth grade. However, bad knees could hinder an athlete. Unfortunately, Stefan was no different. Sport writing was the closest way to be part of the action now and he would often express it.

Hazel was less interested in Donnie's frustration or her brother's lack of it. She was fixed on the court and her interested eyes feasted on the tall, fit ballers cluttering the court. Her eyes were a bit brighter than her brothers and they indeed seemed hungry.

Yvette didn't realize she was staring until Hazel turned to her. "What is it?" Hazel asked curiously.

Yvette always thought Hazel was very pretty. She was lengthy like her twin and had long mode-like legs that she liked to show off. Her short afro was a collection of delicate curls that felt like a soft brush and even tickled to the touch. Boys were always complimenting her and Yvette sometimes felt a bit

195

jealous about it. Still, Hazel liked all the attention while Yvette frankly wouldn't know what to do with it.

"Sorry for staring," she said politely; however, there was a rain of shouts and cheers that showered her words.

Hazel leaned in closer to her. In one hand, Hazel had her pen and pad opened to her notes, but the other rested on Yvette's thigh. *Warm,* she thought.

"What was that?" Hazel asked nearly in her ear.

The crowd died down again so Yvette repeated, "Sorry for staring, I said."

Suddenly, Hazel looked down and surveyed herself. Hazel was a bit more shapely than Yvette was, womanly as well. Yvette sometimes felt a bit self-conscious when around her but Hazel never did it on purpose. Even though she was used to compliments, she was always full of compliments herself and found the beauty in anything or anyone. Her self-confidence was endearing.

"Do I look bad or something?" Hazel asked, seemingly perturbed.

"No, no, no. You look great, actually. But no, I just see that you're very interested in the game, that's all."

Hazel chuckled. "It's not the game I'm interested in." She turned back to the court. "You see all that sweat on them." The hunger returned to her eyes and Yvette smirked, nervously staying quiet.

Soon, the rival team went on a small run as the momentum on the court was beginning to shift. One of their players took a three pointer and it bounced on the rim twice before the ball sank in. Now the other team was up by two. Fortunately, Art brought the ball down but saw his teammates heavily defended. Still, Art psyched his defender, made space and quickly shot his own three pointer. The ball glided through the air then fell through the net. The crowd exploded into cheers before the ball even reached the floor. They were back up but only by one.

The rival coach called for a timeout. Even during the timeout, the crowd was getting progressively more excited by the moment. Students began stomping on the metal bleachers in a steady rhythm and others joined in with their own feet or claps. Even the "crowd-phobic" Yvette was feeling excited, clapping with the crowd and feeling the rumble around her.

Stefan was the loudest in their little group of reporters. "That's what I'm talking about, Art!" Stefan shouted, and Art even pointed at him with his game-face and a smirk.

"I never knew he was so good," Yvette had to admit.

"Who? Art? Oh, definitely. He's short — shortest on the team, I think — but he's one of the best, in my opinion. The best shooter, no doubt."

"He's pretty cute too," Hazel added. Her full lips made a half-smile as her eyes glowed a bright brown while watching the teenage boys on the court carefully. She seemed to be in her own little world.

Stefan snorted at his twin. "Keep it in your pants, Hazel."

"Shut up, Stefan," she replied without turning away from the court.

As the teams take their timeout, Yvette spotted Kevin looking her way. It might have been for her or some other girl in the stands, but the smile he made was very handsome. She even felt her lip curl upward on their own. However, once she knew it was there, she turned away to hide it. When she did, she saw Georgia-Lee returning to the game. She sat on the opposite side of her and the four returned to five.

"I saw that," Georgia-Lee observed as she made herself comfortable beside her.

"Saw what?" Yvette felt herself pinch her ear before her hand dropped to her lap.

"Oooh..." Georgia-Lee eyes widened. "So that's why you came to the game. Because of Kevin."

"Ooo..." Hazel turned to the girls with her interest obviously peaked. "Kevin Kittle?"

Yvette's head flitted to both of them, one after the other. "No. I'm here to support the team."

Georgia-Lee giggled a bit. "It's fine if you like him. Kevin is pretty cool."

Hazel leaned into Yvette. "And he's pretty cute too."

Stefan was a bit annoyed now. "Really, bro?"

Hazel rolled her eyes as she looked up at her brother finally. "Oh, my God. Can you please shut up, Stefan? Talk to Donnie and leave us alone. And stop calling me bro, already. You know I hate that."

Stefan wasn't deterred. "Whatever, bro. Why don't you pay attention to the game and do your job." As he said that, the whistle blew and the game continued. They were up — 31 to 30 — and it was the last few minutes before halftime.

Hazel snorted. "First of all, don't tell me how to do my job — a job I've been doing longer than you, I might add — and second, the players are a part of the job too. Be my twin, Stefan, not our Dad, please."

Georgia-Lee stepped in. "As long as the article is good, I don't care what she watches. The paper hasn't written about a championship game since... since before we were even born. Let her have some fun..." However, she pointed at Hazel with such authority. "But don't forget why we are here, more importantly, why *you* are here."

Just like the twins they are, Hazel and Stefan sulked at each other as they complained in unison. "Whatever." It was a bit funny and Yvette didn't chuckle alone. Donnie was just as amused.

Georgia-Lee returned her attention to Yvette. "Now, back to you."

Yvette wasn't too fond of being interrogated or the center of attention again. "Please don't."

"Honestly, I thought you were going out with Walter."

Hazel's eyes widened a bit and her head tilted downward curiously. "You're dating Walter? The one with the weird name, right? I have seen you talking to him."

"No — well yes, that Walter — but…" Yvette felt a bit flustered but much more embarrassed. "We're not dating. Why are you asking me that anyway?"

Hazel shrugged. "Nothing. I'm just interested."

Georgia-broke in before Stefan could, seeing he and Donnie were listening now. "I see the way you two look at each other. It's not like how you looked at Kevin or the way Kevin looks at you. It's different. A special kind of look or whatever you want to call it."

Yvette squinted her eyes a bit. "Did you get that from a movie or something?"

Hazel was less interested in that. "Who cares? More importantly, are you going to the party tonight?"

Yvette shrugged. "I don't know." If she was being honest with herself, Kevin might have invited her to go but she didn't know if she wanted to or if she should.

Georgia-Lee didn't seem too worried about that. "Well, if you do come and Walter is there then it's perfect—"

"I'm going with Kevin!" she blurted suddenly. The words leaped out of her and it was relieving yet frightening to get it off her chest.

Georgia-Lee seemed a bit bothered by that. "I mean... Not perfect, but... Kevin is pretty fun."

Stefan interrupted once again. "So, you're going out Kevin Kittle?" he asked, seemingly in disbelief.

Hazel pushed her lips outward. "Why? Jealous?"

Stefan was taken aback with his eyes squinted at his sister. "What? Why would I be jealous? You sound ridiculous."

Georgia-Lee took Stefan's question a bit more seriously. "Honestly, I thought you and Walter seemed better together. More... compatible, or whatever."

Stefan nodded. "That's what I think."

Suddenly, the team was up by five and the crowd was getting into it. Hazel and Stefan were paying attention to the game, but the real focus was still on Yvette.

Donnie put down his camera and turned to her. "If you ask me—"

"No one did, Donnie," Georgia-Lee rudely interrupted.

Yvette turned to her. "Let him speak. Go ahead, Donnie."

The freshman brushed it off and continued. "If you ask me, you should be around or with who you feel the most comfortable with. Whether it's Kevin or Walter. They both seem pretty cool, but it's not about that—"

"Dude, you don't know either one of them." Stefan stepped in. "How would you know that?"

"So? That doesn't matter. It's about who Yvette feels safe with, right?" Donnie turned to Yvette. "It's about who makes you feel special. Who cares for you and do you care about them the same way? Are you willing to sacrifice for that person just to make them happy and would they do the same for you? It's like that short story Mr. Burns's class had us read in Literature; about the man who sold his watch to buy something for his wife's hair, but she sold her hair to buy something for his watch. Something like that." When he turned back to Stefan, the twin was nodding solemnly, seemingly impressed.

Yvette felt herself smile as she remembered that story well. "The Gift of Magi."

Donnie pointed at her with a grin. "Yeah, that one."

"Yeah, but…" Hazel was incredulous. "That story makes it sound so easy."

"But it's not easy. That love is rare."

Yvette was still smiling, lost in thought. "But that's what makes it so beautiful."

Hazel started blushing, alone with her own thoughts.

The only one amongst them who had yet to respond was Georgia-Lee. "I never thought I would say this, but… I agree with you, Donnie. What you said was kinda sweet."

"Ditto," Hazel chimed in.

Stefan was still nodding but then added, "Plus, I doubt Walter wants to be just your friend. If you might feel those ways Donnie talked about, probably not the sacrificing part just yet, but you have to ask yourself if you want to be more than friends? Honestly, some of your girls talk like you want a relationship but—"

"Okay, stop right there, you boys act the same way."

Yvette shook her head and tittered, but broke in anyway. "I think that is Donnie's point and the point of the story." After clearing her throat, she continued. "But, I haven't even gone out with Kevin yet. It is so bad to want to see if I really like him or not? I mean… He's cute but—"

"He is," Hazel couldn't help but add.

"—and I like talking to him, but… we are kind of different, you know?"

Donnie shrugged. "They say opposites attract."

"They do," the twins agreed in unison.

Georgia-Lee smirked. "Honestly, I'm more interested in what you think of Walter."

Her voice was a bit too curious for Yvette's liking. "Why?" she asked dryly.

"I can't be curious?"

"I'm curious too," Hazel said, showing her interest.

Just the thought of Walter made Yvette a bit uneasy and even uncomfortable being amongst her friends and their prying. However, she felt a little smile on her lips but instantly bites down on them to hide it. She remembered seeing Walter entering the gymnasium with some other boy she didn't know, along with two girls she recognized but didn't know either. One girl seemed familiar enough and remembered seeing her around Art sometimes. Yvette tried not to stare too long when she saw them, especially the girl she didn't know. Going and talking to him ran across her mind but she wouldn't know what to say. *It wasn't like he came to talk to me though,* she thought sourly. It was all weird and uncomfortable and made her mind swirl.

Hazel was growing impatient. "Cat got your tongue, Yvette?"

She didn't know how long she had been daydreaming, but it must have been long enough. "I..." She was hesitant. "I think so."

Stefan snorted like his twin. "You're lying, Yvette."

That pricked her. "Excuse me?"

"Even I could tell you like him."

Donnie nodded with a few chips in his mouth and powdered cheddar on his thick fingers. "Me too."

Yvette sighed, sunken. "Well, what if Walter doesn't like me and only sees me as some sad puppy he should feel sorry for?" Her question wasn't directed towards anyone. Frankly, she didn't even know if it required a real answer at all. *What a stupid question,* she thought. *You should have kept that to yourself and your mouth shut, stupid girl.* She even grunted a little, but fortunately the crowd masked that.

"Puppy?" Donnie asked, tickled and chuckled. "Seriously?"

"You know what I mean, Donnie." Yvette was rolling her eyes now.

Stefan shrugged. "He's probably just nervous around you. It's happened to me from time to time — well — depending on the person, of course. It's the look, right?" He nudged Donnie for confirmation.

"Kyra Lucas." Donnie nodded. "My first love. She has the eyes of a cat..." his eyebrows rose, "...and a hiss to match."

Hazel chuckled. "You're silly, Donnie."

Yvette was in her own world. None of her friends understood her and Walter's relationship. No one did. It made it uncomfortable talking to others about him, yet he was on her mind more often lately. It wasn't like they were going to the party together... like she wanted. Yvette began regretting not going with him and it weighed heavily on her chest.

The way we look at one another... It was hard not to think of what Georgia-Lee said. The words bore into her, found a cozy crevasse and nestled within a crack. With Donnie and the twins co-signing, that crevasse grew into a cave.

Yvette turned to Georgia-Lee with a thought. "You're going to the party, right? Can I get a ride with you?" Maybe riding with her might make it easier and give her a reason not to be alone with her date.

She chuckled. "Kevin has his brother's old car, you know. He didn't say he would pick you up?"

"Yeah," Yvette confessed, "but I feel better going with you. I can always meet him when I get there, right? Plus, if I don't feel comfortable, maybe I can leave with you?" It wasn't until she said that she realized how selfish and even desperate she sounded.

However, Hazel spoke up. "I think Yvette is right. We should all go together. If the night goes sour, the three of us can leave together. Why not? Honestly, I don't want to have to deal with Jeffery if he gets drunk."

"You sure?" Georgia-Lee asked them both. "Maybe you'll meet Walter there instead." She giggled and Hazel joined in. The chip bag was in her hand now. She took a couple then offered it to Yvette and Hazel who both refused nicely.

"Well, if I go with you then there is less to worry about," Yvette added.

"Sounds fun," Hazel agreed. "We *should* go together. We can all meet our dates at the party. That way they don't think they have all the power. It's good to have an advantage somewhere besides being a damsel under some boy's arm." Hazel rolled her eyes supposedly at some bleak memory she had.

"Sure," Yvette agreed, chuckling. She felt better going with her friends anyways.

Thankfully, the conversation pretty much shifted from her and onto the party itself instead. When she was free from all the questions and comments, Yvette turned into her seat and looked up into the top corner of the bleachers. Cheering with his own friends was Walter. Seeing the big smile on his face and cheering his best friend on was a jovial moment for her. A smile even crept on her lips, seeing how much fun he was having. Be that as it may, she didn't stare long; not allowing Walter to spot her looking his way. Georgia-Lee saw her staring, however — and fortunately — she didn't say anything about it just grinned. Yvette was grateful for that.

A siren sound ran above the crowd as the first half was over. Their team was still winning at this point making the Centralia

High crowd go wild with excitement. Yvette stood and clapped as the team celebrated off the court. The cheering students and teachers even began chanting.

"Let's go, Bulldogs, let's go."

Clap, clap… Clap, clap, clap.

"Let's go, Bulldogs, let's go."

Clap, clap… Clap, clap, clap.

Like a member of the crowd, Yvette clapped and chanted alongside them, adding to the rhythm and song. This lasted for minutes, even when the Bulldogs were in their locker room preparing for the second half of the game. It was crazy excitement that Yvette wasn't entirely used to, but she enjoyed it.

Even so, soon Yvette's excitement simmered as she spotted someone across the crowd from where she was sitting. Dressed in a gray suit and fedora was an unfamiliar man standing across the floor who appeared suddenly. Yvette could feel the man leering in her direction, yet he had no face; no eyes, no nose, no mouth to speak of. But she was wrong. Soon the man's face stretched upward as a waxy mouth melted and separated above his chin, and rows of long jagged teeth poked through his slimy skin. Yvette stared blankly and her breath seemed to disappear. Slowly, she looked into where Walter was sitting, hoping she wasn't the only one who saw the faceless man, but he wasn't paying attention to the court. However, when she turned back, the man was gone.

What was that? Yvette thought, feeling like she might faint. She was hallucinating again, no doubt, but she never saw a faceless man when she daydreamed. Walter didn't seem to acknowledge him — maybe he was just distracted — but Yvette knew what she saw. She left her diary home that day, but something seemed to be following her. *Maybe both of us. Should I tell him?*

Yvette jumped in her seat as a hand suddenly rested on her shoulder. It was Georgia-Lee, and the look on her face showed a clear concern.

"Hey, are you okay?" she asked. "You look spooked all of a sudden."

I have no idea, she thought, wishing she could say it out loud. Instead, she nodded quickly with her lips pressed shut as she thought of a lie. "I'm fine. Actually — um — I'm going run to bathroom real quick." Hazel nearly stood to go with her, but Yvette said she needed to be alone.

A few minutes later after crossing the courtyard and the long hall, her wish was granted. She entered an empty bathroom not too far away from the school entrance. Overwhelmed, Yvette turned on a sink and began washing her face. When she looked into the mirror, she was prepared to be spooked by the faceless man behind her, but all she saw were weary eyes and empty stalls. She found herself leaning against the bowl for a while and unsure how long. It could have been a few minutes or more, but she was so tired and felt like she hadn't slept in days.

A sudden screech interrupted her thoughts as the bathroom door opened and Yvette straightened. Before she saw someone enter, she heard footsteps and a flick of a lighter and thought of Walter. She hoped it wasn't some nightmare she drifted into without knowing — like the night she got her diary back — but she relaxed when she saw Molly Rose instead.

"Molly?" Yvette said as she spotted her with a purple lighter and what looked like a rolled up newspaper in her hand. "What are you doing with that newspaper?"

"Newspaper?" She asked, confused. "This is not a newspaper."

Yvette had turned her body to face Molly completely now. "Well, what are you trying to set on fire?"

"Set on fire? No, it's not... Oh my God. Why do *you* have to be in here?"

Feeling quite guilty but not knowing what she had done, Yvette took a step closer, waving her hands in submission. "No, I mean... I'm sorry. I didn't mean to..." If she were being honest, she didn't know what to say. Maybe seeing Molly with a newspaper rolled up and ready to be lit on fire triggered her.

Molly Rose was quite short for her age and even looked up to Yvette, but when she did, her dark-gray eyes weren't all that kind, to say the least. Some of her blonde locks were tucked behind an ear so Yvette could see the mistrust in them. Be that as it may, this was the girl who wouldn't tell her what she saw with the strange clay dolls and, now, it seemed like Yvette was invading her personal space. Still, when she looked closer and noticed Molly wasn't holding a newspaper and something entirely different, Yvette felt quite foolish.

"I'm sorry," she said. "But if it's not a newspaper, then what is it?"

"No!" Molly nearly shouted and Yvette was taken aback and even two steps back for good measure. "If I tell you anything it will be in the newspaper next week and everyone will know who you got the information from. Everyone already thinks I'm crazy."

Yvette bit her tongue at that, knowing she wanted to yell back, but she thought wiser of it. "I would never do that, Molly. Even if you did tell me anything, I can't put your name as a source unless you gave me permission—"

"And you think people wouldn't think it was me, regardless of a source?"

Yvette shrugged hoping her face was genuine. "You could always lie."

Molly thought of a moment, her eyes still showing suspicion. "Fine, but I swear, if you tell anyone about this, I will deny it to the day I die and your little life as a reporter will be tarnished."

Yvette sighed but was more weirded out than frightened. "Umm… okay," she replied, not really knowing what else to say since she didn't take Molly's threat seriously. Still, the fear and anger in her eyes was nothing Yvette wanted to take lightly either.

Molly handed her the not-a-newspaper and it made a dry crackling sound as she grasped it. It was a large bundle of long gray herbs wrapped together with rows of cherry-red yarn. It had a strange smell to it — like an old but clean rug — and a sharp yet subtle hint of what might have been peppermint. The large end had already been burned, so it had a smoky scent as well. Strangely, the feel and smell made Yvette grin a little.

"What is it?" she asked, taking a second sniff, realizing how much she enjoyed it.

"It's a smudge stick?"

"A smudge stick?" Yvette felt her head to the side. "I think I might have seen one before." She might have been lying — most likely — but she wouldn't admit that to Molly. "What does it do exactly?"

"It's like incense, but it's not for the smell. It's a bundle of these herbs called sage." Molly raised her lighter and ignited it. Gently, she brushed the flames against the burnt end, making certain the bundle was lit. Once a small fire was there, Molly blew out the flames and a large cloud of smoke pushed into the air. "The smoke is supposed to ward off bad spirits and cleanse the air itself."

Yvette was indeed intrigued. *Might be something I might need... just in case.* "Do you think it has something to do with those strange dolls? Do you think some bad spirits are in the school?"

Molly's blonde hair whipped as she suddenly turned to her. She regarded her for a moment then said, "Maybe. I'm not taking any chances. I wish I had enough to smudge the entire school, but everyone wants to call me crazy, so I'll only smudge the places I go and let everyone else suffer. See if I care. Even my mom doesn't believe me and she knows more about this stuff than I do. She can suffer too. I don't care."

A knot was caught in Yvette's throat. Molly was indeed hurt and angry. The last thing she wanted to do was make anything worse for her.

Yvette nodded. "I'm sorry, Molly, and I understand." She wasn't sure if that was a lie or not. Yvette could remember her mother telling her when she was a little girl that what she didn't believe in couldn't hurt her. *That only works with junk in the closet or shadows that seemed like monsters.* It was a white lie, she knew, one of stories parents tell little children to get them to go to sleep instead of worrying about everything else. As it was, Yvette herself had become good at colorless fibs. However, Molly seemed to be quite open with her.

"You're lying," said Molly. She stepped away from her and began waving the smudge stick around the stalls, covering the room in silvery-gray smoke and paying her no mind.

Yvette sighed and said, "I believe there is so much that happens in this world that most of us just can't understand and even more of us can't accept. People who can are special." If she was being honest, people like Molly needed to be protected, not feared. "Can I tell you a secret?"

The girl turned back to Yvette, appearing more sad than angry.

"Sometimes, my mom comes to me at night as a ghost. I don't know if it was really her but… I don't know. It…" She shrugged. "It brings me comfort."

Molly gasped. "But… Isn't that frightening? It's your mom but… I know it would be for me."

Yvette nodded. "At first, but… I guess I just got used to it. I can't tell anyone about it. Not my father or my sister. I tried talking to a therapist about it once, but even she tried to say it was all in my head." She paused for a moment. "I thought you might understand and… it might make you feel a little better. I'm sorry if I'm prying or… if I'm not helping—"

"No," Molly assured her, even taking a step closer. "I… I'm sorry. I shouldn't have shouted at you like that. You've never done anything wrong to me and…" There was a light pause as she sighed. "Thank you, Yvette."

"No problem. Thanks for telling me how you feel. Your secret is safe with me."

Molly smiled warmly. It might have been the first time Yvette ever saw her smile, and she was surprisingly welcoming. "Your secret is safe with me too."

With that, Molly looked down, lit the smudge stick once more and blew a second gust of sage. Thick streams of smoke spread as she waved the sage and silvery-gray filled the bathroom. It bathed the sinks and stalls and both girls basked in it. Yvette only hoped it would keep any faceless men away.

It was hours later when Yvette picked up her head from a silver sink and cleaned her face in the bathroom. The oval glass mirror was hitched to a maroon painted wall and the petite bathroom had a subtle wisp of assorted fruit above the toilet.

The music in the background was loud yet Yvette could hear someone banging on the bathroom door. *Why did I even come to this party?* she asked herself.

"Hey, hurry up," the banger shouted. Another voice responded right after, but she couldn't make out the words.

Even so, Yvette was basically already done. She honestly just wanted a moment alone. The crowd at the game was worth being a part of, but now, at Kevin's brother's party, crowds became increasingly more unbearable as usual. The banging on the door was unsurprisingly incessant. Not even the bathroom was a refuge from the clusters of people and clouds of endless noises.

When Yvette emerged, she was nearly pushed aside by a boy who obviously was about the piss himself. Just that, made Yvette uncomfortable as well as disgusted. Fortunately, Georgia-Lee and Hazel weren't far away. She twisted her shoulders from side to side, pushing through teens with cups in their hands towards the kitchen.

"See, I told you this was the best time to come to the party," Hazel was saying to Georgia-Lee when Yvette approached them.

Maybe I shouldn't have come with them, she began regretting. The three girls had arrived at the party when it was the most crowded and obnoxious. The counters were filled with beer chilling in soft ice while others were either empty or half drank. A few open kegs were in the corner making puddles of homebrewed beer at their feet and Yvette could only imagine who would be cleaning this house when the party was all said and done.

"Yeah, when the animals are out," Georgia-Lee commented.

"Just seems like less time at the party to me." Yvette knew how ridiculous she must have sounded. It was preferable then admitting how annoying the party was. It wasn't as if they had been there long, but it didn't settle her uneasiness. Also, she had yet to tell Kevin that she was there. Prolonging it seemed like the best opinion for now. *However, the last thing I want is Kevin to see me here and I didn't even text him.*

The girls each had their own cup and Hazel had a second for her. "Here. Drink this." It was a pinkish red drink with way too much ice, but Yvette hesitated before taking a taste. "It's a vodka cranberry. More cranberry than vodka though."

Georgia-Lee's eyes rolled. "It's not a vodka cranberry. It's called a cranberry and vodka."

"No, it's not," Hazel debated. "Unless you're saying that my mom doesn't know what she's talking about."

Before Georgia-Lee could argue any further, Yvette asked, "Does it really matter?" As for the drink, it was sweet, but she could taste a sheet of bitterness underneath.

"It doesn't," Georgia-Lee admitted. "We just need to loosen you up a bit."

Yvette took a second spi and it was better than the first. It was surprising how much she enjoyed it. "I'm fine. I'm relaxed." Yvette felt a genuine grin beginning to grow a bit.

"Really? You're the one who took nearly ten minutes to get out of the car when we got here."

Hazel leaned in closer to Yvette and whispered in her ear. "You're not afraid, are you?"

"No," Yvette replied as she tried resting her cup on the table but couldn't find a place where it wouldn't fall. "I'm not afraid. I just… hate crowds."

"Who cares? Once you are with Kevin all that won't matter. It will just be you and him."

That was what she was afraid of. Although Yvette was a bit nervous about being around Kevin all night, she did enjoy him and he was indeed handsome to look at. Even with the overwhelming popularity, Kevin was funny and likable. When it was just the two of them, she felt quite comfortable. She soon realized she was grinning at the thought of it and pressed her lips together.

Even so, ensuing her thoughts of Kevin, Walter came to mind. She had seen him when she arrived. He was around a group of guys and Kevin was amongst them. However, she still wanted to see Walter — to talk with and laugh at his stupid jokes, to watch him try not to blush in front of her, to look into his eyes. But then she didn't and knew Walter wouldn't want to see her either... not really. It was all confusing. Speaking to him might make her second guess who she came to the party with. It would be even worse if she was caught smiling at Walter when she was with her date. Kevin wouldn't like that nor would it be fair to him. However, her thoughts were interrupted by party cheers from the other room. Fortunately, Yvette soon realized she was thinking too much and took a third sip of her drink just to distract her a bit.

Hazel had a good look at her. "She is frightened, Georgia-Lee. Just look at her. I don't think the drink is helping."

"Leave me alone, Hazel," said Yvette, frankly a bit irked. Fortunately, when her cup met her lips, it hid them well.

Hazel shrugged. "Alright, fine. Well, I have to find Jeffery. He just texted me a minute ago. See you around, ladies."

With a little wave of her fingers, Hazel strolled off, leaving her friends behind and disappeared in the crowds she was so comfortable with.

Georgia-Lee was staring at her with a thin grin when Yvette faced her. "You've never really been on a date, have you?"

"I have," Yvette admitted. "I dated the same guy in eighth and ninth grade."

"Boys aren't the same in middle school—"

"Ninth grade is high school."

"Barely. Let me put it this way, I've never dated a ninth grader even when I was in ninth grade."

Without thinking, Yvette chuckled with her cup to lips. "Somehow I know you aren't joking."

"Oh, I'm not. It's like this, dating becomes — well — different when you're older... well, for them, really. For us, it's pretty much the same, we just see it differently because we understand more about boys and what they want and what they won't admit. Kevin should be the one who's nervous, not you. You're not the same girl in junior high. Just be the way I know you can be."

"And how can I be?" Yvette asked, shocked yet a bit tickled.

"Slick." Georgia-Lee snickered. "Just play a little hard to get. Boys hate that they love that. Use that power against them. Trust me, it's fun."

While listening to all this, Yvette realized how manipulative it all sounded. However, with the vodka cranberry or cranberry vodka even sweeter now, her friend's words didn't seem so bitter as they might usually sound. She even felt herself chuckle when she thought of it. Still, she wasn't as witty as Georgia-Lee or as shapely as Hazel, Yvette was just Yvette.

"Now, come on, let's go find your date." Georgia-Lee wrapped her arm around her, ready to beckon her out of the kitchen. However, before they could leave, a tall and slender man cupped his eyes over Georgia-Lee's eyes and said, "Guess who?"

Georgia-Lee bit her bottom lip slightly as she turned around to face him. "Hey, baby," she said before wrapping her arms around his neck and kissing him lovingly.

"Look at you," he said. "Beautiful as ever."

"Oh stop." She gestured to her friend. "This is Yvette. Yvette, this is Levi. He's actually Kevin's brother."

Levi made a light smile as he greeted her. Then his eyes widened a bit. "Yvette, huh? So you're my brother's date? You're a lot prettier than he described."

"Leave the girl alone," Georgia-Lee cut in. "All those compliments are meant for me."

Levi laughed. "You already know that, Gee-Lee."

Yvette grinned nervously. *So, that's why she doesn't like Donnie calling her that. That's her boyfriend's pet name for her. That's a little corny... but cute,* "Nice to meet you, Levi."

"'Nice to meet you' huh? She's polite. Maybe you can teach my brother some manners." He snickered. "You too, Yvette." He took a gander around him. "If you're looking for Kevin, he is somewhere outside I think. He knows you're here, right?"

She shook her head. "Not yet."

With a little snort and smile, Levi said, "Well, let's go find him."

*   *   *

Walter hadn't seen Levi Kittle since the ninth grade, but not during school only after — loitering outside the school yard and making jokes with his old schoolmates. Levi had already graduated by the time Walter got to Centralia High, but at twenty-one years old, Levi still seemed like a senior at times.

Even more strangely, he asked Walter and Art to help him bring in a few kegs from the back of his friend's truck, promising they would have the first taste. It wasn't just a few kegs though, there were more than a dozen and more than Walter and Art expected.

"You're making a champion do manual labor?" Art sulked on their way to the truck. He and Walter had arrived at the party only five minutes ago and were already given a job.

"My own brew, boys," Levi announced. "Well, me and Richie's."

From around the truck came a heavyset man — maybe a few years older than Levi, Walter wasn't sure — with thick cheeks, squinted eyes, massive arms and thick fingers to match. "You better not forget me before I pull off with *your* kegs," Richie said, unsmiling and stern.

Levi snickered unfazed. "You know I'm playing, Richie." Levi then introduced the boys. "Art, Walter, this is my partner-in-crime, Richie."

"What's up?" Richie's voice might have been deeper than Walter's father. As a matter of fact, he was certain it was.

Levi was a slender man, dark locks down to his ears, and a thin goatee below his hooked nose. He wasn't slick dressed with designer jeans or a leather jacket like Richie, he wore a simple white shirt that was slightly too big, along with his bleached jeans that helmed over his leather boots. It was sort of a messy clean, as carefree as careless.

As Walter and Art were climbing into the truck with Levi, Kevin was swaggering over. "Levi, you brought the brew?" he said, addressing his older brother. He slapped Art's palm and they both snapped fingers — a dap only members of the basketball team did with another. Speaking of basketball, it was strange seeing Kevin without one. He would think being the state champions had him glued to the thing even more. However, they were at a party and he realized how ridiculous he sounded.

Levi laughed. "You already know, bro. Who needs fake IDs when you can brew your own?"

Walter had a thought. "Aren't you already twenty-one? Does it even matter?" It seemed queer to him.

With his eyes even more squinted than they already were, Richie pointed at him. "Every party has a pooper. Are you the pooper?"

Levi chuckled. "I'm actually twenty, but soon." That was Walter's mistake.

"Leave him alone, Richie," Art broke in chuckling. "He's my best friend. He's cool."

"Walter's no pooper, just a homebody," Kevin added before bumping fist with him. That never felt weird to Walter until tonight. It might have been because Yvette was still on his mind; heavily even.

Walter felt a hand dropped to his shoulder. It was Levi's. "Well, Home Boy, tonight, I'm going to turn you into a party animal then, Walt."

Walter scuffed. "Please don't call me that."

"My bad, but tonight, I'm bringing out your wild side. Tonight, I'm going to teach you how to live. You're going to drink beer, you're going to get somebody's daughter's number—"

Walter was caught off guard a bit. "Why do you have to say it like that?"

"—and you're going to have a good time. You think you can do that?"

Walter nodded, mainly hoping Levi would let him go. "Sure."

"Yeah, man," Art cosigned. "Forget about Yv—" Walter nudged his friend's arm sternly. The sudden pain seemed to jog his memory. "—you know... What's Her Face."

Levi continued uninterested. "It doesn't matter who 'What's Her Face' is. Tonight will be a night to remember." He pointed a finger towards him. "You remember that, Home Boy. Now, repeat after me. 'She doesn't exist.'"

Walter rolled his eyes. "'She doesn't exist.'"

"Say it again."

"'She doesn't exist.'"

"One more time." Levi's eyebrow rose as Walter faced him. "One more time, Home Boy."

There was a moment of silence between the two, but Walter eventually nodded and said again, "'She doesn't exist.'" Then to myself... *Yvette doesn't exist.* It might have felt real mentioning her name, but won't dare speak it aloud.

Levi nodded satisfied. "Good. Now, come on. Let's get these kegs out the truck. We have a party to officially start."

The group of five boys rose to a dozen. A few of Levi and Kevin's friends helped carry the kegs through the garage and towards the kitchen. There were fourteen kegs in total, so Walter and Art carried one and it was heavier than they expected. Still, Levi was true to his word and opened their keg, filled a cup for two of them first, then to his brother and then the rest. Levi filled his cup last then held it above the eleven.

"Boys! Tonight, we celebrate what none of us has ever been able to celebrate in our lifetime in any sport. Boys, that long wait is over and we are finally champions again!"

The dozen boys were cheering now while others close by joined the cheers.

"Raise your cups, boys." He shouted the final three words. "To the champions!"

"To the champions!" The choir cheered, repeating after the preacher with their own cups of beer.

Walter and Art toasted their cups together before taking a few large gulps.

"Hold up!" Levi got the choir quiet somehow. "First to my brother, the captain of the team; The-Little-Train-That-Could."

A few people laughed a bit and Kevin nudged his brother and smiled. Even Walter felt himself obviously grin in response.

"You told me you were going to be a champion and look at you. You worked your ass off to get here. I planned this party because I knew you and the team would win, but it didn't matter to me. We were gonna celebrate regardless, but you all came this far... plus you are my champion, right?"

Kevin blushed a bit. "You're right."

"I'm proud of you, Kevin. To Kevin!"

"To Kevin!" The crowd cheered back and some took a swig while the brothers hugged tightly.

"I'm not done though!" Levi shouted. "Yo, Art, come up here."

The crowd began to chant Art's name as he stopped next to Levi. Walter was one of the loudest among them.

Levi continued. "To the shortest man on the team yet the killer in the corner." Art started to smile. "Every team needs a general on the court and we had the best general this entire season. To my man, Art, The championship game MVP!"

"MVP, MVP, MVP!"

Art downed his cup as the crowd chanted. When the cup was empty, he held up over his head in triumph. Art wooed over the crowd as they cheered for him. He was pumped and excited and Walter felt it. He was proud of his best friend and chanted with the rest of them. With a large smile, Art returned to his friend and they both cupped their hands together, laughed and hugged. Walter couldn't stop smiling either, showing his best friend all the praise he deserved. After his clutch performance on the court, Art did everything to hold that lead at the end and Walter was proud of his brother like Levi was of his.

While Art was getting praise from his classmates and strangers alike, Walter first saw... "What's Her Face." She was wearing purple again, but a brighter shade than the last. Her short dress wore the color well while her jean jacket hugged her chest. Her dark ringlets were thick and flowed down from one shoulder. She was with Georgia-Lee and Hazel, Stefan Penn's twin sister. He watched them survey the crowds of people, and, unsurprisingly, Yvette seemed a bit reserved, however she wasn't with Kevin which was a bit strange. He expected to see them swooning over one another but instead he saw her duck into the bathroom alone while her friends were making their way to the kitchen.

"You're doing it again," Art said to him.

"What?"

"Staring. Look, bro, just because she's here to party with Kevin doesn't mean you lost your chance. But for tonight, just forget about her."

Walter nodded. "You're right."

Seconds later, Levi found Walter and Art standing around. He was seemingly disappointed. "Art, Home Boy. I know you two aren't going to hug the walls all night."

Art snorted. Though it wasn't too loud to hear, the look on his face was undeniable. "Only for now, my date should be here soon."

Levi shrugged unconcerned, then something caught his eye. "Oh, and speaking of dates, there she is."

"Who?"

"Georgia-Lee Singer."

"Wait," Art interrupted. "Isn't she a junior?"

Levi pressed a finger against his lips. "Keep that to yourself, boys. Now, I'm going to see my baby. As for you Walter, I expect you to be having too much fun the next time I see you."

Suddenly, the unsmiling Richie found Levi and got his attention. "Levi, we have a problem, bro."

Levi turned to him. "What problem?"

"Did you know Linda was going to be here?"

"Oh crap—" Levi flitted his head back to where Georgia-Lee and Hazel were walking towards the kitchen. He stared at Georgia-Lee for a moment before he turned back to Richie. "Okay. I got to get Linda out of here before she gets me in trouble. I'll see you two later, boys."

Levi and Richie left Walter and Art behind.

The boys found themselves outside a few minutes later. The backyard was a pretty solid size, but with groups of party-goers with cups in their hands and smoke pouring from their lips, it made the backyard look more petite than it was. They even saw Lenny, who did say "what's up" to them, but seemed more interested in whatever girl he saw close by. Walter didn't see who the girl was, but there were so many unfamiliar faces at the party that it seemed silly to even guess.

"I think some of these people are in college," said Walter. Some faces he did recognize like a few who graduated last year, and one caught his eye. Walking toward them with such swagger in his steps, their friend Hopper spotted them and opened arms as he approached.

"Boys!" Hopper took both arms and embraced his friends. His arms were unmistakably larger, he was a bit taller now too, not as pale as the last time they saw him. A patch of thick yellow hairs had grown on his chin, yet his mustache had yet to grow a noticeable fuzz. As for his eyes, they were dark gray as always but we're surrounded by a monochrome of red and pink. They didn't talk for long since he was entertaining his girlfriend but he made time to congratulate Art and give his condolences for Samuel.

"I love you guys, man." Hopper and his girlfriend were already drunk and she even gave a drunken congratulations to Art and then hugged Walter as she gave her condolences. The gesture was kind... sloppy but kind.

Soon after, Art got a text from his date and grinned. When he finally saw her, his grin stretched and grew to a smile. Walter was quite surprised to see it.

"Hey, Arthur," she said. Walter nearly laughed hearing his friend's full name, but didn't want to ruin the moment for either one of them. "Congratulations on the game today. You did great... MVP." Her voice was gentle, her eyes held a certain longing and her smile was welcoming.

"Thanks," Art said gratefully. "I saw you at the game. I'm glad you came."

"Yeah, of course," she smiled softly. "I've only seen you play a few times but you always seemed to get better every game."

Walter was about to say he would leave the two of them to talk alone before Art introduced them both. "This is my best friend, Walter. Walter, this is Trisha."

"Hi, Walter," she said. Her tone turned to a more friendly one. "Art has told me a lot about you. Nice to meet you."

"Same but hopefully he hasn't run his mouth too much about the both of us."

Trisha chuckled a bit but tried hiding it. Even so, Art did see it and it made him smile.

"Look, I'll leave you too alone," Walter announced. "I'll find something to distract me."

"Alright, bro," Art replied. He didn't say anything, but his best friend's look spoke volumes. It said, "And, hey, don't forget what we talked about."

"Don't even trip, bro. I'm cool—"

222

As Walter was walking backwards away from them, he bumped into someone. His drink spilled onto his pants while he felt a subtle splash of liquid on his back. Fortunately, his shirt was black, but it didn't make the wet spots bearable. In utter shock, he turned around to see a teenage girl with a blue cast on her arm, that was now damp from her slipped drink. The look on her face was utter shock as well. Her eyes widened and her mouth ajar.

"Oh my god," she gasped. "I'm so sorry."

Walter looked down at the drink on himself and began wiping what wet spots he could reach and shook his t-shirt to help it dry. "No, I'm sorry," Walter said, putting the blame on himself. "I didn't mean to walk into you all backwards like that."

"No, no, it's my fault. I wasn't watching where I was going. Oh, lord." The girl finally took a good look at her cast and saw how wet it had gotten. "I was afraid this was going to happen. I knew I should have wrapped it in plastic or something. And look at your pants. We both look like we can't drink properly. I'm so sorry. Come with me?"

The girl took him by the hand and led him back inside, not without Walter and Art sharing a look. Art seemed proud while Walter didn't know what to say and just went along with her.

The girl had black hair with green highlights, olive skin with a bit of a shine to it, deep green eyes, round lips and her nose had a soft curve on the tip. She led Walter to the bathroom that was fortunately empty. Right away, the girl grabbed a plethora of paper towels and began wiping the drink off his back while Walter had a bundle as well working on the beer on his jeans.

"Damn," she said. "I dropped a lot on you."

Walter snickered. "Yeah. My back feels cold now."

There was a cute chuckle that came between her lips as she tried to blot her drink off him. Luckily it was only a beer. A mixed drink would cause a stain that Walter might not be able to get out. Either way, Walter was happy he was staying with Art that night. *Easier to hide it from my mom,* he thought, already imagining the punishment she would have for him if she knew he was acting out like some drunk idiot. Fortunately, he wasn't the only idiot at the party and not the only idiot with spilt beer.

"I'm Claire by the way," the girl said. "I figured I should introduce myself since we just met and we are already in a bathroom together."

Walter snickered again. "Yeah, I get that. I'm Walter."

Claire nodded. "Yeah, I know. I've seen you in school before — well — in junior high. We never had class together but I knew of you. You're the one with the strange last name, right? Dar something, I think."

"D'Artagnan… and it's not that strange. Is it? Some people say that."

Claire giggled a bit as she finished with his back and threw the damp paper towel in the trash. "Not really," she admitted while grabbing another paper towel to dry her cast. "It's just funny to say."

"So, what happened to your arm?" Walter asked, looking at the many signatures on her baby blue cast.

"Oh, my baby brother fell on my arm."

"Oh. How did he do that?"

"I was trying to play wrestling with him, but he took it too far. He wants to be a wrestler when he grows up. So, I try to support him, but he's so violent. I swear, I indulged him in his antics once and… look at what happened to me."

"I get it," Walter replied. "How old is he? Thirteen or something?"

"Oh no, he's seven." When she said that, Walter started to laugh a bit. "Yeah, I know."

"I'm sorry for laughing," he apologized with a titter left in-between his teeth.

"No, it's fine," Claire assured him. "It's pretty funny now and he's pretty big for his age so… I don't know what I was thinking, honestly."

He wasn't done snickering. "Plus, it's play wrestle, not play wrestling. It's not like a video game."

Claire rolled her eyes jokingly. "Whatever." She was shaking her head now. "Boys."

"So, you have a marker or a pen or something? I could sign your cast, if you like."

Claire smiled lightly. "Yeah. I do, actually."

She went into her pocket and found a black sharpie for him. With all the signatures and get well notes on her cast, Walter had to really search for a space. When he found one, he signed his name — first and last — then wrote a small note for her and finished it off with a smiley face with a wink. Claire tried to have a look at it when he was done, but the position of it was impossible for her to see. Walter had to take a picture on his phone to show her.

"Oh, nice," said Claire. "What does that say? 'Keep it dry.'" Claire started to laugh. "That's funny. It's our own inside joke. I like it. Oh, and you signed with a winky face too. Nice touch, Walter."

"Thanks."

"It's kind of funny that your name is longer than your note."

"Yeah, I wasn't going to, but I already started with the D in my last name. I figured Walter D sounded too stupid just to leave it."

225

Claire laughed aloud. "That's true. Now, let's go get us some more beer," Claire said, taking his hand, ready to lead him out the bathroom. "I want to try some of the beer Levi brought."

"I had some. It's nice." Walter opened the bathroom door for her, letting in a cloud of sounds. "After you," he said loudly.

Claire seemed impressed. Sweetly, she came to his ear and said, "Aren't you a gentleman."

Walter snickered and shook his head. "Oh… Not at all."

Just like Yvette, Claire was beautiful, but this girl seemed to be far more at ease at the party and seemingly unbothered by the many faces. In a way, she seemed more friendly than Yvette. Also, as Walter thought about it, Yvette and this girl could probably be considered as opposites yet, strangely similar.

After that, Walter didn't say much. As the doctor listened to his story, she continued jotting down notes. It was interesting to see his progression from the beginning of his story. He seemed more transparent. However, Walter had not reached the moment that brought him to the doctor in the first place. Well, not yet.

"I'm guessing your parents don't know about your partying that night," Dr. Pierce asked, already knowing the answer.

Walter shook his head. "Thank God. They would probably go crazy if they knew what kind of party it was. Nothing too crazy, but… wild. Well, that's not really true. Art told me about the fight that caused the party to end early."

Dr. Pierce couldn't really believe that he didn't know about the part when he was there. "Did you get that drunk, Walter?

"No!" said Walter. His voice was assuring. "That's not… Okay, first of all, I wasn't drunk. Not really. Tipsy. It wasn't my first-time drinking, so… whatever. I was having fun, you know. Getting out of my comfort zone."

"So, you weren't drunk — and I believe that you weren't, Walter, please don't mistake me — but how did you not see what happened? You were there. A fight breaks out and you are the only one who didn't see what happened?"

Walter fell silent for a moment then sighed heavily. *"It was because of Yvette."*

A bit baffled, she didn't know what he meant. There might be something She missed in his story, but she wasn't particularly sure. *"What do you mean? You told me that Yvette went to the party with Kevin. Levi's brother, correct?"*

"Correct," he nodded.

"And you were trying to ignore her throughout the night, correct?"

"Well, not exactly. I mean... I was... but when I saw her, it was hard for me not to acknowledge that she was there or even look at her when she was aware. I enjoyed my night with Claire, she was fun to be around, but Yvette is the one I liked."

"Liked?" Dr. Pierce asked, catching the past tense. *"Do you not like her anymore?"*

"I do," Walter admitted. His tone was slightly aggressive, but she had grown used to that. *"It's just..."* He paused for a moment in thought. *"It's just complicated."*

The doctor curiously sunk in. *"You say this stems from Yvette. What actually happened to her that night? Can you tell me?"*

"She told me a little about what happened, but.... But I don't think I should tell you" Then Walter chuckled sarcastically. *"Maybe one day, Yvette will be considered crazy too and she can tell you."*

Dr. Pierce bit her tongue at that. Certain things were confidential and she wasn't at liberty to say. Instead, she left it at that.

227

Saturday, April 24th

YVETTE WOKE UP LATE THE NEXT MORNING. SHE
had been used to waking up with the sun, even during the
weekend, but that morning, her bed was too comfortable to
emerge when her alarm went off. The house was still silent. Her
father had to leave earlier for work, while her sister and nephew
were already gone and she didn't know where they might be.
She even fell back to sleep one or two times but got up
eventually. She had homework to finish, an article to write, and
most of the morning was already unused.

Although she knew she had work to do, Yvette's mind trailed
on the party the night prior. When she finally rose from her bed,
she was drawn to the diary. There seemed to be a certain energy
spewing from its cracked leather bindings and stained pages.
The feeling was unfamiliar yet irresistible. Even her pen seemed
to have appeared in her hand rather suddenly. She could feel the
ink and the strokes across the page, like it was seeping through
her fingers.

Traditionally, she began her letter with:

Dear Diary,

The party with Kevin wasn't as fun as I hoped it might be. I was never particularly interested in parties — as you know — but I was hopeful. Usually I attend school events with crowds mixed with students, school staff, parents and whatnot, but I always have my pen and my notepad. I felt a bit more comfortable since I'm there for a reason. The championship might have been an exception, but without my pen and pad, I didn't quite know what to do with my hands. I'm thankful for my friends, especially Georgia-Lee and Hazel. I wouldn't have gotten through the day without them, but, that night, I felt really alone.

The crowds were far from comforting, and Kevin wasn't much help. When he tried to loosen me up with a dance or idle chit chat, it only made me more tense. If I'm being honest, Kevin's excessive friendliness and rapport with so many rubbed me the wrong way. Being so used to story books or articles, dealing with real people's personalities in clusters were just clouds of chaos to me and Kevin was his own overcast. Parties always seem like a collection of things untamed — if that makes any sense. Nonetheless, that was never my specialty; crowds and the like.

Kevin is popular, so there was always someone trying to get his attention. Usually other girls. When people saw me at the party, they would seem surprised to see the "nerd reporter" there as well; not to mention being escorted by one of the most popular boys in school. Some of his friends were trying to put

Kevin and I together like we were some kind of couple. We are far from that and last night made me realize that we aren't really right for each other. Still, people always seem to have a need to put titles on things, hoping it will help them understand. I don't want them to. Beer didn't really help to loosen me up; I was more worried about getting drunk, I suppose. My dad told me once that alcohol gives some people courage. I didn't want courage. That's not what I needed... That's not who I needed.

Yvette paused for a moment, looking down at what she wrote thus far. She wasn't done but she didn't know what exactly she was writing either, and took a longer moment to think of what she wanted to say next. When she did, she continued to write. For some reason, nothing else seemed right at the time. It was unexplainable. The diary had her and she let it.

When I saw Walter at the party, he was with this girl I once had a class with in eighth grade. Claire Davenport is her name. I remember her well. She's very pretty and had that kind of engaging spunk to her that was attractive as well. Even her black hair bounces when she walks. As for her hair, it always had some different color highlights in it. It's green now and was pink two weeks ago, according to her social media. It might be turquoise tomorrow for all I know. She was very talkative and friendly and had a gorgeous smile that I can't deny. I might have been a bit jealous seeing them together. Walter was enjoying his night while I wasn't.

When Walter was close by and Kevin wasn't looking, I peeked over to him a few times with my peripherals. I would even stare a bit, but never long. I didn't want anyone to see.

Including Walter. He didn't seem too concerned with me though. Who am I to try and stop him? I couldn't deny, regardless of the crowds and the plethora of noises, I would have rather been there with Walter. Why did I choose otherwise? Why didn't Walter ask me himself? Was it something I said? Was it something I didn't say?

Yvette remembered running into the bathroom again; the same bathroom she saw Walter and Claire Davenport walking out of together. For a moment, Yvette was feeling overwhelmed; stressed in a way. She was sitting on the toilet with the seat down feeling the ringing in her ears and the pain in her feet. The only thing she needed was her bed. So many voices and noises seemed to batter against the walls relentlessly. It was more than noise. It was a reminder; a reminder that she didn't belong.

The cold wind cut through her when she left the party. She didn't tell Kevin anything when she left the bathroom and cut the date short. She didn't look for Georgia-Lee or Hazel to let either know she was ready to go. Yvette found the front door and put the party behind her. However, she had only gotten several houses down and was several feet away from the streetlight when she heard a few footsteps following her at a steadier pace.

"Yvette."

They didn't hesitate, her feet stopped abruptly. She already knew who it was — the voice was undeniable — but she didn't turn to face him. Her cheeks, they were shivering now and a subtle burn painted her dimples. Melting away seemed preferable to her than being bathed in a spotlight and her shadow being approached by another.

"Yvette?"

Suddenly, Yvette looked up when she heard her name being called. It wasn't the shadow calling this time, that memory faded in an instance.

"Coming," she called back. Turning back to the diary, she saw the words were still there… still staring back at her. The diary wasn't through with her yet.

Swiftly, Yvette made her way down the stairs to see her sister dropping her large pocketbook to the couch.

"I swear," Charlotte said with a heavy sigh as she flopped to the couch and began freeing her feet from her high heels. "I should have told my boss I wasn't coming in today; even with the overtime hours, I should have just stayed home. Do you know how exhausted I am?"

Yvette smiled softly. "Come on. I'll put on a pot of coffee if you like."

Charlotte was slightly taller than Yvette, a shade or two darker and a tad thicker. Her dark brown hair was straightened and hung down from one shoulder; a simple style that Yvette often mimicked. Her business attire was a good look for her, with her long sleeve business shirt and a skimming skirt that displayed her curves. Yvette had forgotten her sister had to work overnight. Yvette watched her exhausted eyes and weary shoulders. *Being a single mother must be hard,* she often thought. Yvette was always willing to pick up where her sister left off when necessary. It was all practice, she knew. The thought of being a mother had been on her mind ever since becoming an aunt, but the thought soon became heavy when she lost her own mother. She tried not to let that sunken feeling reach her face as she helped Charlotte off the couch.

"That would be perfect," her sister said. While being escorted to the kitchen, she asked, "Is Dad already gone?"

232

"Yeah. He was called into work early today. I think someone called out because of some emergency or something." Yvette opened a cabinet and grabbed the jar of crushed coffee beans.

Charlotte wasn't pleased. "I don't know why he still works that stupid job." Sulking, she rested her tired elbows on the kitchen counter while her chin rested on her hands. "All it does is make him miserable and they barely pay him anyways." She sounded as if she would scold their father if he were in the kitchen with them. Although she tried not to think of it often, Yvette sometimes wondered if her father would have returned to teaching.

Yvette began to prepare the coffee maker when she said, "I think it's just like how you hate your job but you still go. You complain about college too."

"This isn't about me, Evey, that's the first thing. Second of all, you will see how annoying college is when you get there. And three, you should convince him to go back to teaching."

Yvette was surprised. "Why me?"

"Because he'll listen to you. I'm the daughter who got knocked up in high school and had to get married right after like it's 1930."

"Good thing you got a scholarship—"

"And a baby right after."

Yvette started the pot and turned to her sister. "Michael is—"

"The best thing to ever happen to me. He's sweet and full of life and strong... Strong like his father. Michael makes life harder, I'll admit it, but... he makes life so much better and worth living. And I always miss him, I swear."

Yvette grinned. "I miss him all the time too."

"Anyways, back to my first point, this isn't about me."

"Well, what if Dad doesn't want to teach anymore?"

"And that dead-end security job is better?"

"Maybe." Yvette felt a bit frustrated, but tried not to show it. "I don't know his salary. You know teachers don't make much either."

"You're right and I don't want to rush him, but he'd be happier where he belongs. He really loved your mom, and I know it will be hard to go back and teach where they both worked but... I don't know... I think it will be good for him. Even if he doesn't teach at the same school anymore, but... I don't know. I'm in college and soon you will be too. He needs some peace in his life. We all do. We can't all grieve forever, Evey. There is too much sadness in this house already."

"You're right," Yvette relented. "Maybe he can teach at Centralia High. It's a different school. As long as I don't get his class."

Charlotte chuckled. "He might be our dad but he is so far down on the list of my favorite teachers. I think he did that on purpose, honestly. I'm still mad you never had his class."

Yvette snickered. "Oh, yeah. You hated that. You used to get so mad when you would check my schedule every semester looking to see if I would have Dad's class and every time you were disappointed."

Charlotte shook her head. "Don't remind me. I remember when your mother taught me English in eighth grade. That wasn't so bad. Better than Dad's class, for sure."

Her sister chuckled a little. "I remember when she taught me English too." Yvette could see it in her mind. She could see her mother in front of the chalkboard, the dark cherry wood desk at the back of her classroom. The classroom was always bright, and so was she, with her warm welcoming smile and motherly tone. Still, just like their father, Mrs. Margaret Anders was far from being a pushover.

"Well, maybe he will eventually," Yvette suggested optimistically. "It's not like we are hurting for money or anything."

"It's not about the money, Evey," Charlotte protested. "It's about his sanity and what will make him happy in the long run. You know that."

Yvette did know that, but she didn't know what to really say. All three of them were grieving and maybe being away from the classroom helped. Maybe the school made him think of his wife too much and he couldn't bear the constant memories. The halls of that school is where Mr. and Mrs. Anders met. It would be hard to be the only Anders there now.

Eventually, she spoke up. "Well, can't we just tell Dad together?"

"Maybe," Charlotte replied, "but doesn't that sound like an intervention or something? We shouldn't hound him or anything. I just want him to go back to teaching where he belongs." She paused for a moment, then added, "But you're right. Maybe teaching at another school would be best. Our old school must be filled with so many memories of her. Sometimes I feel like that when I think of my baby." She sighed heavily, looking through Yvette more than right at her. "I miss my Samuel so much."

Yvette felt a tightness in her stomach when she said that. It made her wonder, *If Charlotte had found the diary instead of me, would she use it the same way I do. This* is *my sister...*

For a moment, there was silence between the girls and only the coffee maker could be heard. However, Yvette felt the next words slip between her words as they broke the silence. "If you were able to see a dead loved-one again, would you?"

Charlotte was in mid-sip but put her cup back down. "See a loved-one again... Like a ghost?"

"No, not like a ghost, but…" Yvette bit her bottom lip, feeling a sense of fear before asking.

"What do you mean?" her sister asked curiously.

"I mean… If you…" She gathered her thoughts a moment then tried again. "If you had a way to see a dead-loved one again, to hear their voice, to smell their scent, to hold them again, would you do it?"

Charlotte was speechless for a moment. She began looking down at the kitchen counter with her lips slightly parted and her mind digging deep. She was silent for a while, so Yvette called her name again and Charlotte looked at her suddenly as if she were daydreaming.

"Sorry, I was just… thinking," she said sadly.

"Would you?" Yvette tried not to seem too eager for an answer, but she was.

"I don't know," Charlotte eventually stated. The look on her face appeared like a woman who was on the brink of tears. "I would love to see my Samuel again. I miss him so much. I wish Michael could actually know his father and have memories of him." Charlotte paused for a moment. "I wish for so many things, Evey; things that I know are impossible. Even if it were possible, I don't know if I would. I don't know if I could deal with that." She paused for a moment then asked, "It wouldn't be the real him though, would it?"

Yvette knew that answer but she lied instead. "Maybe. I don't know."

Slowly, Charlotte leaned up, hugged herself and began smiling sadly. "All I know is that I would never want him to leave me again. It would just make me feel worse knowing I can't have him to myself anymore. Honestly, there are times that I wished he would just haunt me, even if it's just a little bit."

236

Yvette let herself grin at that. "Maybe those shadows in the corner of your eyes are him. Maybe he doesn't want to frighten you but still wants to protect you."

"I wouldn't be afraid," Charlotte assured her. "I would only be afraid of him leaving me again."

Yvette bit her bottom lip. A part of her wanted to show Charlotte the man she loved, but knew that would be a terrible idea. Yes, her son experienced her diary with Yvette, however Michael was too young to truly understand. As for Charlotte, it would be something different entirely.

"Honestly, Yvette, there are times when I wish I could just forget all about it. All the times we shared; the way he would make me feel... his smile. Just forgetting about it seems like the best way to get over all of this."

Gratefully, the coffee maker dinged and stopped so Yvette gave it her attention. She didn't know how to respond to her sister, so the steaming coffee was a savior. Quietly, she simply began filling two clean mugs and kept her thoughts to herself.

"Thanks, Evey," said Charlotte. From the same cabinet, Yvette grabbed the brown sugar and cream, and began dressing their drinks. The first sip brought a satisfying smile to her lips. "Mmm... I needed that."

Yvette needed it to. Just the warm porcelain toasting her palms was comforting. It had a perfect amount of cream and sugar so it tasted like warm joy.

Charlotte cut the tension by asking, "So, what's going on with you? How's school? Still at the top of your class or have you started liking parties all of a sudden?"

Yvette squinted her eyes as she faced Charlotte. "What are you—"

Her sister giggled. "Well, you did go to Levi's party last night, didn't you?"

Yvette gasped as her heart thumped. "Dad doesn't know that, does he?"

Charlotte snorted. "Please. He's too busy and overworked to even know what I'm doing. 'Oh, Charlotte, you're a mom now...' like I wasn't in labor for hours for *his* grandson. I don't need him reminding me of that! I agreed to marry Samuel, didn't I? And now Samuel's gone and 'Father Dear' can't..." Mid-sentence, her vent was clear and Charlotte sighed relieved that she got all that out. "Sorry. It's just the stress. Anyways, how was the party? You didn't get drunk, did you? You were the last one up today, so—"

"Of course not," Yvette replied nearly disgusted. "I mean... yeah I had a drink... then a second one."

Charlotte chuckled with her cup to her lips. "I know you can handle yourself. Did you have a date?"

Yvette nodded with a nervous smile. "Yeah. Kevin was nice, but it was still a bit uncomfortable being there."

"Kevin?" Charlotte put down her cup of coffee. "Which Kevin?"

"Kevin Kittle"

"Kevin Kittle? The baller boy? Really?"

Yvette sighed. "Yes, him. Why?"

Her sister shrugged. "I don't know. Surprised, that's all."

Yvette explained. "I helped him prepare for a test and he asked me to the party sometime after."

Charlotte shook her head. "What did I tell you about helping these boys study, Evey?"

"Really, Letti?" Yvette was a bit confused. Even so, she wore a grin like her sister's. "Isn't that how you and Samuel started dating?"

"Exactly and I got pregnant not long after."

When she said that, Yvette felt her eyes roll nearly on their own. "Letti, I'm not even having sex. I still remember that stupid lecture you gave me."

"Well good."

Yvette went on. "Anyways… parties aren't really for me. At least not like that one."

Charlotte chuckled a bit. "Well, I could have told you that." Yvette didn't know why, but when Charlotte started giggling, she ended up joining her. It all felt so silly for some reason, but her sister was good at making Yvette loosen up. Soon, they simmered down, and Charlotte asked, "So, do you like him?"

"I don't think so," she said, showing her uncertainty. Yvette decided not to tell her sister about walking out on him at the party. That was something she would rather keep to herself.

Charlotte shrugged. "Honestly, Kevin doesn't strike me as your type."

Yvette sipped her coffee and asked, "So, what do you think is my type?"

"Well, you know, those smart boys who plan to go to college and be a decent member of society or whatever. I don't know. Someone boring."

"Boring?" Yvette had to laugh at that. "Are you trying to say that you think I'm boring too?"

"Maybe."

"Whatever. I really just hate crowds. All that energy just drains mine. Does that make sense?"

Charlotte began to chuckle once again. "Trust me, I know what you mean. Your friend though, he can be a party animal."

Yvette snorted lightly. "Kevin is not my friend."

"Well he's not your boyfriend either, so—"

"Can we just drop it?" However, even though her sister did, Yvette said, "I just remembered something."

"What is it?"

"I think Kevin asked me last night if I wanted to go to the movies this weekend. I think I couldn't answer so I ran to the bathroom... I think. I can't remember."

"Oh," Charlotte replied. "Well, just lie to him. As long as you don't kill anyone off — like lying about a funeral or something — you can tell these guys anything and they will believe it... well, if you are convincing enough. You're smart enough for a little deception, aren't you? Lying to high school boys isn't like lying to Dad. Most of them are easy to outsmart or fool. And speaking of our dear old dad, remember what he says..." Charlotte's voice went surprisingly deep. "'A distracted mind is a weak mind, and a weak mind is easily influenced.'"

The girls shared a chuckle, but Yvette already started feeling guilty about it all. She wasn't prone to lying, although she had been doing it more often lately. Even so, when she did, she wasn't really good at it. For some reason, just the thought of it would often make her ears ache. "I don't want to lie to him, Letti," she told her sister.

"Well, either you tell him the truth or you don't. But still, you cancel enough dates and he will get the hint... unless Kevin is an idiot that only knows his way around a basketball court."

Yvette rolled her eyes. "Kevin is not an idiot."

"You are the one tutoring him, so you know better than I do."

"That was one time."

"If you say so. Why are you defending him anyway? I thought he wasn't your boyfriend or your friend."

"I'm not defending him—"

"You're always defending some boy, like that boyfriend you had your freshman year!"

240

"Terrence *was* my boyfriend. Was I not supposed to defend him?" Yvette felt a bit tense now.

Charlotte snorted. She even sounded like her late husband. "Oh I know how much you defended the last one. You didn't want Mom or Dad to know."

"So what?"

"And that boy you liked in elementary?"

"Brayden was cute and smart and very sweet. I didn't like how he got picked on all the time because he was smarter than everyone."

"I get it, but Evey when you get older, you are going to need to find a guy who will defend you and not the other way round all the time. I understand you care about people — I love that about you — but why defend someone who won't do the same for you? You already see Kevin is a degenerate so you can't expect much from him, but whoever you decide to date, they need to focus on protecting you as much as you want to protect them. Now, does *that* make sense?"

There were times that Yvette wished she was the older sister. If she were, she would have been on the other end of these sisterly lectures. Yvette already had to listen to lectures at school along with her father when he was ready. Charlotte got that gene from him, undoubtedly. Yvette wasn't naturally candid like her sister, but she figured it was important to take her advice. Samuel certainly took care of his wife and made her feel protected. Yvette couldn't deny it, she wanted that. She wanted to know that feeling.

"Yvette, wait."

She remembered the voice again; the approaching shadow, the streetlight. Feet away from the party, the approaching footsteps slow down and soften. It wasn't until she turned around to face the shadow that she felt her eyes water and the tears fall.

"What's wrong?" The shadow came into the light with her and the shadow was no shadow anymore.

"I'm leaving, Walter," she replied sternly, arms folded and tears still falling. He was still slowly approaching when she wiped the tears from her eyes.

"What happened?"

"I don't belong here."

Walter seemed a bit baffled by that. "What do you mean? None of us belong here, Yvette. Most of us are underage... even more of us are already drunk... Who cares about what anybody thinks?"

Yvette felt a violent tingle in her gums. "Like you? Are you like everyone else, Walter? Do you *not* care about what I think? Is that how you want me to feel?"

Walter looked even more baffled now. "What do you—"

"Never mind," she said, ready to turn around and walk away, but didn't. "I don't even know why you care."

"You know I care about you, Yvette."

She grit her teeth and goosebumps ran up her arms. "Why don't you go back inside to your date?" she said hotly.

"What are you talking about? I didn't come here with Claire," he stressed. "I literally met her tonight. We're just having fun."

"Exactly. Go have fun with her." Once again, she was ready to go. She starts walking away, but Walter quickly deterred her.

"What are you talking about? It's not like that."

She faced him again. "I saw you coming out of the bathroom with her, Walter. The bathroom? Disgusting."

"We spilled drinks on each— Wait... why am I explaining myself to you? I didn't come here with a date, Yvette. You did."

"It's not my fault that—"

"I'm not blaming—"

"Never mind, Walter. If you're not going to listen to what I have to say, then you can go back to Claire Davenport."

"I'm not going to listen to you turn this around on me," he said, vexed.

"Then go back inside. I'm not stopping you."

"No, you're not. You're not stopping me. I'm here because I want to be here. I'm always overthinking everything that I barely take a chance at anything. I was afraid just to put myself out there. I just wished I had learned that before tonight. I wish I had just asked you out myself. If I wasn't such an idiot then maybe… maybe I won't have to see that look on your face right now."

Yvette bit her bottom lip a little. "Why do you care about me, Walter? Why?"

"How could I not? After everything you told me about you mom—"

"Don't push that back in my face?" she spat.

"I'm not pushing it back — oh, my God — You asked me a question, right? I'm giving you my answer. I don't know what happened with you and Kevin, but don't push your attitude on me either."

The word attitude was a trigger. It rattled her and Yvette didn't know how to respond. She hated seeing Walter this way with his frustration aiming at her. She was already crying from how hurt she was, but now, she didn't know how to feel at all. Yvette's parted lips closed sternly, then, without a word, Yvette turned around and walked away.

"Wait, Yvette."

This time, when Walter called after her, she wouldn't dare to turn around. Her night was over and she was ready to be alone.

Not even her mother could make it any better. At that moment, all she wanted was to forget.

*   *   *

Walter shrugged. "I don't really know what happened with Yvette that night. She could only say for herself."

Dr. Pierce nodded solemnly. "So, besides seeing her leave, you don't know what else happened to her?"

The young man shook his head and rubbed his temples. "I wish I knew," he admitted. "I didn't see her again until school."

"The week of the incident." It wasn't a question. She already knew the answer. Walter nodded. "Let's get into that story before our time runs out today.

Monday, April 26th

IT WAS MONDAY ONCE AGAIN, AND THERE WAS NO
reason to be happy about it. They were dreary, mind-numbing
and overwhelming. This Monday was no different but with an
unsatisfactory weekend it was less than satisfactory. Article due,
homework and occasional essays to turn in, scheduled tests and
unexpected pop quizzes — Mondays were always proving days
in Yvette's eyes.

Maybe that was just her stress doing the talking for her.

Georgia-Lee wasn't at school that day. It was strange and
quite shocking not having her governing the newsroom,
critiquing and accrediting every speck of the newspaper before
publishing. Surprisingly, Mr. Mullen looked to Yvette to fill that
missing link. Excitement and fear rocked her hard. Once the
opportunity was laid before, she was hesitant to claim it. It was
another proving ground that she wasn't sure if she was ready for
when the offer was presented to her, even for just a day.
Nevertheless, she had been waiting for the chance, so, even with

her nervousness, Yvette held the reins. *I thought I could do this better than Georgia-Lee,* she thought with uncertainty. *Maybe not.*

Maybe that was just her stress doing the thinking for her.

Donnie felt proud of his pictures at the game. With all the commotion from the crowd, he caught good shots at different angles. He called every picture a triumph but everyone could be used. Yvette was happy for him. Hazel and Stefan's article on the championship game wasn't just engaging but inspiring. A few sentences were like memories, and Yvette could see it all before her whether she attended or not. Jacob wrote about the lunch ladies overuse of tomato sauce and garlic. It was a bit of yellow journalism for the waters. She supposed that Mr. Mullen himself had to revise it first. As long as her name wasn't attached to the words, she considered herself lucky. Georgia-Lee sent her article that morning about the school donating money and to the animal shelter. Even the principal was praised for adopting a dog, yet she barely highlighted the students who did so as well; a bit more yellow to color the black and white pages.

Maybe that was her stress being spiteful for her.

Before Yvette left the newsroom that day, Mr. Mullen took her aside.

"It's great to have you back, Yvette," Mr. Mullen said joyously. The old English teacher was nothing if not the well-known cliché; a gentle giant. Even with his round belly and meaty hands, he was far from intimidating. In fact, Mr. Mullen was one of the few teachers Yvette felt comfortable speaking to.

"I'm happy to be back, sir," she said, smirking.

"With Georgia-Lee out with the flu, I appreciate you taking over today. I've been very proud of your work since you've been a part of this newspaper. Most certainly."

Yvette smiled, genuinely showed her teeth. "Thank you, Mr. Mullen. I really appreciate that."

The old man nodded with his old man's smirk. "I know your mother would be proud as well. Did she ever tell you that she and I used to argue endlessly when she was Chief Editor?"

Yvette chuckled. "She did."

Mr. Mullen sighed blissfully. "She was always one of my best students and even one of my better adversaries. My most challenging student by far. She always had a pride in her work — too much pride if you asked me — but... she always knew how to use it properly."

Yvette smiled. Her mother never told her how close she was to her old teacher. It was strange when she heard Mr. Mullen speak on it after the fact. Unfortunately, Yvette couldn't get the story for her mother on her own. No matter how real the diary made her seem, it wasn't the same. Sadness shook her and it showed.

"I'm sorry, Yvette," Mr. Mullen said discouraged. "I shouldn't have brought her up. I know this is all still quite new to you."

Yvette grinned, her gritted teeth hidden now. "It's okay," she said, although she wasn't sure how true that was. "I'm okay."

Mr. Mullen nodded. "Well, I know how busy you are. Mondays, of course. So, I'll let you get to it. Once again, you have my thanks, Yvette. And if you need anything or just need to talk, my door is always open to you."

The day had turned to a dry one. Even with the clouds beginning to gather outside, yet the rain never came, so it was gray all around. The morning was boring too. She had a test to take in her World History class that she didn't relish. She had studied and was prepared, but Yvette was tired and didn't care if she passed or not. It wasn't often that she felt that way, but, with her head so heavy, she only wished for her bed and even her nephew to hold as she slept. Soon she drifted off. She wasn't sleeping, but her daydream had conjured so heavy that she couldn't tell the difference. Even so, Yvette slipped into yesterday.

Sunday afternoon was quiet. Charlotte was at work, Michael was spending the weekend with his grandmother, and her father was in the other room getting ready for work. Yvette was in her room, busy painting her toenails. They were already painted orange, all ten, and now she was using black to paint dots and antennas with a joyous grin. It wasn't often she painted her toenails, and it was queer when she thought of it. She only did when she wasn't in the best mood and Walter was on her mind the entire time. The orange ladybugs on her toes were a beautiful and ugly reminder all at once. It made her smile sadly.

Setup on her dresser was a tiny band playing music loud enough to fill the room but for her ears alone. They were all dressed in tiny leather jackets, with silver links hanging from their shoulders and shelves like rings that babies could barely wear. The lead singer strummed his guitar and his lyrics serenaded the tiny microphone before him. Yvette hadn't paid them any mind, simply muttered the words to herself as the miniature band played some of her favorite tracks. *The smallest cover band ever,* she thought. Those same words were still written in the diary in ink and intention.

Soon, her father walked past her room then doubled back. When he poked his head into the room, the tiny cover band took a sudden five. Yvette didn't nod or queue, they just knew.

248

"You haven't seen my tie clip, have you?" her father asked. He was all prepared to leave. His uniform laid upon him well. His tie however, it swayed and swung from his neck without his clip to station it. She was just proud he tied it on his own. *He taught me himself yet he couldn't do it on his own.* If only her mother were here…

Yvette snickered then got up from her bed. In a small clear container sitting beside a half-eaten plate of beef lasagna on her desk were several pieces of jewelry soaking in cleaning solution — bracelets and bangles and, of course, her three silver rings and father's gold-plated clip.

"Did you forget that you asked me to clean it?" She plucked it from the solution then wagged and wiped the drizzle left off from the gold and handed it to her father.

He shook his head. "It slipped my mind."

Yvette chuckled while taking out her bracelets to dry. However, she decided to leave the rings to soak a bit longer. They were always wrapped around her fingers.

He wiped the clip a bit himself and slid it in its proper place. "There we go. Okay, sweetheart, I have to go before I'm late." He kissed her cheek then pointed to the Tupperware container with unfinished lasagna. "Make sure you finish that."

She nodded with a grin. "I will."

"Good."

After, they told each other they loved one another and her father was gone. The silence evened out through the house, only to be interrupted with the cover band playing the next song on Yvette's mind. The inches high speakers on either side of the band. She returned to the black nail polish and continued.

A dozen songs might have played before Yvette was satisfied and the paint dried. She emerged from her bed and the cover band took a much needed rest. She grabbed the diary and the words on the page had already vanished, leaving her dresser free of little speakers and rockers. She dropped the diary on her desk, then grabbed the square container with half a lasagna. Absurdly, it felt lighter than she expected. Yvette did feel a bit tired. She was done with her toes and she had some studying to do, but she wanted to rest; even just for a little bit.

Like most days, Yvette took her plastic bowl of food towards the kitchen. She found a wooden spoon and scooped the meat and cheese off the bowl. It felt too easy as the food flopped to the sink... yet, there was a rattle that vibrated through the metal sink. Pushing the food down the drain was easy as well.

When she clicked the garbage disposal on, the blade spun and screeched. The loud nerve-wrecking sound crashed into her and Yvette quickly stepped back and turned to the bowl still in her hand. However, she was shocked when she didn't see specks or vestiges of meat left behind. Frightened, she dropped the container to the floor. Capsized on the floor, clear colorless liquid slipped and flowed in-between the tiles.

"No!" she gasped breathlessly. She quickly switched off the disposal and ran up stairs, leaving the bowl on the floor. "No, no, no, no, no, no, no!" She ran into the room and her heart nearly sank. Her entire breath seemed to drain from her. "No, no, no." There it was, the bowl with her half-eaten, undisposed food sitting beside her diary. Suddenly, her teeth gritted against one another, her face felt like flames while the rest of the body felt numb. She stared at the leather bindings with anger, agony and disdain.

They were all gone, she thought. Hate boiled within her and it won't simmer on its own. It boiled within her and felt like it was spilling over the brim. Her teeth even gritted heavily as a nasty scowl paid a visit to her face.

With all that anger, Yvette grabbed a pen on her desk and began stabbing the diary as hard as she could. Every strike came down with so much force that it felt she was digging through stone. However, the pen's point broke and a spoonful of ink gave out and splash back in her face. There was a burn and the pen slipped out of her hand as she wiped her eye as clean as she could. However, when she opened them, her body gave out and she fell to knees. *I didn't even hit it,* she thought exhausted. *Not even once.*

It was true. She had missed the diary entirely and left her desk top with sharp dents and a mess of ink. Sitting right beside the mess was the diary, still old with its cracked bindings, but left unharmed and untouched. Not even the ink dared to splatter in its direction.

"No," she said again. Her eyes were wide with disbelief now. The fear made her crawl back to the foot of her bed and held her knees to her chest as if she were shielding herself from the monster perched on her desk. "What is going on?" Tears formed in her eyes and gave out. Even her lips curled in confusion, not knowing how to even feel.

Yvette?

There was a subtle whisper in the air and Yvette looked up around her room. No one was there, but she knew what she had heard. "Mom?" she called, hoping it was just her coming to comfort her daughter, but Yvette was alone and the tears flowed once again like a spigot.

When she felt strong enough, she retrieved her cellphone. Without thinking, her thumb hovered over Walter's name, but then she scrolled back to her father's. However, her thumb hovered over his number as well, hung by hesitation. *I can't,* she told herself. *I can't call my dad.* She needed him but that worried her. Instead, she sat and waited — she didn't know why — but she did. The silence that surrounded her was daunting, but still, she stayed put.

"Yvette?"

The silence was soon broken as she heard her name again. It was her father coming up the stairs hastily. "I got all the way to work when I remembered that I forgot my—" When he arrived at Yvette's bedroom door, she looked at him to see his face wearing a weary look. "What's wrong, sweetheart?"

When she looked at him, her lips curled and shocked as she tried to speak. "D... D... Dad... I... I—"

"Breathe, sweetheart," he told her gently. He approached her slowly then knelt beside her. "What happened? Where did all this ink come from?"

"I'm sorry... so sorry. You told me I shouldn't but... I'm so sorry, Dad. I should... I should have listened to you. I do it nearly everyday, but I didn't expect..." She paused. "Now they are gone and... and it's my fault. It's all my fault."

"Who's gone, Yvette?" His soft voice had turned rough as stone.

Yvette sniffed and wiped her nose. "Not who... what. It's Mommy's rings." Her three empty fingers made her feel... unlucky, maybe... frightened. She couldn't be sure. *Terrible,* she eventually thought bitterly. *I feel terrible.*

"You should feel terrible."

252

It wasn't until Yvette looked back up at him that she knew —
certainly — that it was her father's voice who spoke. The words
rocked her. If she weren't sitting already, Yvette might have
stumbled to the floor.

"What?" she gasped; lips ajar, eyes agape. "How did you—"

"I heard what you thought," said Maurice Anders, stern and
unsmiling. "Now, did you hear what I said?"

Yvette's hands fell to her sides as she slowly scooted away
from him. "You're not my father."

Maurice Anders made a smile. "Of course I'm not. I won't
hurt you. You're father, on the other hand—"

"My father would never hurt me," Yvette said, shaking her
head and gritting her teeth. "So, stop it. You're not helping."

"Really—"

"I know what you're doing. I'm not afraid of my father, even
when he's mad at me... even when I lie to him. He loves me and
wants to protect me. I know that. You should know that too.
Don't you?"

The smile he made was sinister and it frightened her to see it
on her father's face. "We all get carried away sometimes, don't
we?"

"Stop it!"

That smile again; there for a moment, gone in an instant.
"I'm sorry, Yvette. I shouldn't have assumed that—"

"No, you shouldn't have," she spat. "Now, it's time for you
to go. I don't want to speak to you right now."

"Yvette."

It was her teacher calling her now. She had returned to the
classroom. Her daydream — or dream — had come to an end.

They were all watching her now, teacher and students alike. With her ringless fingers, Yvette rubbed an eye and gave Ms. Fitzsimmons her attention.

"Are you here with us or somewhere else, Ms. Anders?" the teacher asked sternly.

"I'm sorry, Ms. Fitzsimmons," she apologized then cleared her throat.

The lecture went on and Yvette tried her best to stay attentive.

It was during lunch time when she saw Kevin. When she did, her tummy tightened into a knot. She wanted to apologize to him for walking out of the party and she felt the courage mustering. Kevin was at his locker when she saw him and, surprisingly, without a basketball in his hand. Yvette tried to smile but was more of a challenge than she thought it would. Even so, she wasn't sure if smiling was the best way to approach.

"Hey, Kevin," she said nervously.

He turned to her with such an interesting look that it was more frightening than a full-on furious face. "What's up?" he said in a tone more cordial than expected. She didn't feel a wisp of anger.

"I know you are mad at me," Yvette said sadly. "I shouldn't have left but I had to. It was all too much for me. I didn't feel like I—"

Kevin sulked. "Is there a reason you are bothering me?"

His tone shifted from cordial to combative so quickly that if she had blinked she would have missed it. Yvette could already spot some students muttering and peaking over at her. The prying eyes were already irritating.

"I already said I was wrong and I was sorry," she muttered to him. "You don't have to sound like that."

Kevin closed his locker and Yvette's heart nearly fell to her stomach from the loud bang. "What do you want from me, Yvette? You decided to leave the party, not me."

"I know, but I—"

Kevin cut in aggressively. "You are bothering me, Yvette."

She tried to hold her composure but she wanted to strangle him. *He might have just been having a bad day.* "Do you need to talk or—"

"About what? You think because you are always on every teacher's top tier list that you could just say sorry like it's nothing? Like you can just talk your way out of it? You really don't get it, huh?" Kevin snorted. "You're right, you don't belong, Yvette. We are not the same and you know that. So, stop pretending. You're not good at it."

With that, Kevin didn't wait for a response. He walked down the hallway of students with their eyes never leaving Yvette's. No one studied or even acknowledged Kevin and he disappeared through the frozen crowd. Her worst fear had come true and now Yvette was in the midst of that terribly unwanted attention. She bit her bottom lip as they tightened. She wouldn't dare cry — she wouldn't let the tears fall, not for Kevin, not for the stupid crowd — but they fell anyway.

She turned to leave in the opposite direction and eyes and heads followed with mutters and muffled jokes. The only one that spoke to her was Molly Rose who seemed more frightened than a few others scattered about.

"Yvette?" Molly came to her with a look of absolute dread. "It didn't work?"

"Molly…" *Get away from me… Leave me alone… I can't deal with your stupid problems right now… Come any closer to me and I swear I'm going to…*

Terrible thoughts swirled through her and pulled at her strings. She turned her back to Molly, turned her back on everyone else and left the hallway swiftly not knowing where she was going.

But then she thought, *How did Kevin know I was going to say that? That I don't belong?*

*   *   *

A baffling feeling washed over the doctor and Walter seemed a bit worrisome sitting on the couch before her. "So, don't you know what happened with Yvette?" she asked, curious of where the story would go next.

Walter was speechless for a moment. He soon turned his attention away from her as he sighed. "What are you not telling me, Walter?"

Walter shook his head then turned back to the doctor. "I shouldn't have—"

"You shouldn't have… what?" She was still baffled and not hiding it now. "You know you can tell me. Remember this is a safe place."

"Can I ask you something?" Walter asked instead. "I need you to answer me honestly."

Dr. Pierce nodded as her legs shifted, the bottom right resting on the left. "Of course."

Walter took a deep breath. "Do you think I am a good person?"

"Do I think you're a good person?" Dr. Pierce was taken aback slightly, frankly surprised. The question seemed sudden.

Walter nodded eagerly while waiting for an answer. "I do, Walter. Although, I also think you are going through some things that many can't even fathom so people's perspective could cause you to be portrayed as something worse than misunderstood. As for me, I do believe that you are confused. As you say, your cousin believed that you know the difference between right and wrong. I believe that. However, life has a way of confusing us. We don't always know that the decisions you make are right even when it seems like it is. The older you get the more you will understand that there is more gray in the world than black and white. Does that make sense?"

Walter smirked and the doctor couldn't tell why, but there was joy in his eyes.

"Why did you ask me that question?" Dr. Pierce eventually asked. "What's on your mind?"

Walter sighed. "I'm thinking about what happened later that week." His eyes were fixed on a corner of the room, seeing memories that only Walter knew. "She told me…"

*   *   *

"Yvette?"

Later in the library, Yvette was curled up on the floor; forehead to her knees and arms hugging her legs. When she heard Hazel's voice and footsteps, Yvette grasped her legs even tighter and buried her head even deeper. There were so many tears falling from her eyes, that she didn't know when they would stop, and now Hazel found her at her most-weakest state.

"What's wrong, sweetie?" she asked gently.

Feeling Hazel's hand rest on her shoulder brought Yvette a sort of chill. The touch alone made her shiver all the more. Hazel sat beside her and slowly rubbed her back. It took a few rubs, but the shivering slowly simmered. When Yvette finally looked up at her friend, her eyes were still watery and she could barely see.

"Shh," Hazel quieted her. She began wiping the tears from her cheeks and moving aside strands of hair from in front her eyes. "It's okay. What's wrong, sweetie?"

Yvette shook her head sadly. "I'm so stupid."

"We both know that's not true," Hazel said, gently but frankly. "Talk to me. What's going on? Is it Kevin?"

Yvette shook her head again.

"Walter?"

"It's me, Hazel," she said, blaming herself. "I know I should have just stayed home."

"Yvette... who cares about some stupid party? So you don't like parties. No one can punish you for it. If Kevin doesn't understand him then that's his problem, and, more importantly, that's his loss."

Yvette sniffed. "I tried talking to him in the hallway today, but he was so mean. I didn't think he could be like that." When she said that, Hazel seemed baffled. "What?"

"You called him, right? In the hallway?"

Now Yvette was baffled. "What do you mean? I talked to him when he was at his locker earlier. It was at lunchtime."

"What are you talking about, Yvette? Kevin didn't come to school today."

Yvette's heart seemed to stop abruptly. Even the tears at her cheeks seem to freeze. Her mind was racing and her skin was turning cold.

Hazel was concerned now. "Yvette, what's going on? Talk to me."

"What are you talking about, Hazel?" Anger was starting to build in her and she was too confused to know what to do with it. "I saw him in the hallway at lunchtime."

Hazel shook her head. "No, you didn't."

"What are you... He was here."

"No, he wasn't." Hazel was certain. "Him and my brother have third period together so you can ask him. Kevin wasn't at school today."

Yvette's eyes seemed to widen on their own. Her entire body felt like it was sinking into the floor. Even Hazel seemed to feel further and further away from her.

"Yvette?"

Yvette could hear her friend, but the voice was muffled and a bit distorted. Her teeth were gritted and her heart... she couldn't remember when it started beating again.

*   *   *

That afternoon, Walter was deep in study. He had another test tomorrow and fortunately for him, it was his best subject, Algebra II. His mother was adamant about him concentrating on his tests and reminded him of his homework as well. His grades had gone back up recently. Even so Harriet D'Artagnan kept her son focused. She wouldn't suffer attending another parent-teacher conference with disappointment in her eyes that usually matched his teacher's. If his father attended as well, it would prove to be worse. *Good thing he wasn't at the last one,* Walter thought darkly. His punishment might have been a more unpleasant one. It was never good to give his father that luxury. Lawrence D'Artagnan was creative with punishment.

The sun was setting when he got a call from Yvette. She was on his porch and asking him to come down. Regrettably, Walter had been keeping his distance from her. Even so, although his punishment was over now, his mother gave him a certain unmistaken look when he told her Yvette was here to see him. However, the look on her face read, "No company today."

Yvette was sitting on the steps when he opened the door. She faced him with an upset or bothering look.

"Hey," Walter said wearily. "What's... What's going on?"

She stood then stepped up to him. "You must think I'm an idiot, don't you?" she muttered angrily.

"What are you—"

"You are clever, Walter, you really are. Like — I was angry with Kevin almost all day... until I found out that Kevin wasn't even at school today. Then I remembered something he said that reminded me of our conversation Friday night. He said, 'You decided to leave the party, not me.' Sounds similar, doesn't it? But... that wasn't Kevin, was it? He got sick yesterday and stayed home. What, you planned on him getting sick too or did you just pick the perfect time to screw with my head?" She paused for a moment. She suddenly turned from angry to sunken and disappointed. "Did you use the pages from my diary to trick me?"

Walter couldn't respond to her question. He was too afraid to. Even still, his silence spoke volumes to her. Her eyes widened, her lips parted as she stepped back from him. The disappointed and angry look she was giving him was unbearable. Even when he said nothing, Yvette knew what the answer was.

"Why?"

"I didn't, Yvette."

"You didn't?"

"I thought about it…" It burned him just to say that. "I wanted you and Kevin to break up so that…" Words failed him.

"You couldn't have thought that," she said grimly. "You and I both know that Kevin and I aren't anything. I don't know why I have to explain that to you."

"But, I didn't do it." Walter was pleading now. He was telling her the truth. Although the thought came to him, it never touched the stained page. "I'm telling you the truth. I never wrote those words down on the page. Hate me for even thinking of it… I deserve that, but don't hate me for something I didn't do." Walter sighed heavily. "I don't understand how any of this happened, Yvette. You have to trust me."

Yvette's lips turned stern and her eyes squinted with fury. "I don't believe you, Walter. I want to, but I don't." Yvette sighed. "Maybe this is a bad time — or maybe just stupid — but… I don't know. I thought we had something. If you had asked me to the party, I would have said yes."

"Then why did you go out with Kevin then?" Walter blurted. It came out more harshly than he would have hoped.

Yvette was taken aback. "Why didn't you just ask me? You could have said something even when Kevin was there. You could have stepped up, Walter. I even gave you a chance. I looked up at you, but… you said nothing."

"I was just about to ask you—"

"Of all the times we were together you could have said something. Why didn't you? You made me look like a fool in school, talking to myself in the hallway. I was wondering out of all people why Molly Rose would be so worried about me after my talk to Kevin. Then after Hazel told me Kevin wasn't even at school today… it didn't make sense to me… until it did. Molly must've thought I was talking to some kind of ghost or I was possessed or whatever that crazy girl thinks. And what about everyone else? What would they think? Overly grieving? Crazy?"

"Like me?" Walter felt cold all over and his words showed.

Yvette shook her head. "I never said that, Walter."

"Then why don't you believe me? We had that whole conversation about trust. You trusted me then. Why not now?"

Yvette fell silent and her lips began to curl as her body shook. Tears began to form in her eyes, but she wouldn't dare let them fall. Walter noticed that. Her voice cracked as she spoke. "You betray me and still try to turn this around on me? I was honest and open with you. I shared my deepest secrets with you and you throw that back in my face? How dare you? You don't have the right to say that to me. You're not my father, Walter."

Then there was a pause as Yvette watched him with painful eyes. "What happened to you? I don't know who *this* Walter is. I like the old Walter. The old Walter made me laugh, feel optimistic, feel safe… safe to be me… I don't know who you are now. If the old Walter asked me out, I would have said yes. I would have loved that. This new Walter, I want to forget he even exists. That would make me feel better."

She was turning away to leave when she stopped herself and said, "I want them back."

Walter was lost. "I don't—"

"—know what I'm talking about?" she finished for him. "The pages, Walter! I want the pages from my diary back!"

The word struck him hard. He might have mistaken them for a slap as it was very much how Walter felt. "Fine," he replied in a more scornful tone. However, that's not what truly baffled him. When he returned to her with the pages she requested, Yvette took them in her hands, lifted a silver lighter from her pocket and lit the pages on fire. Walter's eyes grew wide as the flames began to overtake the parchment. Black specks gently dropped to the floor, but Yvette put a boot into the ashes and kicked them off the stairs.

Yvette gave a satisfying sigh and smiled. "You know what, I do feel better now."

*   *   *

No one was home when Yvette got there so she made all the noise she wanted — stomped her way up the stairs, slammed her bedroom door behind her, threw her book bag at the wall. She was angry and didn't care if the entire neighborhood heard. Flopping to her bed, Yvette felt her entire day weighing on her. But when she thought of Walter, her head began to whirl with confusion. *How could he do that to me?* If truth be told, she was more annoyed than angry and she couldn't fathom any of it. Perhaps Walter wasn't as mature as she thought... *But to use the diary just for some fake break up because of some stupid date and some stupid party?*

She dozed off for some time, waking only to a passing car with loud music playing and felt drool in the corner of her lips. She wiped her eyes and lips and sat up in her bed. The house was still quiet and her mind still hovered over Walter. Getting up from her bed, Yvette grabbed her bag. She fished inside for the diary and wrote her mother's name on a page.

"Hey, sweetheart," Margaret Anders said sadly when she appeared.

Yvette faced her, feeling the tears finally coming. "Why did I do that?"

"You made a mistake, but can you blame yourself? This is Walter you're talking about, don't forget."

Too annoyed to respond to her, she ignored that. "Why didn't I just tell Kevin no? It's not like I wanted to. I wanted to go with Walter. Maybe he was afraid but… but so was I. I just… I just can't believe he would do that."

Her mother laid a warm hand on her cheek. "Sweetheart, you shouldn't be worried about this foolish boy. Frankly, he's pitiful. So undesirable."

"He's not pitiful," Yvette whined like a little girl.

"And if you hadn't gone with Kevin, you would never know how vile the boy is. You should look at it as a moment of clarity. If you want to blame yourself for something, blame yourself for sharing the diary with him further."

Yvette could only agree, hating herself even more for dragging anyone into this with her, someone she realized she truly enjoyed being with. Walter was funny, understanding and even more patient than she was… or at least that was her perception of him. Now it felt like everything was a lie.

"But how was I supposed to know?" Yvette asked desperately.

"If you use the diary on him, you can frighten him so he would never want to use it again. Then we can rid ourselves of him. He doesn't deserve the pages you gave him."

Yvette looked at her mother and gasped. As she bit her bottom lip, Yvette turned away angrily and asked, "What do you mean?" knowing the answer but couldn't say it or fathom what it entailed.

"Sometimes getting someone to feel the same hurt as you is the only way they can truly understand how you feel. You have the diary. It's yours. You can use it against the people who harm you. You just have to be sly and sneaky about it and I know you can do that. Walter can't protect you, but I can."

"So, what are you trying to tell me? What Walter did to me was — what — should be the reason for me to do the same to him? My mom would never say that!" She was facing the woman with a grimace and her heart beating with fear. Suddenly, her bedroom felt bitter cold and even when she stepped back, it felt like she was stepping on ice. "My mom won't say that. My mom isn't that cold."

"You're right," she said dully. "Your mother isn't cold, but it's not your mother that I know, is it? I know your little friend, Walter... and I know you."

Yvette scowled. "I'm not cold—"

"You're not? You, the one who secretly hates a girl because she has the position you want? The one who throws away the food your father makes for you?" Margaret Anders stepped forward. "The girl who wouldn't share her diary with her father, a man who provides for you and suffers even more than his children?"

"But..." Yvette couldn't believe what she was hearing with her mother's voice, but she did remember what her sister had told her. "But Charlotte said—"

"Who cares what Charlotte says or what she thinks. You could've helped your father so many times yet you're more concerned with a boy who betrayed you."

"No, but... I didn't know. I..." Yvette began to shake her head as if it would summon a whirlwind and blew all her problems away. "This isn't right."

She hurried to grab the diary, but, surprisingly, her mother was quicker. Yvette barely saw her move. A blink and the diary was in the woman's hand.

"Give me back my diary."

"Don't raise your voice at me. I am your mother."

"You're not. Now give me back my diary!" Yvette screamed so loud that her eyes wouldn't dare stay open as she spoke. However, when she opened her eyes, her mother was gone, the diary was laying on the carpet and her father stood by her open door with haunted widened eyes. The sight of him made Yvette's heart thump harder, like it was racing in her chest. "D... Dad?"

"Yvette, what..." He seemed frightened and concerned all at once. "What's going on? Who are you talking to?"

"Dad..." she called again. "Is that really you?"

"Of course it is, sweetheart. What's wrong?"

"It's... it's just..." Yvette couldn't take it anymore. She couldn't respond or even speak. Instead, her eyes fell to her knees as tears began to pour down her cheeks and the chills in her body ran through her violently. She began to rub her shoulders, hugging herself until her arms were replaced with her father's. He held his daughter so close and Yvette cried and cried into her father's shirt. *It has to be him,* she thought, grasping him tightly. *It has to be.*

"I'm here, sweetheart," her father told her. "Everything is okay."

Yvette began shaking her head with her nose still in his shirt. "No... No, it isn't. Nothing is okay."

"What do you mean? What's wrong? And your diary? Someone took a diary from you?"

Yvette didn't know how to answer her father. She was usually so careful when she used the diary, but her anger was fierce and a terrible distraction. One thing was certain, the truth was out of the question although she wanted to tell him. She wanted to show her father the love of his life, but even when she first thought of it, she wasn't sure if he would cope with an illusion of his late wife. Now, hearing her mother's voice calling her

266

selfish was painful. *But I am.* A part of her regretted those choices but knew she couldn't take it back.

"No, I… Yeah." A lie came to her. "Someone took this diary I had and… they were talking bad about… my article and… I don't know. I was angry — I'm still so angry — and I was venting and thought I was alone and I just… I just wish I could talk to her sometimes."

"She does know best about the life of a school reporter, doesn't she?"

Yvette grinned sadly while nodding.

Her father matched her grin with his own, showing his understanding. "I wish the same thing too. You know your mother had a few bullies in school who tried to criticize her work; making fun of the nerd. I heard a lot of stories of her fighting back at times. She did have strong hands for a writer."

"She used to fight them?" Yvette chuckled with her eyebrows raised.

"A few times. She was a mess. I don't know if your mother ever told you, but she used to sleepwalk when she was younger too."

Yvette cocked her head. "Really?"

"Anytime she was dealing with high levels of stress, it would happen. She felt she'd rather fight through it — literally — then stress about everything because it was hard to compartmentalize it all. Reading and writing helped, but it wasn't always the solution. You're not a fighter, Yvette, but the point is you always have to find — well — not-destructive alternatives to deal with things sometimes. Your mother had to figure those things out the hard way a lot of times." When he was done, her father was wearing a small grin, but Yvette saw that his eyes were growing wet with tears and melancholy.

Despite how she felt, Yvette felt herself smile hearing her father's warm words. A few times she tittered when he spoke of her mother's teenage antics — her real mother — but it made her think. She never told Yvette about her sleepwalking, but she figured some things were best kept in the past. Still, she could only imagine the fright of seeing her mother sleepwalking about the house. Just like when she died, Yvette wouldn't know what to do. Only then did she remember seeing her mother taking pills earlier that night. *Were those pills for that?* she wondered but wouldn't dare ask her father. *Not now, at least,* she thought, but she couldn't deny how curious she had become about her mother's past.

When her father rubbed her hair, it made her smile warmly. "We all miss her, sweetheart," he said gently. "But she is always with you so you aren't living without her…" Then he pointed toward her chest. "…when she lives here… in your heart.

Yvette smiled warmly at her father. "You're right." Walter had told her the same thing… *Right before he called me unhinged.* That memory still brought a sour taste to her mouth, but she couldn't deny how sweet he was for saying it nor the warm feeling it gave her. However, she often told herself… *But the diary is the only reason I can remember my mother's voice.* She still never told anyone that… no one besides Walter. Even so, she wouldn't share that with her father. *That will only make him worry more.*

Regret began to seep through her from all corners. Maybe she couldn't share her secret with her father, but Walter had been there for her. She began wondering how awful she must have made him feel when he was only trying to help. *How can you be mad at him when you told him your secret?* she scolded herself. *He consoled you and spoke his mind. He tried to protect you. What else do you want? Why do you have to be so angry, Yvette?*

"We should deal with it together," her father went on, bringing Yvette out of her musing. "Your mother always wants what's best for us."

"And you have to go back to school," Yvette said suddenly, looking up at him, her eyes watery. That regret she felt within made her sincerity surge.

Her father smirked with surprise. "What?"

Yvette sniffed and rubbed her eyes. "I know it will be hard to go back to the school where you and Mom used to work but you can work at another school or something."

Maurice Anders was taken aback. "Where is this coming from?"

Yvette shrugged slowly. "Well… Charlotte and I thought you would be happier being a teacher again."

Her father snorted as he smiled. "Charlotte too, huh?"

"We are both just worried about you."

"I'm worried about you and Charlotte more than anything." Before his daughter could plead her case, he continued. "I haven't told you or your sister, but I'm finally finishing my master's courses."

"Really?" Suddenly another surge ran within her, full of excitement and pride.

"You remember that I was hoping to be a professor one day. This is my chance to do that."

The smile Yvette wore made her worries disappear for a moment. "That's great, Dad. I'm so proud of you."

"Thank you, sweetheart." Her father rested a kiss on her forehead.

"Why didn't you tell us?"

"I didn't want you two thinking I'm taking on too much at once."

Yvette thought for a moment. "In a way, you and Charlotte are going through the same things. I think sometimes she feels alone. I know you do. Like you said, we have to be together with everything. I think you two should help each other. And you have me."

Her father said and embraced her once more. "You're right, sweetheart." Soon he was face to face with Yvette again and he was moving the curls in front of her eyes to behind her ear. "As for you, Yvette, I know everything feels strange now... maybe it even feels wrong... like a new normal. But when you feel like everything is swirling around you and out of control, just remember that there are some things that are out of your hands. You don't know how often I wished I could change what happened to your mother, but I couldn't, so I did all I could. Sometimes I wish I could just see your mother one more time, hear her sweet voice, feel her fingers pulling my chin hairs..." Yvette watched as her father smiled from a memory then slowly it faded away. "But we can't change that and we have to live with it and live for her. Otherwise, you're just fighting fire."

"What do you mean?" she asked, feeling like she was seven again.

"We can never change a flame," he said. "It does what it wants and dances how it pleases, and when you try to change the way the flames move, you only get burnt."

"Unless you have water." Yvette didn't know why she said that. Optimism, she supposed.

Her father laughed a bit. "Unless you have water. Well, think of it like this: if a flame is a memory, what happens if you throw water on it?"

Yvette nodded understanding. "So you're saying that trying to change what happened is like trying to change a memory in your head? Even if I want it to turn out differently, it never will and I'll only hurt myself?"

"That's right," he nodded, pleased how well she understood his analogy. "Everything takes time, sweetheart. I have to remind myself of that everyday."

Time, she thought. Maybe the same applied to Walter. Maybe she could just give it time before doing something brash that she might regret. Maybe she was wrong and her father had the right of it.

Eventually, Yvette asked her father something she was always afraid to. "Why do you think she did it?"

For a moment, her father didn't seem to react like he hadn't heard her, but he soon turned to face his daughter and said, "I don't know. A part of me just hopes it was all a terrible mistake."

Thursday, April 29ᵗʰ

WALTER'S BACK WAS PRESSED AGAINST HIS LOCKER when it happened; something he would never forget. He was in-between classes, preparing for his last lesson for the day. Although he enjoyed history and of all its stories, it was terribly hard to concentrate during the final period knowing the day was coming to an end. Usually he could look forward to seeing Yvette after school, but with her angry with him, Walter's afternoons — whether sunny or not — always felt gloomy.

It had almost been a week since the championship game and the party at Levi's house. That didn't stop Art from talking about it all, the game mostly. Although Walter would rather not talk about it at all, it was an epic day for his best friend. Walter couldn't fault him for wanting to brag about it. Before the police shut everything down and attendees began scattering from the area, the party was wildly fun. Walter was a bit drunk that night, but he remembered everything. He remembered dancing with Claire song after song. He remembered chugging down Levi's beer like he was Stone Cold Steve Austin, however, he couldn't remember what made him think to do that; maybe because Claire's arm was broken by an amateur kid wrestler. Walter hardly drank liquor or even beer, but he had more fun than he thought he would. However, there were two memorable occurrences that he could call bittersweet.

The first involved Claire. The two were on a couch in the living room sitting so closely. Claire laughed at Walter's jokes then found herself playing with the little curls behind his ear. Her fingers tingled him a bit — a good tingle though, to be sure — but they came so unexpectedly that Walter was a bit nervous. He only hoped that she didn't see that. Soon, Claire was sitting on his lap and looked down into Walter's eyes longingly. She whispered in his ear that she had been waiting for this for a while. Walter wasn't so sure what she meant, nor did he want to guess. Claire sweetly pressed her soft ajar lips against his own, and Walter received her. His hands slowly wrapped around her waist, and gently pulled her closer to him. The kiss was long and sweet and memorable.

The second came minutes after. Shirtless, Walter ran after Yvette when he saw her walk pass with a stern scowl yet sad eyes. He didn't know what he should say when he approached her outside, but the tears flowing down her eyes made him feel like he should say something... anything... He knew speechlessness couldn't simmer her sorrow. However, knowing what happened when he did open his mouth, a part of him knew he should think more before he spoke. On the other hand, maybe he shouldn't have said anything at all and just watched her go... but he didn't.

"She used to go to junior high school with us, but transferred to the north side before high school," Art reminded him later that night after the party. "Clarie, I mean. You don't remember her? Her brother and I were on the basketball team together." It wasn't until the Saturday after Art reminded him that Walter remembered her talking about her older brother being an athlete too. It didn't matter anyway. Yvette was still whirling through his mind and it was distracting enough. Even so, Walter never met Clarie before the party nor did he remember seeing her in school. Apparently, Art remembered her and so did Yvette, so that seemed to be that. He might have had a good night with her, but in a way, she was still a stranger to him and he might never see her again.

For days, Art pestered him about what happened that night with Yvette, but Walter was tight lipped about it. However, while at his locker one day, Art brought her up again.

"Why are you asking again?" Walter asked, annoyed already.

Art snorted. "You're the one who keeps bringing her up yet avoiding her. How could I not ask?"

Walter sulked as he opened his locker to retrieve his history "Art, we're not going over this again."

"Look, whatever it is you should just talk to her. You're just procrastinating. It's not like she's dating Kevin or anything."

"Procrastinating? That's a big word for you."

"I'm trying to help you—"

"Help me? Sounds like you just feel bad for me because you and Trisha got together during the weekend. You don't have to, bro."

Art sulked a bit. "Listen. You have to give her the look. It's all in the eyes. You have to... Are you listening to me? I'm here spending my time trying to help you—"

"We don't have much time, Art, so if there is a point here can you get to it?"

Art continued. "What I'm saying is that now you have an advantage."

Walter's eyes squinted. "What? What are you talking about?"

"Yvette saw you there with Claire. She probably said something about it before she left the party. Tell me I'm lying?"

"You're not," Walter said, giving his friend a bit of what he wanted. Art wasn't wrong at all, in fact, his comment was quite accurate. "What does that have to do with — what was it that you called it — oh, my 'so-called' advantage?"

"Have I taught you nothing, Walter?"

"Technically—"

"You know what, don't answer that... Anyways, she saw you with another girl at the party. If she really likes you then that would bother her." He raised an eyebrow as he looked up at his taller best friend. "And it did, didn't it?"

Walter rolled his eyes. He was done talking about it. "Just let it go, bro."

His friend nodded. "Walter — I don't want to sound all mushy or anything — but I just want you to be happy. We're boys, right? We can be honest with each other about everything. Claire is cool. Pretty too. But Yvette... Yvette is great... pretty too. What I'm saying is Yvette is good for you. You're more focused because of her and you might even make her feel safe. With everything going on in her life, that's all she really needs is to feel safe and that focus is what you need."

More than you know, Walter thought sorely. However, Art's words were a bit foreign coming from him, but it was profound all the same. "You know what, I appreciate you, Art. Some people won't say something like that. Very... heartfelt, or whatever."

Art shrugged. "What else can you expect? Besides, girls always say I have a way with words. You don't have to take my word for it."

"No, I'll take your word, bro." Walter snickered at that. Art was definitely good with words and far more comfortable expressing himself. Walter always admired him for that.

The bell began ringing through the hall. Walter didn't want to hurry but he knew he might be late from class.

"Come on, Walter. I'm not trying to be late again for Mrs. Dockett's class. I just want to get this period over so I can go home."

Walter nodded his agreement. "I'm right there with you."

With his textbook in hand, Walter shut his locker closed, then he was suddenly spooked and shocked to see who was leaning on the locker beside him. The eyes were leering and below was a sinister smirk, both staring back at him.

"Samuel?" Walter gasped with his eyes so wide, they felt like they might pop out. Even his heart stopped beating and he felt a hard squeeze around his lungs. "What's going on—"

"Hello, cousin."

Art stood beside his friend puzzled. "Do you just say Samuel?"

The feeling inside Walter was indescribable, but his fear was incredible. "How are you—"

"Here?"

Samuel wasn't how he usually appeared. He was wet from head to toe with all his clothes drenched in water and blood.

"You alright, man?" Art was still behind his friend trying to get his attention.

Walter couldn't help but ignore his friend, pulled into his cousin's presence. "Are you just going to haunt me now?"

Samuel shrugged. "Your guilt, not mine."

Suddenly, the entire hallway turned dark and empty. Everyone had disappeared leaving the two of them amongst the lockers. From behind his cousin, a locker door flew off the hinges and an eruption of liquid flames came pouring out. Then another locker, then another and another until the tiled floor was slowly engulfed in flames. Samuel stood, unfazed by the sudden heat, but Walter could see the flames reflecting off his eyes.

"Walter!"

He could hear his friend yelling, calling his name, but all he could see were the dancing flames around him. "Art?" he said, hoping he would awaken from this sudden fire dream and realize that he never left his bed that morning.

"He can't hear you, cousin," Samuel asked spitefully. "And this is no dream."

Soon, the bright reds and oranges all slowly turned darker into deep twilight flames and continued to sway like a dancing night sky.

What is this? Walter asked, but the words didn't come out of his mouth and stayed in his head.

"Dreams are stupid, aren't they?" Samuel complained. "So confusing."

Suddenly, the black flames overtook them both instantly and everything disappeared around him — the hallway, the flames, his cousin — leaving a sea and sky of darkness. Even in the dark, Walter could see black ashes slowly beginning to fall gently down like snow. Even his shoes were submerged in this same ash. His breath began to turn heavy and goosebumps ran across his body like insects.

"Did you see it?"

A voice spoke behind him and Walter quickly turned to see a slender and short teenage girl standing several feet behind him. Her dark skin was quite dry and had a paleness to it, her lips were painted a reddish black and her eyes were a milky, silvery-white. The seemingly blind and malnourished girl was skull and bones, really. Even the dress she wore was faded, and

277

appeared more gray than green. However, the detail that caught his attention were her long curls she wore… and the eyes... It was all too familiar and that frightened him.

"Yvette?" he said, a bit incredulous.

The girl shook her head. "Did you see it?" she whispered instead. "The monster?"

"Monster?" Walter didn't know what she meant, then again, he didn't know where he was or who she was. "What monster?"

"Cloaked in a thousand shadows and speaks with a hundred voices."

"What?" This girl was beginning to frighten him. Her cryptic words gave him pause, but the sad look in her eyes made him think she was saying some kind of truth that he didn't understand.

Another voice spoke behind him. "The girl isn't lying." A man appeared behind Walter, a tall man that towered over him, wearing an old elegant suit that was faded through time and covered in ash as well. He wore a fedora, but when he took it off to bow before Walter, his head was burned and bald as well. The injured skin was peeling off his face, showing half his skull. Beside him a young woman appeared in an old maid's uniform, long ginger hair and a long bloody gash upon her throat. Besides a few stains of dried blood on his apron, the falling ash seemed to neglect her.

"That shadow monster will swallow you too, boy," he said, adjusting his hat. "Maybe it already has."

Soon a few others were appearing all around him, all dreadful and skeletal with their clothes covered in ash or dried blood.

"Don't frighten the boy," said an old slender man, dirty and bald as most.

"He should be afraid," said another bald and burnt woman in all white overalls, that had been stained brown and gray.

"Maybe you can get away," said another woman's voice, but Walter couldn't tell where it came from. There were more than a dozen now surrounding him.

"No one gets away," Half-Skull grunted, seemingly speaking to whoever would listen, "or have you all forgotten that too?"

"The keeper will fool you," said another man Walter hadn't heard before, but now he was surrounded by burned faces.

"Ohh gow—" the young maid with the open throat tried to speak desperately, but Half-Skull held her and rubbed her back as she hunched over and began gagging on her own blood. When she caught her breath, she removed her hand and Walter could see the pink of her open flesh and a bit of blood seeping out.

"It's okay. I'll tell him," Half-Skull then turned back to Walter. "She can't speak like she used to anymore. But that… No monster did that to her."

"Oh, are we to mourn the foolish, as well?" hissed a buxom woman in a jade bustle dress. "You're little maid did this to herself, for all the good it's done her."

Suddenly, Walter felt a skeletal hand on his shoulder and quickly turned. An elderly woman with rotten teeth and red tears on her cheeks grasped his shirt. "Are you my son?" she croaked. "It's been some long, countless years… I can't remember his name… or what he looks like. Have you come to save your mother from this dreadful place?" Her breath was fowl like rancid milk. Just her smell made Walter try to pull away, but his crippling fingers were somehow stronger than him.

I don't… he tried to say, but, once again, Walter's voice was caught in his throat and only rang in his mind.

"I just want to see my wife again," said another man, gasping and pulling onto him, trying to pull him away from the old woman. Walter tried to fight back but it was no use. "I just want to hear her voice again... just so she can say her name... I can't remember any of it. It's been so many years... Too many years..."

"He should be here with me," another woman shouted at him, trying to pull him away as well. "Why isn't he here?"

Soon, they were nearly all upon him, over a dozen creepy cadavers clutching onto him with zombie-like fingers, tugging him in all directions. They waned and wept blood and pleaded for forgotten lovers, forgotten children, forgotten dreams...

"You can't help them."

Walter saw the teenage girls with the faded blue dress and curls. She was the only one standing and watching, never leaving where she stood.

"What do they want from me?" Walter screamed at her, seeing she was the only one his voice could reach.

"It doesn't matter," she said, spreading her hands, showing the open slashes in both her wrists. Shaking her head, the girl said, "No one can help us, Walter."

*   *   *

Yvette was weary. She didn't know why or what was causing the unease, but it was there, feeding her irritability. Everything was quite bothersome for her that afternoon. She barely spoke unless she needed to and even when she did, she couldn't hide her irritation. She was quite pleasant most of her day, but as the day waned to the end, that irritation swelled.

"Are you okay?" Hazel asked as the girls were walking into their final class for the day. "You've seemed on edge all day."

"I'm fine," she lied. "Just a little headache."

"Did you eat lunch today?"

"I had a bag of chips."

"That's not lunch, Yvette."

The girls walked past a few students to their seats in the second row. Yvette slid behind her desk, but Hazel only rested her bag on her own before following her.

"You don't have to eat the lunch room food," she said relentlessly. "If you don't have the money for lunch, you can always ask me."

"It's not that."

"Then what is it?"

Yvette wanted to assure her friend of… something… anything… but she wasn't sure how to answer that. Still, she didn't want to be bothered either. She would rather not talk about any of her troubles, no matter how overwhelming it all was.

Still, every time she thought of Walter, she grew uneasy yet lonely, but she didn't want to admit that. She didn't want to think of him nor talk about him. The days in school without him gave her mixed feelings and she hated that. *I should have confronted him,* she thought. The thought of Walter using the diary on her still angered her, but she still hadn't spoken with him since the party — another burning thought, another burning memory. If she were being honest with herself, she didn't want to see her mother either… or whatever she was supposed to be. She had never felt such agitation and anxiety. *Why didn't Walter just talk to me?* Yvette then realized how hypercritical she was being. *But I didn't talk to him either.* The constant assumptions on her side only made everything worse. Instead, Yvette promised herself that she would try and talk to him… even if it were the last time she ever did.

"I'm just tired and ready for the weekend," she finally told Hazel. It was the only thing she could admit, so it wasn't a lie, not really.

As for Hazel, she eventually let it go as a male student started asking her about an old lesson; probably trying to slyly ask for her number. However, something caught her ear that distracted her.

"I heard he started to see things in the hallway," one female student was muttering to another in the row behind her. As low as her voice was, it seemed to tower over Hazel's. Yvette heard a snort. "Another crazy."

"Wait, so it's true?" a second girl said with shock in her voice. "Is the school really haunted or something?"

"You really believe that?"

"Well… First that Molly girl…" her voice lowered a bit more, "then Yvette and now this… Walter guy."

"Don't blame ghosts when this school is full of crazies," the first girl said harshly but not as quietly as her friend.

Yvette quickly spun around to face them. "What did you just say?"

The second girl, a brunette with a small face. "We didn't…"

"Walter. What happened to Walter?"

Both girls were taken aback by her, the second girl more startled than the bold one. However, she was the one who answered. "They said something happened to him in the hallway earlier. He's in the nurse's office. We don't know anything else. We just heard about it before class."

Yvette wanted to punch those stupid gossiping girls straight in their mouths. Although that probably wouldn't shut them up anyway. When she turned back around, she didn't sit. She began

to grab her bag to leave when her teacher walked into class and
she thought better of it. Instead, she sat and felt her lips tighten
into a grimace. But her eyes were filled with worry. Gossiping
girls don't lie about the stories they hear but not every story they
tell is true. Unfortunately, all she could do for the moment was
wonder and wait.

Hazel leaned in from her own desk and whispered, "What
happened?"

Yvette didn't look at her and just shook her head. "Nothing."

When the last bell of the day rang, Yvette was the first one on
her feet and exiting the classroom. She would have been the first
one to leave as well, however, she nearly forgot her textbook
and the diary stuck inside. Hazel might have tried to stop her,
worried of what was wrong or brought that disquieting look to
her face, but either Yvette couldn't hear her or she was too
perturbed to know what she said.

Yvette moved as quickly as she could to the nurse's office.
When she arrived she asked to see Walter D'Artagnan.

"Mr. D'Artagnan hasn't woken up yet, so…" Nurse Jane
gave a freshman girl her attention suddenly. "Take this for your
headache when you get home. Keep your hands clean and get
some rest, okay? And remember, if you don't feel well
tomorrow, please stay home or keep your mask on. Just make
sure you bring a note from your parents when you come back to
school. Okay?"

"Okay," the freshman girl nodded, then departed the office.
"Thank you, Nurse Jane."

"Good. Now sit and relax until your father picks you up."
The girl did as she was asked then the nurse turned her attention
back to Yvette.

"Well… can I go see him?" Yvette asked anxiously.

Suddenly, Walter's friend Art approached the counter and it gave Yvette a bit of a scare. "Is Walter okay? Can I see him?"

"As I just about to explain to Ms. Anders, Mr. Wright, Mr. D'Artagnan hasn't woken up yet but you can go see him. I'll have to ask the both of you not to make much noise. His mother is back there."

Before the nurse even finished her sentence, Yvette was already on her way down the small hall with steady steps. In the last bed down the hall, she found Walter laying stiff and still like a dead man. At first, she didn't see his mother sitting beside him. However, when Mrs. D'Artagnan saw Yvette and Art approaching the bed, she stood to address them.

"Hey, you two," she greeted them. Her voice was weary.

Yvette and Art stepped forward to observe Walter closer. He was sweating a little and his breath was heavy but steady. Even his eyes fluttered a bit. She thought he might be dreaming, but she wasn't sure if someone could dream when they blacked out.

Art spoke first. "What happened to him? It seems like he blacked out or something?"

Walter's mother nodded. "That's what the nurse is saying. Walter has really been worrying me lately." Mrs. D'Artagnan turned her body to the two of them, giving them her attention. "Were any of you with him when this happened?"

"I was," Art announced. Yvette turned to him. She felt eyes widen and her lips part. "I don't know what really happened, but he was acting like he saw someone or something... Then he looked spooked out all of a sudden at... well, I don't know what it was. I think he was shaking a little before he almost collapsed but Mr. Phillips caught him before he fell. He's the one who helped him here. "

"He saw someone?" Mrs. D'Artagnan asked before Yvette could. "Like he was hallucinating or something?"

Hallucinating? Yvette didn't like hearing that. She didn't want Walter to go through what she had but that might have been her fault anyway. She bit her lip when she thought of it.

"I'm sorry, Mrs. D'Artagnan, but I'm not really sure," Art admitted.

Mrs. D'Artagnan took a napkin and began wiping the sweat from above his brow. "Besides this incident, have either of you noticed Walter being a little... strange lately?"

Yvette didn't know how to answer that. She could tell his mother about the diary, hopefully ease her mind, but... *It will only make everything worse.*

Art's eyes squinted in bemusement. He might not have known what to say either but spoke up nonetheless. "Strange? Strange how?"

"I don't know. Anything... different about him?"

Art shook his head. "No, not really." Then he gave Yvette a quick side glance. She knew what it meant. The only thing that changed recently was her. She never felt more uncomfortable, but wouldn't leave Walter, no matter how much she wanted to run away.

"Arthur, sweetie, can you get a few more napkins for Walter for me?" Mrs. D'Artagnan asked.

Art nodded. "Sure." Yvette watched him go, not wanting to look at Walter's mother.

"What about you, Yvette?"

She wouldn't be rude to her either though. Yvette slowly turned back to her and was met with pleading eyes staring back at her.

"I... umm—"

"I don't mean to put you on the spot, but... well, I know you two have been spending some time together."

Yvette took a deep breath and said, "I think... I think he's overwhelmed and... and I think it is my fault."

"What do you mean?"

Why can't you just leave me alone? Yvette wanted to shout and scream at the woman, but she continued. "After I lost my mom, he's been trying to help me and..." She felt her body fidgeting and her ears burning, but she held herself together. "I couldn't deal with everything on my own but..." *I shouldn't have opened up to him.* "I never should have overwhelmed him with that. He has his own grief. But... I don't know. I don't know why he blacked out or anything I just... I'm sorry."

Mrs. D'Artagnan stood and hugged her. Yvette didn't want to accept it, but she wrapped her arms around Walter's mother and began to cry into her shoulder. It was warm and comforting and reminded her of her mother.

"It's not your fault, sweetheart," Mrs. D'Artagnan assured her and rubbed her back. "This has nothing to do with you. Like you said, Walter has his own grief. So, don't put that on you. Walter is not alone and neither are you, okay?"

Yvette nodded into the woman's shoulder. She felt guilty standing there, knowing she was taking Mrs. D'Artagnan attention away from Walter, but couldn't deny the comfort she felt and decided to enjoy it, even for just a moment. "Okay."

When the two broke away, even Walter's mother was wiping tears away. She smiled at her too and that made Yvette feel a little better.

"Oh, thank you, Arthur," the woman said and took the napkins from him. Yvette felt a bit nervous seeing as though they weren't alone anymore. "What took you so long?"

"Sorry, I thought I'd give you two a moment," he said before returning beside the bed.

Mrs. D'Artagnan sat back beside her son and blotted his forehead again. "Oh lord, Walter. I swear..."

Soon the three heard a grunt. Walter's eyes had opened and he turned in his bed. As they adjusted to the light, his eyes flitted hastily from side to side while his chest rose and fell from hyperventilating. Walter was frightened and fatigued.

"Walter, sweetie, relax." His mother calmed him, even shushed him gently like a baby "It's okay. I'm here."

"M... Mom?" Finally Walter could see everyone around his bed and that's what calmed him. He slowly sat in his bed and Yvette felt a smile pay a visit to her lips. Art even smiled as well but shook his head as he approached his best friend.

"Bro, what happened?" he asked. "You were good then you started... I don't know."

"The nurse said you blacked out," Walter's mother explained. "Do you remember what happened?"

Walter was silent for a moment, seemingly thinking it through. "I think I had some kind of panic attack." Just the way he said that, he sounded as uncertain as everyone else in the room.

"But how and why and..." Mrs. D'Artagnan abruptly stood. "I need to call your father. I'll be right back."

With that, his mother quickly made her way out of the room with her hand fishing though her purse. When she was gone, Walter turned to Yvette and Art. "What happened?"

Art shook his head. "I don't know, bro. You look like you saw a ghost. That's what everyone at school is saying, like the school is haunted or something. What do you remember?"

Walter was hesitant for a moment then finally said. "It was just a panic attack. There were no ghosts. It's all in my head, I think. Thanks for keeping all this away from my mom. She's already worried about—" He coughed. "—about me all the time. I don't want her worrying any more than she already is."

Yvette peaked over at Mrs. D'Artagnan, who was pacing through the hall. One hand had her cellphone to her ear, while the other was massaging her forehead with its fingertips. "She already looks worried and confused," she shared, "and devastated."

Art nodded. "She's right, bro. If you don't know what is going on, we can always figure it out."

Walter peeked over at Yvette, but his eyes lingered a bit longer than when she first caught his eyes. He turned back to Art and said "Bro, let me get a chance to talk to Yvette alone before my mom comes back."

Art nodded hesitantly but understood. "I'll call you later, bro."

Walter nodded. Soon, Art was gone and the two were left alone. A look of guilt frown ran across his face, plain to see. However, what he asked, she didn't expect. "What are you doing here?"

Yvette was taken aback, but the sad look he wore didn't match his question. She couldn't tell if he was angry with her or afraid for her. Confused, she asked, "What do you mean? I heard what happened. You think I wouldn't come see you?"

"No, it's just..." Words failed him. It wasn't until then that she realized he was shivering. Any anger she felt seemed to wash away and Yvette held his hand without much thought. It was as cold as ice and she found herself cupping his hand, hoping her smaller palms would provide some warmth. As she drew closer she saw how pale he actually was. Eventually, he found his words. "I'm sorry, Yvette. I didn't mean for that to happen. I never wanted that."

Yvette felt a bit of air escape her. The thought of Walter admitting that he indeed used the diary against her was frightening. That fear — rightly assuming Walter was guilty — couldn't allow her to utter the words and claimed ignorance instead. "What do you mean?"

Walter cocked his head from side to side, seemingly trying not to remember or stay awake, she couldn't tell. "The time in the hallway. That incident with Kevin."

The words stuck her so hard, she felt she might vomit. Both her hands let go of Walter's as she took a step back; or might have been a stumble. She wasn't quite sure. "So, you did use the diary against me."

"No," he said at once.

"Yes. Yes, you did. You just admitted it."

"No, Yvette, I didn't. That's what I was trying to tell you yesterday. You weren't listening to me then and you aren't listening to me now."

"Yesterday?" She couldn't tell if she had heard him properly. "We didn't talk yesterday, Walter."

"Yes, we did," he insisted. "You came by my house, and you were angry and yelling at me, saying I used the diary against you. I tried to explain to you and—" Soon, Walter paused. No doubt he saw the vacant look on her which deterred him to speak further.

"Walter," she said patiently, "I didn't come to your house yesterday. A part of me wanted to… a part of me wanted to scream at you but… I didn't. I didn't have the courage to come and…" The words broke away from her and she couldn't find them anymore.

"Then where are the pages you gave me?" Walter asked, more worried than angry. "Ever since you burned them, they are nowhere to be found."

"Burned them?"

"You set them on fire right in front of me and now they are gone. I was going to give them back to you if you wanted but to burn them right in my face? Why?"

He's telling the truth. She couldn't deny it. Walter's eyes were unwavering with a shade of anger. *But that was just a thought, I never even...* "That..." Hesitantly, Yvette tried to put her thoughts into words and fumbled with them. "That wasn't me, Walter. I would never... No matter how mad I might get, I could never do that to you, Walter. I... I couldn't." Stepping closer to the bed, she wanted to comfort him, assure him that it all wasn't true, but his eyes — that unsettling look — that frightened her.

Although he was silent for a moment, soon the sternness on his face softened, thankfully. Exhausted, Walter blew a heavy sigh between his lips and adjusted himself in the bed so he sat more comfortably. His eyes shifted back to hers. "I believe you," he said lowly. "I don't think you would do something like that, but I would never do that to you either."

"I know." Once again, Yvette took his hand. She smiled sadly and said, "I'm just happy to be talking to you again."

Walter grinned, even chuckled under his breath. There was a brief silence but then he held her hand tightly and said, "I should have gone to the dance with you, Yvette. I honestly just... didn't know how to ask."

I really wish you did, she thought, remembering how unenjoyable that party was and feeling more like a second trophy Kevin won. "It's not your fault. I think I went out with Kevin just to make you jealous. It was stupid of me." Yvette didn't know how true that was, but she knew who she wanted to be there with. "That doesn't matter anymore. I don't care about any of that."

Walter gave her a smile although it seemed a bit painful to do so. Yvette didn't like seeing that, but didn't know how to comfort him. However, she could provide some closure, something Walter badly needed.

Yvette squeezed his hands a bit tighter. "Walter, there might be something wrong with the diary. I don't know what it is, but there has to be something wrong. It's been acting on its own — like it's being rebellious or something."

Walter thought for a moment. "Maybe it's something to do with ripping out those pages. Like I said, I haven't seen them since then."

"Maybe," she nodded, although there was a strange feeling of doubt within her. Still, she couldn't admit to him that it had been acting a bit strange before he started using it as well. Initially, she thought it might have been her own grief making her see things, but maybe it was something more. Now she knew it was something more. *It's not me. It's not Walter either. It's the diary.* The thought of all of it made her grimace. Even the solace of seeing her mother didn't feel like a solace anymore.

"Hey," Walter murmured sweetly while caressing her thumb gently, "you are not worried are you?"

Yvette grinned. The way his fingers caressed her own did bring her some ease. *He thinks he knows me, huh?* "No, just… just happy to talk to you again."

Walter looked down at her hand. "Your rings?" he said, a bit surprised. "I think this is the first time I've seen you without them on."

"Umm… Well… they were… a little dirty," she lied. "I left them soaking at home today." She couldn't tell him what had happened to them, not now. It was a stupid secret to keep, she knew, but if Walter was beginning to hallucinate, she didn't want him to worry any more than he already was.

They didn't have much alone time after that. His mother had soon returned with Nurse Jane. Yvette already felt like she was intruding and started edging her way out the room. She promised Walter she would call him, but she couldn't linger long. It wasn't until she left the nurse's office that the tears returned. She wiped them away but her watery eyes stood above a stuffy nose and a smile.

*   *   *

"Did you believe her?"

Walter looked up at the doctor as she interjected. However, he was baffled and couldn't hear the question at first. "What did you say?"

Dr. Pierce cleared her throat. "I asked, 'Did you believe her?' Do you think Yvette had anything to do with what happened in the hallway? Do you think she was lying about burning the pages?"

Walter shook his head. "No." There was no doubt in his voice and the doctor took note of that.

"And you said you didn't write it in the diary and you only thought of it. Was that the truth?"

He nodded with certainty. "Yes."

Dr. Pierce nodded then closed her notepad. "I'm glad we got to the incident today, but we'll have to continue on next week."

Walter was a bit surprised. "Oh, time is up?"

"You didn't hear the bell go off?"

He thought about it for a moment. "No. I... guess not"

"It went off ten minutes ago. I tried to get your attention several times but you keep on talking, so I let you go on for a while. You don't remember that, do you?"

Walter stared for a moment then slowly shook his head.

With a solemn grin, the doctor stood from the chair and approached her patient to help him off of the couch. "You need to go home and get some rest. We went through a lot today and you're exhausted. But you're doing well, Walter. We'll tackle more next week."

Walter made a heavy sigh then nodded. "I will be here."

Friday, May 14th

THAT DAY WAS AN EVENTFUL ONE. HIS FATHER HAD
kept him busy most of it while keeping a close eye on him.
Walter didn't care for the work in the mechanic shop and cared
for the watchful eye even less. He couldn't blame him though.
Besides the therapy itself, Walter learned enough from Dr.
Pierce that he was viewed by his parents in quite an ill way.
Sleepwalking and hallucinating, he thought. *That would frighten
anyone.* Maybe it was naïve of him not to be frightened as well,
but he couldn't be. It was too late for fear. Even so, Walter was
exhausted. He hadn't slept well lately and stress ran through him
daily. He never imagined the kind of toll it would take. Bravery
felt more costly than stress or fear itself.

   When he arrived at his father's house later that day, Walter
laid on his bed feeling bothered by everything. He felt so alone
and trapped, and when he looked up at his desk, he found his
jailor — resting on his desk with its cracked bindings and eerie
presence. Walter tried lighting it on fire once, hoping he would

be released from the burden, but the flames did nothing. They soon died out and the diary remained cold and cracked to the touch. He tried ripping out the pages and burning those instead. To his surprise, they would burn; to his horror, the diary's pages would always grow back. It was hopeless. The diary was in Walter's possession now but that toll for it came at a more terrible cost than anything else.

Sometime after, Walter's mother came by. He could hear her giving her ex-husband a gloomy greeting. It wasn't long that he heard her voice again calling up to him at the foot of the stairs.

"Walter!"

He sighed heavily as he rose from his bed. "Coming."

Both his parents were sitting at the dining room table beside one another when their son entered. In place of her glasses, his mother wore sad eyes. As for his father, he seemed disappointed and concerned all at once. The scented candles burning in their glass jars on the table gave their eyes an orange glow, adding to the glow and gloom in the room. Walter couldn't look at either one of them. He slowly felt his head sink into his chest where his heart was beating and quaking strongly. It made evading their eyes even harder to do.

His father gestured to the chair before them. "Take a seat, son."

It was all bothersome, but Walter sat with his father and mother looking upon him. His mother poured everyone glasses of water. It wasn't like they were all sitting down for dinner but it was something in his mother's eyes. As a family, they all looked uneasy together. It wasn't the look they should share, but… it was. Walter hated that.

"Walter…" his mother began — hesitant, but began. "Baby, Dr. Pierce spoke with me today about your progress. How has it been so far? Do you think she is helping you?"

Walter nodded slowly. "I think so."

"We are frightened for you, Walter," his mother continued while his father stayed silent with his relentless stare.

"I'm fine."

"You're not fine and I'm sick of you staying that when I'm sitting here watching you sleepwalk, talking to yourself in your room... screaming in your sleep... I don't know what to do... I don't understand what's going on. You're scaring me, Walter."

To hear that he was frightening his mother made his chest hurt. He couldn't talk about it, but he couldn't look at her frightened face either.

"I... I really don't want to talk about it," Walter said wearily, already knowing that wasn't the answer they wanted to hear.

"You have no choice, Walter." It was his father who said that with his thunderous voice. His disappointment was showing — or it might have been his frustration — it didn't matter nor did he care. He just wanted to be alone now... for just a little bit.

His mother was silent for a moment before taking back the reins of the conversation. "The doctor says you could be a danger to yourself."

"I'm not a danger to anyone. You should know that."

"I don't," his mother admitted; frankly, sternly.

Walter felt hounded now. "Why would she tell you that?" *She's supposed to keep that to herself.* Then he remembered that if she believed him to be harmful to himself or anyone else, she could inform his parents. *Does she really believe that?* Still, he already seemed to know that answer. His head lowered again, not wanting his parents to see the anger in his eyes.

His mother sighed. "If she believes you're a danger to others then—"

Walter had already told himself what she was going to say, so he interrupted. "So, you're going to take the word of some doctor over me?"

"Walter!" His father said strongly. "Settle down, boy, or do you need me to do it for you?"

Once again, Mrs. D'Artagnan waited for her ex-husband to finish scolding their son then continued. "Listen to me, Walter. I need you to take this seriously. I found you once wearing your winter coat opening every window and door in the house, muttering that you were cold. Then I heard you yelling in your room and when I came in you were quickly scribbling words on these old pieces of paper. The entire time you were sleepwalking."

"We can't wake you up when you do that," his father added. "I don't know what will happen. Bad things happen when you try to wake someone who's sleep walking. I should know, you tried to strangle me once." He saw the frightened look on Walter's face and said, "It didn't last long, son. You simmered down and I guided you back to your bed." He paused for a moment. "We didn't tell the doctor because we want to protect you."

Walter's mother turned to his father. "I told you that trying to wake him when he sleep walks is a bad idea. Don't pretend like you knew that already."

Her ex-husband's mouth twisted. "It was too much to deal with seeing him like that, Harriet. You feel the same way too. He can't break stuff in my house and wake the next day like it's nothing. I'm not having that."

Walter tried jumping in. "Wait—"

"It doesn't mean you should be trying to wake him during an episode," his mother nearly growled at her ex-husband. "You don't know what it can do to him. I told you this already."

Walter tried again. "Mom, Dad—"

"What do you expect me to do?" his father barked back. "I don't know what to do about this. You told me Dr. Pierce would help him but all this talking isn't working. You know I don't agree with all that therapy mess."

"Oh… Of course, you don't. You have no conversation skills whatsoever, Lawrence. You don't talk about anything."

"Guys!" Walter blurted out. Finally, his parents quieted down and turned to him. "Why didn't either of you tell me about this before? And whatever you didn't tell, I had to hear it from the doctor? I don't know her. Why didn't either of you tell me?"

Simultaneously, his parents faced one another; both of them seemed a bit ashamed.

"Walter…" His mother started. "We… We weren't—"

His father took over. "We wanted to, but we thought it would be better if we spoke with a professional first. Once we told her about what was going on, she wanted to meet with you. It was out of our hands after that."

"Out of your hands?" Walter's face read contempt. "You're my parents."

"And who else has been affected by your episodes?" his father grunted. "We were worried and did what we thought was best for you, Walter."

Undoubtedly hard to conceal, Walter was as angry. An unrelenting weight seemed to cast over him, as if the ceiling was resting on his head and shoulders. His mouth was bone dry as all the will to speak fell back in his throat. He grabbed his glass of water to wash it down. The glass felt warmer than expected. He hadn't been sitting there long yet he couldn't feel or hear any ice rattling in the glass. Strangely, it felt like there was no ice there at all.

That's when his father shouted, "Walter, what are you—"

It was only then that Walter saw it. His glass wasn't in his hand at all but his father's scented candle. The candle was already tipping over his mouth and the melted wax was an inch from the brim. Suddenly, his palm felt the heat and Walter quickly dropped the candle to the table. It bounced on its side, the table cloth took fire between Walter and his parents. They all found their feet as the flame ignited. However, in quick succession, his parents grabbed their glass and drowned the flames before they got out of control. With a loud hiss, the fire was gone and smoke rose from the burnt hole left behind in the center of the table. No one said a word, just stood and stared, fanning the smoke from their eyes. As for Walter, it was even harder now to look at his parents and it wasn't because of the smoke.

Mr. D'Artagnan eventually grew closer to see what the fire had left behind. Both candles were out. One stood with water mixed with its wax while the other sat on its side; wet, black and cracked with wax poured from the jar and sticking to the tabletop. From his peripherals, Walter could feel his father turning to him. "And you don't think we have reason to be concerned." It wasn't a question and it wasn't kind. His tone was livid. "What the hell just happened, Walter?"

His lips spread ajar. "I thought..." Words tried to escape him, but he was hesitant and afraid. "I thought I saw..."

"Saw what?" his mother asked, nearly out of breath.

Frightened, he suddenly regretted not holding his tongue. "Nothing," he eventually replied. "I wasn't thinking."

His father sighed before leaving the table. "I need some air." With that he was gone leaving Walter with his mother.

I am a danger, Walter began thinking. *I don't even know what's happening to me half the time.* "What's wrong with me?" he muttered to himself.

Harriet D'Artagnan approached her son from around the table. "Nothing is wrong with you, Walter," his mother assured her son. Her eyes were wet with tears. "But now do you understand and see how concerned your father and I are?" She held him by the cheeks. "That's why you need to get better. That's why you need to take this seriously."

Walter sighed and sunk his head. "I understand. I'm sorry."

"It's okay, honey." She planted a gentle kiss on his forehead. "You are our son and we will always protect you. If we can't, they will try and take you away from us. And this diary thing—"

Diary thing? The words rocked him so much that he stumbled where he stood. "The diary?" Walter tried to appear as confused but his mother saw through it. She grew closer. "I didn't tell your father about it. He's stressing himself enough. But this diary—"

"It's nothing," Walter lied seamlessly. "It's just a book Yvette and I share together to write our thoughts."

"What kind of thoughts?"

"Yvette lost her mother and her sister and I lost Samuel. We have a lot of thoughts that we don't feel comfortable talking to other people about, but… but we understand each other… and we both need it."

His mother nodded solemnly. "Have you been helping her?"

Walter grinned, his first in days. "I think so. I'm trying to. She seems to think I am."

"And you? Is she helping you too?

He nodded, feeling it necessary for some reason. "She is."

She grinned. "Good. I'm glad you both have someone to talk to about this. I know therapy… it can be much at times, so I'm glad you have someone else to confide in. But promise me you will take this therapy seriously. Dr. Pierce really wants to help you too."

Walter nodded. He was glad to have Yvette as well. He could suddenly see her in his mind — those big brown eyes and the smile that shone and shimmered. Even so, Walter's sweet bliss was spiced with melancholy. *I almost drank hot wax,* he had to remind himself. He could only wonder if Yvette ever experienced the same hallucinations. *How can I protect her if I could barely protect myself?*

On the other hand, Dr. Pierce was nice enough and was trying to help him; he had to acknowledge that. His mother was about to leave the room when Walter asked, "What else did Dr. Pierce tell you today?"

His mother grinned. "Nothing to worry about, sweetheart. She's worried about you just like your father and I." She sighed. "Speaking of your father, I need you to clean up this mess before he comes back in here."

Walter nodded silently. He didn't know what he felt. There was a numbness everywhere.

"Son," his mother said before leaving the room. "It's not your fault."

Walter didn't understand. "What do you mean?" *Was it the table she was talking about? Is there something else they weren't telling me?*

His mother didn't respond. A soft grin ran across her lips as she slipped under the archway and out of sight. She was gone and Walter was left alone with hard wax on the table instead of melting inside his stomach.

*   *   *

It was an hour after Dr. Pierce's last session of the day. She was enjoying her chai tea while waiting for her guest to arrive. The conversation she was preparing to have was one she never relished. She took a breath, calming herself then sat her mug aside Walter D'Artagnan's file.

Not too long after, there was a knock at the door. "Come in," she called.

It was the first time she'd seen Harriet D'Artagnan in nearly a month. She peaked over to the doctor as she entered and wore a soft grin. "Good afternoon, doctor."

"Mrs. D'Artagnan," Dr. Pierce greeted.

She gave her a sideway wave as she sat in front of the desk. "Please, call me Harriet."

A light smile paid a visit to her lips and it was a welcomed one. "Well then, you can call me Linda." A first name basis could cut through tension like a knife. "I just want to start by thanking you for coming in today. I know it was short notice but I felt it was necessary to speak with you on your son's progression. I was hoping to speak with his father as well."

"Anything for Walter," she said. "His father was too busy at his shop today to be here, but we both just want the best for him."

Dr. Pierce nodded. "Absolutely." She cleared her throat. "I'm going to get straight to it. Walter is a fine young man. Smart, very clever. He has a very interesting mind. However, these stories about this diary are the most interesting part of it."

"Excuse me? Diary?"

"I'm sorry, he's never told you about it?"

Mrs. D'Artagnan shook her head. "Can you tell me?"

"Let me be frank, I don't believe this diary is truly an issue. What I do believe is that it is something he turns to in hopes of making sense of everything that's happening to him. With losing

his cousin and the regret he feels from that, the uncertainty of you and his father's relationship, then there is Yvette..."

Mrs. D'Artagnan sighed. "The poor girl who lost her mother from the pandemic."

The doctor nodded and held her silence. Reaching into her desk, she fished out another file and rested it upon Walter's. A picture of a girl with brown eyes and soft dark ringlets was stapled in the corner.

"Yvette Anders was once my patient earlier this year," the doctor shared with Walter's mother. "Her father came to me hoping for me to help her after the death of her mother. Of course, I can't say much about it with you—"

"Of course—"

"—but what I can say is that the death of her mother took an enormous toll on her. I haven't had her as a patient for some time, but before she left, she told me she was feeling better and she found a way to cope with her mother's passing."

"This diary?" Mrs. D'Artagnan still seemed a bit lost.

Dr. Pierce nodded. "Whatever this is, I believe that they are both using this diary as a way of coping with their grief or other things; things they don't want others to see or know about. Teenage things that they don't want to tell parents, if you will. Walter is an only child and Yvette's sister is widowed and with a young son, she could be considered one as well during this time in her life. I'm sure that there are things that Walter leaves out of his story when we talk. I'm sure the two of them have things that they share with each other that Walter has never brought out in this room. I don't doubt that nor do I expect that he ever will."

As the doctor spoke with Mrs. D'Artagnan, she wasn't quite certain yet if Walter was truly a danger to himself or others and kept that to herself. Telling a parent that their children could be

303

more than just a mere menace, but someone to be frightened of is a hard thing to bear; even for a mere messenger. Dr. Pierce needed to be certain of these things before a contingent response was necessary.

"Reliving such memories without guidance can lead to much regret," the doctor went on, " and I suspect that Walter and Yvette feel much of that. They both have shown signs of that. But honestly, I think they are lucky to have each other." Her lips curled into a grin but faded away quickly. "Still, regret can only be mended if we accept our choices and never forget them. Swimming in regret is harmful, but hiding regret behind stories is dangerous. How could we show Walter that he shouldn't regret the past but learn from it?"

Walter's mother grinned. "Remind him that he is loved." A tear began falling from her eye. She wiped her cheek clean and said, "I think Walter feels a lot of guilt about his father and I divorcing too. More now than ever, I think."

The doctor's curiosity got a hold on her. "If you don't mind me asking, what do you mean?"

Harriet D'Artagnan sighed heavily. "Recently I told Walter the truth about his father and I. I wanted more children and that I was only able to have him. I think it made him feel terrible, like he was never enough to keep his father and I together. That was never the case, but..." She trailed off and left it at that.

"You don't have to say anything else, Mrs. D'Ar—" She caught herself, remembering the knife. "—Harriet. A parent can only do the best you can, and you and your ex-husband have done that. More importantly, you and him are not alone."

Harriet D'Artagnan grinned. "Do you have children?"

"No," she replied. "Maybe one day."

"I hope so." Harriet smiled, but still, she looked tired. "Thank you for everything, Doc. The three of us are going to sit

down tonight and talk. It's been awhile since we've sat down together as a family. It's about that time."

When she was gone, Dr. Pierce could still hear Harriet sobbing. With the office closed and quiet, the cries were easier to hear.

"Are you okay?" Lana asked. Linda looked up and saw her receptionist putting on her coat. "I know that look."

Linda smiled, hoping to ease her mind. "I'm fine. Long day."

"What's on your mind?"

Linda smirked. Lana knew her well. "Before Mrs. D'Artagnan left, she said I would make a good mother one day." Her cheeks tightened and warmed from her large grin. "I still want to believe that. Ever since…" The silence that followed linger as Linda felt the words escape her.

"You don't have to say anything."

She nodded as a tear fell down her cheek. "I know."

"I believe that you will be a great mother," Lana said sweetly. "You're still young. Not too long ago you were in college just like me, right?"

Linda grinned as she wiped her tears away. "Yeah…" she sighed. "Yeah, you're sweet. Go on home, Lana."

"Are you going to write in your diary tonight?"

She nodded. "Yeah. For a little bit."

"Okay." Lana smiled sadly. "Good night, doctor."

"Good night."

When the doctor was alone, she couldn't stop thinking about what Mrs. D'Artagnan said. Being a mother is a dream of hers, but it often felt like an unobtainable thing. Seeing Yvette lose her mother brought her chills, but knowing how her father lost a wife and her sister lost a husband, that was a different cold

305

entirely. Without the marriage, without the titles, without the rings — she still knew what it meant to lose a lover.

Her eyes were growing heavy as she thought of it and even wiped her eyes before tears could fall. Before, she could deal with the grief of loved ones, but now...

Dr. Pierce calmed her mind and took another sip of tea. Walter and Yvette's files were still laid before her. She looked over her notes from Walter's session, and started documenting her final thoughts on her laptop — the thought she was keeping to herself for now.

Walter K D'Artagnan. Diagnosis: Acute Clinical Psychosis.

Saturday, May 8th

WHEN WALTER ASKED YVETTE TO MEET HIM AT THE
park that Saturday, he wasn't sure if she would come. With
everything that had occurred lately among them, he knew she
might not believe anything he said. On the other hand, Walter
was afraid to trust her like he used to. Although no one was truly
to blame, he did wonder if all of this was because of him or
Yvette. Even so, after finishing his first session earlier that week
with Dr. Pierce, he needed to see her.

They met an hour after their phone call. It was a hot day.
With the sun bright and not many scattered clouds, it was
blinding. Yvette was sitting on their favorite bench by the lake
beneath the thick shade of an oak — the same bench where they
laughed and explored the diary together. Sweat began to bead
above his brows but it wasn't just from the heat. He wiped his
forehead dry then approached the bench. When Yvette heard his
steps, she turned around to face him and Walter swore his legs
had turned to jelly.

"Hey," said Walter, not knowing how else to greet her.

"Hey," she said sadly. She wore white today, shoes and shirt, jean shorts, and her curls held back in one.

Walter sat beside her. "You weren't waiting long were you?"

She shook her head. "No, you're fine."

An awkward silence lingered between them for a while and neither seemed too eager to speak but Walter did first.

"I think this is all my fault," he said. "I didn't lie to you, I never wrote that incident with Kevin in the hallway—"

"And I believe you," she said hopelessly.

"I know," he assured her. "But I thought about it." He paused to sigh then continued. "I wanted something to happen between you two, but... but then I didn't. It wouldn't be right... and it would only make you sad or angry... You're been through a lot already. I don't know if the diary can sense these kinds of things but... I don't know. For what it's worth, I wanted to apologize for all of it."

"It's worth everything to me, Walter," she said, her smile still sad. "But it's really not your fault..."

After those spearing words on the steps, hearing Yvette's voice assure him did help put a small grin on his face, but it wasn't there long. "You were right, Yvette. Maybe it wasn't really you, but... you were right."

Yvette seemed a bit haunted by that. "What did I say?"

"You said I should have just asked you to the party, no matter if Kevin was standing right there. That's what you wanted."

Feeling a bit embarrassed, she turned away from him for a moment. "No, I wouldn't want you to do that. Yes, I did want you to ask me, but..." As she spoke, she edged her attention back to him. "Maybe you felt it was the wrong time since I was just crying and... I was being stupid and so impatient with everyone, Walter. That wasn't fair to you. You've been very

patient with me and… helping me." Her eyes looked into his.
"You know how sometimes you find something in your life that
you didn't know you needed before you had it, but… once you
do, you feel like you can't live without it anymore?"

Walter nodded. "I do."

"I guess that's what it feels like."

"You mean like the diary, right?"

Yvette giggled lightly, her eyes still fixed on his. "I'm not
talking about the diary, Walter. I'm talking about you."

For a moment, Walter wasn't sure if he heard her right or if
he understood. His lips were agape now and his eyes were
searching hers. He closed his mouth as he still had no idea how
to respond.

She must have sensed it as Yvette smiled, even giggled a
little. "You don't have to say anything. That's… just what it
feels like."

Suddenly, Walter wasn't speechless anymore. "You know, I
really like you, Yvette. I like spending time with you. You're
fun, I can be myself with you, you're probably the smartest
person I know, which is cool because you don't act like it all the
time—"

Yvette gasped but her smile was still there. "Well, what is
that supposed to mean?"

"I mean…" Nervously, Walter found an itch in the back of
his neck that he didn't know was there and began to scratch at it.
"It's not like you're always spitting some kind of facts to me or
quoting some old dead guy all the time, so…"

Seeing Yvette cover her mouth as she laughed made Walter
shake his head and smirk. "Some old dead guy? Really, Walter?"

"I'm just saying, you're not… What's the word?
Pretentious."

Yvette's laughs had simmered a bit as she caught her breath. "Well... Well, I'd hope not." She was giggling now. "You are so silly."

Walter was still shaking his head and smiling. "What I was trying to say—"

"Oh." Playfully, Yvette rubbed her mouth and tried to appear serious after, but failed to stop grinning. "Do go on, Mr. D'Artagnan. You're such a musketeer."

"You see, now you're being a nerd!"

Yvette snickered this time, a bit slyly. It reminded him of himself in a way and he liked that. "I'm joking," she said. "I'll stop." Quickly, she returned to semi-serious smiling, but her eyes looked up into his with such longing.

"I don't mind just being friends since we've become really close, but I don't want to be just your friend, Yvette. I want more than that. I'd like to be more than just your friend." It was then that the butterflies began flapping their wings, in time with his nervousness.

Yvette seemed nervous as well and she turned away for a moment. When she turned back to him, she was trying to hide her blush. "I... I don't know what to say."

Walter found himself smiling as well. "You don't have to say anything."

A small titter slipped between her lips. "You can't use my sayings." Yvette tried to sound serious, but, as usual, she couldn't without looking silly while doing it. "You already have all the best ones. Not fair."

He laughed. "I'm just borrowing it for a little. Is that okay?"

With a fun smile, she relented. "Yes, that's okay," she said playfully. The two shared a laugh and soon they simmered. They both stayed silent for a moment and she kept her eyes away from him. Eventually, she said, "I'm glad you are okay, Walter.

After... what happened, I was afraid everything with the diary would get worse."

Walter nodded, unsure of what to say but showing Yvette he agreed.

"Even though you are in therapy now, you should be able to hide certain things. You don't want a doctor to think you are going insane. Still, hopefully we can find out what's going on with the diary soon."

Walter knew he should be honest with her about his time with the doctor. He didn't want to worry her further, but felt it would serve as a warning for her. *Yvette has had the diary longer than I have. Who knows if she's experiencing the same... or worse.* With the diary fully in Yvette's possession once again, it seemed more than necessary.

"When I was talking to Dr. Pierce, she told me that my mom found me sleepwalking once."

Yvette was baffled and shifted her entire body his way to see his face clearly. "Sleepwalking? Wait... I remember Art was saying he thought he saw you trying to walk when you passed out or blacked out, but... I guess he wasn't sure."

"Yeah, probably. He tried to talk to me about it but we didn't really get anywhere. But my parents... they knew but didn't know how to tell me."

"How could they? They were afraid. I honestly wouldn't know how to tell you either if I knew, especially if I didn't know about the diary."

Walter nodded and conceded. "Yeah... I guess you're right."

"You shouldn't be so hard on them. They are only doing what they think is best for you."

He sighed. "It's just frustrating. Nobody believes what I say — my mom doesn't believe me, my dad doesn't believe me, Dr. Pierce doesn't believe me—"

"I believe you." Yvette grinned when she said that, still sad as ever, but there was a solace it provided him.

"I know you do," he grinned, "but you aren't them and I don't know how to convince them otherwise. Especially this doctor. My parents already think I'm crazy. What if I *am* going crazy? I mean, what if I attacked someone? What if the diary is really that dangerous?"

"It is that dangerous, Walter," Yvette warned, "but I don't think you would hurt anyone—"

"How do you know that?" She turned away and Walter realized how assertively he spoke. "Sorry. I shouldn't have said that, but you know what I mean."

"It's okay… and you're right… I don't know."

Walter didn't know what to say. He found himself staring at the light reflecting off the lake. A breeze had passed thankfully and made ripples of gold and indigo over the surface. He even grinned a little when he saw the ducks floating over the surface.

Yvette broke the silence. "Walter, I have to tell you something."

He turned back to her. "What is it?"

She wasn't looking at him, instead fixed on the water as he was. The look on her face, it was an unpleasant one. "Before I found the diary, after my mom died, my dad… he had me talk to Dr. Pierce too."

Walter wasn't expecting that reveal and it shocked him. "Really?"

Yvette nodded. "After she died, I did something stupid. We had several pamphlets leftover after the funeral. I was so angry that she was gone that... that I burned all the ones we had. All of them. I didn't want to look at them anymore." She paused to take a breath and sigh. "The last pictures I took with my mom were during my sweet sixteen. Those pictures make me cry, but

312

they don't make me angry. Those pamphlets made me angry. And I know it was stupid and I felt terrible about it after... but I still sat there and watched all of them burn. I didn't really care. My dad sent me to Dr. Pierce after that and figured I needed someone to talk to about it."

"Did she help you?"

Yvette shrugged her shoulders while grasping her ear and grinning gently. "Maybe, she did... or could. I didn't see her long enough to know, honestly."

"Why not?" Walter was certainly intrigued. He would rather have a reason to withdraw from his sessions before they started the second.

Yvette was hesitant for a moment. She turned to him and said, "I found the diary and when I did and I was able to speak to my mom whenever I wanted, I didn't think I needed the sessions anymore. I lied to my father and said I was overwhelmed and couldn't take it. He didn't blame Dr. Pierce, but he didn't want to tell her too much more anyway."

He didn't want to pry, but Walter's curiosity got the better of him. "What do you mean?"

For a moment, Yvette was hesitant again. "Umm..." she struggled, "family stuff."

"Dr. Pierce has her confidentiality thing—"

"I know, but... somethings aren't meant for strangers."

"Like the diary..."

Without a word, she quickly nodded as she was fixed on the grass below.

"I would have never guessed." However, Walter snorted. "Maybe she can help but she doesn't understand."

"I don't know." Yvette let it go then averted the attention to him. "So... what did you tell her?"

"Well, since everything is in confidence, I told her the truth. I told her about the diary. If I didn't, I wouldn't know what else to tell her."

Yvette nodded. "Yeah, you're right. If she thinks you are... We don't want to think about what happens next. I mean... sleepwalking? It has to be the diary that's doing this to you, right? There can't be any other explanation."

Flustered, he simply stayed silent, uncertain of what to say. "I don't know," was the most he could muster.

"What else did you tell her?"

He was silent for a moment before saying, "I told her about you mainly. We haven't talked about everything that happened yet, but I tried to be honest about everything. I tried to keep things vague when it involves you personally, but... I told her how I felt about you. I even told her how we met..."

Yvette started to snicker, remembering that day in the lunchroom. She could never forget that. "You told her about that?"

Walter grinned as he nodded. They shared a laugh but he continued. "But, overall, I told her that... you're just you and I really like how genuine you are. You've been there for me, and I've tried to do the same for you and that I want to protect you the best way I can. Maybe she doesn't understand why because she doesn't believe that the diary is real, but that's what really matters to me."

When Walter was through, he felt so relieved — for a second or two — before the butterflies swirled in his stomach once again, flapping their wings even more viciously. It was Yvette's shock and silence that made him nervous. However, his relief returned when he looked at her more closely.

Yvette was blushing now with a soft smile but she never turned away from him. It made Walter smile to see her all cheerful. "You really said all that?"

Walter only nodded with his smile. "Yeah." He wasn't afraid anymore. Yvette's big brown eyes and her rapturous glee had taken that fear away. He could only wonder if she knew what she was doing to him.

"Walter... I..." Yvette still was lacking the words to describe what she felt. She even shook her head and smiled. "I still don't know what to say... I missed you so much when I barely saw you. When I finally did and I heard what happened to you... I was afraid but happy you were okay. I was worried about you, not just because of the diary, but because of how much you mean to me. You mean more to me than just a friend, Walter."

Walter felt himself smile when she said that, but tried not to show how gleeful she was making him. Feeling her fingers slide in-between his own gave him comfort.

Then she squeezed it as she looked back up at him. "But, that's why I have to show you something," she announced. "I wasn't sure if I should but..." With her smile faded away, Yvette went into her back and pulled out a small folder of paperwork. "I've been doing some research and... well, I found a few cases that might be tied to the diary. Look." Yvette began flipping through copied and printed pages from various websites and articles. "In one case, a man claimed his wife was still alive two years after she died from cancer. A lot of this is really vague, but he started claiming that she comes on her own, even when he asked her not to appear, saying some old book was the cause of it. Maybe he lost control or something?"

If he had any control to begin with, Walter thought bitterly. "Maybe."

315

Yvette shook her head. "I still don't really understand any of this. The news got wrong information and said the diary was a little black book. Like… some people thought he might have been cheating on his wife too. What does some old book have to do with that anyways?"

"I think I heard my dad talking about that once, little black books with women's numbers. It's something guys used to use back in their day or a cliche or something I guess."

She snorted. "I guess we just have phones now. Who knows if he was cheating on his wife or not, but the diary could have created that paranoia. I don't know." Yvette continued on to the next article. "Now, here. There was a woman who claimed she was seeing her nightmares come to life. Her husband admitted her into a psych ward after he found her scribbling in a little leather book. He even found her sleepwalking with a knife in her hand, stained with her own blood. Apparently, they never found this book so no one believed her when she blamed it on her hallucinations. However, not too long after her conviction, she began blaming her husband, calling him a rapist and a tyrant. They were never able to investigate him further because a few weeks later, the husband had disappeared. No one has seen him since."

Walter took a closer look at the article laid out on her lap. "Woah…" he said, astonished. That's… crazy."

Yvette nodded. "I have a few others too, but I've realized that these are all recurring events from different states at different times — four years ago in Texas, eleven years ago in Alabama, twenty-three years ago in New York…" She was skimming through the dozen or so articles she had compiled. "Some of these are from twenty… thirty… even forty years ago. There could be more that no one knows about and from even further in the past."

It wasn't until she said that that Walter thought of what he saw when he blacked out. Not only were there dozens of people but they all seemed to come from different times. "Probably," was all he said, not sure if he should share what he saw.

"And look at this one." Yvette turned her attention to the last article in her bundle and slid it out amongst the others. "I found this one too. This man claimed to see fairies and little green men around his home... even a mermaid that was living in his bathtub."

"What the—"

"Yeah, I know. There were no claims of a little leather book or anything like that. Still, I thought it was interesting. What makes it even more bizarre is, that one day the guy just couldn't remember anything about it."

Walter was taken aback by that. "He couldn't remember? Like he just forgot it all or something?"

Yvette shrugged. "I don't know. I looked at a few more articles to see what I could find, but they never explain how or what happened. There are a few other examples of people losing their memory after, but it's very slim. Like this other woman several years ago who lost her son, claimed she could still talk with him a few years after he died. Then eventually she claimed she didn't even have a son like he never existed."

Walter was haunted by that, but tried to keep a cool head. "Either one of them could have been lying after, right? I mean... how could a woman just forget about her dead son like that?" He knew his own mother wouldn't forget him. Walter could only wonder. If his Cousin Lily had the diary and could speak with Samuel, she wouldn't be able to forget him so easily. No mother would. Walter was not one to judge, but that seemed so cold and cruel to him. Still, it was a situation he couldn't fathom.

Nor did Yvette. "I don't know," she said, shaking her head sadly.

"They had to be lying," he surmised, trying to bite back his frustration. "Claiming stuff like that could cause others around them to think they were going crazy but might prevent people from asking too many questions."

"But more than once? I've found three stories where there was some kind of memory loss and there is no pattern that I could see."

Walter nodded. "No, you're right. That makes sense. I guess the only pattern is that there is none."

"What do you mean?"

"That means that it is the diary that might be causing the memory loss too."

"Maybe," she nodded. "But this guy with the mermaid in his bathtub and the aliens, it stood out to me because he lives just uptown."

"Really?" Walter drew closer to the article, surveying the page for a name. "Who is this guy?"

"George Ellis," they both said in unison; him reading and Yvette reciting.

"Sounds like some grumpy old man," Walter added.

She tittered and shook her head. "Have I ever told you how terrible you were?"

"Once or twice."

"Seriously, Walter, we need to talk to this man and see what we can find out. Maybe when he sees the diary it will jog a memory."

"First we need to think this through a bit," Walter implored. "Maybe do more research on this house."

"Well, I still need find the address—"

"I know, but..." Walter knew they should find any information as soon as possible, but it seemed too reckless. However, he couldn't deny that he was afraid. "What if this is all some crazy ghost story? We go there asking questions about some diary that makes you see things and we're wrong? I... I don't know what to expect after that. Not to sound selfish, Yvette, but if Dr. Pierce finds out about that — that I'm poking around harassing others and disturbing the peace about some diary she doesn't even believe exists in the first place — she would have more reason to think I am insane."

Yvette sighed heavily. "No, you're right. She can't find out." She paused, then suggested, "Maybe I should go alone."

Walter was a bit baffled. "What? Why?"

"You just said it yourself. If anything bad happens we don't know what will happen to you. So, it falls on me. I don't want you to get into any more issues than you are already in. As for me, people can chalk it up to grief for all I—"

"No!" Walter said sternly. Yvette was a bit shocked by it. "You're not going by yourself, Yvette. I don't care what happens to me. We don't even know who this man is, so I'm not letting you go alone. You said the diary is dangerous, right? If this situation goes bad and this man does involve the diary, who's to say he's not dangerous after being affected by it? No, Yvette. You don't want people wondering why you're disturbing the peace because of something they don't understand."

"I can lie if I—"

"No!" Walter never spoke so sternly, but it wasn't a mistake. He was adamant. Then he thought for a moment as he simmered. "You were planning to do it on your own anyway... weren't you?"

The frown she wore as she turned away from him, he already knew the answer. "I thought about it, but I changed my mind—"

"Why?" Then he thought further as she looked at him. "No."

"No?" Yvette didn't understand.

"No, I mean… I already know why. You pretty much already told me." He grinned a little. "It's your way of trying to protect me, huh?"

Yvette gave him a soft grin when he said that. Resting her head gently upon his shoulder, she said, "Trying to."

Walter liked how she felt against him. He wanted to wrap his arm around her, but didn't want to appear too eager. "If we can't find another way to get the information we need then we will go talk to him, but we go together."

Yvette nodded against him. "Okay," she agreed lowly. Hearing how low her voice had gotten made him feel guilty. Still, Yvette found his hand again but began fidgeting with his fingers. She did that for a moment while Walter let her and watched, and eventually he felt her smile against his shoulder. "I feel better going with you."

Walter was sure she could feel him grin, still, he was curious. "What made you change your mind?"

"Everything you told me today. That really helped." They were silent for a moment, until Yvette said, "You never told me about the dream you had… the night before that incident at school?"

A part of Walter had hoped that she had forgotten about that. The weekend of the incident, Yvette had called him, concerned about what had happened that day. Walter had told her he had used the diary to speak to Samuel before, and that he started seeing him in his dreams, even the night before that unforgettable Thursday. Unfortunately, he wasn't able to tell her then, but Walter was foolish to think she would just let that go and not ask again eventually.

"I can't exactly remember how it happened, what I was dreaming before this, but I remember finding myself in this park and… all the trees were on fire but… but, it was raining. There were only a few street lights so it wasn't easy to see and…" He paused in thought. "I was walking and I felt like I was looking for something — or maybe someone — I don't know. But I remember seeing Samuel. He was as if he had just been shot and I could see the blood seeping from above his eye. He looked almost zombie-like and soaked from the rain and… some of his shirt was burning but he didn't seem to notice. Not much happened after that… not much that I can remember anyway." Walter shifted on the bench and looked over at Yvette. "That day in the hallway, I saw Samuel. And there… there was fire again… black fire… and rain." He paused for a moment to think. "No, not rain, ash. Black ash. And there were others. They were asking me questions… they were… I can't remember. Every time I think about it I remember less."

"How many times did you write his name?"

"Maybe twice."

Yvette fell silent as she thought for a moment. "And… you told Dr. Pierce about this?"

Walter shook his head. "I haven't had the chance to talk to her about that yet." Mentioning Samuel brought other thoughts out of the crevasses of unfortunately, unforgotten memories. He was silent for a moment, reflecting.

"I never told you about this," he went on, "but a few years ago, I… I might have told your sister something — it was so long ago I can't remember what it really was — but her and Samuel nearly broke up because of it. It was about a friend of his. It wasn't like he was cheating or anything, but he did have to win back your sister's trust. I never had the chance to talk to him about that." Speaking openly about it was a bit helpful, but the taste was bitter. "He wouldn't talk to me for a long time after that, in fact, we never really talked about it at all. I can't blame him. I should have just kept my mouth shut and stayed out of their business." He sighed. "Anyway, with all the regret that followed and the silent treatment Samuel gave me, I was ashamed about that."

From his peripherals, he could see Yvette's saddened look. "Why?" she asked.

Walter smirked, staring at the lights reflecting over the still water. "Because of his reaction, I know he really loved Charlotte. She made him a better person."

There was silence again, a silence that neither seemed to have the courage to break. Walter leaned all the way back on the bench then sighed. Soon, he felt Yvette grab his hand into hers and rested her cheek back upon her shoulder. Walter shivered a bit when she did, but her touch was warm and comforting. Walter felt his lips curl upward and he rested his cheek upon her hair.

"It's not your fault, Walter," she assured him. "Charlotte and Samuel had their own issues and it was just something else to argue about. One time I picked up my sister's phone and thought it was someone else. You should have heard how upset Samuel was. Automatically, he thought I was talking about some guy she was cheating on him with or something. It was so stupid."

Walter was a bit shocked but that sounded like a Samuel reaction. "Really?"

She looked at him and nodded before laying back on him. "They both had their own trust issues they had to work out before they even were married. Samuel shouldn't have held that against you for so long."

Feeling a bit relieved, a light smile perched on his lips. "I appreciate that, Yvette."

"Plus, you're just an honest person. I like that about you, do you know that?"

His light smile turned to a light chuckle. "I know now."

"Thank you," Yvette said warmly.

Walter didn't know what she meant. "For what?"

"For telling me how you feel about me." Yvette was smiling. He could feel her cheek stretch against him. "That makes me happy because... because I feel the same. I guess I was a little afraid to say it after you did, but... I don't know, Walter. I just really missed you." She paused, then said, "You're the only thing that makes sense to me."

Walter smirked a bit. "I was worried about you too, Yvette."

"What do you mean?" she asked, looking up at him.

"When class started after the pandemic — of course, as you know — we were scheduled to have Biology class together. I knew about your mom already, so... I was worried about how you would feel coming back to school after everything that happened. I know Samuel's death didn't make things any easier. But, for the first week, Mr. Vega would call your name in attendance, forgetting you were doing your lessons at home for a while. A part of me thought you might not come back anytime soon, or might just do home school instead. Honestly, I also hoped that you would come back. Maybe it was selfish of me, but I wanted to see you and just... and just know that you were okay, you know?"

"You're sweet, Walter," Yvette said gratefully. The way her dimples appeared and her cheeks swelled around them, it gave Walter some solace to see her somewhat blissful. "You really are. Have I ever told you that?"

"Once or twice. Just not as sweet as you."

Blushing, Yvette laid her head back on him, nuzzling her body closer and shifting a bit to get more comfortable. Walter finally wrapped his arm around her and rested his cheek gently upon her curls. She began playing with his second hand now and Walter smiled as he let her have her fun. It was very comforting.

However, her voice softened. "I don't want to go home," she said. "I don't even want to deal with all this anymore."

"I know," Walter understood. "Just promise me something. Promise me you won't use the diary until we get some more answers."

Yvette was silent for a moment, but soon she looked up at him and nodded. "I'll try."

It wasn't really the answer he wanted to hear, but he wouldn't pressure her either. "Okay," was all he could say.

"When do you think you can get away again? Once we find him, we're going to need some time to really talk to him."

"I'll find time. My second session with the doctor is on Wednesday. We can try next weekend. My parents have been keeping a close eye on me, but they can't keep me cooped up forever. That should give us a week to track the man down. Should be enough time."

Yvette nodded. "It should. I'll try and find out the man's address. One of the camera guys for the newspaper lives in that neighborhood. Maybe he can help out."

Walter was reluctant. "How are you going to get him to do that? No one can know about this."

"I know," she assured him. "I don't know yet, but I promise I'll tell you before I do so you know."

Walter nodded solemnly in agreement. "We can't let anyone find out. Especially our parents."

"I know. I don't want you to worry about that, Walter. It's our secret and it will stay our secret. I promise you."

- Session Three

Wednesday, May 26th

WHEN THE MORNING OF THE THIRD SESSION CAME, DR.
*Pierce's patient was ill. May 19th was scheduled for Walter;
however, his arrival was replaced by a call from his mother who
hoped to reschedule. The doctor obliged. After the hallway
incidents — Walter's and Yvette's — Dr. Pierce was not
concerned with the time or date, but was more concerned for
them both.*

*The diagnosis of Walter D'Artagnan was documented. If she
were being truthful, after a certain surprise visit last Friday, she
might have counted her conclusion as premature. She couldn't
be sure, but something about that day seemed to be missing;
something important. Branding Walter insane might not be a
diagnosis at all. Still, nothing was scratched into stone... yet...*

*Until proven otherwise, Dr. Pierce wanted to trust her
diagnosis — even if a part of her hoped she didn't have to. To a
doctor, the word "insanity" should be a pretext to assure that
patience is needed for a patient... or even cause for major*

concern. *With that being said, the need to be convinced otherwise still hung in her stomach and swung with such weight. Walter D'Artagnan might be considered dangerous if that feeling were to fall.*

It wasn't until the following week that Walter found his way to his third session. When he strolled inside, he didn't seem sick at all. Although it was a week ago she wondered why she thought so ill of the young man. Gratefully, he didn't seem as upset or worried as he was during their first two sessions respectively. Dr. Pierce was happy to see that.

"Sorry I couldn't be here last week," said Walter whilst sitting in his favorite spot on the couch. "I don't know where I got it from and my mom got sick after, but everything is cool."

"Sounds like you had an interesting week."

"Interesting, yes. Eventful too."

Dr. Pierce sat in her usual chair and rested his files on her lap with her pen tucked between my fingers. For a moment, she observed her patient. "You seem... different. A good different. Pleasant. A bit blissful, if I'm being so dramatic."

Walter grinned. "I feel... okay, I guess. A lot of things are starting to make sense to me."

"Is that so?" The doctor was surprised to say the least, but still didn't know what that meant. "Sounds like you had some clarity."

"I did." He was nodding and a grin appeared soon after. "I finally told Yvette how I felt."

Dr. Pierce felt her lips stretch. Her eyes might have been beaming a bit for all she knew. "That's great, Walter. You should be proud... I'm proud. How did it feel?"

Walter's smile softened. "Good. I felt good about it."

It wasn't until then that she realized what Walter had said. "But you said 'felt.' Do you not have feelings for her anymore?"

She remembered wondering that before, but the young man seemed more open and receptive.

Walter sighed a bit then leaned up on the couch. "Before I answer, I want to ask you a few questions, if you don't mind. And I need you to tell me the honest truth. It's important."

The doctor hummed a tune of interest. "Well then, this won't be the first time. Sure. I'll be honest with you, Walter. What do you have on your mind?"

"I want you to tell me what you think of me," he stated; unquestioned, the doctor noted. "I've been telling you this story, but you don't believe it and I know you don't. So, what exactly do you believe?"

There it was, the question she figured he might ask and even dreaded. Dr. Pierce took a deep breath, knowing she had much to say. Her notes weren't necessary.

"I think you are frightened, Walter. I believe this diary is just a way to hide the mistakes you made. I believe you don't want your parents to get back together knowing you won't get their attention like you have now. You brought up Captain Long Ears too; a stuffed animal that you believe your father took from you and you've been recreating that in your head to make sense where this rabbit could be. Is it strange that it was the first thing you claim to draw in the diary? No, because I believe that a bit of that Walter is still there; the little boy who lost his first friend.

"I believe you hold a lot of guilt for what happened with you and your cousin, Samuel, but you created this hoax to gain attention from both your parents... and Yvette." Dr. Pierce couldn't forget her. "As for Yvette and Kevin, I don't believe you used the diary to break them up. In your own words, you and Kevin seem to have some good rapport. It doesn't seem hard to surmise that you told him something or convinced him of something to keep him away from her. But, even after all that, I

do believe you've been there for Yvette. Knowing this, it's not far-fetched either that Yvette would lie for you to protect you. Maybe even protect herself as well as both of your secrets."

Walter nodded solemnly, biting down on his bottom lip. "I understand. And you still believe that Yvette and I made up these stories, right?"

Dr. Pierce was a bit taken back, but tried not to show it. "What do you mean?"

"You told me you would answer my questions, right?"

She was silent for a moment and observed how still and calm he was. She could only wonder what this questionnaire was leading up to. "Okay, Walter. Yes. I still believe that you and Yvette made up these stories."

"Does Yvette seem like the kind of person who would make up stories?"

"I'm not saying she is..." She sighed. "Honestly, I don't know, Walter. I don't want to think that she would but I'm not sure."

"You said it yourself that trust is important, confidentiality is important. Yvette was your patient once and had that same rapport with her. Wouldn't you know if you can trust her or not?"

Taken aback once more, the doctor couldn't hide it a second time. She put her notes down and shifted in her seat. "Yvette told you about that." This was no question, she already knew the answer. Somehow, she knew it wasn't his mother who told him either.

Walter nodded. "When I told her I was having sessions with you, she told me about hers." He paused for a moment and asked, "Yvette came to see you last week, didn't she?"

She nodded. "Yes, she did." It was once she spoke that Dr. Pierce realized she was wearing a tiny smirk.

Walter went into his bag and fished inside for a moment. From inside, a little leather book rose from his finger. "She told me she stopped seeing you when she found this. Does this look familiar?"

As her eyes feasted on the old crack bindings in his hand, her bottom lip fell agape. She knew what it was, but didn't know how. Not from the stories, but from a memory. She couldn't remember which memory it was or if it was a memory at all... But it has to be.

"It does," she finally admitted. "I feel like I've seen it before. Where have I seen it?"

Walter smirked. "Would you like to see if Yvette and I are lying? You were certain that this story was bogus, so why not prove that you are right? Right here, right now. All it takes is a name."

"A name?"

"You've heard my story and you heard Yvette's." Walter stood and approached her chair holding out the book. "Just write one name of anyone — anyone at all — and you will see."

Frankly, she was hesitant, but took the diary from him all the same. The binding felt heavy; not by weight but by pure energy that felt familiar too. A tingle played with her palms. She didn't know if she could hold the weight of it for long.

Walter sat back on the couch. "I won't lie to you," he said cautiously, "the first time feels... well, strange, but don't be afraid. I'm right here with you." The tone of his voice was assuring. It made the doctor feel like a patient herself, with Dr. Walter D'Artagnan keeping her calm and collected instead.

Nervously, she began opening the diary and saw its stained pages. There was nothing inside; empty on every page, but it didn't feel empty at all. Eerie energy was seeping from the diary. A subtle pulse seemed to be thumping against her skin.

"Just write any name?" the doctor asked.

"Write a name down of someone you wished you could see... but you can't. That will be your proof."

Hesitation still hadn't simmered, but she took her pen in her fingers and pressed the point on the page. She thought of a name... a name of someone she could never see again. She wrote it down. When she was through, her eyes met Walter's.

"So, now I wait?"

Walter gave no answer. In fact, he didn't have to but simply gestured behind the doctor. Before she could turn around, Linda Pierce heard a familiar voice; a warm yet haunting voice that made her heart stop long enough for her lips to part and her eyes to grow heavy.

"Linda?"

When she finally turned in her seat, she was met with those deep gray-green eyes she hadn't seen in years and missed so much. Frightened, she quickly stood from her chair, letting the pen and files tumble to the floor. She didn't have to see her face to know how haunted she looked. Linda's eyes grew moist with melancholy even so.

The man was tall as she remembered, his face was round and olive and held a few grizzled streaks in his thick black beard. His hair was a bit unkempt, his stomach was still a bit wide, but his smile was as handsome as ever and those eyes... those beautiful dreams of green and gray.

"So, you finally did it," the man said sweetly. His voice was spiced with pride... and more. "You did what you said you would. I didn't expect anything different. You see, it doesn't matter what you became — writer or doctor — I knew you would be amazing at it." His dimples deepened as the smile stretched. "Look at you."

"You," she muttered, afraid to say his name aloud. The tears were already falling. "But... But how? How is this..." Possible is what she hoped she said, but it came out in such a whisper that she wasn't quite sure if she said it or not. Even so, she felt it when it ran across her tongue.

A voice spoke behind her and reminded her and she wasn't alone. "Now do you see how powerful the diary is?"

Walter's voice brought Dr. Pierce back down to earth. For a few moments, she was floating in many memories all at once. None of this was right, but her feelings were enemies to that.

Eventually, she couldn't look at him anymore. She turned away from him, even a bit thankful that her tears clouded her vision. The weight fell over her as she dropped into her seat.

"Tell him to go away." Dr. Pierce muttered, her eyes now shut closed.

The man was about to plea. "Linda, I—"

"I can't look at you anymore!" she nearly shouted. "How do you tell him to go away? Do I—" However, when she looked down at the diary, the name was gone. When she turned back around, he had vanished without a sound.

Walter rose from his seat and began picking up the doctor's belongings still spread about on the floor. He didn't even hand them to her and simply rested them on the table beside her chair. Even if he did, she probably wouldn't have the strength to take them herself.

"Sometimes erasing the name works too," said Walter. Gently and gratefully, he took the diary back from her then returned to his seat. "Sometimes the words just disappear off the page because we want it to. The diary has a connection to the people who use it. But... it becomes difficult."

Wiping her eyes dry, a wash of relief showered over her as energy from the diary drifted away. Parched, she had to take a

*sip of water and breathed deeply for a moment. But then, Yvette
came to her mind and that Friday afternoon and the memory of
it seemed to slowly return to her.*

*Slightly embarrassed, Dr. Pierce shook her head a bit. "I'm
sorry, Walter. I—"*

*Before she could say anything, there was a rap at the door.
"Dr. Pierce. Is everything ok?" It was her receptionist.*

*"Everything is fine, Lana. No worries. I'll call on you if we
need anything, okay? Thank you."*

*"Okay." Lana's voice seemed worried, a bit doubtful even.
Dr. Pierce already knew there would be questions later. Her
footsteps descended down the hall slowly, seemingly still
listening and worrisome.*

*Dr. Pierce slowly turned back to Walter. Yvette came to her
mind again, more clearly. It wasn't an old memory but another;
fresh, even. "I remember."*

Walter was baffled. "You remember what?"

*"I remember what it was Yvette came to talk to me about. She
came to show me the diary. I remember now."*

*Once again, Walter leaned up, elbows on knees. "What did
Yvette tell you?"*

*   *   *

Dr. Pierce began to recall that day, but not as vividly as she
hoped. She was in her office after a long session. Her usual
warm tea was at her lips while light music played on her phone.
With a moment to relax after one of her more sensitive patients,
she took advantage of it. There was always one or two that were
more exhausting than most. Wine usually helped, but drinking at
the office was never comfortable to her, even after hours. Warm
chai usually sufficed.

While flipping through the notes of her sessions, Lana informed her that she had a visitor. The doctor was hoping to be done with patients for the day. Although such unexpected visits weren't something she frowned upon — walk-ins were more expensive, of course — but peace and quiet was more desirable that day than a thicker paycheck. Dr. Pierce might not have the heart to send someone away who might need the help, but the thought of listening to another's problems made her half fatigued already. However, when her door opened, she felt her eyes widened as the visitor closed the door behind her. She was a teenage girl who was sometimes shy in their sessions, but seeing her then, the girl looked more sleepless than ever before.

"Yvette?" she said, surprised.

"Good afternoon, Dr. Pierce," she greeted. Even with tired eyes, she held a slender smile.

Yvette Anders stepped into the office and she stood as she approached the desk. They embraced one another and Linda Pierce felt herself smile while holding her.

"Come and sit," the doctor said as she beckoned her to the couch. Strangely enough, Yvette sat in Walter's usual spot on the couch. Grinning, Dr. Pierce sat beside her. "It's been so long since our sessions. I always appreciate a visit." It was a little white lie, but her smile masked it. "How have you been?"

Yvette nodded slowly. "I've been okay. Well, not really. There's just... a lot going on right now and I need your help."

The doctor nodded and understood. "This is a safe place. You remember that, don't you? You know you can talk to me about anything you're having trouble with. I may not be your doctor anymore, but I'm here and your secrets are always safe with me."

Yvette sighed. "That's the thing, it's not about me. It's for…
someone special to me. He told me he was having sessions with
you. His name is Walter. Walter D'Artagnan?"

"So, he told you about his sessions with me?"

"He told me about them after his first session," she said
while nodding. "That's why I am here. I want to show you
something."

"Why? What is it? Is something going on?" The doctor was
curious and a bit worried.

Not paying her question any mind, Yvette delved down into
her book bag until she pulled out a little leather book with faded
and cracked bindings. She held out the book so she could get a
better look. "Do you know what this is?"

Dr. Pierce took the book in her hands. It didn't seem special
at all nor did it feel supernatural of any sort, but she knew what
it was when she saw it. "The diary?"

Yvette nodded. "You might not have believed him but
everything about this book is true. I can prove it to you."

"How can you—"

Before she could finish the question, Yvette handed her a
pen. "If you want me to prove to you it is real, write your name
inside the diary."

She opened the book for her and Dr. Pierce stared at an
empty page before looking back up at her. "Yvette, slow down.
I—"

"If you really want to help Walter like you said you do, then
you have to listen to me. Please, just… just write your name
down in the diary and you will see for yourself. You will see
what Walter and I see."

The desperate look on Yvette matched her tone. It had yet to
abate; a sign that usually mean what was being said was

genuine. The empty pages staring back at her, patiently waiting, so she signed her name down in the diary.

Linda Pierce.

"I remembered being very spooked when I saw myself," Dr. Pierce was telling Walter. "It was a carbon copy... in every way. She sounded just like me too."

"Hello, Linda."

Dr. Pierce was startled by herself. It wasn't a mirror but a clone. When she turned back at Yvette, she seemed less interested in the wonder before them.

"Do you believe Walter now?" she asked sternly.

Speechless, she slowly nodded. She slowly walked over to her copy and slowly raised a hand to touch her cheek. When she did, she could have sworn she felt a tingling feeling on her own cheek. It was strangely satisfying, feeling the skin of her own reflection. "How is this—"

"Possible?" the copy asked and Dr. Pierce drew back. Her own voice speaking back to her and finishing her own sentence made her a bit anxious and disturbed.

Yvette, however, didn't allow the gawking to last long. She began erasing the name from the page. As "Linda Pierce" disappeared from the page, Dr. Pierce watched her reflection fade away.

"It's not good to wish for people who are real for too long. I learned that the hard way. You can lose touch with reality. However, it's easy to tell the difference between yourself and a fake."

Dr. Pierce slowly turned to Yvette as the revelation was now on display. "So… you *have* been using this diary to see your mother, haven't you?"

Yvette was taken aback when she heard that and even her eyes widened in shock.

The doctor sat beside her. "That isn't your mother, Yvette."

"How do you know that?" Lips agape, Yvette didn't seem pleased. "How did you know I was using the diary to see my mom? Walter told you that?"

"He told me you used the diary to cope with your mother's death. Now I truly understand what he meant. Even if he had told me everything, I wouldn't have believed it either way. It didn't seem possible to me."

"Because you thought he was going crazy." It wasn't a question. Yvette's voice was stern and sour.

Dr. Pierce sighed, feeling defeated. "Why don't you tell me everything that happened from your perspective? Help me understand. That's why you are here, right? Well, I'm here to listen."

Yvette was a little hesitant, even a bit angry, but she eventually nodded and decided to tell the doctor everything.

She told it all — the day of Samuel's funeral, the first day back at school, the chess game in the library, the study session with Walter, the night without the diary, receiving the diary from Walter's, seeing her mother after a night without her, Yvette telling Walter her deepest secret, Kevin's asking her to the party, the championship game, the party and after, her heart to heart with Charlotte, the incident with the fake Kevin, losing her mother's rings, seeing Walter in the nurse's office. For over an hour they spoke; longer than a session would be, but Yvette was filling the holes Walter's stories had left behind, while even

337

sharing things he knew nothing about. Even so, Dr. Pierce suspected that she was keeping some things to herself.

Seeing Yvette advocate for Walter so strongly, Linda Pierce felt the girl's deep affection for the boy she liked... or maybe even loved. But no. Yvette's story ended where Walter's did — which was queer when she thought about it. If there was some kind of danger they were in, Dr. Pierce only hoped she would say so and didn't know if she should pry. Still, Dr. Pierce wanted to smile. *She only wants to protect him,* she thought.

"I told my dad one day that I never got to tell my mom good-bye," said Yvette, bringing the doctor out of her musings. "He told me, 'You can, sweetheart. Tell her and she will listen.' But, I couldn't even remember my mother's voice without the diary. So, I did what I thought was the right thing... but I broke my promise to Walter."

Dr. Pierce's head cocked to the side. "What promise?"

Yvette shook her head. "I can't tell you..." She paused then sighed. "When my mom got sick, I was frightened... but when she died — the way she died — I was devastated. That wasn't supposed to happen."

"No. It wasn't supposed to happen that way. Yvette, to find your mother the way you did, frankly it's—"

"Walter knows," Yvette suddenly blurted out. "He knows what really happened to her. He knows my mom didn't die from the virus."

That surprised the doctor. She would have gasped if her lips weren't already agape. "Did you tell him?"

Hauntingly, Yvette shook her sunken head. "No... I... I'm sorry. I wanted to talk about it — I thought I could — but I can't." Tears began to build in her eyes. "It's just really hard to think about. It's something I would rather forget." Yvette sighed.

"My mom died. She wasn't dying… She could have survived. She was strong... at least I..." She paused, her grief plain to see. "And now, I… I'm not prepared to lose her again."

"None of us are ever prepared to lose anyone," Dr. Pierce assured her, hoping the teenage girl would understand. "Even when we know that death might come. It's never easy, Yvette. I know you never expected your mother to pass away; especially away the way she did. It's not your fault."

Yvette didn't stay long after that. She left rather abruptly actually and that worried her. When the doctor finished telling Walter what happened that day, she was overwhelmed but couldn't even imagine what Walter might have been thinking. The silence that lingered in the office weighed heavily. She could feel it on her shoulders.

"She wouldn't tell me anymore than that," Dr. Pierce explained, breaking the silence desperately. However, the doctor's curiosity was far from savored. "Let me ask you… you told me that both you and Yvette tried destroying the diary several times."

"Yes."

"Has she ever asked you about the man without a face?"

Walter suddenly looked spooked as his eyes widened. "No… No, she hasn't."

"She said she thinks she first started seeing him at the game then more often when she tried to stab the diary with a pen. I wasn't sure if she told you or if you saw this man yourself."

Walter slowly shook his head as he bit his bottom lip. "No. She never told me about that." Frankly, Walter seemed tired of talking about it and stood ready to leave. "What matters is that you believe us now. It doesn't make sense being here anymore."

Dr. Pierce shook her head. "You can't leave, Walter."

"I'm not crazy, Doc." Walter stretched his arm out like wings. "I'm fine."

"Walter, we are not done here."

"Yes we are. It's bad enough that I had to show you how the diary works so you can believe me."

Upset, Dr. Pierce stood as well. "Walter, I am your doctor. If you walk out that door with that diary and something bad happens to you, how do you think I will feel? You are still my responsibility."

Before she got an answer, Dr. Pierce went to her desk and pulled out Yvette's file. Inside were articles Yvette left for her to read. "And all this. She showed me these different cases. I remember now. You know about these articles. These people might have been conflicted by this diary and gone insane because of it. Do you want to be on that list too, Walter?"

Walter D'Artagnan's face turned sour like he had swallowed a lime. He had no answer for her and she expected none.

The doctor approached him slowly, calmly. "Walter, regardless of what I believe, I want to help you but you have to understand how frightening this all is. Your parents don't know about this and you have to give them some kind of closure as well. I can be willing to lie to them just to keep them at bay for now, but, based on what you and Yvette told me, that won't work for long. What will happen to you and Yvette if this diary turns you both insane or even against one another?"

"You don't have to worry about that," said Walter.

"I'm supposed to just believe that just because you said it?"

He grew silent and grimaced. "No, you're right."

"Well then, tell me. What is going on?"

340

Walter sighed heavily as he sat back down. "There is a reason why I have the diary now and Yvette doesn't. It started the day we learned why Yvette's mom really died. It was the week that I didn't come for our session.

The real truth? *Dr. Pierce was baffled now. Aside from Yvette and her immediate family, she was the only one who knew the truth about Margaret Anders's death — that it was no disease at all, but not something else entirely. "What truth?"*

"I don't care about anything else," Walter suddenly blurted sternly. "I don't care if you tell the whole world about anything Yvette and I told you, but, what happened to her mom, what really happened, that's different. Not even Yvette's father or sister knows about this and Yvette wants to keep it that way. Tell me that you agree to keep this secret."

Once again, the doctor was baffled and full of questions. "I don't understand. What does this have to—"

Walter interrupted. "Tell me that you agree."

Dr. Pierce had never heard such seriousness coming from him. She nodded. "I agree." However, the questions were still there, every one more puzzling than the last. "I still don't understand why Yvette won't want her father and sister to know, or is that a lie? Is it possible her family actually knew about this and her father lied to me? Did he create a lie to hide the truth... just to win my trust? Why do that if he wants It doesn't make any sense." The thought of it might have made the doctor dizzy so she sat back down. "Why so many secrets? Does this all have to do with the diary?"

"It's a lot to explain. Bear with me."

Sunday, May 16ᵗʰ

THE SUN WAS SHINING; A PLEASANTLY WARM DAY,
and fortunately for him, Walter's mother wasn't home when his
father dropped him off. He quickly grabbed his book bag, then
made his way to the park to meet Yvette at their favorite bench.
When he spotted her, she looked undoubtedly nervous.

"Are you ready?" Walter asked.

"Just a little worried," she replied.

Honestly, Walter didn't expect Yvette to be so nervous. A
few days before, she and a chubby, pink-faced boy approached
him while he was in the lunchroom pulling out his food. The
way she held her folder and the boy held his camera around his
neck, Walter wondered if he was missing something.

"Am I being interviewed or something?" he asked, a bit
puzzled.

Yvette sat beside him while the other kid sat on the opposite
side of the table. "No, don't be silly," she said. "Donnie was
able to help me find the house. Remember I told you I have a

friend who lives in the same neighborhood where the old man lives."

"Oh yeah, the Ellis guy? Perfect!"

Yvette handed him the picture of a white house with blue trim in a boring old neighborhood. Walter might have seen it or even walked past it before. The design was quite common around the city.

"So, do you have time to get away this weekend?"

Donnie spoke up before Walter could. "I know I do." He even leaned over the table and drew closer to them. "So, what's the plan?"

Yvette's eyes squinted. "Sorry, Donnie, but that's all we need. The two of us have to plan something important."

"Some kind of investigative reporting? Getting a scoop? A stakeout?" Both Walter and Yvette peeked at each other but said nothing. "Oh, come on, Yvette. You didn't even tell me what this is all about. I'm curious. Hey, maybe you might still need a photographer. "

"But, this is the only picture we need, Donnie. Sorry."

Walter decided to step in. "You can't help us because we are planning our first date."

Yvette seemed a bit surprised — in a good way — but Donnie was confused. "Why do you need some old dude's address for a date?"

"It's kind of weird," Walter continued, "but we're going on a prank date."

Donnie chuckled his head to the side, his eyes squinting now. "A prank date?"

"You never heard of a prank date? You seem like the type who would know all about prank dates."

"Maybe." Donnie folded his arms. "Go on."

Yvette picked up the story and said, "This guy has been siccing his dogs on little kids in the neighborhood. Your neighborhood. Don't you think it's time for some payback?"

"Yeah, but since it's my neighborhood, shouldn't I help?"

"But it's our date and our first date at that. You can't go harassing the man though or you're going to spoil it."

Donnie conceded, wishing them luck while Yvette chuckled when he was finally gone. "First date, huh?" she said with a light blush.

"I figured it was the best way to keep him from getting in the way. I liked how you took my story and ran with it."

She smiled. "I liked your story."

Now the two were outside the Ellis house gate and Yvette wasn't as motivated or optimistic.

"What if this man doesn't know anything?" she asked, second guessing being there.

Walter shook his head firmly. "Don't worry about that. Let's just focus on getting in there, learning what we can and getting back before either one of us gets in trouble."

Yvette nodded, seemingly shaking off the anxiety. "Okay. Let's go."

The ride to uptown took nearly an hour. They had to take one bus, then another just to get to the man's neighborhood. It didn't take long to find the house however; a boring white and blue two-story townhouse, with a few squares of green in front that seemed more fitting for a small garden than a lawn. Walter led Yvette up the stairs but her nervousness was oozing from her profusely. He held her hand tightly hoping it would relax her a bit.

"What's the man's name again?" asked Walter.

"George Ellis," she remembered.

344

Next to the door, a newly painted slab of wood was hung above a black iron mailbox. There were two parallel screw holes on either side and a missing name plate.

"Donnie said they removed their name plate not too long ago," Yvette told him.

Walter nodded, knowing the man's last name printed big and bold beside their door might bring unwanted snoopers or meddling kids… like themselves. Nonetheless, he rang the doorbell. Neither of them heard anything, so Walter knocked on the door hoping someone could hear that instead. Someone did.

"What?" said an older man with an unkind voice. Just from the tone of it, both Walter and Yvette could tell they were interrupting him. When the door opened, a round bellied man was in the doorway, with a bit of his hairy belly peeking at them from between his old tank top and tight black sweatpants. "Oh lord. I'm not buying whatever you're selling. Raffle tickets, Girl Scout cookies, I don't care."

Walter instantly turned to Yvette. Both were slightly annoyed already. "Girl Scout cookies? No, sir, we wanted to ask you a few questions. You are George Ellis, right?"

Mr. Ellis grunted. "Son, today is Sunday, my football day, do you understand? I don't have time for you or your little girlfriend's questions so—"

Then Mr. Ellis was interrupted by another man's voice calling from behind him. "Pop, who's at the door?"

Mr. Ellis grunted as he returned inside, sliding his feet across the floor. "I don't know. Tell these kids not to disturb me. It's Sunday, Gordon."

"I'll handle it," said the other man. "Go relax and watch the game."

Walter leaned to his side and muttered to Yvette, "I told you he would be a grumpy old man."

"Hush," she whispered while she nudged him with her elbow.

As Mr. Ellis continued to complain his way back to the television, a younger man, no older than thirty-five, came to the door with a bottle of beer in hand. He peeked at both Walter and Yvette with curious eyes sitting behind black rim glasses. "Can I help you?"

"We're sorry to bother you," Walter apologized.

The man shook his head. "Don't worry about it. My dad is grumpy no matter what day it is."

"I thought football season was over." Walter only knew from his father's lack of interest in sports those days.

The man snickered. "Not after he discovered old football games were on YouTube to play any time. Any day can be his Sunday. Anyways, how can I help you two?"

"My name is Walter. This is Yvette. We actually wanted to ask your father a few questions if he didn't mind."

The man tittered a bit. "He always minds. What are these questions regarding anyways? Is this for some kind of survey or something?"

"No, it's actually regarding a book he might know about."

The snickers continued. "My father and a book in the same sentence? That's strange. I would love to see what book you two are talking about."

Walter turned to Yvette. She went into her bag while the man tittered on and fished out the diary. She showed him and the man's amusement suddenly vanishing leaving nothing but a blank stare.

"Where did you get that?" he asked.

"You've seen this before?" Walter was curious but thrilled that someone knew what they were talking about. "Can you help us?"

Gordon's eyes flitted between the two teenagers at his door. "Alright, come in," he said as he led them into the house. Walter and Yvette shared a curious look, but ultimately followed the man.

The house was quaint and cluttered. It had a bit of a sour smell and when they passed the living room, they could see Mr. Ellis with his own beer in his hand, a lit cigarette in his mouth and his eyes glued to the television. Gordon led the two to the kitchen which was a bit cluttered as well. Old beer bottles cluttered upon the table and several dirty dishes were in the sink. Walter had seen worse, but he could see Yvette trying to hide her disgust. Fortunately and surprisingly, the smell wasn't as sour as the one in the living room. The host began to clear the table for his unexpected guests.

"Sorry for the mess," he apologized. "It's just me and my dad, so it's kind of like a man cave in here most of the time."

"Apparently," Yvette muttered, but both Walter and Gordon could hear her.

"Oh, so she does speak." He grinned. "I'm Gordon by the way."

Once he cleared the table, he offered them both a chair. The teens thanked him and Yvette rested the diary between them and Gordon.

Walter began the conversation. "If you know what this is then you know what it can do."

"That book is dangerous," Gordon confessed, "but I'm guessing you two already know that or you wouldn't be here."

I didn't expect the conversation to start this way, Walter thought.

"How dangerous exactly?" Yvette asked.

"Before I answer that, I need to ask the two of you something first. Which one of you is the keeper of this book?"

347

The two teenagers were confused. "The keeper?" Walter asked.

"The owner, I mean."

Walter turned to Yvette before she responded. "I... I guess I am." She was still a bit baffled.

Gordon nodded. "And have both of you been using it?"

"Yes," Walter nodded.

"I had it first," Yvette explained, "then I gave Walter a few pages from it."

Gordon was a bit surprised. "Has the book ever been rebellious or displayed any hostility towards either of you in any way? Especially you, Walter?"

Yvette nodded frantically, "Yes, it has. Walter—" but stopped abruptly. She appeared too haunted to say it herself.

"I've been sleepwalking," he finished for her. Gordon didn't respond with words as he pondered for a moment. This made Walter curious. "What is it?"

"The book only becomes hostile towards its users if it feels like it has been misused in any way."

"Misused?" Yvette said, more offended than curious.

Walter was more curious than she was. "Yeah, I'm lost... How is that possible?"

"The book only recognizes one person as its keeper; or owner, if you prefer. In a way, it's selfish, and now, it's being pulled between the two of you. It might feel misused. This book has its own spirit and it injects itself into whoever or whatever you conjure with it."

"That's crazy," Yvette said tensely.

Gordon agreed with a nod. "I don't know how right I am on this, but I have a theory. I believe this book tries to find its way out."

"It's way out?" Walter asked intriguingly.

"I believe that it tries to make the users succumb to it, eventually, using their body as a conduit or vessel to escape the boundaries of its book, and live inside a human body or as a mental parasite that wants to take control. Sleepwalking seems to be a part of it, but I'm not really sure."

"But how do you know all this?" Yvette asked; eyes wide open, lips ajar.

"And what does this have to do with your father?" Walter added, just as befuddled as Yvette.

"I found this book years ago when me and a friend of mine were cleaning out an old bookstore. I took a few books for myself, but I found it inside one of them. Even before I took it with me, it had a curious energy about it. This was around the time when I first thought about writing my own novels, and once I learned what this book can do, I was instantly hooked. Everything I wrote came to life. As someone who was an aspiring author, it was a godsend.

"However, everything changed after I began using it with my son. He was three years old at the time and I would draw little cartoons for him and he loved it. I became a bit more careless with it after that. I think I forgot it once on the counter and he wrote a phone number down in it or something. After that, everything I wrote or drew in the book he started seeing and it drove him crazy. I knew I had to make sure I kept it away from my son after that so he didn't go through the same things."

"Is your son okay?" Yvette asked empathically.

Gordon slowly nodded. "At the time, my ex-wife and I were going through a divorce, and since we were separated already, my son went back and forth between the two of us. Of course, my son was very young so he didn't know what was really happening, but the book still found a way to him too and made me regret using it with him.

"One night, my ex-wife called me and told me that our son was writing on her living room walls in marker. It took her a while to realize that he was asleep while doing it, but, when she figured it out, she was unsurprisingly frightened for him… and herself."

"How did she find out?" Walter asked. It might have been a dumb question but he needed to know. His own sleepwalking incidents were unknown to him and he hoped for some insight. "How did she know he was sleeping?"

"Well, of course, his mom was angry because of what he was doing, so she was screaming at him but he wouldn't reply or react or anything. When she got closer, she saw the marker was out of ink, yet he was still writing on the walls in an entranced state."

"What was he writing on the walls anyways?"

Gordon sighed. "The same thing over and over. 'It Wasn't Me.'"

A spooky response, Walter thought candidly, but he kept that to himself. Gordon's divorce might have been even worse than his parent's, but just thinking that way didn't seem fair to their host.

As for the host, he paused for a moment and continued. "My son is smart, but he wouldn't know how to write that. 'Wasn't?' A conjunction like that?" He shook his head. "I don't think so… but what I do think is that whatever this spirit is, it was using my boy. Maybe trying to see how much control it can have over him. He was only three so… it might have been easier, but I was never able to figure that out."

Yvette was understandably uneasy. She seemed like she wanted to say something, console him if she could, but by the frightened look on her face, the words might have been swallowed whole before surfacing. Even Gordon fell silent for a moment.

Walter, however, broke that silence. "But there is something I don't understand. Unless it was all a lie to keep people away, how does your father not remember anything he saw anymore? That's ultimately the reason we came here."

"Well..." Gordon looked down at the diary, "it might sound a bit strange — or maybe a lot strange — but I made a deal with it."

"What?" Yvette was taken aback a bit, yet leaned closer in her seat. "A deal? You made a deal with the diary?"

"Diary? Is that what you call it? Clever. But yes..." He coughed. "You can... well... talk to the diary... If you want, of course."

If we want? What else did we come here for? Walter was getting annoyed but Gordon seemed a bit nervous; a bit jumpy even.

"Can you show us?" Yvette asked eagerly, desperately.

Gordon stared at the diary for a moment. "Honestly, I don't even want to touch that thing. I made some terrible mistakes with it. However, as you know the book works off intention. Like I said before, the diary makes a connection to the ones who use it. You can use that connection. The diary will know you have questions — just as it knows your desires... and fears. I found myself writing in the diary hoping for a response."

"Did it?" Yvette asked. "Did it respond to you?"

Gordon nodded. "Yes... but you have to understand, once you open that door or... turn to that page, if you will, there is no going back. So, before you even confront the diary, you must know what you want because the diary will sense that. If you show any weakness, it will use that against you."

Yvette nodded but didn't seem pleased. "So… we have to play its game?"

When Gordon nodded in agreement, she stayed silent, seemingly a bit sunken. Walter, however, shifted in his seat and asked, "What was this deal you made anyways?"

"Right. Since… Since I was the original owner, my father and son's bond from the diary was broken and their memories were erased. However, it wasn't really a deal for me because I wanted sole ownership to unburden my father most of all, but the diary — as you two call it — had certain — uh — conditions… before this arrangement could be made. Um…" Gordon was growing hesitant, but he continued. "Apparently, every deal is different according to the… the owner. So, I signed a contract but… I don't remember much about it. It was a while ago. And it doesn't happen right away, "

"What doesn't?" Walter asked while tilting his head to the side.

"The memories, I mean. If someone were to lose their memories of it, it only happens after you fall asleep. When you wake up, the memories will be gone. My father didn't have any memory of what happened after — when he used it or any people trying to ask him about it or anything like that. I never asked him anything about it either, of course, but he wasn't as anxious anymore. He already doesn't like strangers so it was pretty easy to keep reporters or curious folks from coming back. However, I always thought it was interesting that you only lose your memory after you fall asleep and not right away, like it's baiting you to get back or second guess yourself."

Yvette rubbed an ear while asking, "Your wife. She didn't know about the diary, right?"

"No. Ultimately, my *ex*-wife still knows what happened with our son. She had no connection to the diary so she remembers all of it." He was growing upset now. "She didn't know who to blame, me or my father after his episodes. She believed that once she took my son away from me that everything returned to normal. Well... she wasn't wrong, I'll give her that. Still, she never knew what really happened. Even so, it all gave her more incentive to keep my son away from me." He might have been livid if he were alone, but he progressively calmed down in their presence.

"I'm... I'm so sorry, Gordon," Yvette said sadly. "It must have been hard losing your son like that. I can't imagine how you must have felt."

"Thank you," Gordon nodded. Then he raised his bottle over the table. "Beer helps." He took a good swig — a little more liquor to drown his sorrows in.

Walter broke in abruptly. "What happened after that? Something must have happened, right? Why else would we have the diary now and not you?"

"Walter!" Yvette said a bit prickly as she nudged him in his arm. "Don't be rude. Gordon has been through a lot. We all have."

"I'm sorry," Walter assured both of them. "I am, but there has to be more to the story. Yvette, we've already confirmed that we can't destroy the diary nor can we abandon it. It always returns. You and I both know that Gordon is hiding something. I mean, how does he still remember everything?"

Yvette's lips tightened soon after he said that. Walter knew she agreed with him, but didn't want to say it in front of their host.

"You're right," Gordon admitted himself. "But I'm not hiding something, I'm hiding someone."

Yvette leaned in a bit. "What do you mean? Who?"

Gordon sighed heavily. "Her name was Margaret."

Walter was waiting for more, but he tried not to show it too much. Instead he asked, "Who's Margaret? I'm guessing we're not talking about your wife?" In his peripheral vision, Walter could see Yvette shooting him a scolding look.

"You're right again. I met her when I was going through my divorce, but that didn't last long, however."

Yvette made a nervous smile. "What was she like?" Her voice was gentle.

Gordon smiled softly. "Tough... Tough, but sweet."

Walter snickered. "Reminds me of my mom. Well... sweet to everyone else, really."

Yvette snickered a bit as she elbowed him. "She's not that bad."

Gordon was still smiling. "You must have a good mother, Walter. Those kinds of women have the biggest hearts... but hearts that know an extraordinary amount of pain." He sighed in thought. "Margaret was vivacious and loved to laugh. She knew so much about literature and read so many books. The many things she knew were astounding. I remember meeting her in her English class and she was reading with my niece after school. I really didn't want to pick up my niece from school that day, but I'm glad I did. That was the first time I saw Margaret. I didn't expect to see her again, but I did. When I did, I saw it as some kind of fate, but... I only wished I had met her sooner. Things might have been different. Everything might have been different." He paused for a moment as his musing came to an end. "Oh... sorry. I'm just... distracting myself with old memories."

"This Margaret..." Yvette said less cordially; prying in a way. She even leaned up in her seat a bit more, resting her elbow on the kitchen table. "You said she was an English teacher?"

He nodded. "She was."

Yvette was scowling now. "So, after your wife left you, you decided to pursue a married woman?"

Gordon was taken aback. Even his eyes widened in response. His mouth might have been ajar, but no words came out.

"Yvette?" Walter said, slightly appalled. He didn't expect her to say something so blatantly. The way her eyes bore into Gordon was a side of her Walter had never seen. However, he slowly felt his eyes opening wide.

"I can't believe you," Yvette muttered underneath her breath. Although Walter couldn't be quite sure what she said, he knew what she was thinking. Yvette had told him that she found the diary in her mother's things, but there seemed to be more to that story. He only imagined Yvette was piecing everything together in her head; separating what she knew from what she didn't.

"So, what happened… between you and Mrs. Anders?" Unsurprisingly, Yvette pried curiously and tensely.

"How… How do you know Margaret Anders?" Gordon asked breathlessly.

"Does it really matter?" Yvette responded curtly, her compassion abandoned.

Their host shook his head slowly, the look of shock still on his face. "I… don't think that's any of your business."

Walter grimaced uncomfortably as he looked over to Gordon. "So, you were sleeping with a married woman," he said frankly. "Was that part of the diary's deal? That you would remember all the bad things you did?" He hoped that could deter the conversation a bit before anything got out of hand, but knew he couldn't do the same for Yvette's vexation. Still, he grasped her shaking hand beneath the table and she locked her fingers into his.

"No, that was after I made the deal. I still had the book and my memories."

"But you don't have the book now… yet you still have your memories. That's what I don't understand." Gordon's face turned sour and seemed painful to speak. Walter took note of this. "Something else happened, didn't it? With this woman."

The man took a breath and said, "The book became an obsession for her. I would let her use it from time to time, but it became more like a drug for her that she couldn't have whenever she wanted. Eventually she took it home one day and I never saw her or the book again. Wasn't too long after that she—"

Gordon stopped himself. His lips linger ajar for a time like he might go on but instead he stared at the diary for a time like he was daydreaming old memories.

"She what?" Walter eventually asked.

"She died." Gordon's eyes finally peered into his. "I read the paper and I know what it said, but it was all a lie."

Walter peeked over at Yvette whose face was emotionless yet held angry eyes. "What lie? Mrs. Anders died due to the pandemic. What lie are you talking about?"

"That lie." Gordon nostrils flared up a bit. "Look, I know I'm not the one to take advice from, but I believe Margaret killed herself."

Walter felt a stagger within him when he heard that. As for Yvette, he may have not really seen her face tense up next to him, but he couldn't mistake the tight squeeze on his hand. "Why would you even—"

"She tried to kill me, Walter. The sleepwalking was frightening enough as it was, but when she tried to kill me in my sleep… while in her sleep? While she was sleepwalking, she threatened to kill me if she didn't have the book. I was worried for her when she couldn't remember. She confessed that all the stress and lies and secrets were getting to her. Still, that didn't

stop her from saying threatening things soon after. This time...
she was awake. So, no. I'm certain it wasn't some virus." His
displeasure was plain to see as well as his shame. The man
might have even cursed if they weren't there. Still, it didn't
seem to Walter like Gordon would have a reason to lie to them.
He had already told him such a deep secret not knowing who
they even were. However, he went on to say. "This book is
dangerous and I don't know what it did to Margaret, but... I
promise you two that you have to be careful and make the right
decision when dealing with this... diary. I've made so many
mistakes and... I had a chance to do the right thing, but... I feel
like everything that happened to Margaret is my fault."

"It is," said Yvette; suddenly, sharply. She pushed her chair
back as she emerged with a sour grimace, yet sorrowful eyes. "It
is your fault." With that, she snatched the diary from the table
and swiftly made her way out the house, leaving Walter and
Gordon in the kitchen.

"I'm sorry," Gordon apologized. "I didn't mean to upset your
friend."

Without a word — and no idea what to say — Walter rose
from his chair to leave as well. "Sorry if us coming here was
hard on you. Neither one of us wanted that."

The man seemed quite flustered as Walter was leaving.
However... "Wait." He turned back to face him. "Tell me the
truth. Your friend, Yvette, who was Margaret to her?"

Her mom, he wanted to say but he knew he shouldn't.
Wounds open and fester from the truth. "Thank you for your
time, Mr. Ellis," Walter said nicely instead. "I'll see myself out."

However, before he left, Gordon's eyes widened and he
asked in a dark, desperate tone, "Have you seen him? Does he
follow you too?"

Walter's eyes squinted as they bore into Gordon's. "Who?"

His voice lowered. "The man without a face?"

Watching the man's haunted eyes, Walter shook his head slowly. "The man without a face?"

"If you haven't... then your friend has."

Haunted, Walter slowly turned around and left the Ellis house; never turning back, not even for a moment.

The walk back to the bus stop was quiet. Yvette was sunken and full of sorrow and Walter didn't know what to say, so he held his silence. He could only imagine where her mind was. The bus ride back was more crowded than the first and Yvette laid her head upon his shoulder while Walter put his arm around her to comfort her. Even when they returned to their own neighborhood, Yvette didn't seem any better. However, she did eventually speak.

"Walter," she called as they were leaving the bus stop with her hand in his. "I need to tell you something."

Walter turned to her as they both ceased their steps. "Sure. What is it?"

Yvette sighed. "It's really hard to say. I never told you this — I never told anyone about this at all — and most people don't know since my father tried to keep it a secret. But my mom... my mom *did* kill herself. It is the truth. I... I was the one who found her."

Without knowing, Walter's lips parted and his eyes widened. "Are you serious?"

Yvette nodded while looking down. "Even after meeting Gordon, I still don't know why she did it." Tears started to fall from her eyes. "My father created the lie that my mom died from the pandemic because he didn't want people to know, but... Knowing I have to keep lying to everyone about..." Yvette broke off and sighed heavily.

"Have you talked to your father about this?" Walter asked, "About how hard all this is for you?"

"I can't," she admitted. "If people find out the truth, it would make us all look like liars. What happens when my father tries to become a professor? And Mr. Mullens? He wrote the article about my mother and helped my father spread this lie without even knowing the truth himself. I understand why... to protect my mother's imagine..."

Walter nodded but said nothing, uncertain if he should say anything at all.

"But now... looking at what Gordon said, the truth goes deeper than even my father knew. She was cheating on him... and... well, who knows for how long or what other secrets she had." The more and more she spoke, Yvette's voice grew augmented painfully — dreadfully even.

"I'm so sorry, Yvette," Walter said as he wrapped his arms around her, letting her tears fall upon him. *She found her mom... dead?* What she must have been through then and now was unfathomable. He couldn't blame her for how the diary had become her obsession after that. It was true what Dr. Pierce said: *Grief can be a powerful thing... if you let it.*

Yvette wiped her eyes then leaned up on him to see the wet marks in his shirt. "I'm sorry. I got your shirt wet."

"It's fine." Walter wiped the remaining tears on her cheeks and she grinned nervously as she let him. "All we need to worry about now is confronting the diary and see what kind of deal we can make."

Yvette nodded then was silent for a moment. However, she turned away and said, "Yeah, but... I've just been thinking and... If only one of us could be the owner of the diary... If only one person could keep their memory of the diary like Gordon, then it should be me, Walter."

Walter 's eyes squinted. "What? Why?"

"We've talked about that before. Think about Dr. Pierce. I don't know what she will think if you don't get better. I told you already, I don't want that to happen. Technically, the diary is still mine, so it's my choice—"

"No," Walter responded right away. "I can't let you do that, Yvette. You don't know what deal we can make. You heard what Gordon said, every situation is different."

"Are we any different, Walter? The diary has already taken my mom from me. I want to hate Gordon but... I know the diary had something to do with her death. She wasn't the real owner and look at what happened to her. I wasn't there to help her, but I'm here now, for you. Don't let the diary take you away from me too, Walter. Please don't."

"You won't lose me, Yvette," Walter assured her. "I want to help you. Let me help."

Yvette was silent for a moment then stepped away from him. "I have to go."

"Wait, Yvette." He didn't want to stop her. He was certain she was overwhelmed with grief, but he didn't want her to leave him so abruptly either. "At least let me walk you—"

"I'm... I'm sorry, Walter. I just need to be alone right now."

Walter did understand, but he was still worried about anything dangerous occurring. "Yvette, promise me something. Promise me you won't use the diary until we figure all this out. Promise me."

Yvette nodded with her wet stare as the tears were forming again. Without another word, she nodded then walked away taking her grief and tears with her. Walter only watched as she walked down the blocks, turned a corner and disappeared. For a time, Walter's legs felt numb as he couldn't find the strength to move. He felt a queasiness as his stomach began to stir. He bent over beside a nearby tree and began vomiting, leaving spew on its roots and the neighboring sidewalk.

In no time at all, the pleasant day didn't feel so pleasant anymore.

*   *   *

When Yvette returned home, she buried her face in her pillow and screamed her lungs out. She was so overwhelmed and more saddened and scared than she ever felt before. It wasn't long before she entered the bathroom to clean her face, hoping to wash away how terrible she felt. She began thinking how she found her mother in that very bathroom, her body on the floor with open wrists and blood on and in-between the tiles. It wasn't one of her hallucinations, just the thought forced her to knees. Feeling queasy, she quickly opened the toilet and began vomiting the bit of breakfast she ate. She felt so disgusted when she was through but so tired that she didn't even flush. She wiped her lips clean, but she couldn't stand. A numbness swept through her and her head began thumping. She found herself on the bathroom floor soon after, rolled into a ball; laying and crying beside the blood pouring from her mother's ghost.

Soon she heard noises downstairs while waking from a stone sleep. She didn't know when she drifted off and she felt a bit groggy because of it. However, Yvette closed the door with her foot and rose from the floor as quickly as she could, ignoring the thumping in her worried head. She listened closely to hear her father's steps coming up the stairs and his voice soon after.

"Yvette?" her father called from down the hall.

"In…" She cleared her throat. "In the bathroom, Dad." She flushed the spew down the toilet then approached the sink.

"Well, when you're through, come down stairs. I brought food home."

"Okay, I'm coming." Yvette could hear her father descend back down the stairs, so she turned to the mirror. She washed her face, especially the drool on her lips, then wiped her face dry. However, as she stood in the mirror, Yvette saw how sad she looked. She didn't want her father to worry, so she tried her best to look pleasant. It took a few tries, but she was able to forge a convincing smile in the mirror, though there was sorrow still stuck behind it. Her eyes couldn't hide that.

Sunday, May 23rd

LAWERANCE D'ARTAGNAN KEPT AN EVEN MORE watchful eye on his son now. Walter couldn't argue that — with the scorched marks left on his father's dinner table, of course. He had spent the morning cleaning hard, dry wax from the table. He had to scrape most of it off while trying his best not to take some of the wood with it. Even scratches could cause his father to uproar. He dressed the table in new drapes and all, but it can only cover the marks where Walter maimed the table with flames. Even his father snared when he saw what the burning candle had left behind. All he could do about it now was complain and that he did. Even so, a tongue lashing or two couldn't help Walter with his situation.

Sometimes on the weekends, his father would cut a few yards around his block, mainly to help the young boys of the neighborhood make some extra money. Conveniently, this was the second weekend Walter was staying with him, so as always, he was dragged along. Walter appeared less ready for landscaping than usual, but this wasn't why he looked a bit flustered.

"Just a few lawns today," his father told him, hoping to assure his son that the day was meant to be quick and easy. "It will be just you and me today. After that we can shoot some hoops for a while. It will be a good distraction; get your mind off the doctor and all that therapy. What do you say?"

Walter felt a little smile forming on his lips. "Sounds good… if you're ready to lose again."

His father smirked. "Give me a minute to stretch this time and I got you."

"You need all that, old man?"

"Old man, huh?" His father snickered as him and his son made their way towards the door and out the house with their tools and hard boots. "I'll show you old."

Before he could open the door, Walter got his attention again. "Dad?"

"You're not backing out because you gave it some thought, are you?" His father was full of laughs but Walter was serious.

"No, it's not that." His voice had sunken and his father took notice. "I wanted to ask you something."

His father nodded. "What is it?"

"I want to take Yvette on a date tonight."

His father turned to him with intrigue. "Well then, the famous Yvette, huh? I see you found the confidence to ask her out."

Walter smirked. "It wasn't easy, but I did. I'm glad I did." It felt good saying it aloud.

Walter's father nodded. "I'm glad you did too. Life is too short to be afraid. Disappointment, rejection — these are only lessons. But life… life is full of possibilities and you passed an important test. I think you are starting to really understand. Just remember that confident feeling you got when Yvette said yes and stay positive." Then he poked his son right between the eyebrows. "Don't let it go to your head though."

Walter smirk rose to a snicker. "You're right, Dad."

"You really like her, don't you?"

"I do."

"Well, get her out of your mind for now," his father said. "You'll have more time for that tonight when you see her."

Walter grinned contently, feeling a bit more up to their work day together. "Thanks, Dad."

To be honest, Walter tried — often throughout the day — but he couldn't. Yvette was constantly on his mind. He couldn't stop thinking of what it would be like to forget all of it; everything that happened with the diary and Yvette. He was afraid she might shun him in fear that the same unfortunate events would repeat, but content that she might be better off. Walter only hoped he wouldn't forget what he learned about Yvette, and regress back to the fool he was before. That made him angry. *Could losing my memory do that?* His thought boiled his anger and he nearly snipped one of Ms. Lipschitz's roses. His father was right, Walter had to get Yvette out of his mind.

Anyhow...

It was mid afternoon when Walter arrived at Yvette's front door. He had his bag on his back — strange for a first date, true — but had freshly picked roses from work today in his hand as well.

"A carnival?" Yvette asked curiously.

It was three days ago and she and Walter were hanging out together after school. They were sitting on their favorite bench by the lake. Both of them were given a day off from mechanic work, therapy, articles and babies and decided to spend that time together. The two of them went half on a pizza and a couple drinks. Yvette even brought a blanket for an impromptu picnic as the day was quite pleasingly sunny. Walter played a bit of music on his phone and the two talked about the diary a little, but it was hard to plan out something without knowing what to expect. Just talking about it after a while became draining, so Walter changed the subject some time after.

"Well, no, it's not really a carnival," he explained. "It's the food fair they have every year in the park downtown, remember?

"Oh yeah," Yvette said. "I forgot that was during this time."

"Sunday is the last day so it probably wouldn't be too crowded."

Yvette grinned with a blush on either side. "That would be fun. I think my sister and Samuel went on a date at the fair once in high school."

Walter shrugged. "Should be fun, but you can't come if you're not going to eat though," Walter said frankly yet smiled when he did. "You have to promise you will try some food with me, okay?"

Yvette pouted. "Aww... Do I have to?"

"Yes. I'll let it slide today since you only ate a slice and a half of pizza, but you can't be too picky. Try a few things with me. You don't have to try everything, but it will be fun. I know this lady who makes these kabobs. Trust me, they're really good."

Yvette chuckled and nodded. "Okay, I promise."

Walter shrugged. "Still, whatever we do or don't do, we should just have fun together and we'll handle everything with the diary after. I think we deserve a bit of fun, don't you?"

Yvette was still chuckling a bit, but smiled a sweet smile then nodded. However, she shyly asked, "So... is this like... a date?"

Walter snickered and nodded. "Yeah. Like a date."

It was a good feeling, finally asking Yvette out. However, knowing either might forget all the time spent together, and all those sweet memories might soon fade was saddening. One last night is all Walter wanted. He only hoped she felt the same and the feeling they shared would remain. Even since that day when they met Gordon, Walter often thought of the woman who lost her son and the memory of him. *Was that a choice she made herself,* he thought, *or did she not have a choice?*

He rang the doorbell and it was answered soon after by Yvette's older sister. For a moment she nearly forgot who he was until she had a good look at him.

"Walter?" Charlotte said surprised.

"Hey," he greeted. "Long time no see."

Charlotte nodded with a grin. "I was about to say the same thing." She examined a bit and her head tilted to the side. "So, you're Yvette's date, huh?" She snickered. "That's so cute. So, are you staying out there or are you coming in?"

When he was let in, Walter saw Yvette's home for the first time. It was quiet and quaint. Shelves of books hugged the walls, while a few titles perched on the coffee table between the couch and the television. Barely any of the walls were bare as family photos were hanging around the room, while others sat up in cubbies above the flat screen. Walter found himself staring at the family moments for a bit. Younger Yvette was indeed smaller but her smiles were even wider in the past. Walter could see most of her teeth when she smiled — sometimes in such silly manners. However, even within those silly moments, there was always a twinkle in her eyes; invitingly bright. Walter smiled and chuckled as his eyes flitted from picture to picture.

Suddenly, Walter heard a deep bark behind him. He turned around to see a large and scruffy black and white dog that was watching Walter curiously.

"Hush, Po, Michael is sleeping," Charlotte scowled. "Walter is a friend. Leave him alone."

Po whined a bit, but his attention never left Walter.

"Evey!" Charlotte shouted up the stairs. "Walter is here."

Calling back down to her sister, Yvette replied. "Give me a minute. I'm coming."

Walter was already nervous, so knowing he had a bit of time before he saw her somehow made it all easier. Even so, there was still her sister who he already expected an unduly amount of questions from. Walter was used to it before from other prying siblings of past dates, but Charlotte was different just like her little sister. Charlotte knew Walter pretty well, but he didn't expect to be let off the hook easily because he was familiar to her.

"Oh, wait," Charlotte said intensely, facing him. "I have to take those."

She snatched the flowers from Walter's hands and began making her way towards the kitchen. Baffled, Walter followed with his eyes squinted and his brisk steps trailing behind her as if he was trying to follow her phantom footprints on the floor. Even Po followed behind with his long furs swaying beneath him.

"What the..." Walter's voice turned impatient. "Charlotte, what are you doing? The flowers aren't that ugly. Yvette will—"

"No, she won't," Charlotte affirmed. "These have to go in the trash."

"What?" Walter nearly snatched them back before they fell from her fingers and into the bin. In response, he was more confused than angered. "She might not like them but you didn't have to throw them away."

Charlotte approached him, nodding her head sincerely. "Yes, I did. We can't have flowers in the house."

Still confused, Walter asked, "Why?"

"Because Yvette didn't tell you that she's allergic to flowers. I mean, badly, badly allergic. Plus, it reminds her of funerals. Lord knows we've had too many of those lately."

"Oh..." Walter didn't know what else to say. He thought of the orange rose he gave the diary's Yvette and how much she loved it. However, that no longer mattered. *That Yvette doesn't exist.*

Charlotte smirked. "Don't worry about it. She won't find them. I'll make sure of it. She goes woozy and the rashes are terrible, believe me. You don't want to see that. She gets very irritated too and you won't be here to deal with it like I will have to. So, yeah... it is sweet and Yvette would like it but no flowers, Walter." Then she examined him for a moment. "But look at you. You're looking... older."

Walter glanced down at himself and spread his arms to his sides. "Well, I hope so."

"Taller too. Why do you have your bag on you though?"

"Oh..." Walter peeked over at the strap on his shoulder. "We have plans."

Charlotte gave him a small shrug then leaned a bit and gave him a little whiff. "Well, you do smell good too. Yvette will like it."

"Thanks." Walter chuckled slightly, not really knowing how else to respond. "How about you? How have you been?"

"I'm fine," she said with a tired shrug. "Getting back to work. Maybe back to school too. I don't know yet. Just trying to figure everything out right now."

"No need to rush, right?"

"I wish there was no reason to rush, but I have to get back to everything. Samuel wouldn't want me to be sad forever either — as hard as that is. I miss him... but I have to do what's best for our son and this family." Charlotte was silent for a moment; Walter regrettably didn't want to say anything either. Soon, she was examining him once again.

"What?" he asked, curious.

"So... you and Yvette, huh?"

Walter shrugged sarcastically. "I guess we will see, right?"

Suddenly, Po rubbed his nose against his hand, seemingly warming to him. Walter began rubbing his head and Po sat beside him, enjoying being petted by a new palm.

"Just make sure you look out for her," Charlotte told him. "I'm sure I don't have to tell you that she has been through a lot lately, but if she's going out with you. I'm sure she'll be fine. Just be a little patient with her for me."

Walter was flattered but curious. "You seem to have a lot of faith in me."

Charlotte snorted a bit. "You're a good kid, Walter, and I think you're good for my sister. I don't really think that too often, so don't let me regret saying that."

"Thanks, Charlotte." Still flattered by her blessing — as Walter liked to see it — was something he wasn't expecting, and didn't realize it was something he wanted. Seeming, only Mr. Anders's approval remained.

"And, Walter, I want you to know that Samuel was stubborn, but he couldn't be mad at you forever. He had his own demons you had nothing to do with, and he might've not said it aloud, but he forgave you. I forgave you."

"Yvette told you, didn't she?" Walter had suddenly realized this.

Charlotte nodded. "Maybe I should have known she was interested in you when she brought that up. It bothered her because it bothered you. I just wanted to tell you that because... well, we all have to move on. That's what my Samuel would want. I know that."

Walter felt a subtle smile poke out between his cheeks, but he couldn't deny the sour taste coating his lips. Charlotte's words reminded him of his cousin Ciara's when he saw her at Samuel's funeral. Even now, Samuel's death was still affecting them all.

"So," Charlotte said, back in her pleasant tone, "when was the last time you saw Michael?"

Charlotte led him back to the living room. Laying on the couch and beneath a gray blanket checkered with yellow ducklings was Charlotte and Samuel's infant son. He was sleeping soundlessly, his breath barely made a sound. It made Walter crack a small side smile.

"He's getting big," he whispered.

Charlotte smiled and thanked him. "You should come to his first birthday party next month. It will probably be boring with a bunch of little kids running around the house, so I don't expect you to stay long, but Michael would be happy to see you, not to mention Yvette would too."

Walter smirked. "She's been helping you plan the party, right?"

"Help me? She's been handling most of the party plans herself. I don't know how she does it all. Trying to keep herself busy, I suppose. So, show her a good time tonight, Walter. Help her get her mind off things and just have some fun. Can you do that for me?"

He nodded solemnly. "Of course."

Soon, he and Charlotte heard footsteps descending down the steps and saw thick curls bouncing down Yvette's back. She wore baby blue — on her short cotton dress, her fitted jeans jacket that hung above her waist and her low-top white Converses. When she saw him, Yvette's eyes brightened above her gentle smile. He stared for a moment, memorized by her welcoming smile, and wouldn't dare turn away.

"Hey," Walter greeted.

"Hey," Yvette replied with her grin. She seemed a bit nervous the way she grasped her hands together. However, her nervousness seemingly simmered as Walter approached and embraced her. Around his waist, her fingers intertwined and grasped him lovingly as her cheeks pressed against his chest. They held each other close, their embrace feeling like neither had seen the other in ages. Even so, it felt right.

"You smell good," she smirked.

That made Walter chuckle a bit. "So do you."

Charlotte, on the other hand... "Didn't you two just see each other in school?" she asked, but neither were bothered by that. "And why didn't you tell me that Walter was your date?"

Yvette ignored her with a roll of her eyes. "I hope you two weren't down here talking about me."

"What else is there to talk about?" Walter said slyly while smiling. "You ready?"

Yvette matched her smile with his. "Of course."

The two were making their way out the door when Charlotte warned, "You better not keep my sister out too late, Walter, or I'll come looking for you."

He chuckled. "Don't worry, I won't."

"You won't?" Yvette asked; playfully, desperately.

Walter whispered, "Yeah, but I'm just telling her what she wants to hear."

"I hear that, Walter," Charlotte scolded before turning to her sister. "Be safe and have fun. I'll be here when you get back, Evey. I'm not going anywhere tonight."

Yvette nodded. "Okay. Tell Dad I'll see him later."

When Walter and Yvette got outside the house, they were both a bit nervous. Yvette had a grin on her face but Walter couldn't tell what was underneath. For Walter, he'd hoped that this day could have been the beginning of something he coveted for some time, but, in reality, it all just felt like everything was coming to an end — unforgettable moments soon forgotten.

Yvette found his hand and held it there. "So, how far is the carnival from here?"

"It's not a carnival, Yvette," he laughed, "it's a food fair. Anyway, it's just a bus ride and a small walk away. It is the last day but if it gets too crowded we can find something else to do. No worries. We have a lot of time."

She giggled a little as her grasp on his hand grew tighter. "It doesn't matter what we do."

The bus ride was only a few stops away, so they arrived at a food fair not long after. The large city park was covered with tents, with striped pavilions and colorful booths with their colorful strobe lights. There were several mobile rides that dotted the park like bumper cars, a few family coasters and swing rides, a few kiddie rides not worth mentioning and the large Ferris wheel. Around the grounds were dozens and dozens of food booths while a few sold children's toys or held carnival games for various prizes. It wasn't too crowded and Walter was happy about that. Besides mainly chattering and screaming children, there was feel-good music playing throughout the grounds as well as jingles coming from the rides. Yvette seemed pleasant and even enjoyed the lights and colors. Every corner of the carnival was full of distractions; just enough to keep Yvette's mind away from grief — even just for a time.

Walter was happy to see the many foods, sweets and delicacies put a smile on her face. He even laughed uncontrollably when the pumpkin punch gave her a thin orange mustache. Soon she was laughing back at him when his kabob left BBQ sauce all over his lips and cheeks. Yvette went on laughing as he struggled to get all of it off.

"Aww… look at you," she said when she finally took a napkin and finished up for him. "So messy."

"Oh, shut up," he replied as she continued to titter and tend to him.

After trying a few different foods, the two began walking through the grounds a bit. Yvette was always pointing at the many bright ornaments they saw, and Walter liked seeing her so gleeful. They even saw a few others from school, and even stumbled upon Donnie. He was on a date too with a girl neither of them knew. However, before he and his date walked off, Donnie gave the couple a wink and a smile. Walter and Yvette shared a confused look then laughed once their schoolmate was gone and out of earshot.

"So, how about we go on a ride?" Yvette asked some time after strolling through the grounds.

Walter was a bit surprised by this with the lines and all. "Sure. Which one should we go on first?"

Yvette tapped her chin and looked around and stopped at the pirate pendulum and watched it sway and swing. "I've never been on a pendulum ride before."

"Really? Then come on. Let's go."

The pirate ship pendulum was fun, so was the "Colossus" Drop Tower and the Whipping Tilt-a-Whirl. After every ride, Yvette would end up apologizing for how loud she would

374

scream or the many times she clutched onto him when she was afraid. On the other hand, the wacky funhouse was strange, shocking and silly all at once. Walter had her on his radar while playing bumper cars, and crashed into her relentlessly while Yvette was no doubt the better shot and bested him at the duck hunt. Funny enough, she was even better at gloating than he was but it wasn't enough to win the large fluffy pink kitten she had her eye on. Walter even tried again, not backing down, but he couldn't win the pink kitten either. Even so, her smile never wavered. Instead, it grew, even when they only won a small purple giraffe.

When they were walking past a crane machine, a short kid was crying as he lost all his money trying to get a small stuffed animal himself. Neither Walter nor Yvette could understand the boy when he tried to show and tell which animal he wanted. He was sobbing too much. However, Yvette eventually offered him her purple giraffe.

"Really?" the boy said, his eyes watering. Fortunately, he stopped crying. "I can have it?"

Yvette smiled and nodded. "Sure. I want you to have it."

The boy hugged the giraffe tightly. "Thank you, miss."

Before she could respond, the boy ran off and disappeared.

"Well, look at you," said Walter.

"You see, I'm just the sweet one between the two of us," she chuckled.

"No, I was talking about him calling you 'miss.' I thought that was funny."

"Oh, shut up." Yvette nudged into him and it only made it all the more funnier.

She chuckled. "Whatever. I'll probably lose it before he does."

375

Slowly but surely, there were less open spaces within the grounds as the crowds began coming in to enjoy the last day of the food fair themselves. It didn't seem to bother Yvette though, yet they evaded as many people as possible. However, regardless of how long the lines became, Yvette was willing to wait to get on the one ride she wanted to take, the Ferris wheel. Her eyes gleamed at the rainbow of lights that flashed and danced in various patterns with the rhythm of its music. Less inviting however was the length of the waiting line itself.

"I haven't been on one since fifth grade," Yvette told him excitedly. "I love to see the lights from that high up. Come on before the line gets longer." Yvette grabbed both his hands and led him as he faked an annoyed look.

It was nearly thirty minutes before their turn was up, but the time was spent laughing, joking and apologizing for bumping into others. The time might have slugged on or the line was moving slowly, but the couple were more interested in each other than how long it took. Even so, soon they were strapping in and waiting for the wheel to climb.

The Ferris wheel was undoubtedly tall, Walter couldn't tell the amount of stories either. Being able to see the many streets and buildings from so high up was a crazy sight. The sea of lights below made Yvette's eyes glow with a brilliant twinkle. The higher they climbed, the more the fair below seemed to vanish as if Walter and Yvette were the only ones for miles. After the second go around, the wheel stopped at every seat, giving the riders a chance to view the city from the top. When it was their turn, Yvette leaned up a little to feast on the countless lights below.

"Beautiful," she observed wondrously, nearly muttering her amazement.

Walter smiled. "It is." When he looked over at her, the thousands of lights reflected off her eyes and made them sparkle orange and gold. "So are you."

Yvette blushed as her eyes met his, but, unlike Walter expected, she didn't hide it from him or suddenly turn away. Her shoulders rose slightly and her head sank shyly, but, those big brown eyes, they never left him.

"Thank you for bringing me out tonight, Walter," Yvette said warmly. "I needed it... and you're the only person I want to be here with."

Walter grinned, his eyes deeply into hers. "I feel the same way."

Yvette's smile was brighter than the lights below, and her eyes shined the brightest. They were deep and flit back and forth between his own, searching in a way; even when her smile simmered and lips slightly parted. It was at that moment, the world seemed to come to halt. The music had stopped, the shattered voices below had ceased and everything seemed like a distance memory. Walter and Yvette only saw one another and Walter began to lean in closer to her. Yvette shifted backward slightly and nervously... but was undeterred. Her eyes were still searching and her parted lips showed a speechless desire. Once again, he leaned in and his lips found hers. Yvette nervously drew back when their lips met, but soon she opened her lips to his and their eyes shut together. Walter felt her palm against his cheek and her fingers gently caressed the peach fuzz beneath his ear. Slowly, he wrapped his arm around her in response and held her closely as if she might fall. She felt so soft and weightless against him that he held her tenderly.

"I like your lips," Yvette whispered when she found the chance, her bottom lip perched between her teeth. "You're a really good kisser."

Walter made a soft smile before finding her lips again. He embraced her closely, holding her lovingly while her fingers ran gently across his ear and to the back of his neck. At that moment, they were vulnerable and wicked, yet, even at their age, they didn't care who saw. Neither wanted the kiss to end, but soon they realized they were both descending back down to the bottom of the wheel.

While wrapped into one another, Walter and Yvette stared at each other until they shared a light laugh together. It was all so wonderfully silly and nothing else seemed to matter.

When they exited the ride, Yvette asked, "Can I show you something?"

Walter grinned. "What is it?"

"One of my favorite places. I haven't been there in months. Do you want to see it? It's not too far from here."

Walter nodded. "Sure."

Yvette took both his hands again and led Walter out the fairgrounds and deeper into the park. The large ground dotted with various trees was darker and cooler as the crowds and music behind them slowly faded. The scattered streetlights glowed over vacant areas, and a few other people were walking across the field or occupying park benches. They soon walked off the path into a small clearing of dark grass. Walter felt a certain uneasiness as he soon realized where they were. It was the dream all over again, with the same dying streetlights and the ominous gloom. The only thing missing was the rain… and the ghost.

Not too far from the fair, they soon arrived at a wide wooden bridge stretched over a narrow lake. Dimly lit street lights dully shined above, but the moonlight picked up the slack. From both ends, vines wrapped and stretched throughout the stony arch of the bridge, some digging deep in-between the stones but either side had yet to reach in the middle. Yvette smiled softly and slowed her steps as their feet touched the wooden deck; her fingers still intertwined with Walter's.

"I loved coming to this bridge," Yvette told him. "My dad used to teach a class around here and would let me read in the park sometimes. That's when I found this bridge. I would always come here when I can. It's peaceful and a perfect place to read. It's better in the daytime too, I promise."

Walter smiled as he put his bag down against the stones. "It *is* peaceful here." Even the water below was still as if the night's cold had frozen it. Sometimes a gust of wind would swoop by and a few ripples would drift across the surface, but it was mostly still. "I like it. Why did you stop coming?"

Yvette shrugged. "I don't know. School and studying, mainly. Well... that's not true. Mainly the newspaper and having to stay after school some days. Then my dad stopped teaching too, so... there's that."

Walter walked along the bridge and looked down at the moonlight shining upon the lake's soft ripples. All he could hear were crickets singing nearby, along with a few distant frogs belching along the coast.

"This place seems like you," Walter went on. "A quiet place to just be alone. I can see you sitting down here, reading or studying."

Yvette made a silly snorting sound. "You realized that, huh?"

"I realize a lot."

"Oh really?" Yvette's hands fell to her hips. "A lot, huh?"

"Yeah. I realized that I've only seen you eat a few times."

"Good." She chuckled.

Walter smiled. "I know you have a fear of being misunderstood. Not like most people, but I think it's somehow different for you — not only being misunderstood but someone thinking you don't understand something. Like how you ask me, 'does that make sense' sometimes? I guess what I'm trying to say is you like to be considered one of the smartest in the room and not the other way round."

Yvette sighed but couldn't help but grin. "Not one of my best qualities."

Walter smiled. "I realized that what you wear kind of expresses how you feel at the time. Well... the color you wear."

She chuckled. "Yeah. I usually wear certain colors depending on how I feel that day. I'm not really a fashionable kind of girl, but... you know."

"You know, huh? You should like me now."

"Shut up!"

Walter chuckled. "But honestly, you always look good to me."

Blushing, Yvette chuckled and turned away from him a little. "Oh, really?"

"Really." Watching her blush and grasp on her ear, still trying not to let Walter see much. "And that."

"And what?"

He smiled. "You always play with your ear when you are nervous."

Yvette was chuckling now. "You realize all that?"

Walter stepped closer to her in the center of the bridge. "Yeah. I do." She looked at him as he gently rested a hand upon her cheek. When he leaned into her this time, she raised her lips to meet his right away. They were even softer than the last — more relaxed, even — yet Walter felt her nervous fingers clutch behind his back. With barely any space between them, Walter was a bit nervous himself but the way she kissed him, it only made him hold her closer.

When they broke apart for a breath, Walter caught Yvette staring up at him, not hiding the dimples or blushes on her cheeks like she usually does. Her eyes were bright and unblinking.

"What is it?" he asked, smiling.

"Nothing..." Yvette shook her head. "I just like looking at you." Heat rose from Walter's cheeks as a tight blush ran across them when she said that. "You know what else I like?"

"What else?"

"Everything." Yvette smiled then drew him closer to her, their lips meeting once again.

The trees, the critters, the water, the moon... the diary — nothing else existed. A vast emptiness took its place... an emptiness only fit for the two of them. Their lips conjured a sweet nothing, and, when they separated, the world returned with a satisfying exhale. Both their eyes were closed however and Walter gently rested his forehead on hers for comfort.

They stood in silence for a time, wrapped in one another when Walter asked, "Are you ready?"

Yvette looked up at him with sad eyes and nodded. "Yes." However, once it was fished out of her bag, she grew weary. "Wait... I... I have something to tell you."

"What's wrong?"

She sighed. "I went to see Dr. Pierce on Friday."

Walter was taken aback slightly. "Why?" Prying further for answers came to mind, but he waited patiently for her to respond.

"I had to tell her," she said, lowly and desperately. "I had to make sure that you were fine. If you both lose your memory of the diary then everything might go back to normal."

"If she doesn't remember? What do you—" His words failed him as his mind was pulled elsewhere. He realized why the

381

doctor's memory might vanish. "You let Dr. Pierce use the diary, didn't you?"

Yvette nodded briskly. "I had to. If she doesn't remember anything about the diary then it should help you, right? I thought about it. I don't think memories just cease to exist. There is always something left in the brain. A piece of a memory. But if you both don't remember then how could it resurface? She might just think you're grieving after that and nothing else is wrong."

"But wouldn't she remember you came to see her and vouch for me?" Walter wondered. "What if it doesn't just work like that?"

"This works, Walter, I know it does. Forgetting about the diary will make her less suspicious. She will know I came because I am worried about you, but that's it."

"Maybe but..." Walter sighed heavily. "Yvette, we are talking about a supernatural book. We don't know what we're messing with here. And my mom... she knows about the diary."

Yvette was shocked. "What?"

"She doesn't know what it is and hasn't used it or anything, but Dr. Pierce has asked her about it and she asked me about it too. She thinks it's a book we use to write down our thoughts that we can't tell to anyone else. But my mom never used the diary. If she doesn't lose her memory too, what happens then? If my mom goes and asks the doctor about it some other time, what is the doctor going to say? How can I prove it to her if I can't remember the diary either?"

An incredulous gasp left Yvette's lips as she realized the mistake she might have made. "But... I thought if she didn't know either then... it could be avoided."

"You don't need to worry, Yvette. Yes, we don't know what could happen, but..." He held her gently by the shoulders. "I know you want to help, but I'm afraid too. I…" Walter shook off the hesitation and continued. "When you agreed to go out with me, before we learned so much about Gordon and… I wanted to just spend this night together because… I don't know if I'll feel the same way about you after… I don't know if you will feel the same about me either. I've thought, 'Is it all because of the diary… everything between us?'"

"No," she said breathlessly as she grasped his hand. "It's not because of that stupid book, Walter."

He smiled as looked into her eyes. "Yvette, I've liked you for a while now and all the time we've spent together makes me like you even more. I don't care if it's some diary that brought us together because it happened, but… I don't want this stupid book to be the reason why all those feelings go away."

Yvette looked up at him, her eyes glossy and bright. Without preamble, she held Walter by the jacket, pulled him into her. She kissed him again; strongly, deeply, more passionate than the first. Walter kissed her back and held her close to stop her shivering. "I'm sorry."

Walter wiped the falling tears with a grin. "It's okay, but we are supposed to be a team—"

"And we still can be. I will be there for you regardless of what happens. I could forget the diary, but I can't forget how I feel about you, Walter."

There was a knot in his throat and Walter didn't know how to respond to that. Soon all that might not matter and that worried him. Instead, he nodded. Yvette grinned anxiously before resting her cheek on his chest. Hoping to calm her, he combed his fingers through her curls slowly.

I love you, Yvette, is all Walter wanted to say. "Everything is going to be okay, I promise. You believe me… don't you?"

With a little sniff, she nodded against him. "I do."

For a moment, the two were silent. Walter and Yvette stayed in each other's arms not saying a word and enjoyed the warmth of one another. It was exactly where Walter wanted to be.

Yvette nuzzled into him then paused before asking, "Can we stay here forever?"

Walter felt himself smile as he cupped her head and held her close like a baby's. "Yes."

Even though neither wanted to move, they both knew it was getting later in the night and neither could linger long. A sheet of melancholy spread above them, but they both felt safe; something they hadn't felt in a while.

"Ready?" Walter asked.

She took a moment, but Yvette eventually nodded slowly and sniffed again. "Yes."

In due time, they separated and Walter made a half grin. "You can get it."

Yvette made her own half grin before walking toward his bag and pulling the diary out of it. As she returned to him, her eyes dwelled on the diary a bit; grasping it with both hands as if it were already open. Everything seemed to turn silent at the moment. All Walter could hear was Yvette's sad sigh.

She opened the diary and it rested above both their opened hands. "Thanks for holding the diary… after—"

"You don't have to talk about it," he assured her. "It's okay."

She smiled nervously. "Thank you, Walter… for everything. I don't know what I would do without you. I hope you know how much you mean to me."

"Well, isn't that sweet?"

A sudden voice came out of thin air beside Walter and Yvette. Standing in the center of the bridge was Samuel. Although the lights above were dimly lit, the smug on his face wasn't hard to see.

"Samuel?" Yvette muttered.

The dead man's smug turned sinister. "How are you, Yvette?"

She never replied, simply gasped heavily as she stepped back.

Walter stepped in front of her and began shaking his head slowly in disbelief. "How did you—"

"Like I told Yvette before, there is more to this tome than just being your little play thing."

"Why don't you tell us then?" Walter insisted. "Tell us what we don't know."

Samuel smiled as he slyly ignored him. First, he cleared his throat. "So, you have a deal for me?" Walter and Yvette faced one another nervously. "Do you have a deal for me tonight?" he reiterated impatiently.

"I want to know something," Walter spoke up. "Who are you, really... and what exactly do you want?"

Samuel grinned once again. "Your desire is mine."

"That's not an answer," Yvette sharply chimed in before anyone else could.

Then suddenly, Walter remembered what Gordon told him. "You are the faceless man, aren't you?"

Yvette slowly turned to him. Her face seemed like she was close to vomiting. "You... You've seen him too?"

Walter could have told her the truth just then, that he never did, but it would be too much to explain. They had already agreed to never speak of Gordon again, so he lied and said, "Yes."

Speechless, Yvette's lips lay ajar and silent, her body seemed to go limp but the brown in her eyes were shaking with fear. Samuel began to chuckle at that, even growing to quite a maniacal laugh. This caught both their attention.

"Secrets," Samuel sneered. "Neither one of you can save the other from them. And as for you, cousin, still a little liar as always." Taking a few steps forward, he continued. "You have never seen the faceless man."

There it is, the moment where the Samuel and spirit of the diary met. The façade was starting to crumble before them. Yvette's eyes had widened now as everything that was being revealed was glass scattering.

A wicked smile perched upon Walter's lips anyway. "Yes I have. No matter what mask you wear, you're like a faceless spirit wearing whatever face we tell you to. You don't even have a face for yourself, do you?"

The man in the Samuel mask made a grin. "Yet you both fear me. Isn't that why you are here?"

He snorted confidently. "Why ask questions you already know the answer to?"

Samuel smirked then gestured to the diary. "Open the tome."

Furious, Walter tried to simmer himself and he turned back to Yvette. There was fear in her eyes but was visibly trying to keep everything together. Her fingers trembled as they both held the diary. Walter opened the front cover and a contract was written in an unfamiliar and possibly ancient cursive.

I hereby take on the keepership of this tome. From this moment forward, I am responsible for this tome and any secrets the spirit of the tome might possess. I understand that the diary must protect its keeper from any the tome deems a threat. I also understand that this tome can only be used by the keeper, and if anyone else were to do so and/or the tome feels misused by anyone, including the keeper, the tome will be forced to protect itself and seek a new keeper elsewhere if necessary.

*Signed:*_____

"Whoever takes ownership will keep their memories of the tome," Samuel explained. "All other bonds will be severed. Once they awaken from their next slumber, their memories will be gone."

Walter instantly felt nervous hearing that. A few swoops and swirls with ink and everything would change. One nightmare might come to an end only for another to begin. Yvette would be alone to endure the grief of her mother along with everything she now knew about her death. Walter could only wonder, *If I'd never found the diary, would Yvette be better off? Would any of this ever happen if it wasn't for me?* A part of him had to know that he was to blame, but he felt some solace knowing that now Yvette realized the diary could never fill the hole her mother left behind. Still, the unsigned contract in shimmery gold ink was haunting.

Yvette looked into his eyes, speechless and sobbing.

"It's okay, Yvette," he told her.

"I know what you are thinking, sweetheart."

When Walter heard the voice speak, it startled him. It wasn't Samuel who spoke, but the voice was still familiar. From the corner of his eye, Walter saw a woman standing on the opposite side of the bridge. She wore a familiar black dress with tiny red roses that seemed to match her rouge lips. Her ringlets laid on her left shoulder and sharp eyes were fixated solely on Yvette. "Should I remind you what that boy did to you, sweetheart?"

Walter felt himself gasp as he said, "Mrs. Anders?" Seeing the woman conjured without preamble made his mouth twist in anger. The diary was toying with Yvette.

The woman went on. "It doesn't matter what you feel for this boy," she said coldly. "He's dangerous. You know this."

This made Yvette scowl. "*You're* dangerous. Walter didn't do anything, you know that. But it doesn't matter. It doesn't justify why you betrayed me. Did you forget how you tarnished my mother's memory? How you tried to drive us both insane? Me and Walter? Give me one reason why I should trust you again?"

Samuel broke in instead. "Just think about what happened to your mother, Yvette," he said curtly. "Imagine that happening to you. Do you think she would want you to share the same fate as her?"

Yvette was livid now. "How dare you? You don't know anything about my mom."

"Well…" Mrs. Ander chimed in with a red smile. "I know what you know."

Walter felt himself growl, but before he could react, Samuel asked, "What about you, Walter? What happens if you hurt her?"

Walter grimaced with an incredulous stare. "Hurt her?"

"You can't hide what you want. You want the diary for yourself, don't you?"

It was Mrs. Anders who added, "You're just as selfish as Samuel says. You don't want to protect my daughter."

"I'm not your daughter," Yvette said furiously, nearly screaming across the bridge.

"And you are sure you won't hurt her?" Samuel continued coaxing his cousin condescendingly.

When Walter turned back to him, he saw something laying a few feet between them. Eyes widened with shock, stepped closer and saw Yvette's body; bloody, mangled and even malformed. Her big brown eyes had turned to a ghostly pale while the corners of her lips had streams of petrified red tears frozen on her cheeks. Her curls had become a tangled mess and her clothes were tattered with scattered stains of blood. Everything about her was still and dead.

Samuel shook his head solemnly. "What a shame."

Speechless and nearly gasping for air, Walter fell to his knees. Desperately, he crawled the few steps towards her, suddenly feeling too fatigued to walk. With every inch, his arms gradually felt weaker like they might fall from under him. Inches away, he raised a hand to reach out to her, but then he was suddenly struck with horror. He slowly brought both tired hands closer and saw what he feared. They were both covered in blood. The pain in his hands worsened by the slight of it. Large bloody marks were even stained all over his shirt causing his heart to begin pounding and pulsing against his chest.

He didn't know if the tears had come before or after, but Walter quickly pushed himself away and crawled until his back met the rocky archway hard. He had forgotten it was even there and the sudden pain was payment. As the tears forming in his eyes began to blur his vision, he quickly muttered. "This... this isn't real... This isn't real..."

"Is it?"

Trying to ignore Samuel's voice, he cupped his ears tightly and repeated, "This isn't real... This isn't real... This isn't real..." over and over under his breath. The more he said it, the more he believed it. His breathing slowed along with his heart rate and that fear began to slowly abate. "It's not real." With his lips tight and a grimace, Walter wiped his eyes then slowly opened them.

He found himself alone. The faceless man's puppets were and Yvette had vanished. There was some solace with that and, looking down at himself, the red stains were gone as well. Still, the solace was short-lived. Grimacing and rubbing the stinging pain in his head, he slowly rose. It wasn't until he found his footing that he saw the diary laying on the wooden bridge where he and Yvette were standing. He grabbed the diary from the ground and gripped it tightly. Instinctively, he flipped through several pages back and forth through the entire book. The contract had vanished. Angrily, he slammed the book shut then began surveying his surroundings thoroughly.

"Yvette!?" he yelled hoping for a response. There was none. The entire park was dead with silence. Not even the crickets or the frogs had anything to say. He couldn't even hear the wind. Silence was so engulfing that all he could hear was his own ear pulsing.

Suddenly, the silence was pierced with a harrowing scream. Without thinking and with the diary in hand, Walter ran towards the scream and uncharted darkness.

The further he ran, the more trees he passed. The woods grew thicker and darker as there weren't any lights blinking about. The thick branches and clusters of leaves let in little moonlight for Walter to see. Soon the scream came again and he stopped abruptly as they seemed to have migrated away. *Is she running from something?* he wondered, even so, he seemed convinced. *But from what?*

His question was answered right away. A heavy stomp quaked behind him and Walter couldn't help but jump in fright. Large orange eyes were lurking towards him. A shadowy four-legged gargantuan beast seemed to be burning through the trees; a black fiery mane whipping violently with every step. Beneath the orange eyes, a ghostly mouth opened where dozens and dozens of ghoulishly gray skulls made up its teeth and gums. Instead of a roar, the many heads turn to Walter in unison and hundred voices wail a whirlwind of agonizing screams. Swiftly, Walter shielded his eyes with his arms as small stones

390

and twigs began flying past him. Some collided with him, sliced through his clothes and even slashed his skin, but somehow he never fell or tumbled. The gust of wind of screams were seemingly endless, but when he got his bearings, he began sprinting in the opposite direction.

His mind might have been racing even faster, however. He first wondered where Yvette was, now he was just hoping she was somewhere alive. But, he couldn't daydream. He kept running and evading the trees, never turning back. He didn't need to. Walter could feel the ground rumbling and trees breaking behind him.

Soon, he quickly spotted a fallen tree in his path. With his adrenaline skyrocking, he heaved over mid-stride, however, the drop back down was farther than he thought. Walter fell a few extra feet deeper in a dark ravine. He could feel the jagged edges on his way down scraping at his legs, but when he hit the ground, he collided hard, tumbled and his knees and back took a bulk of the pain.

Darkness now surrounded Walter as well as protruding rocks. Even his loud, rapid breathing seemed to bounce off the jagged black walls. It took a moment for the pain in his wounds to simmer a little, but he soon reached outward hoping to stand. The sharp jagged stones might have aided him to his feet, but it felt like it was cutting though his skin as he rose. Walter unfortunately drew too close to the wall and another sharp stone snagged at his leg; through denim and skin. His body nearly buckled beneath him but then a hand caught him by the shoulder and balanced him back to his feet.

Walter let out a gasp. "Yvette?"

She shushed him as the shadow's quaking steps were growing louder and closer. "Don't move."

Walter froze suddenly. The eyes of the shadow crawled and gripped at the edge of the ravine and everything shook around him. A bellow of a hundred rang in Walter's ear. Everything seemed to rumble around, but the ravine held. The shadow's large head lurked around for a moment before turning and stomped off. Walter let out a exhale, realizing he was holding his breath the entire time.

"Are you okay?" she asked him.

Even nodding his head was a challenge. "I'm fine," Walter lied. He couldn't admit how much pain and fear he was feeling. He could only imagine what she was feeling as well. "Are you?"

"Yes. Do you have the diary?"

The diary. Only then did Walter realize that the diary was no longer bundled under his arm. "I did," he admitted, "but I think I dropped it."

"Do you think you remember where?"

"Maybe," he lied again. He had no idea where the diary might have dropped. He could only muse on all the zigzagging through so many trees and bushes. Then he thought of what Samuel — or whatever he was — said about keeping secrets and decided not to lie anymore. "I think I dropped it when I was running," he finally told her. Still, the thought of scouring through the dark made him weary, queasy even. It didn't matter how daunting it all seemed, they had to get the diary back. "We have to get out of here."

"No," the girl said suddenly, her voice impatient.

Walter turned to her, barely seeing her though the dark. "What do you mean?" No answer. "We can't stay here. Day or night, that shadowy… thing will chase us… or worse."

"But… Can't we just stay here?"

"Stay here?" *That doesn't sound like Yvette.* "We have to get the diary and sign the contract. You know that."

Suddenly, a pair of orange eyes glowed within the dark and a light giggle filled the ravine and grazed across the ragged rocks. "I thought being alone with me… is what you always dreamed of."

Walter suddenly shifted away from her, pain and all. As he backed away, those large orange eyes followed him. They grew brighter as she stepped closer and she revealed herself more clearly in the dim moon-blue glow.

"Why so surprised to see me?" she asked sweetly. "You were just calling my name." Then her face turned puzzled and her head cocked to the side. "Weren't you?"

He gasped. "You knew where I was all along… didn't you?"

She smiled at him. When she opened her mouth, a collage of voices spoke in unison "Of course I did."

Quickly and with his bare hands, Walter began to climb the ravine, using sharped edged stones to hoist his mangled body up the walls. It wasn't long after that he felt a strong tug at his heel like his foot was being ripped off. His fingers dug into the sharp rocks but he wouldn't falter. Her eyes and lips were scowling while her nostrils flared viciously. Steam might have been pouring out her nose but it was too dark to see. He was able to get halfway up the edgy slope, but his grip was weakening. It might have been the last stretch he could muster, he extended his arm and felt a warm hand grasp his tightly.

393

"Hold… Hold on," said Yvette hoarsely, her voice straining from above him. Her second hand clinging onto his hand with all the strength she had and pulled.

When Walter looked back down at the orange-eyed doppelganger, he scowled even deeper.

"Kick her down," said Yvette, still trying to pull him up.

She didn't have to tell him twice. Walter's free foot kicked straight to her nose several times until the doppelganger lost her grip and fell. When she hit the ground, she bursted into a thick, black smoke that blossomed and slowly rose from the ravine like ink in still water. As it dispersed, the black slowly formed into a dead rose.

"Are you okay?" she asked while helping Walter to his feet. The cuts upon his palms were deep and terrible. Gobbets of sore meat were protruding from his palm or holding on by a sliver of flesh. "Stupid question," she surmised.

"It's nothing," Walter assured her through his gritted teeth as he gripped his wounded hand tightly. Fortunately his other hand didn't feel as much pain. *Luckily it's my writing hand that's still good,* he told himself.

Suddenly, Yvette's eyes widened as she watched him. "What are you… Don't…"

Annoyed, Walter ripped off the hanging meat with his teeth and spat it out. Somehow, it felt better after. Yvette gritted her teeth in shock when she saw that.

Walter wiped his lips clean. "Sorry," he said.

"You sure you're okay?"

He nodded, trying to ignore the pain running through body. He was trying his best not to worry her more than he already was. "I'm fine. We need to find the diary. I had it but… I must have dropped it."

"Find the diary?" Yvette asked, puzzled. "I have it here." It was true. He had just realized his bag was on her back and, sure enough, she fished the old brown book from inside.

A sigh of relief graced his lips. "I thought I felt it in my hand."

"And I thought you disappeared or something. I was distracted by… her."

"It's okay. Samuel distracted me too, trying to separate us. I thought I heard you scream, so I ran towards your voice."

"And I thought I heard you calling my name. So, I ran after you."

"It doesn't matter now. Once we sign the contract we'll be fine."

She nodded. She opened the diary and found the contract and its cursive. She fished for her pen, with eagerness permeating her brown eyes. Walter wanted to sign it himself, but, with fear in his stomach, it didn't seem to matter anymore.

Suddenly, a thick shadow cloaked over them. Gray clouds swallowed the moon above and the darkness below thickened, covering the contract in black. Neither of them could see but they both began digging for their phones. Unfortunately, Walter's phone's screen wasn't responding and he nearly flung it into the ravine.

"Yours isn't working either, is it?" Yvette asked, her breath growing heavier. Panic was starting to settle in.

"The closest lights are at the bridge," Walter said, still applying pressure to his hand. "Do you know the way there?"

She nodded with a grimace. "I know the way, but does it matter? The diary is controlling everything around us."

"It's just trying to scare us," Walter said boldly. He couldn't tell how much he even believed that. *I don't even know what we are dealing with*

Walter felt Yvette press the diary against his chest. "You should hold onto the diary," she said, frightened and forceful. "I don't think it can hurt me so you should hold onto it. I'm still the keeper of the diary so it needs me."

Her hands were shivering as she held it. Even with the pain, Walter didn't take the diary just yet but grasped her hands instead and rested his forehead on hers. She was shivering. "Everything is going to be fine," he told her. "I promise." Without a word, Walter felt her nodding her head against his. Only then did he take the diary and slip it under his arm, then take her by the hand with the other. "Alright. Come on."

Suddenly, an ominous rattle began to play from somewhere not too far off. That wasn't the only one. A second responded from the left then another from their right.

Yvette tightened her grip on his hand. "What is that?"

The rattles were growing closer, but the rattles sounded more like chuckling now; chuckling bones. Walter didn't want to wait and find out. "We have to go. We stay close and keep moving. That's our only choice."

Yvette nodded but he could sense the uncertainty.

The dark was unkind. Besides silhouettes of bushes and trees, it was even harder to see than before. They nearly slipped and fell twice then thrice, but never slowed. The rapid beats of Walter's heart seemed to thump in his ear which was out of sink with the many rattles following briskly behind.

Suddenly, Walter felt an abrupt tug at his arm as Yvette halted. "Wait, wait, wait…" she shrieked. "My foot. It's caught in a root."

Walter quickly drew closer to her as she found his shoulders. Holding her stead, Yvette yanked her foot several times until she was free. Walter grabbed her waist before she fell.

"Are you okay?" he asked.

However, when she nodded instead of speaking, they realized the rattling had stopped… but they weren't alone. From the dark, a pair of smoking eyes suddenly appeared within the outlines of the trees like bright red embers. Several low squeaking sounds seeped past the trees and reminded Walter of old door hinges. There was another chord of creepy chuckles coming through the trees and every note closer than the last. His eyes were beginning to adjust to the darkness, he realized the slender and dark figure.

"Come on," he said. "We have to keep moving."

Walter pulled her closer to him, beginning to flee the opposite direction, but it wasn't long before something suddenly whipped past their feet and knocked them to the ground. He felt his shoulder scrap against a protruding root while Yvette nearly fell on top of him and groaned as she hit the ground. Walter grasped his shoulder in pain feeling the light slash through his jacket.

"Are you okay?" he asked Yvette, trying to quickly regain his bearings.

"Yeah," she whimpered. "Just my leg. You?"

"Shoulder, but fine. Wait…" Suddenly, Walter didn't feel the diary in his possession anymore. Walter hadn't realized it right away, but had no intention to make the same mistake twice.

"The diary. I think I dropped it when we slipped." He was already beginning to search the darkness around him and he could hear her searching as well, but the rattles and squeaking were still coming their way.

"Oh no, no, no…" Panic rumbled in her voice. "Where is it?"

"We'll find it," he promised, a little more roughly than he intended. Losing the diary was his fault and felt the tension growing within him. His fear was showing more than he wanted. His phone was already out of his pocket but he had already forgotten that it had proved to be useless. However, his eyebrows rose as he felt his father's lighter in his pocket. Walter felt a rumble within him as his hand dug in his pocket. The fears caused his fingers to lock up and he could barely grasp it.

"I can't find it," Yvette nearly shouted, still searching through the dark. "I can't find it… I can't…"

Walter hurried, one hand in his pocket and the other surveyed and searched through the dirt, the roots and the bones of dead trees. Then he felt something rough and bound in leather. It had to be the diary. Fortunately, his lighter was out of his pocket by then. "I think I found it," Walter said and flicked the lighter.

The flames sparked and burned still. The diary was where he thought it was, but it wasn't alone. A thick foul breath brushed his fingers and Walter was met with a gray skull staring back at him with smoke pouring from its eyes. As the skull's mouth opened with all its broken teeth, Walter quickly tried to pull the diary away. Instead, its clawed skeletal hand dug into him and began to heave and pull him away.

"Walter!" Yvette yelled. Slightly dazed, she found her feet and ran after him.

Stones and perturbing roots snagging into his body as he was forcefully dragged away from her. Walter looked up, trying to see how to release himself from his attacker. The darkness seemed to recede and he was able to see it; a fully-structured skeleton who's bones seemed to be melting away yet never fell apart. His hand felt like it was ripping apart and blood was already pouring from his skin as the unbearable pain caused tears to pour from his eyes. Unfortunately, Walter had already dropped the lighter, even so, he didn't know if the skeleton could feel pain or how well fire matched against bone. However, he still held onto the diary for dear life but needed Yvette to take it.

"I'm going to let go of the diary," Walter shouted so she could hear him. "Grab it." He didn't wait for a response. The pain was too great and was no use fighting back. He let the diary go and he saw Yvette scoop it up. He only hoped her theory was right. It should give her the time she needs.

"I got it," she announced.

"Sign it," Walter nearly screamed. He couldn't deny the pain his hand was in. But it wasn't long before the skeleton let go of him but its smoking eyes were now set on Yvette. He tried to get up to stop it, but was slower than he hoped. "Hurry! Sign it!"

With a scowl, Yvette swung after the skeleton who avoided it. It didn't matter. Another chuckling skeleton was upon her, creeping on all fours.

"Behind you," Walter yelled, but to no avail. The skeleton had already jumped and tackled Yvette to the ground. She screamed as its clawed fingers dug into her shoulders, stopping her from shielding herself with the diary. Her theory was wrong. The diary was willing to hurt her.

399

Grimacing, Walter sprinted towards the skeleton who dug his sharp fingers into his arm and tackled it to the ground. Walter quickly grabbed and raised his pen in the air and plunged it right into a smoking red eye. Those chuckles turned to a screech as the skeleton clutched his eye as Walter quickly stood. The way it rolled to the ground and screeched in pain, Walter had proven that they do feel some kind of pain.

Yvette's attacker was up immediately and Walter stared him down, not sure of what to do next. Before it could attack him as well, Yvette quickly grabbed its leg and it toppled to the ground. It tried to bash its foot at Yvette, but she quickly let go and the foot missed. Walter quickly grabbed a fist full of dirt, and, before it could get to its feet, Walter pushed the dirt deep into its eyes. Walter flung his hand away as it screeched and fell back to the floor. It rolled back and forth several times then puffed into inky black smoke.

"Walter!" Yvette ran up and wrapped her arms around him and hugged him tightly to hold him up.

However, the wellness check was short lived. The two saw as the same skeleton was now standing and now one-eyed. It stood still before them and it wasn't alone. A few others began stepping forward from behind it. They were all cackling their teeth together, but the one-eyed one was silent. Not only was its right eye gone, but what looked like glowing lava or red-orange ink was pouring from the back socket down to its chin.

"I… have an idea," said Walter. His mind was racing but he wouldn't hesitate. "Quick, open the diary for me."

In the dark, Walter pressed his pen against a random page in the book while Yvette — terrified and peaking over at the creeping skeletons — held it up for him with shivering hands.

400

He scratched in the words as fast as he could, hoping he wrote them correctly. However, a few skeletons grew impatient and came up behind One-Eye and threw themselves at the two of them. Before long, two were pushing Walter to the ground, digging their claws into his arm to keep them spread apart, while another pair was forcing Yvette away from him.

"Walter!" she whined. "Please... Why are you doing this?"

Ignoring them both, One-Eye walked towards the diary. However, a sudden large stream of light shot down from the sky, through the trees and crashed into the ground before One-Eye could grab the diary. The impact caused the skeletons to let them go and even stumble. Walter and Yvette both shielded their eyes but Walter smiled as he looked up at their sudden arrival. The bright bluish light rose into a giant nearly as tall as the neighboring trees. The mouth of its helm was caged and a downward arrow-shaped slit showed its tiny white eyes. The giant dipped its head down and roared towards One-Eye, sending the skeleton off its feet and several feet back. The others reacted and all began attacking the giant at once.

Hoping to hinder him and find weaknesses in his armor, the skeletons climbed and crawled all around him. However, the giant grabbed them one by one and slammed them into the ground, the trees and into one another.

Yvette quickly grabbed the diary then ran to Walter. "You okay?" she asked while helping him to his feet.

"Yeah," he nodded although he was breathing through his teeth. However, the sight of her injured shoulders and the blood. "It's going to be okay. Look and see if the contract appears and we can sign it."

Yvette nodded. "Right."

But the light wasn't there for long. Soon, the shadowy thing had returned, its eyes were now red like blood. It washed over the giant like a wave of darkness. A wail of hundreds poured as it shadowed the giant whole, leaving nothing but darkness behind. Then suddenly, it was silent. All Walter could hear was his panting matching Yvette's. Neither of them moved an inch. The entire forest seemed as petrified as they were. There were no glowing eyes, no silhouette of trees, and Walter couldn't see Yvette right in front of him.

"Where did it go?" Yvette asked, whispering and weary.

"I don't know," Walter admitted. Even though he had lost his lighter, he still had the diary and his pen. "I wrote in the dark already. I can do it again."

"Let me. You are in a lot of pain."

Walter couldn't argue with her. He simply held the diary steady for her. Soon, he felt the pen pushed against the page and heard the scratching, and when she was done, she announced, "I think that should work."

"What did you—" A sudden burn ran through his wounded hand. He would have dropped the diary if Yvette hadn't taken hold of it.

"Raise your hand in the air and open it," she told him. "Trust me. It shouldn't hurt after."

So he did. As his arm lifted above his head, a large ball of fire busted above his bloody palm. Flames of red and oranges burned round and round and even seemed like it was melting into one another in endless swirls. Once the fire was burning, his palm wasn't. His fingers even grazed against the ball and it felt more like warm snow than fire.

402

"Yes," she said with such excitement. Even so, she wasted no time and began flipping through the pages to find the contract. When she found it, she smiled from ear to ear.

The flames made the cursive words glow gold. Yvette pressed her pen to the line and Walter felt a bit numb at once. He didn't want Yvette to take ownership, that hadn't changed. Everything she had suffered through with her mother would never go away. Still, he brought the flaming ball closer. The flames made the words glow an even brighter gold. However, before she could sign, the flaming ball began making a violent spark. Walter stepped back quickly as the ball was startled. Flames were beginning to wipe and whirl wildly out of control.

"What's happening?" Yvette asked, frightened.

"I don't know," he admitted. Unbearable heat began cooking his palm and boiling the blood. He tried to endure the pain and bring the flame back to Yvette to see, but suddenly the flames lifted from his hand and began to swirl around them. Like water, flames streamed from one tree to the next and Walter and Yvette were swiftly surrounded by a ring of fire. The two drew closer trying to escape the flames and heat, shading their eyes as embers and burning specks were jumping in all directions.

Suddenly, Yvette shrieked and the diary fell from her hand. Embers had found their way onto the pages and small flames were slowly overtaking it.

"What the—" Walter already fell to his knees. Even with pain running up his arms — one worse than the other — he tried to extinguish it. "Yvette," he called. "You don't have any water or something?"

"The diary…" She shook her head in disbelief. "It can't be burned," she said breathlessly, her eyes vacant yet filled with fear. "The diary… It can't—"

"Yvette! Look at me."

"No. Look at me."

Suddenly, Walter was struck in his side and was lifted up from the ground. He landed on the ground hard and quickly looked up towards Yvette. Standing next to her was a tall figure with long arms, crippling fingers and his nails were long and sharp. His back was hunched while his shoulders were thick and spread outward like small wings. He wore a tattered suit over his skeletal body and a fedora with a dead feather on top. But his face, there was no face at all; only veins stretching from where his eyes should have been. Somehow, that was the most terrifying part.

But he spoke and his voice was a thousand in one. "I told you… everything burns around him, didn't I?"

Yvette was petrified at the faceless man before her and seemed to be struggling to breathe.

"Yvette, don't listen to him!" Walter shouted. "It's not real!"

The faceless man ignored him. "Don't you understand?"

Yvette's began turning vacant as she stared at the blank face. "Understand? Do I… understand? Am I supposed to? Does… Does that make sense?" She seemed to be in a trance.

The flames were still spreading on the diary but Walter couldn't stop it no matter what he did. Soon it will all be ash. "Why are you doing this?"

"Sacrifice," said Yvette. Her voice was a whisker above a whisper. Even with the world burning around them, Walter could hear her like her lips were at his ear.

The face stretched upward — a smile, Walter presumed. "I always liked how bright you were. You might be my favorite keeper."

A grimace so tight stretched upon Walter's lips. "Keeper? What does that really mean?"

The faceless man turned to him with a lifeless glance. "My desire is hers."

Walter flitted his attention to Yvette whose unblinking eyes were staring back at the faceless man. "Yvette, snap out of it."

The faceless man made an ugly chuckle. Seeing his cheeks stretch where his mouth should have been was uncanny. "How about this? Yvette?"

When Walter turned back to her, Yvette was going into Walter's bag and pulling out his knife. Hauntingly, Yvette slowly turned to Walter as his bag fell from her fingers; her eyes unblinking.

The diary is still caught on fire, but he won't dare move with the blade in her hand. Yvette was vacantly staring at him but on her cheek was a single tear shining orange.

"Break that bound, Yvette," Walter shouted. "Only you can do it."

"Kill him, Yvette," the faceless man commanded, his eyeless stare still upon him. "Only you can do it."

She gripped the hilt tightly and held the knife at her side. Yvette's eyes never left Walter.

"I wish I had told you a long time ago…" Walter didn't know what else to say. The words were tumbling out of him.

"W… What…" Yvette struggled to speak. "What… What did… did you say?"

"I said, I wish I told you a long time ago that... that I love you, Yvette... and I would die protecting you if I have to."

Yvette's single tear was followed by many. Her lips were stern and the knife was still held tightly in her fist, but her eyes were flowing with tears of melancholy.

"R... Really?" she sniffed. "I..." Then a thin smile paid a visit to her as her tears flowed unhindered. "I love... you too, Walter."

"We have no time to mourn," the faceless man told her calmly. "Kill the boy... Now."

"I... I... I can't."

"Then allow me." Suddenly, the faceless man lunged after Walter with his fingers spread. He collided with Walter and his back met the ground hard. He quickly shielded his face and the monster crawled at him with wild arms.

"Get off of me," Walter yelled, trying to push the slender monster away, but with no avail. The monster's clawed hands were around his neck. If he had moved too quickly, they could break through Walter's skin. When he looked up at the faceless monster, the place where his mouth would have been began to melt and spread apart. Long jagged teeth broke through the melting skin, and the conjured mouth looked like it might eat him. Walter couldn't help but scream at the most frightening thing he had ever seen.

Suddenly, however, the faceless man froze. The terrible smirk had vanished but his teeth remained bared. Walter gasped as a trickle of black blood began falling from a sudden rip through the faceless man's skeletal body. "What? What is going on... I can't..."

"Sacrifice."

Both Walter and the monster struggled to look at Yvette. Walter's eyes grew wide as he saw his knife was still in her hand but the blade was resting upon her neck. Her tears still shined orange on her cheeks. However, she wore a smirk and her eyes were locked on Walter.

"I understand now," she said tensely. She turned to the monster with no face. "My mom didn't just kill herself, she hoped she would kill you too. But, she wasn't a keeper so it wouldn't work... but I am. I won't make the same mistake. I'm not afraid of you, not anymore, and I'm not afraid to die. If killing me will kill you then—"

"No, Yvette!" Walter shouting, forgetting about the monster and the diary entirely.

The faceless man with his menacing smile said, "Not unless I kill your precious Walter first." Ignoring his seeping blood, The faceless man raised an arm bringing all his nails together to stab into Walter... but he was stopped again.

With tears still running down her eyes, the knife's point slowly stroked on her neck. Walter could see her blood trickling down and the monster's neck began pouring thick black ink from a similar cut. Walter couldn't watch Yvette kill herself. He couldn't let that happen, so he couldn't hesitate. He had to get to the diary, but he didn't get far. Even with the inky blood pouring down his neck, the faceless man stopped Walter in his tracks. Walter swung his feet to get away and grabbed the burning diary but the monstrous faceless man nearly broke his leg from how hard he grasped it. Walter could even feel the nails piercing into his skin.

"No!" Yvette screamed. Before the monster could strike Walter's chest, she raised her free hand and leaned forward like she was going to run towards them. This was when the faceless man's arm froze in mid-attack.

Struggling to turn, the faceless man slowly faced Yvette. "What are you doing?"

Walter couldn't describe it, but somehow Yvette had the monster in her grasp like a puppet with invisible strings.

"I…" Yvette looked just as shocked as Walter and her monster. However, her head cocked to the side curiously. "I don't know." Quickly, she whipped her hand back and the faceless man suddenly picked up from the ground, and flew deep into the fire, making an explosive crash. Walter's eyes widened as all he saw was Yvette and flames. "Walter," she cried. "Get the diary and sign the contract."

"What?" Walter didn't understand. "Yvette—"

"Please, Walter." Seeing her crying with the knife still at her throat brought tears to his eyes as well. Even so, he quickly turned to the diary. "We don't have much time. I have to hold him off. Sign it!"

Walter felt tears building in his eyes, but she was right. The bindings were nearly garbed in flames and it burned even more by the touch. Grimacing, Walter mustered all his strength and grasped the diary tightly, even with the heat as intense as it was. He struggled to open the diary as the bindings were not just scorching hot but felt like they were made of black stone. His hands and arms were burning and bloody and shook uncontrollably.

Suddenly, the monster crashed through the flames. His body was made of molten lava and his tattered suit and hat had melted away. He was trying to hurry towards Walter but he could get far. Yvette still had an unseen grip on him.

"Hurry!" she wailed. "I don't know how long I can hold him." She was wiping her hands and waves of flames collided with the monster. With all her power, she did everything to hold him back since they couldn't destroy him.

Walter hurried through the pages and found the contract glowing gold. As the diary opened, gales of winds and fire whipped and twisted around him and the pages danced dangerously nearly flipping away. Walter used all his strength to keep the bindings at bay. With his pen and the wind growing stronger around him, Walter grit his teeth and growled like a madman as he held the binding open. Shaking, the pen finally found the page, and the point began to rise and fall into a W.

"Walter!!" Yvette was screaming even higher now. He couldn't see her as the wind and flames were so strong. He could barely open his mouth to respond so he didn't... he couldn't. He concentrated on the page which had his first name sloppily written on the line. Feeling the need to curse for having nine letters in his last name but he couldn't be deterred. From his back and trailing down to his legs and arms, a numbing feeling was taking over. He could feel his nerves shutting down around him. Soon, only his arms seem to work. Right before he felt like he might suffocate, he finished his signature and the feelings in his fingers gave out.

Then suddenly, the winds, the burns, Yvette's screams, it was all replaced with black and silence.

Suddenly, his eyes snapped open, he was breathing heavily and his heart was thumped even harder. Across from him was Yvette who seemed just as shocked and was hyperventilating even. Somehow, they were back at the bridge like they never left. Even the frogs and crickets could be heard again.

Walter saw the knife was still at her throat and a trickle of blood was on her neck where the blade left a small nick. No other injuries had appeared on her and her clothes were still clean. However, Yvette seemed too frightened to move her hand on her own. Slowly, Walter slipped his fingers in-between hers and guided her hand away from her neck, allowing her hand to finally give in and his hand to grasp the hilt.

Once the knife was safely in his pocket, only then did he feel the diary being held up, opened and laying on both their hands like before… and there the contract was. Surprisingly, Walter's name was written neatly on the line and in his best cursive. Seeing it made Yvette gasp. When she looked up at him and her lips were wearing a thin smile. "You signed it."

He nodded slightly. "Yeah." He didn't have or couldn't find the words to say anymore.

Suddenly, the diary began to hiss. Black smoke rose from the words of the contract and disappeared leaving only Walter's name on the page. The page absorbed the name, leaving the diary empty once again. Without a gust of wind, the diary quickly turned all the way to the end, then back to the beginning and slammed closed into Walter's palm. *It's mine now,* he thought wearily.

Suddenly, Walter felt Yvette tugging at his clothes and examining his body for any of his wounds. He even let the diary fall to the floor when she examined his arms and hands.

"It's okay," Walter assured her. "I'm not hurt." He was more concerned with her. "Hold on." He remembered he still had some napkins from when they ate, so he cleaned the blood for her then held it down on her wound. "Just hold it there."

Yvette didn't take the napkin from him. Instead, her fingers slipped in-between his and held his hand down on her thin wound. When tears began to fall again, Walter smiled and wiped them clean once more with his free hand. Before he took his hand away, Yvette held it and kissed the tears on his thumb while staring up at him longingly. Walter leaned in to kiss her and Yvette lifted her head to meet him. The taste of her tears on her lips... somehow, they were sweet.

When Yvette's phone began to ring her, she apologized then answered. "Hey. Sorry. My phone was on vibrate." She paused for a moment. "Yeah, I'll be home soon, okay? Okay." She hung up and put her phone away. "My sister."

"Wondering where you are, huh?"

She nodded. "Yeah. She called a few times but... we couldn't hear it. She'll be okay." Yvette wrapped her free hand around his waist and rested her head upon his chest. "Don't worry about her."

He held her closer, enjoying the feel of her against him. "I'm not worried."

"Thank you, Walter," Yvette said blissfully.

When he heard that, Walter felt quite guilty about what happened and frightened about what might happen. If he were being honest, Walter didn't know how to respond or what he was being thanked for. He wanted to tell her how much he wished everything were different. He wanted to tell her that nothing will change. He wanted to tell her that she had nothing to worry about. But he didn't... he couldn't...

Yvette looked up at him with a warm smile, but seeing his weary and vacant eyes unsettled her. "Hey... Where are you?" She gently brought his face closer to hers.

Walter made a grin for her. "I'm right here with you. I just… I don't know what to say, I guess."

Shaking her head, Yvette grinned at him. "You don't have to say anything."

When they kissed again, Walter savored it, knowing that it could be the last time… knowing that once the night was over, she might not see him the same… knowing that no matter how many kisses they shared, none of them might matter after… knowing that he loved her.

Instead, he held her close. The last thing he wanted to do was let go of her. Still, he couldn't be selfish and wouldn't keep her out for too long.

"I have to get you home," Walter said lightly while his fingers gently played with her curls.

Yvette snuggled into him a little then nodded. "I know… I know. Do you know a long way back?"

"A long way back?" Walter grinned. He let go of the napkin on her neck and took her hand in his. "I know a way that will last forever."

Yvette giggled. "Corny."

He laughed lightly. "I know." However, when he looked down at the diary, it simmered off. "I almost forgot."

Yvette sighed but was quiet. Neither seemed to know what to say or do. A part of him wanted to leave the diary where it was. There were enough times that proved the diary couldn't be abandoned. "If only I could just leave the diary here."

Yvette sighed. "I know."

Walter decided to pick it up and put it back in his bag. "Even if it stays here and doesn't follow me, someone will use it. I would rather not hallucinate someone else's fantasies."

Yvette nodded. "Agreed." When Walter wrapped his arm around her, she grinned and coiled her arm around him as well. Walter was more content than happy, but Yvette's safety was all that mattered. With their arms wrapped into one another, Walter ushered her away; away from her favorite place and his worst nightmare.

When they returned to Yvette's block, the two were strolling hand and hand. They had stopped at a gas station on the way and now Yvette's cut was covered with a smiley face-clad Band-Aid. Walter picked it out as a joke, but she took it anyway. "I won't forget when I look in the mirror." Soon, Yvette was smiling and laughing again. The night will still end, tomorrow will still come, but, at that moment, Walter just wanted her to feel some bliss for a time. He only hoped that it would last when the morning came.

"So, you brought flowers, huh?" she asked, her hand in his while she gently massaged his fingers.

"I brought flowers," Walter admitted. "If I had known—"

"I'm really sorry, Walter. I should have told you but I didn't think you would get flowers and all that."

He snickered. "It's okay. I was going to say, 'If I had known, I would have brought fake flowers or something.'"

Yvette blushed. "Fake flowers would have been cute, but you wouldn't have to, Walter." Her teeth were showing now. However, she turned on a silly sense of suspicion. "Just because I'm curious, what kind were they?"

Walter smirked slyly. "And why so curious?"

"Well, you can't blame me, can you?"

He smiled. "They were roses. I got them from my dad's neighbor."

413

Yvette gasped and her lips opened agape. "Not roses." She sulked. "I wish I was able to see them, even from a distance."

Walter thought for a moment. "Maybe if I put them behind some glass."

She snickered. "Like Beauty and the Beast." That made Walter smirk and nod. "I would love that."

"I should have known. Such a girl."

"Of course. Remember when we wrote that little love story in the diary when we were in the park that day?

"Oh, with the forbidden love story between the princess and the angel?"

"Yeah, and you said you liked it." Yvette was snickering a little. "You even came up with the end, remember? The princess has to renounce her claim to the throne and the angel gives up his wings to become mortal so he could be with her."

"Yeah, because sacrifices like that work best in love stories. It was like... half a comedy and half a tragedy..."

Yvette was smiling at him. "People do crazy things when they are in love, don't they? We did."

Walter felt himself chuckle. He nodded and agreed. "We did."

With her smile remaining, Yvette began to caress his fingers in between hers. "There were a few things I wanted to tell you. Just a few things before tomorrow comes."

Walter nodded solemnly, deciding just to listen.

"Well," she began, "you now know I'm allergic to flowers; been that way forever. Umm... I like scary movies but only at the movies or with my dad. I'm a bit claustrophobic, but I think I just don't like dealing with people in small spaces. What else... what else... Oh yeah! I don't like to be surprised either but I do like the unexpected..." She paused for a moment. "Does that make any sense?"

Walter snickered. "Yes... Well, not really. It's... kind of weird, if I'm being honest, but I wouldn't expect anything different from you."

"Is that so?"

"Yeah, but... I like your weirdness."

"Only you like weird stuff." Yvette giggled then spun away from him. Her curls flew and fell to her one shoulder in a smooth flourish, hugging her face beautifully. Her brown eyes watched him sharply. "So... you like Weird Yvette, huh?"

Walter shook his head playfully. "And Smart Yvette, and Silly Yvette—"

"Going overboard again?" She giggled and it made Walter smile. "I just wanted you to know these things about me," she told him. "I never really had the chance to tell you with everything going on, but I want you to know." She paused for a moment then said, "The time we spent together with the diary meant more to me than anything. If I could help it, it's something I never want to forget."

Walter nodded. "Do you hate me for taking ownership of the diary? Maybe everything could have played out differently. Maybe—"

Yvette was already approaching and she placed her finger against his lips before he could go on. "I could never hate you, Walter. I never have. You protected me, and, for the first time, I want to allow someone to be there for me." She chuckled. "Maybe this is cheesy to say, but I'm just glad that that someone is you. I wouldn't ask for anyone else."

Yvette's words rested warmly within Walter. "I'm happy to be here with you, Yvette."

The Anders house seemed to appear beside them. Just the look of it made Yvette weary. "We're here," she said lowly.

They were standing beneath a streetlight, so Walter could see the sorrow across her face pretty clearly.

"Hey," Walter got her attention. "I want to give you something." He went into his bag and Yvette stared in wonder.

"What is it?"

Rested between his fingers was an old black binder that he pulled from the crevasses of his bag. He handed it to her and Yvette seemed curious enough. She gave him a sly silly look before opening the folder. What she saw inside replaced her chuckle with a gasp. She slowly lifted the single piece of paper, feasting upon it with tearing eyes. She saw herself sketched with her bright smile and wide eyes while her mother happily hugged her from behind with joyful eyes and a wide smile to match.

"When you look at this," said Walter, "I want you to remember that your mother is always there for you... because she never left. I figured it would be nice to remember. I wanted to write a message or something, but the whole memory thing... I just signed it instead. I didn't really know what to say. I guess... with how everything happened, I wish I did."

"Walter, I..." Yvette speechless, mouth still ajar as her eyes looked up into his. "I don't... I don't know what to say."

"You don't have to say anything," he said warmly. He could feel how nervous he must have looked and the awkward smile he wore in front of her.

"It has been so hard to look at the picture of my mom lately, but this... I love this. It's honestly the best gift anyone has given me. Seriously... thank you, Walter."

Her free hand wrapped around his neck, welcoming his lips to hers. Walter's hands found the small of her waist and held her closely and lovingly as they kissed.

"I don't want to go inside," she eventually told him, her tears beginning to fall again. "I'm still worried about tomorrow. Tell me, what are you going to do about the doctor, Walter? I know you have some kind of plan or something. Tell me."

Walter had no plan. He knew he would eventually have one, but he kept that to himself and simply kissed the tears on her cheeks. "Don't worry about the doctor. I can always pretend like I didn't know what I was talking about. I could say I was acting out for attention. I will say whatever I have to say. You don't have to worry about it anymore. I promise."

Yvette smiled then nodded. "But Walter... Can you promise me something else?"

"Of course. Anything."

"Promise me that kiss won't be our last one."

Walter grinned then leaned in once more to get one final longing kiss to finish their night. Her lips were moister and softer than before. The taste was indescribable. "I promise it won't be the last," he said. "Neither will that one."

"Unexpected," Yvette hummed; her smile even brighter, her big brown eyes slowly opening. "I like it."

Nose to nose, arms wrapped into one another, Walter said softly, "I think I'm starting to get it."

Yvette looked up into his eyes deeply. "I think... I... No... No, I know."

Walter tilted his head to the side, baffled. "Know what?"

"I know that..." She was a bit hesitant but said, "I know that I love you. I said it before but I was frightened and... Now we're here and safe and... I just wanted you to hear me say it again before you wake up tomorrow." Yvette's eyes were shining now. "I just want you to know how much I love you and I never want that to change. Promise me, Walter. Promise me that you will make sure that never changes."

Walter smiled softly then whispered to her. "I promise."

A large smile reached her lips as her fingers grasped on his shirt. Now Walter was being pulled into her once again. Her kiss was more inviting than the first, and somehow it felt so familiar, like they had been that close for years.

It was long, it was deep, it was satisfying.

At this point, neither Walter nor Yvette could stop smiling. Their foreheads were pressed against one another. As they stared into each other's eyes, they enjoyed that moment alone for a little longer. However, soon Yvette's fingers slipped out of his as she left his side to push the small gate open. Walter kept his eyes on her as she began walking up the walkway. However, she soon turned back to him.

"So, I'll see you tomorrow?" she asked.

Walter nodded. "Of course, you will," he assured her.

"Don't forget your promise to me."

"I won't," Walter assured her. He held her hand and kissed her once more with the gate standing between them. "I'll never forget."

When Walter arrived home, his father awoke to the sound of the front door closing. He lifted his head from the back of the couch with drool painted on his bottom lip. When he got a good look at his son, the man wiped his mouth and sat up.

"There he is," his father said. "So, how was it?"

Walter felt himself sulk a bit from exhaustion, but he still smiled. "It was good," he said, fatigued. "Can we talk about it tomorrow though? I'm tired. I just want to shower and sleep."

Lawrence D'Artagnan yawned into a sleepy grin. "Sure, son. I'm proud of you."

"Thanks, Dad."

It wasn't until after he showered and dressed in his comfortable clothes for bed, Walter opened his bag. He fished out the diary — still cracked, still old, still haunting. *What am I going to do with you now?* It made him weary to think about that, knowing what the diary can lead to. He might be wise to never touch it again, but he couldn't be certain if only that will keep the hallucinations and the faceless thing at bay.

"Have you seen him?" Gordon had asked. Walter could still hear his words. "The man without a face?"

More than just the words, Walter remembered the fear in his tone. *Does the faceless man still haunt Gordon?* He hadn't thought of that before — until now since Walter had seen the faceless man for himself. It worried him, knowing he might suffer the same fate. Still, he was alive and, as keeper, the faceless man needed Walter to stay alive. If only he could bury the diary deep; deeper than a corpse, deeper than death.

It wasn't long after that Walter was laying on his bed and staring up at the ceiling in silence. With his mind swirling with memories, it was hard to do anything else; such sweet memories with Yvette's eyes and smile in every frame, he just missed her voice to go with it. He contemplated whether to call her or not, but then remembered he wasn't going to hesitate... *Not tonight,* he thought. *I can't...* With that, he stretched for his phone on his end table and made the call. Two rings and she answered.

"Hey." Yvette's voice was sweet, supple and massaged his ear. Just the sound of her made him smile.

"I thought I'd call before you fell asleep," he answered, his voice a bit lower and soothing.

A gentle giggle chimed in the receiver. "I'm glad you did."

He hummed as he got more comfortable in his bed. "I just wanted to hear your voice again before the night was over."

"Me too. I wanted to call you but... I was a little afraid to. After tonight... I just knew that I couldn't go to sleep without hearing your voice again. I guess just knowing what will happen tomorrow makes me… uneasy." She chuckled lightly. "Calling you and sounding all depressed on the phone didn't seem like a good way to end our night."

Walter grinned. "Tonight was fun… for the most part." He chuckled a bit. "Hearing your voice could never spoil my night."

Yvette smiled and he could hear it as well as her shifting in her bed. "I love how sweet you are, Walter."

"Well… you make it so easy for me to be."

Yvette was giggling again and that made Walter feel good about himself a little. He liked making her blush, even if he wasn't there to see it.

She made a blissful hum then asked, "How are you feeling?"

Walter nodded. "I think I'm fine. How about you?"

"I think I'm fine too."

"What are you doing?"

"I'm just laying in bed… in a shirt and… my… smallclothes."

"Smallclothes?" Walter wasn't sure what she meant until she heard her giggling again. That excited him. "Oh, I get it."

"I'm feeling pretty comfortable," she said sweetly. "My sheets feel nice against my skin."

Walter could imagine her laying down with her bare legs barely hidden by her sheets. The picture in his mind spark a bit of fire within him. He said, "Paint me a picture," then he tried catching his words but it was too late now. "I mean, paint me… a picture of you in your bedroom," he corrected. Too bold too quickly could be too undesirable, he knew.

Yvette paid no mind to it and was still giggling . "Oh, me in my bedroom, huh? Curious, Walter?"

"Maybe," he said slyly. "You've seen my room but yours… yours is a mystery, wouldn't you agree?"

She hummed in the receiver. "I do. Okay. Right over me are my Christmas lights."

Walter smiled, imagining lights above her and reflecting off her big brown eyes already. "They must have come in handy last year."

Yvette chuckled, "You can say that."

Walter knew what he meant but didn't speak of it. Yvette went on about her room, describing her separate study and lounging areas as well as the colors and designs she and her mother picked out several years ago. Walter just liked listening to her voice. She even asked several times if he was still there or if he had fallen asleep, but every time she asked, he was right there taking in every word.

Eventually, she told him. "I had to delete our thread of text messages on my phone; too many messages about the diary and it would take forever to delete all of them. I know I might frighten myself if I saw them tomorrow. I didn't know if I should tell you or not... but I wanted you to know."

Walter snickered. "I can imagine you seeing them and calling me tomorrow asking me about 'some diary.' That would be an awkward conversation, won't it?"

She chuckled a little. "It would." Then Walter heard Yvette sigh. "Even more awkward than when we first met."

Walter snickered, hoping to keep his laugh down. "Something told me to call you. I'm glad I listened."

They shared muffled laughs for a moment until Yvette said, "I was thinking—" Then she stopped herself and was quiet for a moment.

"About what?"

"Oh, sorry. I was still thinking." Another snicker reached Walter's lips. "Don't laugh at me. Anyways, I was thinking of

writing a letter to myself… just in case I wake up a bit... I don't
know."

Walter pondered a moment. "Don't you think it might be a
bit weird if you find a letter to yourself that you don't remember
writing?"

"Yeah." Her voice had sunken. "I thought of that too.
Honestly, I can't think of anything better. It might be a bit
strange, but…"

"True and the memory won't be because of the diary. That
shouldn't matter anymore. Maybe just a short letter to make sure
you don't feel… too lost? I don't know how to explain it but you
know what I mean."

Yvette giggled. "I do."

"I mean, who do you trust more than you, right?"

"Maybe you."

He smiled. "Well, you can't mock my handwriting, so—"

She was laughing now. "No, I can't. It's terrible."

Walter snorted. "Maybe I should become a doctor then."

"Mmm… Dr. D'Artagnan. Sounds kind of sexy, exactly."

Hearing her whispering in his ear — so sweetly and so
wickedly — brought a boil within him. It wasn't nervousness
but a longing. Walter wanted to grab her and kiss right then and
there, but could only chuckle through the phone.

Slyly and in a flirtatious tone, he deepened his voice and
said, "The doctor will see you now."

That brought a little laugh to Yvette's lips. Walter only
wished he was there to see it.

"Anyways," he went on. "If you do write something, I think
it should be something for… I guess if you ever feel a little lost
or like something is missing. I don't know if that would be a
good idea or not, but…" He thought for a moment, but couldn't
be sure whether he should agree to it or not. All he knew was he

wanted to provide her with some solace if he could. "If you do… you should tell yourself what you think you need to know; what's important. Something to help fill those missing pieces or empty spaces. Something to guide yourself to… to…" He didn't know how to finish, but he already started. "Honestly, I don't know."

"To you?" she asked sweetly. "Only you would be able to help me. Only you would know what I'm going through."

Walter couldn't stop smiling. "I think you know what to write then. If you need me to, I will paint a picture for you. Or sketch it, whichever you like."

Yvette hummed then he heard her emerge from her bed softly. "You have to promise that you won't fall asleep while I'm writing."

"I won't. I'm not going anywhere."

So, that's what they did. Yvette sat at her desk working on her letter while Walter sat at his own desk and sketched. The night was quiet on his end and hers. Yvette would ask him his opinion on what she said and the wording, but other than that, they both scribbled on their desk silently. His mind was drawn to the diary again, tucked up under his bed. Once the contract was signed, he didn't even want to see it or mention it. He began wondering if he could forget the diary in time as well and let those memories die with Yvette's.

Eventually, as he was working on his sketch, he heard Yvette yawn in his ear. Walter snickered lightly. "Don't yawn or you're going to make me…" And just as he thought, he cupped his mouth as he yawned right after.

Yvette giggled as she flopped back to her bed, exhausted. "I think we are both tired now."

Walter laughed lightly. "I'm blaming you."

"You better not," she scolded, so silly and sleepy all at once. She stretched and yawned again as she snuggled into her bed. "Hey, Walter," she muttered, "do you remember when the monkey was scratching his butt on Mr. Vega's head?"

Walter chuckled. He had returned to his bed as well and closed his eyes to imagine it. "Yeah, I remember that. It was hard not to laugh. Too bad no one else could see it."

"Everyone looked at us like we were crazy."

"Especially you."

Yvette chuckled on before she snorted. "You nearly caused me to be sent to the office. I have never... ever been sent to the office."

Walter snickered. "Why am I not surprised?"

Yvette giggled into another yawn. "Can you tell me a story? I just want to hear your voice until I fall asleep."

Walter nodded. "Of course."

So, he did. Yvette grew silent and he started telling a silly story about four mice, trying to steal a wheel of cheese from an old woman's mansion — all without waking the two Siamese cats in the grand kitchen. Yvette giggled a few times, but after minutes passed, Walter could hear her soft and steady breath in the receiver.

"Yvette?" There might have been a small disturbance in her breathing, but there was no answer. It was time he let her go, he knew this, but thinking about it brought a sad smile to his lips. There was a bittersweet taste in his mouth, but one taste was stronger than the other. His smile grew wide knowing Yvette would be safe when she woke up the next morning. "Good night, Yvette," he whispered. "I love you."

Hesitant, Walter sighed sadly. He was about to move the phone from his ear to hang up when he heard her bedsheet moving, a light yawn, and Yvette murmured sweetly, "I love you too, Walter. Good night."

Overwhelmed, Dr. Pierce sighed and leaned back into her armchair. The bittersweet tale had come to its end and the taste . However, Walter didn't seem upset by any of it. He seemed quite content to her.

"So, that's how it happened?"

Walter nodded.

"Did it work?"

"I don't know. She hasn't been to school all this week. Her friend Hazel told me that she hasn't been feeling well. I wanted to call, but... honestly I wasn't sure if I should."

A sad smile crept up to her lips. "I understand. Sometimes being patient is the hardest thing."

"I know," Walter admitted. "I just hope I didn't make everything worse."

Warmly, the doctor said, "You should call her Walter. She probably wants to call you but is afraid to."

Walter nodded his head slowly. He even stood and paced around the room for a moment but he eventually sighed sadly. "No," he finally said after thinking it through. "I'd rather see her in person. I want to see her face, not just hear her voice... I have to know if she still..."

Silence fell for a few moments before Dr. Pierce finished the sentence for him. "If she still loves you."

Overwhelmed, Walter folded his arms while leaning on an empty space on the wall. "I just want her to be happy and not have to worry about everything that happened with the diary."

Dr. Pierce made a gentle smile. "I'm very proud of you, Walter." Saying that caused Walter to give her a curious look.

"You have come a long way. Even though this diary never consumed you, you were able to get through it. You have found closure in multiple ways and it has made you stronger."

Walter nodded with a tiny smile. "That is a little sad to think about, but maybe you are right. Thank you, Doc."

Dr. Pierce smiled sadly. "And, I have to apologize to you. I didn't believe you and I should have—"

"No," said Walter sternly. "You shouldn't apologize. No one believed me. The difference is that you tried to; you wanted to. You might've been just doing your job, but you forced me to look back at everything and it really helped. So... thank you."

With that, the bell rang and the third session was over. They both acknowledged it, but neither made an effort to leave.

"I guess... that's our time for today," the doctor accepted. She stood and approached Walter who still stood stiffly against the wall. Resting a hand on his shoulder, she said, "Yvette was right, no memory simply disappears. What we feel is far more potent than what we remember. A memory might escape the mind for a time, but a feeling never escapes the heart."

Walter grinned lightly, hopefully feeling better and even optimistic. "Thank you, Dr. Pierce."

"Listen to me, Walter, I know you feel like you don't need me anymore, but I'd hope you would come back next week for another session. I would like to follow up with you with everything and see Yvette is able to cope with everything. If the diary is still in your possession, you could always use someone with you that understands what you are going through."

It took a moment or so, but when Walter nodded, there was a small grin there as well as a single tear. He wiped it away and said, "Sure. I'd appreciate that."

Dr. Pierce smiled sadly. "Would you like a hug, Walter?"

He nodded and nearly fell into her arms. As Walter began to weep, she rubbed his back and he let the tears come. She told him everything would be alright and he nodded, but he wept all the same.

Before he left her office, Walter cleaned up in the bathroom. When she was alone, Dr. Pierce remembered how she felt when Yvette left that day; like she failed her when the girl stormed out and demanded her to believe Walter. Now, the doctor only hoped she was able to help him, even after she didn't believe him initially.

Then there was the diary, sitting on the couch and staring back at her. The eerie feeling still permeated from the binding and its presence was even stronger than when she first witnessed its abilities first hand. Now, Dr. Pierce truly understood the burden that had been weighed upon them both, and realized, now more than ever, that there is only so much she could do to help them.

Thursday, May 27th

THE DAYS THAT FOLLOWED HIS THIRD SESSION SEEM
to pass by in a blur, even more so than the Monday and Tuesday
before. It had been a week since he saw Yvette, and that
emptiness might have contributed, but that didn't change
anything. The courage to call her was already far from his grasp.

When he woke up Thursday, he felt weak and feverish and
stayed home the rest. Walter felt it was a sign to let it be. He
didn't want to revert back to his old cowardly ways yet overly
eager self and figured that what was best for Yvette was space.

With his fears out of sight, Walter's fever felt like a detox.
Yes, his body stiffened and his head seemed to pulse from every
corner. It was so sudden and Walter couldn't remember how he
felt this way initially. Still, he was pretty happy to be away from
school for the rest of the week, even if it meant he couldn't see
Yvette. Even during the weekend when the fever began to
subside, his longing for the girl he loved never did. The way
Yvette permeated his thoughts, it all seemed to burn within him

relentlessly. This made him often wonder if she was thinking of him too, but he tried not to think of that

Still, Walter imagined seeing her in the halls early one morning before the bell, spotting her innate ringlets bouncing beside her shoulders as she walked. In his daydreams, he would call her name and she would face him slowly. With her shining eyes and her stunning smile, she would beckon him boldly, and, without preamble, she would wrap her arms around his neck, claiming his love as hers. She played with his ear, just the way he liked, and even in a daydream, he felt the tingle of her fingers. However, what he missed overall was Yvette being her sweet and silly self.

Monday morning came and he hadn't seen her yet. He didn't see Art yet either strangely. Usually in the mornings, the two would have spotted each other in the hallway by then, but he did see Hazel. When she saw him, she could have simply waved or greeted him as he walked by, but Hazel moved through the crowd and approached him directly. This caught him off guard a little.

"There you are, Walter," Hazel chimed, strangely happy to see him.

"Here I am," Walter replied awkwardly. "What's up?"

"We were looking for you last week."

"We?" His awkwardness turned to curiosity.

"Who else? Me and Yvette." Suddenly, Hazel's excitement turned to suspicion. "She won't tell me what happened last weekend, but she didn't have to tell me anything. I already know."

Now, Walter was indeed suspicious, his curiosity completely replaced. "Know what?"

"What do you mean 'know what?' You and Yvette got together last weekend, right?"

Nervousness finally claimed Walter and he hated how uncomfortable it made him. Yvette wasn't even there yet he felt his heart pumped harder than before. However, Walter was able to hide it well behind his side smirk. "I mean... I... guess so."

Hazel snickered and shook her head. "I swear, the two of you are perfect together. Both cute... and clueless." She then put on a warm smile and said, "Yvette really needs someone to be there for her. I mean... I saw her crying in the library not too long ago and I've never seen her cry. I don't have to tell you how much she's going through — you know how private she can be with things — but she seems to be more open and comfortable with you. I know we don't really know each other, but I see how much Yvette likes you. It's kind of cute the way she tries to hide it." Hazel giggled.

Walter chuckled with her. "Yeah. You're right. Thanks."

"You're serious about her... right?"

Walter smirked as he nodded confidently. "Absolutely."

Hazel smiled brightly. "Well, what else is there to say, right?"

Suddenly, Walter spotted Lenny proceeding down the hall and towards them. Although he saw them both, his attention was drawn to Hazel.

"Well, good morning to you," Lenny said smoothly. The way his suave tone tickled Hazel's ear, it made her giggle and smile. Walter suddenly felt like interrupting them and not the other way around.

"Well good morning, Lenny." The sweet ring in Hazel's voice was sweet. "How did you sleep?"

Lenny smiled as playfully drew closer to her, nose to nose. "Wonderfully, thanks to you."

If Walter hadn't felt a bit strange before then he most
certainly did now. "So—"

Eventually, Lenny turned to him. "What's up, Walter?"

"What's going on here?" Walter asked as the corners of his
lips rose slightly.

Lenny laughed, pushing his glasses up his face, while Hazel
giggled with her eyes staring up into his. She couldn't stop
smiling. Looking into her eyes he said, "Just making some
hallway rumors. It's a long story, but Hazel and I just... kind of
connected after the party. So... you know."

Hazel turned to Walter the first time since Lenny arrived and
said, "Yeah, Walter. You know."

It was a bit strange, but he was happy for them. The way
Hazel looked at Lenny was even cute to Walter; the brightness
in her eyes that matched her smile. Walter thought of that,
wondering if Yvette would look at him the same way again.

Fortunately yet unfortunately, Walter didn't have Biology
class that day. Some solace came from that, seeing as though he
wouldn't have to deal with Mr. Vega, but he still hadn't seen
Yvette either. He preferred his Algebra II class to Biology any
day, but Algebra II didn't have the girl he loved.

When the lunch bell rang, Walter found Art by his locker, but
he wasn't alone. Leaning beside his locker was his date from the
house party. *Trisha*, he remembered. They seemed blissful
together and Walter was happy for his friend. However, when
Art saw him, his face seemed a bit sunken.

"You haven't seen Yvette, huh?" Art asked him. Walter had
told him that he and Yvette were going through a little...
uneasiness, was the word he used. He didn't want to say much
more than that and Art seemed to understand. It was a white lie,

Walter knew, but it was enough to deter his friend from constant questioning.

Walter shook his head. "Not yet. Hey, Trisha."

"Hey, Walter," Trisha said. "I didn't know you and Yvette were dating. I thought you went to the party with that Claire girl. What happened to her?"

Walter shrugged. "We just hung out with each other at the party. That's really what it was"

Art turned to Trisha. "No, *Yvette* is the girl he spends a lot of time with lately."

"Oh," Trisha seemingly grasped the situation. "Sounds like a love triangle."

"No, it's not like that," Walter said, hoping to make it all clear. "I barely know Claire."

"Oh." Now, Trisha seemed to be caught up. "Oh, well that's a good thing. Sounds like you really like her, Walter."

"Oh, he does," Art replied. "The question is: can he admit it?"

Trisha faced Walter again. She didn't say anything, but she didn't have to. The curious look on her face told him what she was gearing up to ask him.

Walter gave no thought before nodding. "Yeah, I do. I think I love her."

With wide excited eyes, Trisha bounced a bit with delight. It wasn't until then when Walter saw her beside his best friend, that he realized she was a bit taller than him. That made him chuckle a little inside. Even so, the joy in her voice, the way she looked at Art and how she smiled and made him blush — it made Walter think of Yvette.

"That's so amazing. I always love a good love story. So, do you think that—"

Then suddenly, Trisha's words trailed off. She stared somewhere past Art and Walter and both were concerned.

"You okay, Trish?" Art asked her, leaning a bit closer to console if he must.

However, her gawking ended and Trisha turned to Art. "Oh, nothing," she said aloud. "I was just thinking… that I think Yvette feels the same about you, Walter."

Confused, he wasn't sure whether Yvette and Trisha even knew each other, or if she was just being nice to him. He didn't pry, instead saying, "Yeah, maybe."

Without preamble, Trisha whispered something in Art ear. In response, Art's eyes widened. "Oh, it's that so?"

Still confused, Walter asked, "What is it?"

"A girl's intuition," Trisha replied with a shrug. Then she turned back to Art. "So, are you ready?"

Art nodded. "Yeah. Let's go." Then he faced his best friend. "Don't worry so much, Walter. Everything will work out. Anyways, we have to go. We're meeting up with a few of her friends today for lunch."

"Oh, cool. Umm... Trisha, would you mind if I borrow Art for a minute before you go?"

"Sure," she replied, "just not too long."

"I got you." Walter led Art a few lockers away. When Trisha was out of earshot, he asked, "So, it's official, huh?"

"Official?" Art asked, unaware of what Walter meant.

"You and Trisha?"

Art peaked over at her. The two shared a smile before he returned his attention back to his best friend. "Yeah," he nodded. "Ever since the championship party."

Walter smirked. *Well, that party really was unforgettable — for Lenny and Hazel, for Art and Trisha...* "I'm happy for you, bro." Walter said before leaning in a bit closer. "What did she tell you?"

Art snickered. "I can't tell you that. Apparently… it will ruin the surprise. I'll say this: last week, I saw how you looked when Yvette wasn't around, but, more importantly, I saw how Yvette looked when you weren't around. I'll keep it at that." Then Art smacked his best friend's shoulder. "I got to go. Pick-up game after school? We haven't played in a while."

That was true. With Art preparing for the championship game, they hadn't had much time to even have a one on one in months. Because of this, Walter agreed at once. "Cool. You might have won the championship but—"

"Stop right there," Art interrupted and pointed at him with a sly smirk. "Keep it on the court."

"Later, bro," he chuckled.

Walter was happy to see Art together with his lady. Trisha seemed to make him happy, and she always seemed to be smiling around him. It was a good thing.

Walter found a vacant area of the cafeteria and sat alone. His mother had packed him leftover dinner from the night before; jasmine rice with grazed chicken and steamed vegetables. The Tupperware his mother used to keep his food warm did its job. His mother was happier than expected when his father finally brought them back. Then something happened that Walter hadn't seen in… well, he couldn't remember the last time he saw it. Anyhow, a few nights ago his father came by for dinner. They hadn't all sat at the dining table together since their interrogation a few weeks prior. Fortunately, there was less tension in the air that night. Although they both asked him about Dr. Pierce and his sessions, Mr. And Mrs. D'Artagnan didn't pry… strangely.

However, that wasn't what Walter remembered most about that night.

His father eventually left after the three of them watched a movie together. It was Sunday night, so the night was cut a bit short when it started getting too late. He gave his son a big hug and said, "I'm proud of you, Walter." It made him feel proud of himself, knowing he had gotten better in his father's eyes and that made him happy.

When his father was walking out the door, his mother followed him. Walter had an eye by the window and saw the two talking then slowly wrap their arms around one another. His father held his mother by the waist with her arms lovingly wrapped around his neck. They even swayed a bit from side to side, as if music were playing that only the couple could hear. When they kissed, Walter felt like a kindergartener again, watching his parents trying to conceal their intimacy. He always saw them even when they tried to hide it. Once he thought it was all nasty and icky, now, kisses made him think of Yvette.

As he sat musing over his meal when he heard a voice over him. "Do you mind if I sit here?"

He began to say, "No. I don't—" Then he paused, stared and smiled. "—don't mind."

Dressed in a white sweater and skin skimming jeans, a pretty teenage girl sat in front of him. Her shoulders held up her ringlet curls and her eyes were soft brown, bold and beautiful. When they found his eyes, hers danced back and forth in-between them. The best thing of all, she wore the warm welcoming smile he loved.

Walter's mouth must have been ajar as she giggled and said, "You look like you saw a ghost."

"You are wearing white so..."

Yvette chuckled. She made herself comfortable on the lunch bench. She pulled out a small paper bag, already wrinkled from the crevasses of her backpack. It surprised Walter slightly, seeing her pull out a bagged lunch. It even made him snicker a bit.

"What?" Yvette asked, fishing out a peanut butter and jelly sandwich.

Walter gestured to her lunch. "You made that yourself?"

Yvette giggled. "I did, actually. You can have a bite if you ask nicely."

He chuckled. "I'm always nice—"

"When you want to be." Yvette already knew what he was going to say. That made him smile. "Did you make that yourself?"

Walter looked down at his plate. "You know it."

Yvette shook her head and smiled, acknowledging his lie. "It does look good though."

"Want to switch?"

"Shut up, Walter." Yvette turned away but with a playful grin she couldn't hide. "Just save me a bite, okay?"

Walter nodded and snickered. "Sure."

"Good." Then Yvette took a bite from her sandwich, trying to divert her eyes a bit.

"So, where have you been?" Walter asked curiously. "It feels like I haven't seen you in weeks. Been playing hooky?"

"Without you? Never." Yvette giggled. "I've just been a little under the weather last week. I came to school Thursday but you weren't here. I wasn't sure if I should call—"

"Yeah, me too," Walter nodded thoughtfully. "I thought you might — you know — need some time before I call you."

She nodded and surprisingly smirked. "Yeah. I felt the same way. I'm fine though and I'm glad you are too. Sorry if I worried you."

Walter shook his head. "No, it's fine. I'm just happy to see you."

Yvette nodded. "Did you miss me?"

"I did," he smiled.

"I missed you too." Yvette was blushing a little now. "My dad asked about you? Seems to be interested in getting to know you better."

Walter smirked. "Should I be worried?"

She shrugged. "I don't know. I guess we will see." Then she giggled playfully. "No. You have nothing to worry about, Walter."

Walter snorted sarcastically. "Good, because... I'm not."

Yvette smiled when he said that. "Good. Oh, I wanted to ask you, have you ever thought of writing a comic?"

He chuckled a little, placing his fork back on his plate. "Yes, actually. Have you?"

"Kind of... Yeah. I don't know... I was thinking... I always wanted to write a novel one day and sometimes being able to see what I wrote... that would be amazing. You're very creative, maybe we can write something together. I can help with some of the drawings too. You can't do all of it, right?"

"I'd like that." He snickered. "And you're right, but I'm sure we can use some crooked stick-men drawn in there somewhere. Who else is better at that?"

Yvette grinned, even blushing a little. "Don't try and flatter me, Walter."

When Walter smiled, felt his cheeks blush as she indulged him.

Wide-eyed and with sudden elation, she said, "Oh, guess what? I heard it! My mom's voice. I heard it yesterday!"

"Really?" Walter smiled merrily, feeling her exuberance.

She nodded. "I thought of her — I was feeling down, I guess — but then I heard her voice so clearly in my ear. It wasn't, like… a memory or something like that… I don't know. It felt like… like she was talking to me herself. It was kind of weird but… it gave me a warm feeling. I guess you were right, Walter… she *is* always with me."

"Of course she is," Walter assured her. "That's what love really is. 'The dead don't create barriers, the living do.'"

The quote caught Yvette a bit off guard. "Where did you get that from?"

Walter shrugged. "Probably a book. I can't remember. Probably some—"

"Some dead guy, Walter?"

Walter chuckled when she said that. "Possibly."

Yvette shook her head gleefully. "Who is this 'dead guy' you're always talking about?"

"I don't know. Some dead guy named Benedict or Chauncey or someone. Sounds like a name for a wise guy, doesn't it?"

Yvette laughed and nearly dropped her sandwich. "Have I ever told you how terrible you are?"

Walter snickered. "Once or twice."

"More like five times."

Even when her laughs simmered and her dimples softened, Yvette's smile remained. Her eyes might have shifted away for a moment and she couldn't hold eye contact for too long, but her gentle smile was still there.

"I really missed you, Walter."

"I missed you too."

Yvette shook her head as she snickered as she took a bite of her sandwich; uncertain of what to say, possibly. Walter didn't care. Being with her was enough.

Nervously, Yvette swallowed, then said, "I hope you are coming to Michael's birthday party. It will probably be a bit boring with a bunch of little kids running around, but we don't have to stay long, right?"

Walter nodded with a grin. "Right."

"Great. It's this Saturday... Wait... I'm sorry. I was just making plans and I didn't ask if you were busy or anything."

Walter felt his grin stretch as he laughed. He could see how excited she was getting. "No, you're fine. I should be free."

"Great," she repeated, feeling better about it all.

Walter suddenly realized how Yvette wasn't hiding her blushing cheeks as much. He liked that. However, she soon cleared her throat, fixing her face to seem less excited.

"So, Dr. Pierce?" she asked before taking another bite.

Walter nodded, solemnly smiling. He began playing with his food, but he didn't really care to eat anymore. "Yeah. It's been good."

"Good," she said, chewing and shielding her lips with the back of her hand. "Good is good. I was worried about you and how that all might end up."

"I know, but... everything is fine."

"Oh, you know, huh?"

Walter grinned. "You're always worried about me, Yvette."

Yvette smiled, shifting her eyes down to her food. "That's true."

"And I like it."

Slowly, her eyes rose to meet his and they stayed and stared into his own.

439

Walter wasn't deterred. "What is it?" he soon asked, his eyes beginning to squint a bit.

"We went to that carnival together, didn't we?" Yvette asked, smiling with her head tilted. "Our first date."

Walter chuckled. "Yeah, we did… but it wasn't a carnival."

"It kind of was though," she giggled. "But we had a lot of fun."

"I'd like to say we did."

"We rode the Ferris wheel together too," she said, her eyes never leaving his.

"We did."

"And then..." Yvette grew speechless again for a moment. "And then… we kissed."

Walter nodded. "And then we kissed."

"Our first kiss."

"First kiss."

Yvette smiled, her eyes still fixed onto his. "And I liked it."

He smiled as well, matching hers. "And you liked it."

The way her eyes danced and flitted between his gave Walter the warmest feeling he ever felt. From that moment, he was truly certain how much she loved him too. Soon, however, her lips softened and her eyes dropped to the table so he couldn't see them.

"Did you mean what you said?" she asked sedately, her eyes now lifting to his once again.

Walter smirked gently, wondering if his memory had failed him. "What did I say?" he said, possibly more curiously than he should, but Yvette didn't seem bothered. He was thankful for that.

Now, her softened smile stretched, showing a bit more teeth. "Well, when you were in the hall, you told Art and his girlfriend that you loved me. Did you really mean that?"

Then it came to him; Trisha's abrupt pause, her stare. *She was there.* Trisha saw her and Yvette heard him. There was a sudden nervousness he felt but he kept it in his back pocket.

"I did," Walter nodded, eye to eye with her. "And I do."

Yvette was speechless, eyes wide and lips parted. "Well... you don't have to go overboard."

"You asked," Walter replied, beginning to laugh and she couldn't help but giggle.

Yvette's eyes were looking deep into his eyes when she said, "I love you too, Walter."

Blissfully, they both just sat there for a moment; face to face, smile to smile.

"Hey," he muttered gently. "Close your eyes."

Yvette smiled nervously. "What? Why?"

"Trust me?"

With a light chuckle, she said, "Of course I do."

"Then..." Walter took two fingers and slowly swiped down and shut his eyes behind them. When he opened them back up, her eyes were closed while her hands were on her lap. Her dimples were dug deep as her grin was outstretched. She even wiggled her shoulders playfully as she waited.

Walter got up and sat next to her, all the while Yvette's face followed. He suddenly spotted her tiny scar; where a blade bit at her neck and left a tiny smile.

She tried to peek but Walter caught her, so she quickly shut them and smiled then chimed, "Don't keep me wait—"

Right there in the cafeteria where any wondering eye could see, Walter cut her words with a kiss; softly, lovingly, wicked and wanting. Slowly, Yvette's hand rested gently on his cheek while the other found and caressed his arm, lightly brushing her fingers against his skin and hairs. Walter's hand grazed beneath her chin; his thumb felt the tiny smiling scar on her neck, and rested his fingers between her baby hairs and that ear she always played with nervously. Yvette shivered a little from his touch, but she never wavered,

"Unexpected," Yvette gasped, opening her heavy eyes with her lips moistened and resting softly ajar. "You remembered."

"I did."

Yvette blushed deeply, as deep as her dimples could go. "I loved it."

Walter matched his smile with hers, and her eyes wouldn't dare turn away. "I knew you would."

After that kiss, they both stared into one another for a moment... or longer; neither could tell. Even with a teacher or two scolding them from across the cafeteria for indecent exposure and the scattered gasps and astonishment from students around the tables, neither could care less about it; any of it. There were no secrets here. Walter and Yvette both felt happy and free and whole — far from empty.